I0649789

Life's
Vagabondage

David Stoeckl

3rd Retelling

ALBEDO BOOKS
SEQUIM, WASHINGTON

Life's Vagabondage. Copyright © 2003 by David Sterling.
Second Retelling, Copyright © 2013 by David Stoeckl.
Third Retelling, Copyright © 2024 by David Stoeckl.
All rights reserved.

Published by David Stoeckl and Albedo Books

All rights reserved. No part of this publication may be reproduced, stored in a retrieval system or transmitted in any form by any means, electronic, mechanical, photocopy, recording, computer scanned, or otherwise, without the prior permission of the publisher, except as provided by USA copyright law.

Cover photo and book design by: David Stoeckl

First printing, January, 2003
Second printing, 2023
Third printing, 2024

ISBN 978-1-967695-04-1

* This book is a work of fiction. Names, characters, places and incidents are products of the author's imagination or are used fictitiously. Any resemblance to actual events or locales or persons, living or dead, is entirely coincidental.

Forward/Backward/Whatever

Hi, I just had to mention that I've re-edited a whole bunch of this novel for the new Retelling. You can still buy the original printed version first released in 2002, but it will be very different from the later version.

Chapter One was completely re-worked. I never fully liked the printed Chapter One. So, there are some changes, at least a character or 2 changed or added, and I'm much happier with this new version of the book. (Hence, it's called the 3rd Retelling.) You can also get this updated version in print.

I understand that I'm in good company. I've read a few times that renowned author Ernest Hemingway continued to edit and improve his work, even after it was published. I likewise want this to be the best work I can create. I expect I'll have more changes in the future, but for the most part, I'm really pleased with this work of Christian, allegorical fiction and expect that any further changes will be little tweaks that would go pretty much unnoticed. It's time to work on my next book.

I pray that you really enjoy what the LORD has brought me through all these years to create and compose and publish.

Be blessed, always and all ways, David Stoeckl

To My Dad

*(But no sojourner had to lodge
in the street,
For I have opened my doors
to the traveler);*

Job 31:32

Chapter One

Leonard Lamb laughed, (like a bald and seeping re-tread, out of balance and out of alignment. Alone; driving; the moonless night became a wallowing fog surrounding the lonely traveler, raking its cold, numbing darkness across Leonard's little pickup as he sped along the highway. Yellowing headlights, each on a nose dive, weakly wedged through the gooey, gelatinous pitch of night which neatly filled-in behind the small vehicle at the speed of light.

Leonard barely noticed.

Dozens upon dozens of flitting accusations darted past the bastions of his mind like road-embedded gravel, rapidly appearing before him, blurring and disappearing under the old pick-up. The countless accusations pricked and prodded the memory foam surfaces of his brain, wire-whisked his emotions, and poked the charley horses of his soul. Despite the barrage of sublime accusations, he had trouble deciding on a reason for his present funk. The white lines of the highway hypnotically flicked past like silent movie projections. With a full bladder of brainwaves to keep him company, he settled back for a long, throbbing drive.

"What happened back there?" he demanded aloud, speaking for the first time since the onset. "Not a care in the world one day; not a burden withheld the next." The words erupted like a whooping geyser, shuddering against the seams of his soul, stressed and leaking.

All over the map, mental images clumsily danced across the stages of his mind like little angels in tutus, stopping briefly to curtsy while they bounded and hopped and pranced about his cerebral playhouse. Abstract pictures flitted by, drawing close, barely brushing his psyche like the cheeky kiss of the hummingbird.

Subconsciously distracted, he considered holding a hummingbird by its bill with a finger across the opening of its beak. Would the suction cling to his finger like a straw? He wondered. He wondered why when cartoon characters got hurt and saw birds flying around them, they never saw hummingbirds? He wondered if hummingbirds were ever diabetic? He wondered if hummingbirds ever sprained their wings and could only maintain 20 beats a second instead of 60 or 80? He wondered if they ever heard music in their hum? Could different hummingbird wing pitches be recorded and fashioned into a symphony with four part harmonies?

Leonard imagined The Blue Danube hummed by bird wings.

He also considered whether hummingbirds could give cheeky kisses since they arguably lacked cheeks.

Then, he wondered if there were hummingangels? Put them in the Heavenly Choir. They could beat wings to beat the band. They could sing harmony with themselves. They'd be the only angels able to fly backwards. Still messengers, they could tickle our ears with their 'beaks', delicately inserting past our headphones so we could actually hear God's will through our chosen, perpetually loud, drown-out-the-world noises.

And, Leonard wondered what hummingangels would wear? Robes definitely wouldn't work. Of course, why do angels wear anything at all? It's not like they chomped on Eden's apple and discovered they were naked. It's also not like they have anything to be ashamed of, have to dress for the weather, have vanity to appease, or work in spiritual textile factories. Needle and thread in Heaven? Ever seen an angel with patches?

Do our Heavenly mansions have washing machines?

Leonard chuckled at the thought of a Heavenly Laundromat. Coin operated? Likely not. An alternative to baptism? Particle Accelerator spin cycle? Super Collider dryer? God's Merry-Go-Round? Why not? Leonard imagined it'd urgently become the ultimate prayer meeting if he ever found himself inside such a machine.

Such were Leonard's thoughts, poking and withdrawing like an obnoxious squeak somewhere in the back of your car. Pure intolerable energy.

Leonard smiled, or would have, but he drove over a huge pothole that bounced and jerked his memories into far off places; such as driving rutted pathways in the fields near his home as a teen, or visiting Pittsburgh to attend a wedding of people he didn't know just to have a road trip with his friend, Reuel. BIG potholes in Pittsburgh. Reuel was right. Pittsburgh roads were worse than Whatcome County where Leonard lived.

Lived?

How did Leonard think he lived anywhere? Here he sat, driving, no destination in mind, and no clear, sequential memory of where he'd been. Good way to never be late. Likewise, impossible to be early. Or, even on time. He would've glanced at his watch if it'd mattered. He watched the gas gauge far more diligently.

*****

"Getting low."

Leonard nodded towards Reuel. Their coffee cups were indeed almost empty and they'd not seen Belinda, their waitress for quite some minutes. Probably on break.

Leonard knew she was just wearing her work face, but she had a distinctly nice smile; lots of clean, white teeth holding up rubbery cheeks and spit-polished, blue eyes framed in a pulled back mane embellishing an unnumbered variety of blond and reddish colors. Leonard mused that she'd donned it all specially for him.

"Well, why not?" he thought. It wasn't like he couldn't dream...

Of course if she really thought that much of him, Belinda would've brought him more coffee before now, break or no break...

Maybe?

Maybe not.

Leonard felt like the petals on a lover's daisy being removed, one by one.

"She loves me."

"She loves me."

"She loves me."

"She loves me."

"She loves me."

Leonard liked that version better than the usual. Better odds.

"She loves me not."

"She loves me not."

"She loves me not."

"She loves me not."

"She loves me not."

Not as much fun, but probably more accurate. Same odds as the other game.

Ah, here she comes, steaming pot in hand. Same dazzling smile. Same heart melting eyes. He wanted to cast a mold - I mean, mold a cast, not that he had any idea what he'd do with such a sculpted item. A photo would capture her image even better and fit in his pocket. He glanced at his cell phone on the table. He'd not yet found a cell phone that could cast a mold - I mean, mold a cast.

"Are you listening to me?"

Leonard looked over at the young man beside him. Actually, he'd not heard a word, but nodded yes.

"What'd I say?" asked Reuel.

"When?"

"Just now."

"You asked if I was listening to you."

"Before that."

"You said my coffee was getting low."

"After that."

Leonard grinned at Belinda as she smiled, poured, smiled some more, said delightful, chirpy words that neither man absorbed using higher brain functions. Both watched as she departed to serve another tableful of patrons. Still beaming, Leonard turned his head towards his friend.

"You said you wanted her number." Slight head nod her way.

Reuel knew that wasn't it, but decided that sounded better than what he'd actually been saying, and from that moment, couldn't remember what he'd actually said, what they were talking about nor if he even wanted to try to revive the topic of conversation at this point.

Reuel sipped his coffee while idly gazing out the large picture window, watching a young man on the busy street corner, dancing and cavorting and flaunting a large, yellow sign. Reuel couldn't tell from their angle if the sign advertised some Pizza Special, Used Car Extravaganza, or the never ending 'Mattress Sale.' It didn't look like someone Going Out of Business, offering 50 or 75% off during the 'Last, Final Days', nor was he pointing towards a gun shop. The dancer would've been dressed in camo or some costume to make him look like a huge, Chewbaccy shrubbery.

Too bad it wasn't for a Car Wash fund raiser. He eyed the swirling patterns of dirt adorning his little car out the shaded window.

Leonard followed his friend's gaze.

Belinda returned, check in hand, which she laid on the table.

A grin, (I'll let you guess from which fella).

"We didn't order this," he said, nodding towards the check.

Belinda puzzled over the intent of his words. The perfect teeth smile almost floundered, then she got the joke, perked up again, scolded him teasingly with her eyes.

"Compliments of the restaurant," she bantered before slipping away just as gracefully as she'd arrived.

"Come on," he said, sliding out from the booth. "We're needed there on the street.

Reuel grabbed the check. It'd been his turn to buy the coffee. The two longtime friends used to have one pay and the other leave the tip, but with the creation of debit cards, paying both at once became the norm.

Leonard led the way out of the restaurant to maneuver down to the sidewalk behind the sign carrying dancer. Reuel followed, still unsure he deduced Leonard's plan.

Corner of Telegraph & The Guide; Denny's across the street. McDonalds up Telegraph a tad. Banner Bank beside them. Burger King and Rite Aid and Shari's. Red Robin across the street. Boston Pizza just past Mickey Dee's as well as the mall which also had a Mickey Dees.

The dancer moved around rapidly. His headphone wire whipped him mercilessly. His head bent down most of the time, perhaps concentrating on his rhythms and flowing movements, he didn't detect the two mischievous men approaching him. They could hear him singing brokenly along with his headphones.

From behind, Leonard started mimicking the dance moves. Like an echo of an echo, Reuel fell right in line and started dancing not quite alongside Leonard. Each held a make-believe sign, bouncing left and right and left and twirling their transparent 'signs' around clockwise, then counter-clockwise, then clockwise again. Big smiles beamed from behind the invisible signage as they watched for the responses of the countless faces inside passing vehicles.

Some ignored them. Some smiled, amused. Some looked puzzled. Some honked. A couple held up thumbs. One pointed his hand like a gun, aimed with one eye closed, and fired, kickback and all.

The sign bearer continued his dance, mostly oblivious, even after the lights changed. Traffic stopped before him, he made doubly sure the drivers could all read his sign.

Leonard and Reuel continued to dance, getting a bit more aggressive. They switched sides, back and forth a few times. One went forward and the other back. Just having fun.

Leonard wondered if the beggars with their handmade cardboard signs shouldn't try dancing while panhandling? Maybe he'd try it some time - check the response. He could sponsor his own personal sociology experiment, (though he wouldn't do it around here - he knew too many people. Maybe down south in Mount Burnem.)

The sign man spun around.

All three men stopped dancing, like a stunned silence that had been waiting to pop. Signman started to speak, but instead shrugged, and started dancing again, this time in bounding circles around his new dance partners.

All three took position around each other. Leonard started singing. The other 2 joined in.

Ring around the rosey
Pockets full of posey
Ashes. Ashes.
We all fall down.

The three crashed backwards like blooming petals in a time-exposed video. Signman tossed his sign upward as he collided with the concrete. His sign spun in a controlled stumble before returning downward. He caught it, but just barely.

Rising and gasping for air from the impact, he pulled an earphone away and rose to continue the dance. Some cars, still stopped at the light, honked to applaud - or so the three men preferred to believe.

"Having fun at my expense, eh?" asked Signman, spinning around a full 360 in rhythm with 120 beats a minute.

"Need ye ask?" replied Reuel, brushing himself off. He'd landed off sidewalk in the landscaped loam. Flecks of gravel. Some wood chips. A few pine needles. The rest humussy dirt. Cigarette butts optional. He noticed a brown paper lunch bag he'd almost crushed, upright and clean and open. Penciled words on the side. Leonard gave his friend a helping hand up.

"Praise Jesus!" Signman spoke with gasps, a tad out of breath from his boogier moves. "That's great."

Turning towards the sign dancer, Leonard noticed the Denny's sign across the street. At a glance, it seemed to spell Danny's? He wasn't sure. Weren't those lions dining inside by the window?

Certain his eyes were playing tricks, he stepped closer. No lions. Just patrons. Or, um????

The paved streets looked like flowing rivers. Cars and trucks and bikes atop the dirty gray fluid, rising and dropping with the ebb and flow. Leonard looked over at Reuel who was still brushing himself off. Signman continued his dance moves.

"Do you...?" Leonard began to ask his friend when he spied Nebuchadnezzar strolling into Burger King. Or perhaps it was Belshazzar. Or Cyrus. He couldn't tell. Probably not Solomon. Definitely not Herod, the Great or otherwise.

Spinning around, Banner Bank suddenly read Baptism Bank. Hence the watery boulevard? Shari's read Shadrach's. The Mall like Malachi. Bank of America became Bank of Amorites. Home Depot, Hosea Depot. Yet, to stop and focus, each business name returned to normal. Oddly, Boston Pizza read Lost In Pizza and Red Robin didn't change at all. Go figure!

There are a few rare moments in a person's life when whirling-twirling perplexity, ardent amusement, inquisitive curiosity and nagging impatience all try to crowd the brain at once. This could've been one of those moments, but Leonard's brain was moving too crookedly fast, like bouncing balls inside a Bingo cage, to track down and capture even one thought or idea long enough to dwell and examine and see which, if any, of those categories it may've birthed from.

"Okay-ay!"

It was Signman. He'd somehow resigned to something. Leonard didn't know what. Maybe just singing a song, but it didn't sound like that. His sign lay on the sidewalk beside him. For the first time, Leonard could read it: WE BUY GOLD AND SILVER, or was it WE BURY GOLD AND SILVER? Or was it WE BUY GOLDEN SILVER? Leonard was sure he'd read it right each time as Signman picked it up to resume his advertising.

Reuel sat on the curb tying a shoe.

Two middle-aged men passed them to wait at the curb for the light to turn. Barely feet away, Leonard and Signman couldn't help but hear the conversation between the 2 men.

"I don't know what he wants from me," complained the First.

"Explain," prodded the Second.

"Okay," began the First. "Uh, I guess I was filled to overflowing, but I'm so shallow that my cup doesn't hold very much, and it's not stable, so it's easily spilt. And, you know what a neatnick I am. When God's grace overflows my cup and gets my fingers wet, I tend to try to clean up the mess as well as wipe my fingers on my pants 'cuz I don't always have a holy napkin. It's very embarrassing, I'll tell you."

The Second was unimpressed. "That's nothing. You should hear what I have to deal with."

"If I must," sanctioned the First.

The Second took a deep breath, then sniveled, "A hundred-thousand-million-billion-bajillion people are crying out to me for help, but a hundred-thousand-million-billion-bajillion voices is a lot of voices and I have to admit that I don't always listen as attentively as perhaps I should and well, I confess sometimes my mind wanders and when the TV's on, I get hypnotized and don't hear anything else, and my TV screen's only a nineteen inch, so it can't fit a hundred-thousand-million-billion-bajillion people. Maybe if I had a 70 inch flat screen HDTV – or larger, then I might fit them all in. And, my nineteen inch TV only has one small mono speaker. If I'm going to hear a hundred-thousand-million-billion-bajillion voices, they'd better at least be broadcast in stereo with subwoofered surround sound if they really want to catch my ear."

"So," asked the First, "if you had the big screen HDTV with stereophonic sound, how you gonna help a hundred-thousand-million-billion-bakillion people?"

The Second didn't flinch. "I'd see their need n' pray for 'em, of course."

"Wow!" bowed the First.

The Second donned his 'gratefully longsuffering' mask.

"Wow!" echoed Leonard.

"Wow!" mouthed Reuel, who'd arisen after tying his shoes. He kept flapping the lower pant legs to get them to fit property over his high tops.

Both First and Second glared at Leonard before glancing at Signman and Reuel (who'd stood upright after flapping his pant bottoms into submission). Signman vortexually moved his sign forward and back, from chest to arms length and back again, over and over in tempo with some invisible melody. The two passersby stepped off the curb to cross the boulevard rather than hassle with those three weirdos.

*****

"What person can reflect upon their life and ever be satisfied?" Leonard wondered aloud, speeding along the dark, open highway. "I wonder..." He blindly felt his way through gnarly mists clogging his cranium. The fog opened up a slit to display a vision, real but still vague, flagging down his complete attention. Unrolling like a sticky cinnamon roll between pinching fingertips, he fought to capture the jigsawed images of Self and Purpose and Direction and piecemeal Incompleteness, flitting up, drawing close, barely brushing his psyche like a timid feather duster.

As Leonard raced along, thousands of trees near the roadside waved hello and good-bye, their branches flailing in the brisk breeze like a class full of struggling non-swimmers. A few small, black tail deer grazed just within the peripheral vision of the fleeting headlights. Huge, black mountains loomed ahead like slumbering giants under uncounted layers of coarse, wool blankets. Topped with countless evergreens, the behemoth silhouettes propped-up against a backdrop of hot stars and hypothermic sky. It surprised him, the solid sky, so alive with light, even at night.

*****

Apparently a danceaholic, Signman resumed his addictive ways.

"Gotta run," turned Reuel. "Next week, same time?"

Leonard affirmed with half a nod & more than half a smile.

As Reuel pivoted, Leonard did one of those moves of utter, naked surprise when your head lurches forward until it has to stop. Your eyebrows rise just a bit, widening your eyes. Sometimes your breath pauses, but not this time. Leonard had already had lots of practice today doing double takes. This merely became the latest occasion.

"Wait!" called Leonard a tad louder than needed.

"What?" Reuel turned back. Signman kept dancing behind Leonard, almost a dubstep, pieced together like flowing chain links.

"Your jacket," pointed Leonard, taking Reuel's shoulder to turn him around.

Reuel resisted lightly, but turned while wondering if this was another one of Leonard's jokes.

"What?" he repeated.

"There's some writing."

"Someone wrote on the back of my coat?"

"No," corrected Leonard, reading the words with awe and disbelief. He muttered the printed words before adding, "Look," and started to nudge Reuel's jacket off his shoulders. Reuel complied.

"Carefully," urged Leonard.

"What?" Reuel queried for the third time.

"Careful." Leonard kept the back of the jacket flat as he set it on a drab green electric power box. "Look."

The words could not have been an accident. As though a silhouette made of flecks of gravel, some wood chips, a few pine needles and the rest humussy dirt, (cigarette butts not optional this time), lines of text clearly projected from the back of the navy blue jacket. Both men stared in disbelief for a few more seconds as they read aloud the words together.

Brother Reuel, Friend of God, The salutation of Paul with my own hand, which is a sign in every epistle; so I write.

"What's that supposed to mean?" both men asked, almost as perplexed by the message as the way it appeared on the jacket.

Signman turned towards them.

"Oops!"

He grabbed the jacket, aggressively shook off the letters and helped Reuel put it back on.

"Wrong scripture. Here." He nudged and shifted Reuel back towards the landscape.

"Lay down again," he ordered, and pushed him onto his back. The fingers touched Reuel lightly, but he flew back to the raised ground with striking force, forcing some air from his lungs upon impact, and again missing the brown paper lunch bag with penciled writing. Signman helped him to his feet, brushed him off again, and checked the back of his coat.

"That's better."

Leonard stepped around to look. "Huh?"

"What?" said Reuel for the fourth time.

"It says, "*Reuel, But as for you, brethren, do not grow weary in doing good. [14] And if anyone does not obey our word in this epistle, note that person and do not keep company with him, that he may be ashamed. [15] Yet do not count him as an enemy, but admonish him as a brother. [16] Now may the Lord of peace Himself give you peace always in every way. The Lord be with you all.*"

"Let me see it," demanded Reuel, starting to take off his jacket.

"Wait," ordered Signman. "1st take a picture."

"What?" asked Reuel, wondering if he'd now said the word "What?" in virtually every human intonation possible?

"You have a cellphone. Take a picture before you take off your coat."

Reuel handed Leonard his phone. After some fumbling with sliding buttons, Leonard figured out the camera and took a shot of the back of Reuel's coat. Handing back the phone, Reuel checked out the pic while letting the 2 men help him remove his jacket.

Reuel looked, just as flabbergasted as the first time. Correction - even more so. He read and re-read and re-read, gathering the intent of the message as well as wondering how such a thing could happen.

"Who are you?" he turned to Signman.

"Apparently a messenger," answered Signman, tilting his head slightly to the right. His sign dangling from one hand perhaps read REVLIS DNA DLOG YUB EW. Reuel could not recall previously seeing an arrow at one end as Signman added, "but, don't you gotta go?"

Reuel checked his phone for the time. Signman was right. He was late and had to run. And with that, he was gone. (Well, he was gone after he bumped closed fist knuckles with both men, strode the incline to his car, double checked the writing on his jacket and tried setting it carefully in his trunk but some of the landscape and dirt was already flaking off. He checked the restaurant window to catch another view of Belinda, but she was nowhere to be seen. In the parking lot, he turned towards Leonard to wave bye, but Leonard was talking with an Asian couple and pointing towards McDonalds or the Mall or Boston Pizza or Red Robin or maybe he was just pointing west. Who could tell from this distance? Reuel still waved. No response, but he didn't expect one and wondered if anyone in the restaurant noticed him waving to no one, or maybe they thought he was in fact waving to someone they just couldn't see. It might give the diners something to talk about.

He unlocked his car door, sat in, opened the sunroof, and waited for the heat to dissipate. Starting the car, checking the mirrors, clicking his seat belt, adjusting the radio volume, checking the mirrors again, seeing his reflection and smiling, shifting into reverse, driving down and honking and waving at Leonard who grinned at him as he turned onto the busy boulevard and with that, he was now actually gone, (or at least driving away and still in sight for a couple more blocks if Leonard had kept watch, (he didn't))).

"Is Reuel gone?" called Signman, still dancing and waving his sign with his back to Leonard.

"Don't ask."

*****

Red, sizzling taillights played peek-a-boo up ahead, regularly disappearing behind the next curve. Leonard followed, as much as a quarter mile behind, mile after mile along the winding, mountain road. He couldn't see the car to which they were attached, so the scarlet pair led the way like a disembodied laser light show. He watched the lights with the same mesmerizing gaze as one who'd suffered a major jolt, and wasn't yet willing to let go of his previous, now fleeting scraps of sanity.

Turning onto a straightaway, the road flattening out and, leaving behind the mountains, he noticed for the first time the tail lights reflected off the highway. He slowed slightly, watching for the water, but none appeared. Regaining speed, he again saw the phantom lights wavering on the asphalt.

Mirage?

It seemed like a mirage, but late at night? He'd never known of a mirage at night. It also intrigued him that a mirage could reflect light. He studied the migrating marvel mile after mile until his own eyes felt as hazy as a New York City inversion.

"Lord, where'm I goin'?" The words dribbled off his lips like flat, soggy basketballs.

He watched for an answer, and only saw the same dark, impersonal road pierced by the pair of wavering, red eyeballs looking back at him from the phantom lead car. He felt for an answer, but only felt the weak blow of the heater fan. He listened for an answer, but the endless drum roll of the truck motor only served to keep his nerves on edge.

He wondered about the sign dancer on the boulevard who'd sported an expression somewhere between carefree euphoria and fervent sorrow. He wondered about Reuel's jacket? He also wondered if he needed an oil change and if George Bailey ever really told his wife Mary about Clarence? It's a Wonderful Life had a better ending than The Bishop's Wife (or The Preacher's Wife) where no one remembered Angel Dudley. Next, he wondered why the Mariners never won World Series and why the Sonics went to

Oklahoma? At some point, he likewise wondered where he was going and realized, no matter how planned and mapped out the route, nobody ever really knew where they were going until they got there.

No plan is complete before it's carried out.

A yawn like Samson stretched wide his jaw. After some miles of lost thought, he checked his bearings, and could not remember where he'd just been. The road behind him seemed as alien as the road ahead, and he mused how the auto-pilots of his mind needed to keep a more accessible log.

*****

Where're you from? asked Signman, seated on the rock wall of the bridge overlooking Whatcome Falls.

"Acme," answered Leonard. ."It's a tiny town – just a wide spot along the highway, here in Washington. I'd give you directions, but you can't get there from here."

"And, you're not working?"

"How'd you know that?" turned Leonard.

"And, you say that you're a student, and between quarters, but you haven't been to class for over two years."

"And, how'd you know that?"

"And, you're unmarried, and even homeless, mooching off friends."

Leonard paused, still waiting for the answers to his first two questions.

"I'm guessing you weren't always this flaky," commented Signman. "Why the erosion?"

Leonard suddenly saw himself as a stranger and wondered that they were talking at all.

"I don't know," Leonard eventually thought aloud. Tinges and twinges of embarrassment cushioned his next words. "I had my career and my home and I loved attending the biggest church in town, but now I just don't care anymore. It's like I got worn out, or tired of the everyday cycles. For a change, I tried going back to school, but it didn't help."

"I can tell," Signman's voice a mosquito buzz. His sign leaned concavely against the wall, pointed upward. All Leonard could see was the word 'Gold'. Signman rubbed his nose with the back of his hand as he announced, "It sounds like you could use a real change."

Leonard's silence and the sounds of crashing water answered affirmatively.

Signman chomped on a sandwich. Tuna on dill rye by the looks and smells of it. The brown, paper lunch bag dangled from his left hand. Finishing his sandwich and grabbing a swig of water, he handed Leonard the paper bag.

"I think this is for you."

Leonard took it blankly. The bag was folded flat, but Leonard still opened it and looked inside.

"It's empty," he looked towards Signman questioningly.

Signman tapped the other side of the bag and stated, "It's a letter. Better than a fortune cookie."

Leonard had not noticed the writing, in handwritten pencil. Collapsing the bag he turned it over. In handwritten pencil. it read:

Dear Leonard Lamb,

I know your works, that you are neither cold nor hot. I could wish you were cold or hot. So then, because you are lukewarm, and neither cold nor hot, I will vomit you out of My mouth. Because you say, "I am rich, have become wealthy, and have need of nothing" – and do not know that you are wretched, miserable, poor, blind, and naked – I counsel you to buy from Me gold refined in the fire, that you may be rich, and white garments, that you may be clothed, that the shame of your nakedness may not be revealed; and anoint your eyes with eye salve, that you may see. As many as I love, I rebuke and chasten. Therefore be zealous and repent. Behold, I stand at the door and knock. If anyone hears my voice and opens the door, I will come in to him and dine with him, and he with Me. To him who overcomes I will grant to sit with Me on My throne, as I also overcame and sat down with My Father on His throne.

Sincerely, Jesus of Nazareth

PS, Like Ephesus, you lost. Love, JC

Leonard read the letter again. It didn't sound much better the second reading.

Signman jumped down from the wall and started to leave.

"Wait!" called Leonard.

The man turned.

"Is this a joke?"

"Could you laugh at it?"

Leonard sunk down, collapsing on the pieced rocks.

"No."

A couple passed talking about gas prices and yelling for the kids to slow down. They stopped to snap a quick picture of the falls before moving on.

Signman leaned in, eye level with Leonard.

"One made of light and love wrote it. He knew I would pass it along to you."

"What does it mean?"

Signman shook his head. "Must I trust your intelligence more than you yourself?"

Leonard groped. "Uh, have you read the letter?"

"Yes."

"What'd you think?"

"I agree with the author." Signman wasn't joking, but Leonard sniggered.

"Okay," considered Leonard. "Most of it's straightforward enough, but I don't understand the post script. What like Ephesus have I lost?"

The Signman spoke easily. "God's word will answer that one..." He smiled and took Leonard's hand, "...if you care to look. Fear not, Mr. Lamb. You shan't be alone."

Leonard listened to the rush of water vibrating the bridge they sat upon. Signman's eyes, big and deep, nodded assurance, then grabbing his sign, he scooted off. Leonard sat, detached, on the bridge till the sun gave way to the clouds and the northwestern drizzling rains began.

*****

The truck swerved to find the road. Shaking his head sharply, Leonard roused himself, stretched and strained his back muscles and sat up straight. The night had already been so, so long, and it wasn't over, yet. Still, part of him hoped that it would never end; that this was his Heaven as well as his Hell - forever lost to roam the same roadways, over and over, round and round and round, whirled without end, amen.

Both his stamina and his gas gauge suggested otherwise. His journey wasn't going to last much longer if he didn't get both some sleep and/or some gasoline, and his absentminded prayers for a gas station included one with hot refills on coffee.

He picked up the letter Signman had given to him. It'd rested all night, untouched, on the bucket seat. He couldn't readily read it in the weak light, but knew the harsh words were still ingrained on the brown paper. More scary than that, he felt those same words etched to his shabby, neglected self, nagging him worse than the first day his teeth had been fitted with braces.

He also wondered about the stranger who'd given it to him. He could see the vulnerable power behind his eyes. If Leonard didn't possess the letter, he would've dismissed the whole incident as fanciful. He'd long recognized that he possessed the 'gift' in his life to make something out of nothing or to see more than was actually there. He didn't see that indication here.

The pair of red taillights ahead continued to reflect off the migrating mirages. (Actually, it was a different pair of taillights on a different car, but they weren't any more interesting than the first, nor any more or less pertinent to the story.) But, the image ahead had changed; it'd grown larger, like he'd suddenly shrunk to half size, and the wavy heat rising off the road reminded him of the I Dream of Jeanne dance, or a wide court of flags, all unfurled, pointing straight up to the sky. He would come much closer to the mirage before it disappeared. Heat rose through the carpeted and matted floor of his pickup. He slowed the truck, coasting, in exercised temperance, partially to put some distance between himself and the car up ahead, and partially to examine the changing tenacity of the mirage.

The watery likeness seemed thicker, as though rising off the road like a waving wheat field. Leonard, still coasting, opened his car door, and hung his hand down near the pavement. Besides expected heat and wind, another impression seemed to caress and dance along his fingertips, and slide up and out between his fingers. He pulled back, and the effect quit. Down again, and the feeling returned.

He stopped the truck. Right in the middle of the highway, he hit the brakes and clambered out. The air seemed cool, but the roadbed felt cozy warm. The edges of the mirages floated barely yards off. He wondered if he could sneak up and capture the mirage if he stayed low to the ground. He laid down on his belly to get close to the surface, and looked up the road. Ebbing waves of bulldozing heat rolled over him, like the surf, and he became immersed in the liquid-like appearance. It wasn't wet; nor did he submerge, but he felt like bodysurfing, and wondered if he had not re-entered the womb. His senses numbed, the rock-hard asphalt felt comfortable and he seemed to actually float, as though riding the thermals rising off some deep canyon on a bright, hot, sunny day. The impressions suddenly, joyfully overwhelmed him; a gargantuan tidal wave of divine power and grace that filled and inflated him as happens when one unexpectedly touches the dark matter of eternity.

White, intruding headlights appeared a couple miles back. He could already feel the bark of the engine vibrating the road around him.

Sadly, he sat up. Cold shivers grabbed hold as his upper body returned to the common, cool air of the night. Only by force of will could he stand. Returning to the familiar shell of the truck cab, he resumed his journey while wondering what powers of life he'd encountered back there on the road. His mind tingled with childlike questions all the way till he found the open gas & groc. Filling the tank with gas, the travel mug with coffee, and seeking a washroom, he watched the first rays of morning light seep over the flat, two-dimensional horizon. Paying the man, he took off down the highway with renewed verve. He still didn't know where he was going, but wherever it was, he expected quite the reception.

Chapter Two

Leonard squinted against the brilliant sunlight. The high, canary yellow sun coated endless miles of gritty, corn meal sand, rolling upward and downward and over and over like tidal ocean swells. The mounds seemed to flow and shudder just outside his regular vision, becoming stationary as he turned to look. It was distracting and he wished he could find some blinders or a hoodie to block peripherally.

The sudden blast of heat smacked him surprisingly hard, especially after his cool, night drive. The ferocious sun beat down on him in the still, baked air. He looked down to see his feet and ankles buried in the blistering sand. He jumped out of the hole, his feet bare though he remembered donning his shoes. He searched for cover as he gingerly tried to dance over the tractable, scorching sand.

"Jesus," he cried, as much out of habit as in conscientious prayer.

He hastily plodded to the top of a dune and stopped. The sand covered the land, from horizon to horizon in all directions. No mountains. No vegetation. No haze. It felt both awesome and scary. He wasn't thirsty, but suddenly realized that he had no water. Somehow the predicament did not yet alarm him.

"Don't panic," he spoke aloud. His words felt small against the vast desert, but they were real and thereby lightly reassuring.

"Think," he added, not to specifically conceive a plan to traverse or escape the desert, but simply to assess his situation and act as necessary.

He looked all around him again. The dune he was standing on seemed to rise one direction more than he remembered. He looked down into the canyon he'd just climbed out from. It seemed so deep, and he couldn't recall climbing so high. "A quarter mile down," he estimated. "At least." He could see his footprints where he ascended. The view was frightful, and he imagined falling down, down, down into the deep, burning ravine.

He then remembered his burning feet, but he was already wearing his boots, laced and tied, knew it to be right, and again recalled donning his shoes.

He started up the dune ridge. His shadow was shorter than himself. He peered towards the general direction of the sun and wondered if it was late morning or early afternoon, so that he could determine his direction of travel. Not that he had any idea whether to head north, east, west or south.

The ridge leveled off as he found what looked like English words written into the sand.

"What, the...?" he wondered as he bent towards the writing. He watched his steps to make sure that he didn't step on any. Maneuvering over a few lines of writing, he started to read. The words were hard to make out, losing form in the granules.

Sheila Hanson asked the Lord's forgiveness this 3rd day of March for her lifetime of sin. The Lord honored her sincere petition, forgiving her for: Her adulterous relationship with John Beeman; for her idolatry towards shopping and daytime serials; for her vanity and superiority image, especially during social occasions, starting from when she was four years old...

"A list of forgiven sins?" said Leonard. He noted that the list was rather long, and seemed to dissipate in the sand, forgotten and unrecoverable.

He turned and saw more scribbled words all around him, mostly illegible. The words were all over, as far as he could see.

He climbed back onto the ridge, destroying Sheila's immemorial. There was more writing on that side, down & up the next side; some more readable than others, but none destined to last for many more hours.

"Who would do that?" he wondered out loud, "And why?" He continued along the ridge some miles, seeing more areas of writing in the sand. Much was already illegible and he did not stop to read.

A strong wind abruptly arose. It was hot and felt like he'd sat down inside a blow dryer set on 'high', but the moving air felt better than the still, crushing sunlight. The sand also responded, drifting smoothly across the surface. Within moments, the surface was clear and flat, without any evidence of the doomed graffiti.

The breeze stayed with him as he walked. He breathed long and hard, and listened to the sounds of wind, his breath, and his feet on sand. He looked to the sky. If the sun had moved, he couldn't tell. His shadow also seemed the same length.

He stopped to ponder this, and was surprised to hear a voice. A human voice, singing – singing a familiar, old hymn. The Old, Rugged Cross.

He couldn't tell exactly where the voice came from. If he moved, he couldn't hear it. He waited, and opted to walk into the wind. Dropping down, then up the next sandy mound, he stopped to listen. The voice was louder. He still saw nothing, so continued, down and up onto the next dune.

There he saw him.

He was a small man, dressed in dark pants, plain collared shirt, his pants held up by suspenders. He wore a straw hat more yellow than the sand with a thin, black band. He had a grey beard, no mustache, and black shoes. Leonard watched as the man knelt in the sand, ignoring the sun, and writing the list of forgiven sins for a man named Todd.

"Hello," approached Leonard.

The man turned and smiled. "Hello Leonard."

Leonard began to ask, "And, you are?" but the man answered, "Henry," before the words finished the journey to his lips. His voice had an odd and distinct quality. German farmer? He wasn't sure. Leonard looked at his face again – something wonderfully familiar, but he couldn't place it.

"Henry?" Leonard sputtered.

"Yup," he smiled, then turned back to the sand.

Leonard considered numerous ways to begin the conversation – "Can you help me?" – "What are you doing?" – "Where are we?", etc. He instead knelt down next to Henry to watch him write.

Henry scribbled words on the sand with his finger. Some places the sand was so soft, the words were never legible.

"I see what you're doing," began Leonard, "but, I don't understand why."

"Why?" Henry chuckled. "So, their sins will be forgotten." He beamed at the thought.

"What?" pondered Leonard. "Just by jotting down some words in the sand?"

"Did not Jesus our Lord write in the dirt before the woman caught in adultery?"

Leonard nodded, but didn't see a correlation.

Henry continued, "I'm not just making a written record, like a ledger. Do you know where we're at?"

Leonard's face answered before his head oscillated.

"This is the Sea of Forgetfulness."

Leonard glanced around briefly at the endless drifts of sand, then back towards Henry.

"It looks more like a desert," Leonard spoke blandly.

"Yup, I know," admitted Henry, waiting just long enough to peak Leonard's interest, "and, I record the forgiven sins of every man or woman who comes to our Lord Jesus with a penitent heart."

"Why?"

Henry chuckled again. "So, they'll be not just forgiven, but also forgotten." He removed his hat and held it to his chest before beginning the next sentence.

"Didn't God promise that He would forgive us all of our sins and remember them no more?"

Leonard nodded.

"So, this is where those forgiven sins are sent. Only God can forgive the sin. I record each sin as His Holiest Spirit directs." He replaced his straw hat on his tanned brow.

"And, this is the Sea of Forgetfulness?"

"Yup," Henry chuckled. He retrieved a white handkerchief stuffed in the side of his pants, and wiped the perspiration from his face. He glanced up at Leonard, still smiling, and replaced the stained, white cloth. Leonard suddenly noticed that there were no pockets on his pants.

"So, if this is a sea, where's the water?" Leonard thought the question too obvious to put into words.

Henry answered, undaunted, "Underneath us," continuing to jot down a few more sins for a man named Huver. Graft. Embezzlement. Tax evasion...

Henry explained, "This area used to be nothing but water, as deep as it was wide."

"Okay," urged Leonard.

"Well, it's said that each grain of sand is one of the forgiven sins. Since the days of Adam and Eve, God's been forgiving our sins, without fail and completely true to His Word."

Leonard looked all around himself again in inconceivable awe. He stooped down to pick up a handful of sand. As he brought the bland, selfsame grains closer to his face, he saw an extraordinary array of colors. Each grain was as unique as a snowflake.

"Do the colors mean anything?" asked Leonard.

Henry watched him a moment. "How do you mean?"

"I mean," Leonard looked up, then paused as he looked closely for the first time at Henry's deep, moving facial features. His darkly tanned skin. His hazel eyes. His cleanly shaven upper lip and parched corners of his smile, all encased in a face heavily lined, yet beautiful.

"I mean," Leonard re-composed his question, "Does a black grain mean a particular kind of sin, like murder or theft or idolatry – a brown one a different sin – some are marbled, and could represent, say, fornication or spite or... you see what I mean?"

35

Henry nodded and scratched his head.

"Don't know," he admitted. "Frankly, I never thought about it before." He looked up at Leonard, "But, my best guess – probably not. I doubt that if God really wanted the sins forgotten, that he'd categorize them. He's certainly got bigger affairs to direct his energies towards."

Leonard nodded. Fair enough. He looked around at the endless desert, and imagined it, full of water, but filling up with sand, grain by grain, until the water was lost deep below. He wondered how deep, not that it mattered. He also wondered at how many sins humankind had committed over the centuries. These were just the *forgiven* sins. How many more were still out there in the world, un-forgiven, and what shape did they take?

"How big is the Sea?" asked Leonard without looking at Henry.

Henry finished recording a few more sins for Mr. Huver: hatred – contention – vengeance. He rose to his feet and brushed off his pants and hands.

"Can't rightly say," he admitted. "I'm also just like a man, but I can point you to Psalms 103:17."

Leonard waited, having no idea what that scripture would be.

Henry continued, "*The mercy of the Lord is from everlasting to everlasting on those who fear him.* That's how big the sea is – from everlasting to everlasting."

Leonard sighed, and his gaze picked any horizon. He had an endless trek ahead of him, and for the first time, he began to wonder if he would make it.

Henry caught the gist of his thoughts.

"Actually," Henry interrupted, you're right and you're wrong. The Holiest Spirit told me that you were coming. He wants you to know that you have a great and terrible journey ahead."

"I think I see that," interjected Leonard.

"LET ME FINISH!" Henry's demeanor was direct and peppered with urgency, but not hostile. "Your journey began the day that you were born, but to date, you've done foolish little with it."

Leonard began to speak-up – to defend himself, or get more details, but looked again at Henry, shut-up and nodded for him to continue.

"You're not unique, I'm sad to say. You've been a pig fattened and ready for slaughter. You have enough tools and training to build the highest spiritual tower, or the longest bridge. Yet, like so many, you don't use your gifts, but instead ask for more."

He spit out the next words.

"Woe to you!"

Leonard stood back, a bit stunned. Part of him was irritated in the way that nobody likes to have their hands slapped. He fought back, swallowing hard, to squelch his pride and asked, "What do I have to do?"

"That's it," answered Henry.

Leonard gazed at him dumbfounded, and clearly did not understand.

"Do," urged Henry.

Leonard waited for more. After a spell, he spouted, "Isn't that rather – vague?"

"Only to one who has seldom done," smiled Henry. "Once you get started doing, you'll see that it's not as vague as you may presently imagine."

Leonard dropped the handful of sand and pondered which direction to set out. He was about to thank Henry for the good advise, mostly out of politeness, when Henry added, "One more thing. A very important thing."

Leonard waited.

"You've been conquered."

"Conquered?"

"And, you're occupied."

"Occupied?"

"Absolutely. I see it with my own eyes. The Spirit of Defeat has had hold of your life for years – perhaps all your life. He probably also controlled your parents and their parents. He, like all immortals, has been in business for all generations."

"Who is he? What does he look like?"

"As to what he looks like, whatever he wants, but even his best disguise is still a counterfeit. As to whom he is, he's the demon that not only wants to keep you separate from your Savior, (for all demons want that,) but he also seeks to isolate you, or keep you in check, or keep you confused, or down and depressed, or strung-out, or drunk or angry. Anything that will destroy your abundant life on Earth.

"Abundant life and God's holy kingdom starts in this life – not just after your spirit departs this life."

"I know that," popped Leonard.

"Understood," acknowledged Henry, "but, it also goes for Hell's kingdom. The unholy kingdom of Hell also starts during this life. The first way to fight against this demon is to *do*, but I warn you, he will take notice, absolutely without exception, and he will strike at you – hard – knock-down punches."

Leonard appeared to recoil.

"But," urged Henry, "have no fear; stay in prayer; and keep on doing."

Leonard peered up towards the sun. If it'd changed position, he couldn't tell. His shadow appeared about the same length. Henry resumed writing in the sand, this time for a woman named Rita. Idolatry. Pride. Not keeping the Lord's day holy...

"But," started Leonard.

"Don't accept 'but' as an answer," Henry quickly answered without glancing up from his task. "No buts. Do." He paused a moment to look Leonard in the eye.

"Take heart," he smiled. "I know that this seems superficial, but if I gave you some elaborate scheme, you either wouldn't do it, or do it with spite. Either way is wrong." The smile stayed planted against his face like clinging ivy.

"So, take heart, go forth, and do – and watch out for the spirit of defeat. I promise, I'll tell you more soon."

Henry rose and looked up towards the sun. Leonard followed his gaze, and thought that he finally detected modest movement.

Looking back towards Leonard, Henry pointed. "You've got to go – now."

"Where? Which way?"

"Go – now! Wake-up!"

"Huh?"

"Wake-up, Leonard."

Leonard shuddered. He heard the voice again, deep inside his head. "WAKE-UP, LEONARD."

Leonard looked and was startled to see the open highway racing before and beneath him. Shaking his head to push the sleep away, he swerved left, leaving the shoulder back onto the highway. Another second or two and he would've been off the road. He shuddered as he saw the forest of large trees not far off the road. His "doing" days would've rapidly ended if he'd plowed headlong into one of those.

Tired from driving all night, he knew he had to stop. He found a highway off ramp, exited and made for a nearby campground. An hour's shut-eye would revive him. Parking out front to avoid paying fees, he settled back against the deep, high backed bucket seat and soon drifted off for a quick nap.

Chapter Three

Leonard awoke with a real start. He sat up, gripping the steering wheel, and looked around. The sunlight was almost gone, and night rapidly filling in. At first, he couldn't believe that he'd slept so long. His head felt so heavy and groggy, but he also felt quite hungry, and lastly, urgently had to find a bathroom.

He clambered out of his pickup and locked-up. Entering the campground, he was certain that there'd be some sort of facility, however crude, that he could use.

The place was cold; terribly cold. A brutal, freezing wind came up, gnawing away at his clothing. It seemed hellbent to suck all of the warmth from his body. He buttoned the top snap of his coat, lowered his head, and picked up his pace.

"Henry," he wondered, his steamy breath sucked away by the icy blast. Just the name sparked a myriad supply of questions.

"*Do,*" he added aloud.

The ticklish wind penetrated through to his skin. Drifts of old leaves pelted him. His face turned a fiery red, and his jaw stiffened as he gritted his teeth. He could feel the skin on his face harden like an ice sculpture - well after all, we're mostly made of water. Tire tracks followed the thin, packed topsoil filling in the gravel roadways. Snuggling with himself, he couldn't wait to return to the warm compartment of his truck cab.

The area appeared deserted. Leonard passed numerous vacant campsites. Each had its own fire pit, picnic tables and parking space. Numerous trees decorated the landscape. Deciduous trees, skeletal and barren, offered a few brown leaves, like tokens of memorabilia, flopping around limpwristlike at the end of a shivering branch.

He found a restroom. It was locked. He went around to the other side and found it open.

Exiting a few minutes later, he felt surprised to see the nearby sky filled with light, bright and flickering. The light glowed high over the treetops. He secured his coat against the obnoxious wind and, with moth-like curiosity, began to weave his way towards the light. A towering campfire loomed ahead, wrapping his senses with its welcome heat. Roughly the width of a small house, it towered, stories high, leaping and bounding, warm like mother's womb.

Only a couple/three dozen people gathered around the magnificent blaze. Some danced. Some sang personal psalms of praise. Some knelt in reverent worship. Some played instruments to both lead and accompany the songs. One performer caught his eye. Twenty-ish, mid height, medium build, dirty blond hair and large brown cow eyes. A scrap of goatee clung to his chin like an indecisive stalactite. He possessed such youthful cockiness and his huge, brown eyes didn't blink as often as Leonard preferred. The young man displayed enviable talent as a guitar player. Extremely talented, as far as Leonard could tell, but even if he could only play three chords, he had that distinct, charismatic quality that can't help but steal the show.

Leonard stood at the trail's end, or opening, depending on which way you were going. For quite a spell, he comfortably watched the small congregation. The fire felt good, even from such a distance, and he briefly wondered how those so close to the fire could stand the heat. It lit the sky all around them, and burned with joyful intensity. Euphorically mesmerized, he loved to watch it as it leapt and danced and played, right along with the songs of praise.

After the service, the gifted, young guitar player approached him.

"Welcome."

Leonard nodded.

"Is this your first time here?"

Leonard nodded again.

"I'm Ty," he introduced. "Ty Lourdes." He extended his hand. Leonard met him, firm, full grip, warm and alive. Leonard did not want to let go, but still released first.

"Nice name," complimented Leonard.

"My folks idea," Ty explained. "Ty is short for Thank You."

Leonard nodded. He wouldn't have much trouble remembering Ty's name.

"They say," snickered Ty, "that the first time here is the last time somewhere else.

Leonard heard a voice behind him say, "Go on." It did not sound like Ty's voice, nor did Ty look like he said anything.

Both men moved close to the fire and knelt down beside a couple, holding hands and bowing deeply. Leonard closed his eyes and waited, feeling the incredible warmth of the sky-scraping fire. He raised his hands, fingers straight up, palms forward. The fire also took hold, caressing them with its life. It was then that he opened his eyes and realized that the terrible wind just a hundred yards back was virtually absent. He looked up at the treetops to see if it was still blowing way up high. Both the spindly and the evergreens, illuminated by the inferno, seemed still and untouched. He seemed to remember, even on approach towards the campsite, that it did not seem nearly as cold. As he pondered this, Ty rose and turned to introduce a newcomer.

"This is Pastor Pete," Ty introduced. "We call him Pastor Pete the paraclete. If you'll notice, he resembles the Little Rascals' dog."

Shaking hands, Leonard noticed the same impression to make this handshake last, yet again, he withdrew first. He didn't see the resemblance to Pete the dog.

Rather, Pastor Pete was a big man with plenty of round features. His hands pudged. His cheeks nudged the bottom borders of his eyes. His waist didn't exist. His short, neatly cut and combed hair and beard were as black as his eye glass frames. Only his feet and ears appeared small attached to his hefty boned, rotund frame. All the same, the biggest thing about him was either his smile or his heart.

"Welcome," greeted Pastor Pete, and meant it.

"Greetings," answered Leonard, accepting a seat around the fire.

"Coffee? You look like you could use a cup."

Leonard nodded.

"Ty?"

Ty didn't need another word.

"And, be sure to get one for yourself." He turned back to Leonard. "So, Mr. Lamb, how do you like our little campsite?"

"Looks like it keeps the reign on your heads."

"You could say that," he checked the glittery stars framed between the treetops. "You travelin' through or come to stay with us for a spell."

Leonard answered uncertainly, trying to recall if Henry had given him any applicable direction.

"Traveling through, I think." Ty handed him the styrofoam cup, dangerously full of coffee, overflowing with steam. "Thank you," he added as Ty nodded and sat beside him.

"So, you're heading home?"

"Was. Not anymore. This morning, God told me to start a pilgrimage."

"What kind of pilgrimage?" asked Ty, taking note.

"You know, I don't know," admitted Leonard, "but, a pilgrimage typically involves some element of discovery, so I'm trusting that I'll first discover what it is I'm supposed to be looking for – or supposed to be doing, then do it to complete the sojourn."

"Not a clue, huh?" checked the pastor.

Leonard wasn't sure whether to nod yes or no. Either answer could be mistaken and misleading.

"Actually," Leonard fancied aloud, "I may not know exactly what I'm supposed to be doing, but I know that I've been Christian all my life; reared in the Church. My folks were both great people, and I joke that I was raised by Ozzie and Harriet. My grandpa's a pastor, so I've been in and around the Church my entire life. And, that had been fine, till this last year or so, then something inside told me to get off my cushion and go see something I've never seen before, go talk to someone I've never spoken to before, and go find something I've never found before. Even then, I only started the search when it suited me. Now, I think it's finally for real."

"So, how far along are you in your pilgrimage?" asked Ty, intrigued and attracted by the concept.

"Not very far," admitted Leonard. "Of course, like I said, it only started this morning, so I don't think that I'm too far behind schedule, yet." He savored the cranky smell of the coffee billowing up each nostril as he slurped a flat layer of hot fluid, spread evenly across his palate.

"That's quite a fire," Leonard complimented, still unable to take his eyes away for very long. He thought that he saw a burning bush appear briefly in the flames. The impression disappeared as quickly as it appeared, and he watched more intently.

"Thank the congregation – and, of course, God's Holy Spirit. They're the ones who really built it."

"Must take a ton of wood to keep it burning so big."

Pastor Pete laughed, a robust laugh as big as the wind. "What wood?"

Leonard looked away from the flames to question the pastor.

"Look."

Leonard re-examined the fire, and he realized that there was no wood at all. Actually, the fire seemed to hover just above the ground. Pure flame and heat and illumination, all feather light, bobbing like a flock of hummingbirds.

"What is it?" Leonard queried, as much to himself. "I've never seen a gas fire out here in the sticks."

Pastor Pete laughed again. "It's the presence of the Holy Spirit. Or, at least that part of His Spirit sent to dwell in the hearts and minds and bodies and souls of His people, the church.

"So, you can't roast a hot dog or marshmallows on it?"

"Nope," chuckled Pastor Pete, "but, that doesn't keep you from wanting s'more. You've no doubt read Genesis, Chapter One?"

Leonard nodded.

"*In the beginning, God created the Heavens and the Earth, and the Earth was without form, and void and coated in darkness.* But, right off, God's Spirit is there, hovering over the formless void of water. So, He first created light. Before He created us, he knew the need for light, lest we whither and die. Have you ever tried to imagine what this planet would be like if the sun suddenly disappeared?"

It was Leonard's turn to laugh.

"Uh-huh," he snickered. "One time on an all night drive. I was depressed, so pretended the sun had already went out. It was silly, but it probably helped me to stay awake."

He thought a moment, then added, "But, my imagination made it cold and bleak and unbearable. Seeing your light, it wouldn't surprise me if the shining, warm light of the Holy Spirit descended like a dove to keep us alive and warm as long as need be."

Pastor Pete chewed his lip a moment, then said, "Come on." He stood and headed towards the road. Leonard followed.

"You may notice," Pastor Pete pointed out as they strolled along the gravelly road, "that we're quite some distance from our Holy Spirit campfire, but the sense of warmth and joy hasn't dissipated. If this was a regular campfire, we'd feel the cold of the night."

Walking, Leonard noticed various camps, some with large bright lights, and others with small fires, or even no fires. It irked him. None of these had been here during his first tour of the campground.

"Look," pointed Pastor Pete. A very large group of people were praying and singing around the fire pit. Two men knelt down beside the pit, one striking a flint and stone, causing a spark – the other drowning his spark and kindling with buckets of cold water.

"Holy water," said one.

"Living water," declared another.

"That church has been around for hundreds of years," explained Pastor Pete. "I'd bet anything that their fire was bigger than ours at one time, but all that's left are some cold, wet ashes, and heartless traditions to keep them going. Our Lord have mercy! I pray that someday their fire will be restarted. Then, watch-out! But, until then it appears, at least to me, that it will take a serious drought in that church to get the flame to catch."

They walked along a little farther, passing another group, dancing, screaming, and jumping wildly. Some rolled around on the ground. Some barked, or roared, or whooped. Their fire was very low, but widely spread throughout much of the campsite.

"Lots of hype. Not a lot of depth," commented Pastor Pete. "I could probably yell, "Jesus had ear wax," and someone would answer, "Amen." Still, if that works for them. . . They're not violating scripture. It's just not my favorite flavor of worship."

Leonard noticed another congregation. They had a respectably sized fire, but they asked God's guidance regarding just about everything, including probing questions like what to wear or when to go to the grocery store.

"I certainly believe in petitioning the Lord with all your cares and troubles, but sometimes prayers become more like shopping lists and God is treated like a superstition."

"A superstition?" double-checked Leonard.

"You bet. That's where you try to get God to react to the whimsy of your will by following a formula each time. Find a penny from Heaven - pick it up, and all the day you'll have God in your pocket."

Leonard didn't answer. Pastor Pete turned. Leonard had left the road. He watched as Leonard approached the largest campsite.

"Do," thought Leonard, heading in, making no bones about his arrival. He pressed on through the crowd until he found the fire pit. The pittance of warmth rising from the weakly glowing embers wouldn't keep even the closest members warm through this chilly night. Yet, the group huddled about together, reciting well practiced prayers and most behaving as though they were there just to put in their time, such being their weekly commitment.

"Where's your fire?" confronted Leonard.

The mesh of faces, barely discernible in the bleak light, seemed to disbelieve the merits of the question. The answer was too obvious. They all saw the fire. He was standing right by it. Why couldn't this intruder see it?

An elderly gentleman, robed and finely dressed, took a cautious hold 'on Leonard's arm, politely leading him away from the pit. Leonard shook him off, and addressed the congregation.

"My name is Leonard. Leonard Lamb. I'm just passing through. I saw your camp and wanted to stop. I see that you are all decent folk, well dressed and productive. But, I fear that you could be more - much more. You came together to worship and praise God, but your fire has gone out, and you have no light to guide you.

Know this now," he continued, "That your Lord and Savior Jesus wants you to know His Spirit more intimately, and His majestic light will return to your church home."

"Sir, you're wrong," challenged the robed man, and the congregation muttered agreement.

"We are a progressive church with missions in one hundred and twenty two countries worldwide. We have the largest congregation, the largest campsite in the county, and the largest tithe to match. Our Sunday schools are bursting full; our outreach ministries are unparalleled in this corner of the earth, and our fellowship group meets weekly to hike or bowl or dine out. No sir! You are wrong if you think that our church is dead."

Leonard faced the man, long and hard. Neither flinched for an entire hour. The congregation watched anxiously, waiting for one of them to respond. As though on cue, Leonard moved, turning away from the robed clergyman.

"Hey!" he protested, but Leonard ignored him. He knelt down beside the fire pit and studied the dying fire, about to breathe its last. He gently blew on the ashes. A few coals glowed a Hellish red. All watched as Leonard knelt forward and placed his lips against one of the hot coals. He kissed the ember. Immediately, it leapt to light. A small flame came to life, bouncing back and forth, as though joyously liberated. Though small, Leonard could feel the added heat. Though small, Leonard could better pick-out the faces around him as the scant light reflected in each set of eyes.

He straightened up, and dusted himself off. Ash clung to his lower face and lips. He smiled, but received no such warm response. Peering from blank face to blank face, Leonard nodded as a sign of respect, then wound his way through the crowd until he found Pastor Pete, still waiting on the street.

"Wow!" admitted the pastor.

Leonard lamented with a sigh. Looking back towards the campsite, he could see the small flame already flickering and dying. Soon, all was as dark as when they'd arrived, and services continued as before, now that the disruption had passed.

"I wasn't ready to believe," started Leonard as they walked back towards Pastor Pete's camp, "that those who lived without the light would prefer the darkness once they caught a glimpse of the light. I'm still not ready to believe it."

He kicked an old pop can. It bounced and boomeranged ahead of them before finding rest. Pastor Pete raised his arms in praise and thanksgiving as the first light of morning began to peak over the nearby mountains. Leonard joined in, but felt nothing inside. No matter how fervently he prayed, he felt like an old story that still had a bad ending no matter how often retold, provoking a sanitary void that taunted him the rest of the morning.

Chapter Four

"Had enough?" heaved Leonard, halfway up the mountainside, determined, but completely out of breath. "You call yourself tough and mighty and formidable? Think again, buckaroo. You're nothing out of the ordinary, so when ya gonna admit that you been beat & give up? This is your last chance and I ain't takin', '*No*,' for an answer."

He stopped, leaning into the mountain. His head spun dizzily and lungs ached with each groping breath, not unlike the effect kids feel when they take their first drag off a cigarette. His heart rebounded off his sternum with each aggressive, pounding beat. Sputtering, barely able to enunciate anything remotely close to English, he added, "You hear me, mountain? Had enough?"

He looked up to the next peak, only a stone's throw away, not that he could throw any stone any direction at that point but down. He also knew that what he saw was not the peak, but only a ridge. Such progress could be so deceptive on a mountain trek. It looked like the pinnacle till you got there and found the next ridge high above. A dozen or more ridges lay ahead that he still could not see.

Like pudding as it boiled, the Mountains of Perchance shot up from the valley floor. The graven slopes seemed rough and dispassionate as though formed through a mean meat grinder. Up they went, higher and higher, punching huge, irreparable holes in the blue. Nobody knew how deep nor how far back the mountains went, although many believed that they climbed to the doorways of Heaven itself, for those who tried to find out never came back.

Turning outward, he beheld acres upon acres of sun drenched valley, carpeting the expanse before him. Leonard studied the town off to the south; the flickering activity, so minuscule and insignificant. Roadways stretched like electrician's tape into and out of the city, and flowed like arteries, delivering and redistributing life. He watched an impressive performance from his vantage.

He easily spotted the campsite. The huge fires of the Holiest Spirit light rose above the highest trees. He picked one out and imagined it to be Pastor Pete's church. On a whim, he'd decided to hike, and bid his hosts adieu.

He'd heard the many tales and legends that hung from these mountains. One tale told of the Snow Owl Kingdom that guarded the entrance to the peaks. He'd been warned of the goblin' raids and as a lad he'd hunted the elusive Quail Baby, but the latest fables preyed to an old man named Carnibal who had checked-out of society to live in the Mountains of Perchance not twenty years past. Many had known him personally, or so they claimed. Every year or two, someone reported seeing the old prophet as his memory ever haunted the valley folk.

"I'm too young to feel this winded," he chastised himself; one of those few times in his 32 years when he would not have minded being much older to account for his lack of physical conditioning. Rounding a rock, he startled a few grazing deer. They bounded up the side of the slope almost effortlessly, topping the ridge within the next minute. Leonard watched with a renewed sense of awe at how skillfully they climbed, and wished that he could take lessons from them.

"What d'ya think, Lamb? How high you want to go?" Reaching the next ridge, he sat down on a rock to rest, his feet dangling over the side. He noticed a lone man climbing, not far below, coming directly towards him. Watching the climber, Leonard's fingers found rough grooves in the rock. After idly tracing the contours of the grooves, he looked down and found the carvings. He'd been sitting on someone's fish. Standing, he saw that the entire rock shelf was roughly carved. A fish   <')))>< topped the picture. There was an Alpha and Omega on each side, (Ἀ Ω) and small letter T or Roman cross in the center (✝). Arrows surrounded the picture, pointing up the peaks behind the words, "THE WAY." In the lower right hand corner, Leonard read the capital letter C, probably the signet for the sculptor, followed by the copyright symbol © and the number 1929. He wasn't sure he was ready to believe that the rock had been carved over seventy years past.

"Too bad I couldn't ask the author," he mused, wondering whom the "C" might have belonged to.

"Carnibal?" came to mind, but that didn't make sense. Carnibal came to these mountains less than twenty years ago, if at all. The other climber interrupted his speculations.

"Wow! Hi."

A young man, little over twenty, brown hair, freckles and glasses, rounded the rock and just about walked into Leonard before stopping, startled.

"I didn't think I'd find you so quickly."

Leonard looked him over. Nobody he could recall. The young man set down a boda bag, lunch bag, small spiral notebook and pencil with a Yoda shaped eraser on the carved stone.

"M'name's Charley. My friends call me Chuck, but my mom calls me Chuckles. Been doing some writing?"

Leonard glanced down at the old lettering, then back at Charley.

"No. Just admiring it."

"Wow!" Charley repeated. "You did a good job."

Leonard let it drop, and started seeking an escape.

"Mind if I sit with you awhile?" He took a seat on the carved stone.

"Actually," Leonard prepared to bow out...

"I know, I know," continued Charley. "You value your solitude. Me, too. We can appreciate it together."

Leonard stretched his face upward, brows raised, mouth pursed to say to himself a disbelieving, "Okay-ay!"

He turned to go, but Charley continued, "What a great day for a hike, huh?" He sighed, breathing in the view. "I just love to come up here and play What If..."

"What if?"

"Yeah. Like what if we slept up here and when we awoke, the town and the valley and everything was gone, and instead there was another mountain, and we climbed over it and headed down into San Bernardino, California, and nobody ever heard of our town and it wasn't on the map?"

"Okay-ay!" answered Leonard, on the fringes of leaving without being rude.

"Or, what if we slept up here and in the morning we were awakened by water lapping at our feet, and when we looked, the entire valley was full of water, and the water was still rising, but above us the mountain was packed full of people and we were gonna be the next one's to have to go into the drink, and treading water, we watched as all the mountains became islands until they eventually disappeared?"

Leonard was about to comment on Charley's overactive imagination.

"I know," sniggered Charley, twisting around to look up at Leonard. "That's what everyone tells me. They look at me and say, "That's what you think about?" It's like I get started and can't shut-up, 'cause my brain just takes me for a roller coaster ride, and I set my sights high above, and it's three, two, one, blast-off, and, and..."

"...and your brain frees itself of..."

"...no, not a brain freeze. It's more like lift-off. I'm riding high."

"No, I mean like when you climb up?"

Charley frowned. "No, the climate doesn't matter – I mean, I don't go after bad weather."

"No, I mean you're up to it."

Charley paused. "Well, I'd like to see Europe, but that's not what I'm talking about, but what about you? Aren't you the intrinsic illusion, the man of ineffable mystery; the one of a thousand and one lights; the shining ideal of truth and love and perfection, and...???"

"Woah!" corrected Leonard.

"Woe," agreed Charley, "Like Don Quixote. I like that."

It took Leonard a few seconds to dissect that one. Before he got it all sorted in his own head, Charley rose and continued.

"That's why I had to find you. Can I ask you a question?"

"You just did."

"Oh. Uh, can I ask you two questions?"

"You just asked your second."

"And you didn't answer either. I've been in such woe, wondering about life." He gazed intently towards Leonard. "If I can tap your vast resources of knowledge; if you have any cubic zircs of sparkling light to share, you have to tell me."

Leonard massaged his lower lip with his finger and thumb, not about to say something else that could be misconstrued.

Charley interpreted his silence as invitation.

"Tell me," he sighed, "how do we know that we have a soul?"

Leonard started to formulate in his head a treatise based on scripture regarding absolute proofs of the human soul. While composing his thoughts, he opted to use the classic public speaking index standard where he could introduce the subject, tell the audience what he was going to say, tell them again what he was going to say, then present three to five arguments to support his point, then summarize what he'd just said before closing. In turn, he gave himself a moment's reflection by flippantly answering, "How do we know we don't?"

"How-Do-We-Know-We-Don't?" Charley was awed by the response, and sought no further insights from his recruited mentor. Gathering up his few belongings, he turned to head back down the mountain. He stopped and turned back just long enough to offer his thanks, "That's great! I'm in awe. Thank you so much, Carnibal." He proceeded on down, muttering to himself about clear-cut evidence for the existence of the soul in terms of deduction by elimination.

"Charley," Leonard called, "I'm not Carnibal," but, Charley didn't seem to notice, knocking dirt and rock down the trail in front of himself. Leonard could not decide whether to pursue it further or enjoy the misunderstanding. He favored the latter. He also felt downright glad that Charley was gone. Gathering up his strength, he resumed ascending the rocky mount.

Approaching the next escarpment, he came upon a man setting on a huge stone overlooking God's valley. This man wore deer skins. His skin looked darker than chocolate milk, his face boldly freckled, his hair and beard more salt than pepper. He seemed virtually unconcerned that another had joined his company.

"Carnibal?" wondered Leonard. "This must be the holy dude that Charley was looking for."

He nodded greeting to the old prophet.

The prophet nodded back and smiled, his yellowed teeth like aged picket fences, his eyes the color of the rain-stained granite.

"What a day for a hike, huh?" Leonard opened with small talk.

The man slightly shrugged.

"Uh," Leonard continued, "Do you know who did the carvings in that rock down below?"

Again, the man slightly shrugged.

"I thought that it might be you 'cuz there was a letter C in the lower, right-hand corner of the tablet."

The old man didn't seem to understand.

Leonard glanced down hill. He could see Charley tumbling down the mountain too fast till he fell on his back side, making an impressive dust cloud that snowed all around him as he scrambled up to brush himself off. Mostly out of curiosity, Leonard wondered how old Carnibal would answer Charley's question.

"Can I ask you a – theological question?"

Shrug.

"Sir, how do we know that we have a soul?"

The man gazed at Leonard a very long time before answering, his voice sheer rasp, "Without a soul, there would be no Faith, no Hope, no Selfless Love."

"Without – a – soul, – there – would – be – no – Faith, – no – Hope, – no – Selfless – Love," muttered Leonard, surprised by the impact of the words. He wanted to repeat them with that same chafed voice. It sounded so wise and antiquated, but would have to practice it later when he was alone.

"Thank you, Carnibal," he added, and with the replication safely tucked away in his heart, he turned to head back down the mountain. Before he'd gone very far, he realized his presumptions. Maybe this dude wasn't really Carnibal, either. At very least, he could've asked the stranger's name. Starting back up, he looked to see the stranger climbing up towards the next ridge.

Chapter Five

Leonard awoke with a start. The last that he remembered, he'd been climbing up the Mountains of Perchance, following someone, he couldn't remember whom.

"Odd," he thought. Life didn't usually resemble dreams as much as dreams resembled life. The big difference was that we don't know that we're dreaming while we're dreaming, but recognize the dream when awake. In turn, when awake, we know that we're not dreaming. Now, groping for memory, he feared that he'd lost part of his ability to discern reality from dreams. His reality had certainly been more dreamlike lately.

Even his surroundings were unfamiliar, though common. A city park, with trees and grass and a small pond carpeted with duck feathers, (some still connected to the birds,) barbecue stands and playground for the kiddies. Judging by the position of the sun and by the dew sparkling on the grass and by the mild nip in the air, he guessed that it was before mid-morning, then wondered if he'd been out here all night.

His joints felt stiff. He tried to stand, and fell back. His left heel screamed with pain. He rubbed the foot to coax away the pain, then stood and hobbled over to a picnic table. The pain stabbed, but became tolerable as the ligaments limbered.

The Mountains of Perchance rose not far from the park. He felt sure that he must've been here before, but nothing - absolutely nothing seemed familiar. There was no way that he would sit here all day, but he didn't know where to go nor which way to get there.

Isolation was no stranger. He'd spent numerous times alone and on his own, fully invested in life's experiences. But wounded and lost, the loneliness became amplified, and he closed his eyes to chat with Jesus about it.

"I'm confused, Lord," he opened. "And, I'm lost, so I'm trusting you to... y'know, Lord, I don't have any idea what I need, so will praise you since it seems to me that that's the best that any person can do when they know not what to pray for. I pray for Pastor Pete, and Ty Lourdes, and Charley and even," - he couldn't place either name nor face, "whomever that was - that your Spirit will ever be with them, in your name, Lord Jesus, I pray. Amen."

He smiled, and the sun shone, warm and alert. He resisted the call of the lizard, to bask away the day, and rose to hobble. He figured, if he walked away from the mountains, he'd head towards town, or at least happen upon a highway where he could hitch a ride. He also expected to find familiar landmarks, but as he glanced up and around to record his bearings, a flash of inspiration totally knocked him back down on the hard bench.

The sun was rising on the wrong side of the valley.

Yesterday, it'd first peered out over the mountain tops. His mind went to work, considering the possible explanations for the sun being on the wrong side of the landscape.

The Earth could've completely stopped turning, and started revolving the opposite direction so that the sun rose in the west and set in the east. He fretted undecidedly on that one. Also, east and west would be reversed if the Earth was flipped over so that the North Pole was now the South

Pole and vice versa. He wasn't ready to adopt either explanation without further investigation.

For example, if the earth now stood on its head, he'd be in the new Southern Hemisphere. Water would drain circularly in the opposite direction. The sun would sweep across the northern sky, but at this time of day, he might think the northern sun was still the south side. Leonard also considered that he would've suddenly moved from the start of summer daytime to the start of winter daytime. It should take some weeks for the air currents to catch up with the topsy-turvy change. It wouldn't turn to winter weather within twenty-four hours, but the days would immediately become much shorter, like a photo negative. Instead of the sixteen hour day, and eight hour night, they'd have the eight hour day and sixteen hour night. He checked the sun's position once more. It seemed to be crossing over his hemisphere. The more changes he considered, the more he verified that the Earth had not been turned over on its head overnight while he slept.

He couldn't be so immediately sure that the Earth's revolution had not just changed direction. Summer would still be summer. Air currents would still be air currents. He'd have to check the stars tonight to see which way they spun. If clockwise, there'd be no doubt that the planet stopped spinning, then began spinning the opposite direction.

Until then, he was more willing to accept the third explanation that he was on the opposite side of the mountain range. Still, the realization of such a trek seemed just about as difficult to believe as imagining the Earth got turned over. While musing over the impossibility of tramping over hundreds of miles of mountains un-remembered, a vehicle stopped on the street beside him.

"Leonard!" called Rodger, falling out of Leonard's pickup. "Glad I found ya, man. Glad I found ya. I've been driving around all morning trying to find you."

"Rodger?" blinked Leonard, stunned and dumbfounded. Suddenly, a flash flood of recollections drew in around his brain like the fisher's nets.

How far back had it been? Days? Weeks? He sifted through the pile of memories.

Carnibal!

He'd started down the mountain, then saw Carnibal climbing to the next level of insight. It wasn't long before Leonard lost sight of him, obscured by rock and trees and height. A tug-o-war emerged inside his head. To climb meant following Carnibal and higher insights into that which were divine. To descend meant following Charley down to the common graze. The concept of 'following Charley' didn't repulse him, but it bugged him enough that he opted for the ascent.

He searched the mountain face for the best way to climb. He climbed from ridge to ridge, keeping an eye out for Carnibal. Eventually, he came to a near sheer rock wall, rising higher than the clouds. While wondering which way to go, he spied a man scrambling over the surface with the graceful ease of a spider. Leonard immediately saw that it wasn't Carnibal, nor anyone else he knew. He watched with awe and admiration as the scaler seemed to defy gravity.

Soon, the rock climber saw Leonard. Leonard gasped as the man seemed to jump out as though repelling down the cliff, but Leonard could not see a rope, above or below the climber. Still, he flowed down the face for numerous feet, his fingers ever gliding over the rocky surface, then he stopped, repositioned, and bound down again until he settled on the platform beside Leonard.

He was short and lean, displaying the muscles of an acrobat. Thirty-ish. He wore soft, rubbery rock climbing shoes, baggy camo pants and a sheer, brown tanktop that matched his deeply tanned skin. His eyes, the edges of his nose, the tips of his mouth, the flow of his brow; every feature was bold and deep, framed in dark red hair and beard.

"Greetings," he puffed, his voice as deep as his features. "M'name's Rodger. Come to do some climbing?"

"Not like that," Leonard motioned upward.

"Why not?" mocked Rodger.

Leonard began to formulate an explanation when Rodger answered, "Fear?"

Leonard was a bit taken aback, but for such a stark, blunt answer, he had to admit that he'd found the bottom line.

"Fear is a lie," challenged the climber, leaning casually against the rock wall. "It causes your gears to seize and your brain to freeze while all reason flees. So, we fail and we die 'cuz we didn't really try, so I'm telling you straight – fear is a lie."

"I don't know," mouthed Leonard though he readily recalled dozens of personal, integrated incidents. "But," Leonard audibly added, "it's so incapacitating when it does grab you, and no matter what you say to yourself, your emotions are still held hostage. How can you shut it off long enough to get the job done and still be safe?"

He didn't wait for an answer.

"I remember one time," continued Leonard, "when I was hired to help re-shingle a roof. It was a two story home, so we were a little ways up. I worked all over that roof just fine until I came to one section that hung out over the fenced patio. The family dog was below me, barking and getting all excited whenever he'd see me.

For some mysterious reason, I could not make myself go out on that section of roof to work. It was the same slope as the rest of the roof. There were plenty of high drops, but the fear that I could fall down on the concrete pavement, maybe straddling the chain link fence, and likewise be attacked by the family hound caused my emotions to panic each time I tried to step out there to work. I tried over and over, but could not make myself go out there. It got so bad that I became the greatest danger to myself."

"That's what I said," agreed Rodger. "Fear is a lie. So, how'd you finish the roof?"

Leonard chuckled, still chiding himself for being so terrified. "Actually, I was standing there on the roof telling myself how stupid I was being when I saw the home owners turn onto the street. As soon as I saw them, I knew that I had to behave like a professional, so without further hesitation, I walked out onto the forbidden zone and started shingling. Isn't that crazy?"

Rodger laughed appreciably. "Been there a thousand times. But, y'know, someone told me God said to be strong and courageous, I don't know how many times. Fear not! Do you think God wasn't kidding?"

"No," peeped Leonard.

"So, ya ready?"

"For?"

Rodger's eyes motioned up the rock wall.

Leonard recoiled. "No way I'm going up there, at least not that way."

"Why not?"

"You know why not."

"Come on. Climb to new heights. Progress. Your God never said real progress would always be easy."

"But," spouted Leonard, "It also wasn't supposed to be impossible."

"What if I showed you that it wasn't impossible, and the only thing harder to overcome than this mountain is your fear?"

Leonard didn't want to know the answer. He also didn't want to be baited. The more he objected, the more his objections could be challenged. Just say no, and don't give 'em a reason.

"Really," urged Rodger. "I'll show you."

He climbed up ten to twelve feet and looked back. "This ain't the Eiger – or El Capitan. It's angled. It's a steep slope, but it's still an angle. Try it – just a step up or two."

Leonard knew that he was crazy before he touched the stone, but he slipped a foot against the rock and easily lifted himself up the first step. He looked down, examined the rock and took another step, then another.

"Wait," commanded Rodger dropping down beside him.

Leonard seized up, six feet from the base.

"No," responded Rodger. "You're doing great. I just wanted you to take a step to the left."

Leonard complied, then another.

"See?" suggested Rodger, following beside him. "I promise, if you can maneuver at this height, it's no harder when you're farther up."

"Just a lot scarier."

"Fear's still a lie."

"Understood," nodded Leonard, "but, the danger is still greater, and fear is still very real, lie or no lie. I don't want new proof of the existence of my soul as I watch it leave my broken, bleeding corpse..."

"Fair enough," agreed Rodger. "You decide – up or down?"

Leonard paused briefly. He thought that he might go up a bit more, and retreat if he found fear pouncing on him. He also knew from experience that it's typically easier to climb these steep parts of the mountain than safely go back down. Perhaps he could move left and right, like a switchback if he could not safely drop straight down. He moved around the lower mountainside, then dug in and started moving upward.

"You're doing great!" called Rodger and meant it, climbing alongside.

Leonard did fine and avoided looking down until they reached the cloud level. Heading into the thin fog felt more isolating. He could clearly see their direction of ascent, but everything felt less certain.

He stopped to catch his breath.

Rodger recognized the signs.

"It's not much farther."

"Really?" Leonard gasped.

"You'll see." He looked up. "Veer right. The climb's a little easier."

They both moved in unison. The slope graduated, and Leonard continued to climb until he scampered onto the next ridge.

Standing, he whooped, loud and shrill, as the hill leveled out, still coated within the clouds, and he did a little dance.

Rodger nodded appreciably.

Still dancing, Leonard's foot caught a loose rock, bending his ankle. He fell towards the cliff.

Rodger tried to dive for him, to catch him, but knew he wouldn't be there in time.

Leonard flipped over and slid down the hill. Rodger lost sight as he went over the edge. It became deathly quiet. Rodger listened as he raced to the edge.

He searched for Leonard.

Finding him, he started to laugh. Dropping down another twenty feet, he came alongside Leonard.

"That was dumb," proclaimed Leonard, hugging the rock.

"Where do you hurt?"

"No where – so far."

"I can't believe that you stopped yourself."

"Ditto," agreed Leonard, still breathing aggressively. He explained, "My roofing days came in handy. I knew that if I totally relaxed – just flopped against the rock so that I got the maximum amount of body contact and friction against the rock, that it'd probably stop me."

"You were lucky."

"Amen."

The two men took time to catch breath.

"Think you can climb? Looks like your ankle took a nasty turn."

Leonard carefully moved. The ankle seemed fine. He felt around with each hand until he found a cut in the rock to hold onto. His clothes were bunched up with the gravity of his body. He felt around with his right foot, trying to find a foot hold.

Rodger dropped down to place his foot on a meager step. Leonard raised up and studied the rock to see how he could head back up.

"We'll get there," Rodger was undaunted. "Just take your time. You already know that it's not far."

Leonard placed his left foot on a secure foothold, but couldn't seem to raise himself. He tried again, and slipped again.

"I can't make it," he cried, falling back against the stone face. "Just go on without me. Save yourself."

"Are you serious?" challenged Rodger.

"No, of course not," converted Leonard. "I just always wanted to say that line. It always sounded so dumb in the movies. It sounds even dumber now."

"Then, don't waste my ear space," agreed Rodger. "Now, let's see..."

Both men were interrupted by a sound beneath them.

"Look," pointed Rodger.

Leonard didn't want to, but did. Two figures amply climbed the sheer rock face towards them.

"Know them?" asked Leonard.

"No. Don't look familiar."

Both men glanced at each other. Their expressions told the same story. Get to safer ground before the two below caught them. They might be friendly, but they didn't know, and the sheer side of a mountain was not the place to find out.

It felt like slow going, but both men reached the ridge well ahead of the approaching visitors. There they waited, resting until the pair topped the ridge.

Leonard wasn't sure he saw the two properly. They seemed human, but had faces that somewhat resembled mules. It was repulsive, but both smiled as they approached.

"Good afternoon," panted the leader. "What a climb!"

"And, what a day!" added the second.

"Quite," agreed Rodger, then introduced himself and Leonard.

"I'm Grief," brayed the first, and my friend is Pain." He spoke, not with a whine - not as a nag, but in a perpetual apology, or as one who asks permission and doesn't trust the affirmation.

"Maybe you've heard of us?" asked Pain, plopping down to massage his swollen ankles.

"I've seen you around," acknowledged Rodger. He recalled from personal experience that these two were typically the type most selfish and sane folks preferred to avoid. "What brings you over the Mountains?"

"Assignment," sniffled Grief, pounding the rocky floor with his forehead.

"The Perfect Shepherd summoned us," explained Pain, moving up to rub his calves and knees. They creaked as he bent them back and forth. "We need to take someone up to the Elevated Peaks."

"In the Mountains of Perchance?" checked Leonard.

"We wish," whined Grief, tossing handfuls of dirt in the air to land on him.

"Nah. Up the Peaks of Seasonings," coughed Pain. "Place smells like a potpourri factory next door to a spaghetti cook-off. We need to take a new convert, young woman named Lotsa Frump up the Peaks to the Elevated Spots for the Perfect Shepherd." He checked his pulse, pressing two fingers against the left side of his neck.

"We're her tour guides," added Grief, foraging the dirt from his eyes.

"Bummer," said Rodger, "- for Lotsa Frump."

"Yeah," affirmed Grief. "I wouldn't want to travel with us."

"But," hacked Pain, "if she makes it, she'll be so light on her feet, Fred Astaire would be jealous." Leonard noticed Pain's temples pulsed like erupting migraines.

"Are you all right?"

"Never," admitted Pain, rising to go while stretching and twisting and snapping spinal vertebrae into place with the expertise of a floundering chiropractor. "But, no complaints. That's Grief's department."

Grief ignored the prudence to ignore Pain.

"I don't know why you treat me like that." He stomped away, hiking along the ridge. The others followed. With Grief's hunched over back facing them, he added, "Fate, I guess..."

"Actually," interrupted Pain, catching up to his companion, but still addressing all three, "Fate told me about the time that the two of you tried to get Solomon to change his answer when God asked, "What shall I give you?" And Solomon asked for wisdom, but you two tried to get him to ask for Noah's Ark."

"I didn't know you knew about that."

"Uh-huh. I also seem to recall that Solomon almost went with it." Pain mined his pockets for nail clippers to trim back the bamboo under his nails.

Grief explained to all three men, "Fate thought it a shame to leave such a famous relic glacially impacted on Ararat where only a handful of people could see it any given year." He pulled out his bandana to blow his nose. Replacing it in his back hip pocket, it trailed out resembling a flag at half mast. "Personally," he added with smothered elation, "I'm blessed that they did not succeed."

"Why 'cuz?" asked Rodger, tossing an impish side glance towards Leonard who was too busy hiking to notice.

"Simple," answered Grief in his perpetual gray tones. "It would grieve me to see it splintered away by pilgrims and sightseers seeking souvenirs and mementos until it collapsed - that's right collapsed on some obnoxious tourists who had a vicious attorney and they provoked the powers that be to condemn it and eventually dismantle it so that during the upcoming centuries, false theologians and critics to the faith would point to that day as proof that the ark never could have been built or used as a floating zoo; as though their pride filled foolishness would be enough to disenchant one of our Lord's greatest miracles acted out upon this planet."

He stopped to catch his breath, peering from face to face with eternally somber eyes.

"I dunno," Leonard thought aloud. "It seems to me that Solomon might've also changed his mind from a purely human stand point. I'm sure that there are tons of people, thousands upon thousands - even millions who might want the ark, but very, very few of them would make it their first choice if God asked them how he should bless them. I know I wouldn't.

"Likewise," he smirked, "where would most of us keep it?"

"It wouldn't fit in my backyard," quipped Rodger, "but if it did, bet I wouldn't have to mow my lawn."

"You probably don't mow your lawn already," crooned Grief, still leading the way, searching for something along a rock wall.

Rodger grinned, "You're right. I pay the kid down the street."

Tramping right along, Leonard caught sight of something, moving to his left. He looked. Nothing there. He kept pace with the others, then saw it again, and again, it disappeared as soon as he looked straight on. Rounding a corner, the image slipped by just inside his peripheral vision.

"What is it?" asked Rodger.

"Nothing," Leonard lied, not wanting to sound silly. Grief and Pain turned, their strange features questioning him.

"What did you see?" pressed Pain.

"It's just my imagination."

"What's just your imagination?"

Leonard looked at Rodger. "I dunno," he admitted, "but, I keep seeing something out of the corner of my eye. When I look, there's nothing there, of course."

Grief and Pain nodded appreciably to each other, then continued checking through the foliage along the mountain rise.

"What?" asked Leonard.

"A gift," answered Grief, not looking, almost sounding happy. "A very special gift."

"It's a nuisance – and a distraction so far."

"Many new gifts can be like that," commented Pain, rubbing a kidney, "at least until you learn how to use them. Then, you wonder how you ever got along without them. Reminds me of the first time I had cruise control. Never wanted it till I had it, and now I'd hate to give it up."

Leonard noticed something odd about Rodger. The entity suddenly slid by just past the corner pocket of his vision.

"What?" he asked Rodger.

Rodger pressed his lips together before answering. "Sorry to tell you this, my friend, but I think that they're pulling your leg."

73

"Go on," scoffed Leonard, "You think?" Without looking, he felt the presence of something seated on the rock above him. Peering upward, he saw that the rock was bare but he also knew it pointed to the left side of a ravine.

He looked back towards Rodger who added, "I just think that, if anything, it's your imagination running rampant, and playing mischief."

Leonard thought a moment, then said, "You might be right. Or, you might be wrong. I don't know. I just wish it'd go away right now." He looked left, but knew this time it really was his imagination. Grief and Pain continued to examine the wall.

"What're you looking for?" Leonard asked.

"A cave opening," answered Pain, dabbing tissue on a razor nick.

Leonard pointed towards the ravine. "I think it's to the left up here."

Grief sneered, then turned down the ravine, grumbling to himself why he listened to anyone.

"Is this it?" called Rodger, pulling back a bush planted next to a small opening.

Pain stooped down and slithered through the small opening. Bumping his head as he withdrew, he nodded, and went to work rubbing the maturing goose egg.

"Come on," led Grief.

"Where?" checked Leonard, sure he didn't like the answer.

Grief didn't move, but his body english urged them to follow him through the opening.

"I can't fit through there, protested Leonard."

Grief would've laughed if he'd known how. "If I can fit through, so can you. Haven't you ever wanted to try spelunking?"

He didn't wait for an answer. Dropping down to all fours, he slid his arms in first, then head, then wriggled the rest of his body through the opening.

"Come on," he called, his voice a hollow tooth.

Pain followed.

"What about you?" Leonard asked Rodger.

"Wouldn't miss it," he chirped, cavalier as ever. "It looks like the opening's tight, but it opens up once   inside."

"What about light? I didn't bring a torch, or flashlight."

"A torch is a flashlight," said a voice. Leonard turned towards the source. No one there but some red and black ants, skittering and racing to and fro.

"We'll see," urged Rodger. "Come on!"   He didn't indicate hearing another voice.

Leonard said nothing, in response to either.

"You coming?" called one of the voices inside.

"Suit yourself," Rodger shrugged, then practically dove into the hole in the mountain.

Leonard stood outside the hole. He stooped down and peered into the darkness. He looked around at the thin clouds caressing the peaks around him, and wondered which direction he'd go to get back down.

"What the heck!" he said after some minutes, and wriggled himself through the opening.

As expected, the cave opened up. He stood alone in the dark, a troglodyte not anxious to leave the security of the light seeping in the small hole. He could not hear his companions as he waited for his eyes to adjust to the darkness.

"Hey!" he called.

"This way," called Rodger.

"Keep talking," Leonard called back, feeling his way along the wall as he hoped his eyes would adjust to the darkness. The cool, dank gloom seemed to draw in around him as he wondered what in the world he was doing. He looked back at the entrance. It seemed so bright, but so small, and he wondered how he'd ever squeezed through. Visions of getting stuck while exiting, or worse, closed in, plowed through his hyperactive mind. He looked away from the hole. A void of absolute black, colored only with stark imagination.

"This way," called Rodger. "We can hear your steps. And, your breathing. Sounds like a vacuum cleaner. Just keep coming."

Leonard followed the voice, but kept track of his steps in case he had to make a solo retreat. His skin was alive with goose bumps, like massaging fingers up the back of his scalp, tickling hair follicles. The room was cool. The walls were clammy, and the floor uneven. He'd toured caves before, such as Timpanogos, Minnetonka, and the Indian Echo Caverns. Those trips were well lighted. In each, the tour guides ordered the patrons to not touch the walls, and he wondered what walls he was now killing with his greasy fingertips.

"Come on," called Rodger. "You've got to see this." His voice sounded muffled.

Leonard wondered what any of them could see. He came to a sudden right turn. He couldn't feel the wall to his left without letting go of the wall to the right. In the darkness, he wasn't about to venture out, lose direction and gamble that he would not get lost. At the right turn, he stopped, unsure he should go one more step. He recognized the rush of panic flooding his being.

He closed his eyes and prayed, silently, his lips moving.

"You're almost here," called Rodger. "Come on."

The voice sounded close. Leonard opened his eyes, took a deep breath, gauged his movements, made sure that he could find his way back, kept his right hand against the wall, and took that first step to the right.

The light was dazzling. Shadowless. Intoxicating. His eyes ached, resetting aperture. He wondered why he couldn't see the light barely a step away. Backing up a couple of steps, he re-entered the suffocating darkness. Nothing to show for it. He still couldn't believe his eyes. Turning around again, he returned to the light. Rodger, Grief and Pain stood across the widening room.

He took a moment to let his eyes adjust before joining them. It was a common cave with stalactites and stalagmites throughout, covering white, limey rocks.

"I'm confused," he admitted, joining his companions. They stood by a huge, wooden table, loaded with food, hot and delectable. Each ate and drank and motioned for Leonard to join them.

"About the light?" choked Pain, waving a roasted hind chicken quarter around the cave, minus a couple of bites.

Leonard nodded, though the table of food was just as much a mystery. Something about Pain seemed different.

"You're in the Spiritual Realm," answered Grief. Leonard looked at Grief with a different eye as well.

Leonard's blank face gave answer.

"Read your scriptures," answered Grief pouring him a tall glass of wine.

"I do," spurred Leonard, taking a sip. "What part?" The wine was good. Really good. Top quality, as far as he could tell.

"The verse about the Kingdom of Heaven and the mortal, human world being separated by a sheer veil. You just passed through the veil.

Leonard took another sip, and let that sink in.

"So, this is Heaven?"

"Uh, no. Not exactly," answered Pain, planting jumbo, pitted olives on each finger. "It's more like the Outskirts of Heaven. I've never been there, of course, Heaven that is, but I'm sure that it's much more glorious than this feast in an isolated cavern."

Leonard was unconvinced. He looked over at Rodger who shrugged while munching on delicate, cream-filled pastries.

"Um – ," continued Pain, "think of it as being on the outside of a glass, t'where some of the foam drips over. You get a taste, but it's not the same as taking a real drink. This light around us is like that foam." He dipped each olive in a cheesy fondue before popping the fruit in his gingivitis-riddled mouth. "Heaven's Godly light is all around us, but in this sin filled world, it's obscured. We have to die to the world to enter within."

"So, you're saying that we're dead?" muddled Rodger, slurping the cream filling off his callused, dirty fingers.

"No," laughed Grief. "Just blessed for a short time, to be filled before we continue our journey."

Leonard cut into a leg of lamb. It fell apart, steam rising, as he first smelled, then tasted the succulent morsel.

"Nah, I don't think so," argued Rodger, twirling veal bratwurst dipped in brown mustard between his fingers like a cigar.

"What?" both asked.

"I think that the light's just broken."

They waited for explanation.

"If the light was working, it would also make shadows. There are no shadows here, so the light must be broken."

"So you say!" muttered Grief, still not sure he'd heard right.

"And how do you explain this repast?" asked Rodger, looking at Leonard who took his turn to shrug, his mouth full and moving, his face coated with a muttony euphoria.

"Book of Isaiah, Chapter Twenty Five," answered Grief, refilling his glass.

Rodger moved his arms, hands, neck, head, shoulders, and other parts of his body in a jumbled fashion to communicate that he didn't have a clue what Grief was referring to.

Grief quoted by rote, "Verse 6: "*And the Lord of hosts will prepare a lavish banquet for all peoples on this mountain; A banquet of aged wine, choice pieces with marrow, And refined, aged wine.*

Verse 7: *And on this mountain He will swallow up the covering which is over all peoples, Even the veil which is stretched over all nations.*" It goes on. You get the idea."

Rodger tried to act like he was unconvinced. "It's nice that he mentioned the wine twice. How much farther does this cave go back?"

"This is it," answered Pain, patting his stuffed belly and checking the table for some Jell-o.

"Well," reasoned Rodger, "if this is light from Heaven, it seems like we should be able to follow it to its source."

"Probably not," deduced Leonard, realizing for the first time that the hue and glow around them resembled the campfires ~~back in Chapter Three~~ in Pastor Pete's camp grounds.

"I'm gonna find out," declared Rodger, setting down his glass. Like one who knew how to successfully take the bull by the horns, he headed off through the cavern until he was out of sight.

Leonard wondered if he should accompany him, but dismissed the idea. Turning towards Grief and Pain, he was surprised to see them dropping to the hard floor, kneeling, arms and hands raised, hands open, giving praise and glory to God Almighty. They thanked him for the banquet. They praised him for the light. Mostly, they praised him for being their Savior, and asked for insight, direction and understanding in the mission set before them.

Leonard knelt down behind them, closing his eyes, raising his arms to join in the worship. He prayed fervently, but felt nothing.

Nothing!

It exacerbated him. How could he be in divine light, and feel nothing? How!!?? How??!! It didn't make an ounce of sense. How many times had he prayed for just such an occasion? He couldn't guess. It'd been so many. And now, instead of entering the giddiness of worship, his mind was focused about as well as a cockeyed kaleidoscope. It occurred to him if a person could spin a kaleidoscope around and around fast enough for centrifugal force to apply - an impossibility really, but if a person could, the picture would never change.

Leonard opened his eyes. The two figures before him seemed brighter in this already brilliant grotto. They almost seemed transfigured as they prayed in unison.

No, he decided. They weren't transfigured, like he'd imagined Jesus on the mountain with Peter, James and John. But, something was definitely different... what the?

Halo?

He hadn't seen a real halo before. For that matter, he had not believed that they really existed, but he studied Grief and Pain, their entire heads crowned with light. It wasn't the silly little oval drawn over comic strip caricatures. It wasn't the flat, two dimensional yellow or gold leaf border around the heads of saints in medieval paintings. These flowed around each head, like a luminous globe making their odd, bestial features attractively bright and incandescent.

Radiant!

He reached forward to touch the light. Grief didn't flinch or move as his hand passed close to Grief's head. He hoped to feel warmth, but instead felt nothing. It seemed he should've felt something.

Then he wondered if that only reflected his own lack of spiritual acumen. For the *nth* time in years, Leonard seriously brooded on the lack in his spiritual walk with Christ. Again, he wondered how he could be here and not be touched. He prayed for God's blessed grace, and echoed a clanging cymbal. He spoke and petitioned and eventually begged for God's burning fire within. His words just bounced back at him, flat and listless. The only change he could finger was that his attentiveness towards his two comrades exceeded the attention that he gave his pastor last Sunday. The idea was not encouraging.

"Amen," they together closed and stood.

"We must go." Grief and Pain turned to leave, their haloes dimming. Leonard also rose.

"What about Rodger?"

"He's already gone," eulogied Grief as though that would satisfy Leonard's concerns.

They again thanked the Lord for his hospitality. Leonard followed them into the demon darkness. His left hand feathered along the invisible wall, though he could still see the faint, but glowing heads before him. Soon they reached the small hole.

Suddenly, something clamped down on Leonard's left heel. He yelped and jumped, but it remained attached, sinking pressure into the foot, stressing the bones. He landed, and it released hold, and skittered off as Leonard fell back on the jagged rock.

"Leonard!" called Pain. Both jumped back and brought him to his foot.

"What was...?" started Leonard.

"OUT!" pushed Grief, jamming Leonard through the exit first. His belly full, it was harder to squeeze through, but he felt the hole release its hold, and he landed in a pile.

Leonard sat up and waited for Grief and Pain. His foot throbbed, and he tied the laces of his boot as tightly as he could. It seemed like a very long time before Grief wormed forth.

"What took so long?"

"Conference," answered Grief without color. Pain soon appeared, and they helped him slip out like a newborn at birth. He emerged blue and pasty and reached up with both hands to press his conehead back to normal shape. Filling his gurgling, asthmatic lungs with air, he hacked, "Talk about being born again!"

Chapter Six

"What the heck was that?" cried Leonard as Grief carefully removed Leonard's footwear to examine the wound.

"You shouldn't say that," answered Grief, tears flooding down both cheeks as he lifted the foot and looked underneath at the heel. The injury appeared obvious - red and swollen.

Leonard bent forward to also get a look.

"Say what?" he asked, gritting his teeth against the pain.

"Expressions," Pain jumped in as he finished suturing his abdomen after removing his appendix. "Expressions that use variation words like 'heck." He clipped the catgut and dabbed the stitches with the dampened tail of his shirt.

"I wish you wouldn't do that?" snapped Grief.

"What? Clean it with a dirty shirt?"

"No, bite the catgut with your teeth to clip it."

"Sorry." Pain looked at Leonard, lying on the ground. "Force of habit. My father was a tailor."

"Heck?" puzzled Leonard, rolling onto his back as Grief continued to lift his foot, raising the back of his ankle to get a better look.

" 'What the Heck' instead of 'What the Hell', 'dang' or 'darn' instead of 'damn,' 'gosh' instead of God... - you get the idea."

"That's silly," Leonard protested, looking up from his spot on the rough ground.

"Is it?" challenged Grief, sniffling. He started to blow his nose on Leonard's sock, then stopped. He felt around and squeezed the area around the wound, watching for Leonard's reaction. Leonard obliged.

"Sure, I watch my language," argued Leonard, teeth clenched, "but..."

"...Heck is being nitpicky?"

He looked at Pain who retrieved an endoscope to search for an ulcer. "Yeah," Leonard finally answered. "It seems so to me."

"Just for the record," mumbled Pain, "language is a God-given gift, as is all of life. If such words have their roots in words, or more exactly, concepts meant to hurt and/or destroy and divide human souls from your Savior, you might consider different ways to express yourself."

Leonard thought for a moment. "Okay," he rephrased, still seeking answer to his original question, "What in the world was that?"

"Serpent," rued Grief, laying down Leonard's foot. "Big one. Struck ya good."

"Didn't break the skin, fortunately" added Pain appreciably, removing the tube from his mouth. "That's what took us so long to exit the cavern. We had to make sure it didn't attack again. Here. Try to get your shoe back on. We've gotta get you off this mountain."

"Totally caught me off guard," admitted Leonard who paused from dressing, freshly re-seized with shivers as his mind replayed the unexpected attack in the dismal cave.

"Yeah," smiled Pain, "you crushed him good."

"What?" turned Leonard. "You mean the serpent? I don't recall stepping on it. Didn't feel anything."

"You didn't step on him with your foot," informed Grief, his voice a tired triumph. "You got him with your prayers."

"What prayers?" He knotted the lace and carefully straightened the leg to rest his foot.

"In the cave, of course," pointed Pain, sipping a Mylanta cocktail.

"I'm confused," admitted Leonard.

The other two waited.

"I didn't feel a thing, no matter how hard I prayed."

"That doesn't mean that your prayers landed on fallow ground," answered Pain, popping his shoulder in and out of socket while helping Leonard to his feet. "Your prayers hit their mark, apparently hard enough to spark a counterattack. Do you think the Israelites always felt like God heard their prayers when, generations after generations, they lived under repression and slavery in Egypt? Yet, not one prayer was missed, and when the time came for God to release them from their bondage, he had an arsenal of prayers deep enough and wide enough to separate the seas and defeat Pharoah's army."

"So, what should I do?" muttered Leonard, trying to put weight on the foot.

"Keep on praying," both answered in harmony. Each helped Leonard, slinging an arm over their shoulders to start the trek down.

Leonard looked to one, then the other, then smiled. "I can do that. But, let me ask you, even if I didn't feel anything in there, what were *your* impressions while you knelt there and prayed. Did the Holiest Spirit touch you in some tangible fashion?"

They nodded.

"A lot?"

"Floodwaters," answered Pain.

"A complete tune-up, preparing us for the assignment we're about to start," added Grief. "It seems to me that you, and our not-coincidental contact with you, is part of God's preparation for our upcoming assignment."

"So," considered Leonard, "do I get anything out of it?" He paused, then continued. "I don't mean to sound selfish. I'm merely asking for information."

"Of course," answered one, and the other nodded. "Haven't you received already?"

Leonard thought about the climb, the cave exploration, the Heavenly light, the banquet, the assistance by these two unlikelies. The answer seemed to speak for itself before the dust from the question collected.

"But," added Grief, "it sounds like you may be a bit crusted over."

Leonard's eyes questioned him for more info.

"Maybe even solid through and through."

"Hope not," added Pain, checking his blood sugar. "It's just like humans to get so involved and so busy with life that they unwittingly close off the channels to the Holiest Spirit. Then, one day they awaken, totally surprised that they've gone spiritually deaf. Meanwhile, there's this God-shaped void in their being that cannot be filled by anyone or anything else, and the saddest thing of all is that, though they make the big wall to keep the world out, the wall also locks their past hurts inside where they churn and gurgle and choke the life out of their host like a chemo-defying cancer, killing the host organism that gives it life."

"So," closed Grief, "if you're feeling alone and untouched, keep praying with everything you've got, and I promise, our Lord Jesus will answer you in ways that will knock you on your behind."

Leonard nodded a silent, "Amen," and realized with the serpent attack, he'd just been knocked on his you know what... Continuing to stumble along, connected to his companions and his focus on walking, it took a while before he noticed that they were going the wrong way.

"Shouldn't we be going the other way?"

Grief checked their bearings before continuing.

"It's not far," assured Pain. Side by side, Leonard noticed for the first time Pain's blistering, class C sunburn.

Topping a rock hill, the hikers saw two trees, unseemly large for that high on the mountain. The first tree had broad, green leaves and lots of ripe fruit, blue in color, but half of the tree looked dead and gray and without bark. The second tree also had lots of ripe fruit, a golden orange color. It's leaves were long and a sweet, rich yellow color. The narrow trunk spread out towards the top. The branches swept out, drooping near the ends like a birch. Leonard noticed a nub or point of new growth rising at the middle top of the tree.

"Some things never change," complained Grief.

"You've been here before?" asked Leonard.

"These trees are why we came this way," answered Pain as he carefully set a fractured femur in his right arm.

"At this rate," observed Leonard, "you won't have any parts left to fix before you get down the mountain."

"Probably," applauded Pain.

"Typically," barbed Grief.

"So, what's so special about them?" Leonard pointed to the two trees.

The two allegoricals peered at one another questioningly.

"You came all this way, and don't even know why you're here?" stabbed Grief. They gazed at one another. A smile bent Pain's chapped lips. Suddenly, both released their hold on Leonard as they fell back, rolling on the rock, laughing on and on until their sides hurt.

Leonard hobbled over to a boulder to sit. Watching the pair until they let up to catch some air, he exclaimed, "I have no idea what's so funny."

The pair started up again, rolling around like balls, guffawing insanely.

"Stop it," snarled Leonard. If his ankle had not been injured, he would have stormed off in a huff.

"I'm sorry," chortled Grief after a while, wheezing, not used to such regale. "We thought that you were on a mission, so we were dutifully ready to assist you, but instead we find that you're just on a pleasure cruise."

"What mission?" demanded Leonard.

"As a Picker," snickered Pain. "A Harvester. This fruit's gotta be picked before it sours."

"And, you thought I climbed this darn – sorry, – this, uh – delightful mountain to pick fruit?"

"Uh-huh," answered Grief, wiping tears from his eyes.

"Well, what trees are these?"

Pain, (who's sides usually hurt anyway,) still chuckling, clutched his stomach as he snorted, then pointed an arthritic finger towards the first tree with the half-dead section. "That is the Tree of College, and the other is the Tree of Golden Eagle."

Leonard still peered at them more blankly than Grief or Pain expected or would have preferred for that matter. Grief prepared to explain, but held his tongue as Leonard rose and tottered over to the Tree of College. He saw that the tree was good for food, that it was pleasant to the eyes, and a tree desirable to make one wise, so he reached up and yanked off a piece. The royal blue, round fruit seemed about the size of a tennis ball, and just about as fuzzy. He smelled it. Raisin-ish. Digging in his thumbs, he roughly split the fruit. Juice ran down his fingers and arms. He took a bite - almost more a drink. Blue nectar oozed down his chin. Rubbing it off with his sleeve, he looked at Grief and Pain.

"What d'you think?" asked Pain, pulling off a boot.

"Bittersweet." He took another bite.

"I just ate - in the cave, so I'm not really hungry, but I could get used to this very quickly." He slurped the juice flowing down his hands. Suddenly, a thought occurred to him.

"I'm puzzled. If this is the Tree of College, shouldn't I feel wiser or smarter or something? Plus, isn't this like forbidden fruit so I should feel shame and guilt?"

"We wondered about the same thing," admitted Grief, his face in his hands.

"And considered," gritted Pain, biting a bullet as he clipped an ingrown toenail, "two possible explanations. "The first was that God didn't specifically tell *you* to not eat of the fruit, so you're not violating His divine command. That always struck me as kind of a wimpy explanation."

"And the second?"

"That you were already born to sin and fear, including guilt and shame. You've lived with it all your life, so eating the fruit doesn't make you more you. We definitely lean towards the second explanation." He replaced his boot.

Picking more fruit, Leonard considered, "That would be awesome, to be outside fear and sin, even for a moment. I cannot imagine what it'd be like.

"It seems like I should've been free and unencumbered there in the cave, lit by Heaven's light, but I was still duct taped to the floor with my woes and fears."

Grief looked up to add, "And, as far as feeling wiser or smarter, wait and see when the occasions arise. You don't really need the ticket until it's time to board the plane."

Leonard finished the blue fruit and moved on.

"What about the Tree of Golden Eagle?" He hobbled over to pull down some of the pear shaped, yellow orbs. They were smaller and harder than the royal blue fruit; little smaller than a golf ball, and much harder to break into. He retrieved a small pocket knife and opened up the fruit. Inside, he found a single, burnt orange colored seed shaped like a hook.

"That's the other reason we brought you here," approached Grief and Pain.

Leonard smelled the fruit. Not much aroma. He looked up towards his companions.

"For your wounded heel," Pain pointed.

"What?" Leonard looked down towards his foot. "Will it heal my ankle or something? Is it a salve? Or a holistic analgesic?"

"No, no, no," answered Grief. "You're injured, and this will help you get off the mountain."

"Eat the little, hook shaped fruit," urged Pain.

"The seed?" asked Leonard, digging it out with the point of his knife.

"It's not a seed," answered Grief. "It's a fruit, like a cashew."

"A cashew?"

"Yeah," nodded Pain, rubbing his neck. "Ever see cashews in the shell? Cashews are a fruit. They don't have a shell. Walnuts, yes. Pecans, yes. Pistachios, yes. Not cashews. Next time you're in the produce section, ask the grocer for cashews in the shell and see what he says. You can have lots of fun with it if he's new."

"Oh," muted Leonard, his brows popping up and down once. He chewed up the little hook and swallowed. It was soft and tasteless and a bit chalky and pressed down into the canyons between his molars. Swallowing, his tongue went to cleaning out the bits.

"I like them a lot better roasted with barbecue flavored salt," commented Pain, just packing up a root canal. "Grief likes them with lime and chili."

"Now what?" asked Leonard.

"It won't take long," answered Grief.

"What won't take long?"

"You'll see."

Pain explained, "We were going to personally escort you down. That's what we do, but we have to get on to the Peaks of Seasonings and Lotsa Frump, so don't have the time. The Perfect Shepherd told us to get a move on."

"So, what? You want me to stay here and harvest fruit?"

"Not even an option at this point," answered Grief, tears filling his big, ochre eyes.

"I still don't know why you were laughing at me."

The two metaphors glanced at one another, and again started laughing.

"We weren't laughing at you," cackled Grief.

"We were laughing at ourselves," augmented Pain. "We both thought that you were here to harvest the fruit, so were attending to your every need, and found out that we were totally mistaken."

"But..." objected Leonard when they heard a voice.

"Hey!"

The three turned. It was Rodger, topping the hill, clothing torn and ragged, but a huge smile crossing his dirty face. He waved and started to jog towards them.

Leonard started to wave back when he felt the distance rapidly expand between them. The world promptly rushed away; a feeling like the frightful start of a fast ride at the amusement park, only multiplied as the world backed off in all directions at the same time. His last thought before they disappeared witnessed Rodger's smiling face turning to awe as Leonard vanished from sight.

It took quite a spell to figure out where he went. Difficult to reconstruct, but as best as he could figure, Leonard recalled turning into a puddle of water to where he seeped into the earth, collected for a few eons on the bedrock beneath, then felt the movement of tectonic plates that pushed him to flow downhill to a stream. Meandering with the flow of the water, he eventually shot off the side of the mountain in a magnificent falls, dividing into thousands of dancing drops. He landed in the flow and froth and gathered along the banks of the stream for miles and miles only to evaporate, floating haplessly across the range until he collected, once again becoming humanly intact, as part of the morning dew on the lawn of a city park.

He looked at Rodger, falling out of Leonard's pickup truck, with a renewed sense of sputtering amazement. He also wondered that his foot had not healed after all this time. Next, it also occurred to him he could've been brewed and served in Reuel's coffee cup for all he knew. He wasn't sure he wanted to know his friend that well, and wondered what was going on in Reuel's life. Their next meeting was sure to be an extraordinary discussion.

"How'd you find me?" gulped Leonard, his mouth full of over-easy eggs and hash browns.

Rodger boldly shrugged as he took another gulp of coffee. "I wish I knew," he admitted, gnawing on a chunk of bacon. 'Lumberjack' breakfast, only seven ninety-nine. Included coffee and juice.

"I was on the mountain one minute. The next, I was in your pickup truck driving. I didn't know where I was at. I didn't know where I was going. But, I knew I had to drive around till I found what I was looking for. It was that same feeling I get when I wander through the aisles at the grocery store 'cuz I can't remember what I came to buy." He set down his cup to massage and flex his right hand.

Leonard watched him. "Hurt it?"

"Uh-huh. In the cave."

"The last I recall," recalled Leonard, "was seeing you by the trees on the mountain just before I disappeared."

"Yeah! Blew me away. I'm walking up, and you just kind of dissolved."

"You should've been the one dissolving."

"I'll bet."

Leonard took time to eat, then looked across the table. "Tell me what happened in the cave. You took off to find the source of the light."

"Never found it," admitted Rodger, a distant gaze settling over his features. Leonard unexpectedly noticed a vague resemblance to David Carradine.

Some yards past the banquet room of the cavern, the divine light disappeared, just as through the opening passage. One moment, Rodger walked in full light. The next step, he encountered utter darkness. He stopped, of course, and took a moment to recall the layout of the terrain just before he left the light. He recognized how easy it would've been to get turned around in the utter darkness, and wind up walking blind for hours and even days.

He seemed to recall that the closest wall posed to his left. He didn't need to close his eyes, but did. It seemed to help his equilibrium. He extended his left arm. Still no wall. He kept the arm extended as he took a step backwards. Nothing. He took another step back and re-entered the light. It didn't seem right, since he could clearly see the corridor ahead. He extended his arm straight out. It never disappeared in the darkness. But, he leaned forward, poked his head through, and couldn't see his body. Nothing. Not one micro-ray.

"That's so weird!"

Straightening up, he looked around to see if he'd missed anything. He figured that most detours to Heaven should be easy to spot. Satisfied that he'd not missed anything, he retrieved and tested a flashlight, then boldly ventured into the darkness.

Even with the flashlight, the darkness was a stark contrast to the brightly lighted cavern. He took time to weigh his options and let his eyes adjust. The cave continued straight away a few hundred feet, then opened into another wide chamber. He took note of various fixtures, then took the first corridor to the right. Thus far, since entering the cave, he'd stayed with the right side wall. If his flashlight gave out, he could probably turn around and feel his way back to safety.

Sounds arose, indistinguishable, up ahead. He instinctively lightened his steps, silencing his footfalls till he could determine the source of the sound. The noise increased, in volume and frequency as he continued forth. He detected a light ahead. Turning off his flashlight and slowing his steps, he crept forward. He started to make out the sounds of tools against rock. His heart started beating like a dribbling basketball.

"Can't wait to see what it is," he whispered to himself as he tiptoed along with the anticipation of a child escaping his bedroom to peek at his Christmas presents. Reminded him of the time in high school when he and his friend Sam stole the battery out of that Monte Carlo. Now he couldn't remember why they stole it.

The noise increased in volume as he got closer. He heard axes burrowing, and a sound like air escaping.

A voice called, "Look."

"Good one," answered another voice.

Slowly approaching, the light told Rodger he was close. He carefully peeked around the corner. Two mantled lanterns hissed – the air escaping sound. Two men pounded against the rocky wall with a pickax and sledgehammer. They were shirtless. Dirt swirled designs in the sweat on their backs. They worked on the same spot, one pounding, then the other, back and forth, taking turns. When the metal ax dug in and brought up a chunk of stone, they both stooped down and carefully examined it.

"Wow!" admired the larger man, a large scar crossing his left brow. The other grinned proudly. As far as Rodger could tell, it was just a chunk of rock. Nothing remarkable, but in the rapidly pulsing light, he could be wrong. His first impulse suggested he step out and greet them. His second impulse wondered if they'd go crazy and attack him mercilessly just in case they thought him a thief come to steal their treasures. His third impulse had nothing to do with the men, the rocks they were digging, or the caves. He thought of Mary Lou Riddick whom he'd had a secret crush on in junior high school. He didn't tell her at the time, and regretted his silence thereafter. These guys didn't look anything like Mary Lou Riddick, but he'd learned to not be silent lest he lose out on what might have been.

"Hi," he stepped out, loudly and clearly, walking towards the pair.

The two men, righteously startled, just about knocked each other down with their implements turning around towards Rodger.

"Who're you?" confronted the bigger one, stepping up out of his hole, sledgehammer ominously pointed in his hands. His voice rumbled deeply, like thunder singing falsetto.

"Rodger Spears' the name," he answered, extending a hand. "I was just touring the caves when I heard you working, so stopped by to say hi and see what you were doing."

The bigger one glanced at Rodger's hand and just about knocked it off with the sledgehammer. Rodger leapt back and nursed the throb in his fingers.

"An!" scolded the smaller man, ribbing him with his elbow. "Whatcha doing?" He set down his ax and went to meet Rodger who dropped his injured hand to his side.

"Sorry. My friend is a bit temperamental." He looked at the bruise on Rodger's hand. "An, look what you did. You gave him owees and booboos."

An suddenly looked whipped.

"Me sorry," he started to snivel.

"Sorry don't cut it, pal. You have to be careful *before* you hurt someone. My Lands! I'd hate to see what you'd do if you were really trying to hurt someone." He looked at Rodger. "Sorry about An. He's..."

"I already see," interrupted Rodger.

"I'm Ki-Æffuss. This is An, spelled A-N. Means 'peace' in Vietnamese."

"Is he Vietnamese?"

"Does he look Vietnamese?"

Rodger looked once more before answering. "No."

"He's not. His dad just liked the name. You wouldn't believe how many people think Vietnamese doesn't have a word for peace, don't you think?

"Your hand okay? If I could, I'd reverse time and take you back to just before An hit you. That way, you'd know to pull away, don't you think?"

"It'll heal. What're you digging up?"

An bristled at that. Ki held him at bay, but didn't answer.

Rodger explained, "They just look like common rock to me. I don't mean to impose, but since I already did, I thought I'd ask. Or, I can be on my way so you can get back to work."

Ki mellowed, and went to pick up the stone they'd just liberated. He hefted it over to Rodger who moved closer to the light, examined it, and concluded the same as before. It was just a chunk of granite, and he said so.

"You're right," affirmed Ki. "But, what's impressive is what you can make with that chunk of common stone, don't you think? "

Rodger handed back the stone. His expression asked Ki for answer. Somehow, he knew the man did not mean sculpting.

Ki puffed out his dinky chest. "The Children of Abraham." An started to jump up and down and squeal with glee.

"Say again?" checked Rodger.

"The Children of Abraham," he repeated, taking back the stone and wielding it around in the glaring lights. "From stone we were created, and to stone we shall return. We seek the perfect, chosen rocks to make the Children of Abraham. Remember where John the Baptist tells the Pharisees and Sadducees who came to get baptized that God could make Children of Abraham out of stone?"

Rodger knew he'd never heard anything even remotely close, and said so.

Ki studied him with hard core scrutiny.

"You Jewish?"

"No."

"Muslim?"

"No."

"Well, you sure ain't Christian."

"So?"

Ki's aggression stopped, stunned, as though unexpectedly slapped in the face with the full force of the fire hose, but quickly recovered as though suddenly still thirsty for more.

"So, you can't be a Child of Abraham, don't you think?"

"I know," jabbed Rodger, and scratched an impish itch. "But, I thought it was Moses who chiseled stuff out of stone."

"You bet," bantered Ki.

"He was a Child of Abraham," added An.

"Okay," Rodger couldn't argue, not that he knew the first thing about either Israelite or pre-Israelite genealogy.

"Come. I'll show you." Ki grabbed a lantern. An stayed to dig. The musical rhythms of his sledgehammer tolled behind them.

Rodger walked with Ki some yards till they came to a pile of stones, most roughly the size of a Thanksgiving turkey.

"God, the Jehovah Jireh, has ordained these to become Children of Abraham."

Rodger wasn't impressed.

"How?" he asked blandly.

"Miraculously," called An, way down the corridor.

"Uh, how does the miracle work?" Rodger asked, a bit impatient. "What? Do you see them rise or transform to become Children of Abraham before your eyes?"

"Oh, no," answered Ki incredulously, as though the idea had never crossed his mind. "No, we dig them all day, and the next day they're gone."

"So, how do you know that they've become Children of Abraham?"

"Scripture says so," yelled An, still digging.

Rodger looked at Ki who nodded a supportive Amen.

Rodger wanted to laugh and say, "Okay, you're kidding, (don't you think?)" but held his tongue - literally. He reached up and grabbed hold of it with his thumb and index finger knuckle. His dry tongue made it easier to grab and hold. He held it tightly clamped till it began to numb.

"You should try digging with us."

Rodger let go of his tongue. "Why?" His answer had already been made up even before anyone thought to ask or invite.

"Cuz, you won't find a ministry more fulfilling - or challenging. Life should be made up of fulfilling challenges, don't you think?"

"Definitely," confirmed Rodger, "but, pounding common rock isn't my idea of a challenge, and I don't know about ministry."

"You'd be surprised," assured Ki. "In fact, it can seem more important than anything else you could be doing while you're doing it, don't you think?"

Rodger wasn't about to touch that one.

Ki jogged back to retrieve his pickax. He handed it to Rodger, handle end first.

Rodger stared at the tool, then took it, more out of politeness, (not that he typically oozed with urbanity). He checked An's progress, and swung the pickax a few times against the solid rock. It bounced harshly, and Rodger responded just as harshly, pounding it again and again and again with both strength and verve. He saw, heard and felt the wall give way.

"Don't get the pick stuck in the fissures," warned Ki. "It'll hold on tighter than all three of us could muster to get it out."

Rodger and An continued to take turns pounding the rock till a sizable chunk lifted. They pried it out.

"Oooh!" An complimented himself, and hefted the rock to the pile.

Rodger still couldn't figure it out, but dug up a few more. He decided that Ki, though undeniably dotty, still made a valid claim as he reveled in the challenge. He extracted a few more chunks of rock.

"Impressive," compliments Ki. "Look An. He's a natural."

"Ugh!," An responded, as Rodger raised his tool for another burst of power. He felt the lone tine of the pickax wedge into the stone.

"I warned you," scolded Ki. "In the shadows, each man pretends that he's mightier than Hercules, don't you think?"

Rodger scoffed. He tried to pull out the pickax.

No go.

He pushed against it.

Nothing.

He wiggled the handle.

Nada.

Grabbing the handle with both hands, he started pulling with all his strength. His feet slid, so he stood against the wall, suspending his entire body, and pushed against the handle.

"You'll break it," opposed Ki and tried to stop him.

Rodger ignored him and kept pushing, harder & harder, eyes closed, teeth clenched, lips slightly bleeding with the effort. Both Rodger and the tool quivered. Eventually, the rock cracked and began to separate. Ki stared in veneration, and An squealed and danced with delight.

The boulder rolled up out of its hole. Rodger landed on the hard, rock floor. An and Ki immediately fell to their knees to brush it off, as though cleaning a newborn calf. Rodger rose to brush himself off. He looked down at his hand and discovered that it was bleeding.

"What happened?" asked Ki.

"Owee and booboo," answered An, tapping the gross scar on his forehead.

"Not sure," Rodger admitted, dabbing the blood flow with his shirt.

"Here," Ki grabbed Rodger's wrist. "Let me help."

He placed Rodger's hand against the rock wall of the cave, and explained, "The cool rock will help the bleeding."

Rodger felt an odd sensation; a cold, hard feeling, as though the blood filling his veins began to granulate. He yanked his hand away from the wall, and saw the deep, red stain in the stark light.

"Aurghhhh!"

Suddenly, he lurched forward from a fierce blow from behind as An smacked him across the head with the handle of his sledgehammer. Rodger fell forward and crashed headlong against the rock wall. Stunned, he tried to rise. An whacked him again. Ki joined the attack.

Crash!

Struggling, (Smack!) but hopelessly disad- (Pow!) -vantaged, Rodger felt ready to (Boom!) black-out. Though injured and angry and (Klunk!) scared and increasingly incapacitated, he (Biff!) still marveled at the feeling of (Bam!) losing consciousness. He'd never blacked-out before, (Zowee!). One more blow, and he went down for the count. His last thought, (besides fleeting pics of Batman reruns,) slithered through his mind as carousel colors and shape and smog gathered around his failing vision asking why they didn't hit him harder? To wound, not kill, and he entered nothing wondering what lay ahead.

A dream, or two, or ten or twenty, each the same; each offering explanation for the pains covering his head and neck and back and sides and shoulders. One such dream finally landed on the earlier attack, replaying details with livid brutality. Rodger jerked awake.

Through the haze of pain, he saw as best as he could tell, that he was still in the cave, not far from where he'd blacked-out. Only one mantled camping lantern remained lit, hissing and sputtering and scattering light. Despite the weaker light, Rodger could see his attackers. Though he could see his attackers, he didn't believe what he saw. Each stood, backed against the wall across from him, yet part of each, roughly from the waist down, disappeared.

No, that wasn't right. He continued to stare. As they moved, their upper bodies seemed to be connected to the rock wall. Ki looked over at Rodger.

"Sleep well?" He smiled. His smile was neither insidious nor villainous, but it disgusted Rodger.

"Go to Hell," he cursed.

"Not possible," Ki answered smugly. "We're ministers. We're providers, working for our Lord. This is what we do, and now you can be part of the ministry."

Rodger glared at him. He tried to stand, and found himself already standing. He tried to move and found his body also attached to the wall. He looked down and saw that his feet, legs and most of the way up his back were embedded into the wall. He tried to get free.

No go.

He tried to bend down.

Nothing.

He pressed his hands against the wall.

Nada.

Not only that, but his hands stuck. He couldn't remove them, no matter how hard he pulled.

"See?" called Ki, most of his body now part of the wall. Rodger noticed some lines scratched into the wall below Ki's head and arms. He saw similar abrasions beneath An who appeared to be sleeping as he sunk into the wall. Rodger looked back at himself. He, too, was being absorbed into the wall. Frantic, he fought to break away, struggling and thrashing and practically breaking his bones to escape, yet each new part of his body that touched the wall became hopelessly attached.

"Relax," assured Ki watching Rodger's exertions. "It doesn't hurt, though it does feel very odd at first, don't you know?

"Let me go!" blared Rodger.

"Too late."

"I said, 'Let me go!' "

"Can't," admitted Ki. "I have no control over it at this point. I couldn't free you now even if I wanted to, which I don't. But, not to worry. You'll be free soon enough, and you'll be part of the cave and won't be able to leave, and you can mine rocks with us to produce Children of Abra–"

"SHUTUP!!"

Ki stopped, gazed at Rodger a moment, then sighed. "I know," he confessed calmly. "An was the same way at first, but he's turned into a top rate miner and minister, and I have no doubt you will, too."

Rodger continued to struggle as he glanced at An and Ki. An's sleeping face was all that remained of the big oaf. Rodger noticed the lines beneath him, and gasped.

Stick People.

"You're petroglyphs."

"We know."

Rodger tried to find words. Glancing down, he saw the color of his feet starting to fade from the rock. He couldn't feel them. There were no toes to wriggle, or ankles to flex. Only artistic scrapes remained.

"See?" called Ki. "You too can be one of us."

"No way," Rodger snapped. "As soon as I get free, I'm out of here. I don't care how..."

Ki hung his head. "I was honestly hoping that you'd see it my way. An's such an invalid, and not much company."

"Great," scoffed Rodger through gritty clenched teeth, "like you had your pick of the litter down here. It's a wonder you found someone with his IQ."

"Actually," corrected Ki, "An was sharp as a whip when I met him, don't you know? Smarter than you, I'd bet. Also, a real go-getter, much like you, exploring the caves, ever seeking new adventures. Subduing him alone was much more – uh, challenging, and I knew that he'd take off as soon as the stone released him, so I did what I had to to ensure he'd stay with me."

The tone in Ki's voice, as much as his words, caused Rodger to pause. He peered at him, deep eyes narrow, sunken brows furrowed.

"What did you have to do?" He already suspected the answer.

Ki's gaze remained cold as he answered, "Think of it as a kind of frontal lobotomy."

Rodger glanced over at An. He could still see An's facial features, but they were flat - a fading fresco or montage; two dimensional. The roughly hewn outline of his head appeared. In the left corner of his head, Rodger noticed a fissure chipped out of the rock.

"You did it," muttered Rodger. "You chipped the rock while he – slept."

Ki didn't answer. Both already knew he was right.

"Am I next?"

Only the hiss of the lantern answered for the longest time. Ki looked down towards the harsh light, resigned.

"You give me no choice."

"Wrong!" spouted Rodger as best as he could with less than half his lungs. His broken voice bounced off the walls throughout the cave. "You definitely have a choice. You can let me go. You can leave my brains intact. The two of you could certainly subdue me tomorrow, or whenever you get out of here."

Ki looked towards him. Rodger's body was mostly absorbed. His head seemed less than half in. He stalled.

"I'll think about it, but I'm not encouraged. You could definitely get away at some point if you wanted, don't you know? An's big and fast, but easily fooled." He sighed. "I'll think about it."

Rodger studied him. He wanted to reach out and strangle him, but had no arms. He tried to bend over, but there was no body to bend. Though he detected no feeling throughout his body, his mind was still alert.

Ki made a small scratch in the rock near his waist, then reached down to extinguish the lantern.

"What was that for?" asked Rodger, clutching at straws.

"What?"

"The scratch in the rock on your waist.

"Oh," smiled Ki, "that's my match."

"Huh?"

"My match, to light the lanterns. I scratch a line in the rock everyday before retiring, and when I awaken, I have one fresh, unused stick match to light the lanterns." He reached down with his one free arm, and turned down the flame. It flickered, then extinguished. Rodger watched the dull glow of the cooling mantles until they became part of the absolute darkness.

The darkness.

He could hear Ki breathing. His own breathing already obsolete, he could hear water dripping somewhere; likely from some tiny embedded crack in the wall behind him. He tried again to push against the rock, but had nothing left to push with.

"Think, Rodger, think," he scolded thoughtfully. Struggling was useless, lost in the total darkness. He'd faced fear without compromise or reservation so many times, he thought himself impervious.

He was wrong.

Well, almost.

"Ki?" he rasped through the pitch.

"Yeah?"

"You win."

Ki didn't answer.

"I'm yours."

"We'll see."

Rodger cursed to himself. His body, especially his head, still throbbed with pain. A tear coated his eye. Then another. He felt the warm fluid flow down his cheek.

"I can't..." he cried. Then, he thought of the Heavenly light in the banquet cavern. He'd never prayed a day in his life, but he had no other ideas.

"God? Help." He waited.

Only the coldest darkness.

"God. Help!"

Darkness, still, but also renewed warmth.

"God, I need your help. I can't..."

He didn't hear a voice. Nothing audible responded within his being, but he seemed to hear a Moving, Booming Voice.

"I heard you the first time."

He wondered if he wasn't imagining. He wondered if he wasn't just under duress, and willing to believe anything. Since he had nothing to lose, he opted to believe he'd been answered.

"Any ideas?" he prayed.

It seemed like a long time of silence, and he wondered how much of him still protruded outside the wall. He couldn't tell. Maybe nothing. Maybe he'd become totally absorbed, but could still reason. He felt an itch on the back of his leg, but couldn't scratch it.

Then, a divine idea occurred to him, as though it tapped on his shoulder and requested the next dance. Maybe he wasn't imprisoned at all. Maybe Ki only depended on Rodger's ignorance to contain him. The idea perked his imagination. How did they get out? Even dimwitted An could do it. Brute strength didn't work.

He thought to himself, "Time to get up."

Something felt different, so he tried again.

"Time to get to work."

Something definitely felt different. He stayed with the thoughts. He couldn't see the progress, but sensations began to return to his body as it slowly oozed out of the wall. It was slow, and he was anxious.

After some minutes, Ki called through the darkness, "What are you doing?"

"Checking out," Rodger muttered, denying the temptation to try to pull out his arm. He just had to focus and let it happen. He heard the rustling, and knew that Ki also started on his way. His already sluggish progress slowed briefly as he wondered if Ki, well accustomed to the rock bed, could escape much faster. He still had no arms or legs as far as he could tell.

"An," yelled Ki. "An, wake up. Rodger's running."

A groan resounded, muffled, probably from within the wall. It shivered Rodger's immoveable spine, and freezing, slimy sweat dripped down his nose. He tried to relax, overcome the pain, and think as hard as he knew how. Come on, now. Gotta get to work. There're stones to mine. Need my hands so I can use the pickax. Come on, little doggie. We're burning daylight, and have work to do."

His left hand and arm came free. Then, the right. The process seemed to accelerate the more he approached freedom.

"You almost out, An?"

"Coming," answered the goon. Rodger wished he could see how far along they were.

"You can't get away," challenged Ki. "Another minute, and we'll be out, ready and waiting to put you back in the wall."

Rodger tried to ignore him. He checked and rechecked the direction of his flight. Even in the pitch, he'd have to make a run for it, leaving no room for distractions, misgivings, or mistakes. He couldn't tell exactly how long the entire process lasted, lost in the darkness and duress and intent upon the endeavors of freedom, but it wasn't nearly as long as it felt. Ten, maybe fifteen actual minutes, he guessed, as the *flow cries*. He grew giddy as he felt his legs released in one full height motion.

Immediately, he fell to the ground.

He tried to get up. His legs didn't work. Neither did anything else. He felt paralyzed, but still struggled to get to his feet. He heard another body drop to the ground. Judging by the fall, and the sound of his breathing, Rodger guessed that they were barely feet apart. He also heard Ki struggling, and realized that they were on the same playing field. He had to let his body adjust, too.

Rodger started rolling down the way. He heard An's big frame drop to the ground like a bag of old concrete. Rodger knew that he barely had an advantage, and tried to exploit it was much as possible. Another minute, and he could rise to hands and knees. Every step resembled a work-out, but he pressed on, crawling, as though he raced submerged in a pool of mud.

He heard Ki get to his feet, and start walking slowly towards him. Rodger wanted to use a wall to help him rise, but didn't dare. It might grab him and hold him, and he didn't have time to try to get free. He forced his extremities to push him up. He arched his back, a project all by itself, and somehow made it to his feet. His wounds throbbed and tried to hamper his efforts. Ki was closing in. He tried to take a step, almost lost his balance, so tried small steps, constantly stretching himself to a longer step and faster pace. It was so weird trying to run, moving so slowly, completely blind, with his pursuers just a dozen or so regular steps behind him.

True to life, the feeling progressively returned to his joints. Each step became a little easier than the first. He already felt winded, but dared not let up. He ran into a wall, and turned immediately to the right, hoping that his memory led him back down the trail. He knew that he had to feel his way along, while his pursuers could home-in on the sounds of his feet and breathing. He could already hear An, growling and angry, starting to follow. If he made even one mistake, it would undoubtedly give them time to catch up.

Still, he was also reassured. He had run into the wall, but didn't stick to it. He felt for the left wall with his fingers, and used it to guide him. He wished that he had his flashlight, left back in his coat pocket. Needless to say, he had not had time to search for it.

In the darkness, the cave seemed much, much larger than he'd recalled. He pressed on trying to keep his distance between Ki & An. It sounded like they were getting closer, but he had to keep pressing on. The cave opened up, and he felt a structure of stalactites hanging down. He slowed to make sure that he didn't get tripped. Suddenly, he felt Ki's small, but strong hand whisk across the back of his shoulder. He wrenched to keep away, and lost his balance. Hitting the floor, he rolled to the right.

Ki just followed the sound.

Suddenly, Rodger stopped, dead. Not a sound. Not a breath. Ki kept coming, and passed him, barely an inch away, but didn't detect him. Rodger waited, and smiled. He'd pretty much never played the mouse before, avoiding and even taunting the cat. An approached, though still, he guessed, some yards off. Ki hit the wall, turned, and passed by again.

Rodger waited, controlling his lungs to take long, slow breaths. He just knew he would burp or sneeze or cough or whatever. He felt stronger, and judging by the length and ease of Ki's footsteps, he guessed that he was pretty much fully restored, and would be able to make a break for it, or fight if necessary.

Ki continued to wander, feeling around with his feet, hoping to come upon Rodger.

"Where Rodger?" called An, approaching.

"Shhhh!" Ki whispered, "Hiding. Feel around for him."

The pair wandered about in the dark, coming closer, drawing away, never quite finding him.

Suddenly, a scratching sound, and the small corridor became alive with light. Ki held his lone match over his head, and quickly spied Rodger who rolled around to his feet and rose to flee.

An tried to grab him, ripping Rodger's shirt and receiving a swift kick to the mid-drift. He flinched, then went after Rodger. Rounding the corner, Rodger tripped on a rock. Ki's match went out, and An tumbled over Rodger, landing hard. The two wrestled, Rodger with everything he had. An mostly held on, actually getting dragged. Rodger heard Ki approaching through the darkness. He dug in with both feet and lurched forward, trying to break away. Suddenly, he and An crashed into the banquet room, flooded with light. An immediately let go, covered his eyes, and half stumbled back to the darkness just as Ki rushed in, caught sight of Rodger enough to know he'd made it, then also covered his eyes and backed out of the light.

Rodger backed away from the veil, and rising to his feet, started to breathe easier. He could see both of them clearly in the divine light, and felt assured neither of them could see him without crossing the veil.

"You can't go," called Ki.

"Why not?"

"We need you – for the ministry."

"Sorry, bub," Rodger gibed.

Ki sat down in the corridor, and became quiet. Hanging his head, he started to sob. An joined him.

"I even used my only match," Ki rebuked himself. "Now, we shall ever be in darkness."

Rodger listened to them weep a while. He reached into his pocket, and returned to the edge of the light.

"Hold out your hand," he called to Ki. "Just your hand."

"Why? So you can lop it off?"

"No, of course not," he thought. "I have something for you. Something that you need."

It took quite a spell until Ki leaned over and extended his arm. Slowly, the hand opened.

"That's far enough." The hand stopped.

Rodger silently approached from the side and carefully dropped down his arm till it hung just above Ki's open palm. In it he dropped a book of matches, then flitted away back to a safer position. The hand retracted.

"Scratch that into your belt before you go to sleep."

"Thank you," squeaked Ki, still grieving.

Rodger watched them wander blindly back through the cave till they rounded the corner, disappearing out of sight. Turning to go, he saw the banquet table, and gasped with amazement. It was covered with dust, thick and gray. The food was old and spoiled and dried up, as though left out for months or even years. He recognized bites taken that he'd tasted and left. He knew that he had not been gone that long. He ran a finger through the dust, and rubbed it between his fingers, and pondered the mystery. No answers came that satisfied his mind.

He left the Heavenly light, fingers still following the left wall, to traverse through the darkness to the small opening. Squeezing through, he fell to the ground and reveled in the warmth of the outside. Standing, he brushed himself off, inspected his ripped clothing, and ventured up the hill, tracking the trail left by Leonard, Grief, and Pain.

*****

"So, what happened to you after I dissolved?" asked Leonard, tipping his coffee cup way back. One lone drop fell on his tongue, and he wished the waitress would bring more. Where was Belinda when you needed her?

Rodger wiped his mouth, washed the last of his breakfast down with ice water, and rubbed the wet beads covering both his forehead and the exterior of the glass with his callused fingers.

"I saw you three, so started jogging up, and stopped when you suddenly started to fade from view. From down below, you looked like the edge of the steam blowing out of the kettle. It took all of you at once. None of this foot then leg then knee business. You were there, then evaporating all at once. I just about lost my lunch.

Waiting for me, Grief and Pain started gathering up to go. They could see the astonishment on my face."

*****

Rodger stuttered, trying to force-out the question to Grief and Pain. "Wh -Wh- Where's Leonard?"

Grief looked typically woeful. "We sent him down the mountain."

"He was injured," explained Pain, reclined, rubbing the paddles together before placing them on his chest.

"Clear!"

WUUMP!

Levitating, then landing, Pain took a full minute before continuing. "Leonard was attacked by a serpent in the cave. It got his foot. He'll be okay, but we had to get him off the mountain quickly."

"But," sputtered Rodger, "Where'd he go?"

Grief and Pain looked at him blankly.

"You know, we really don't know. But, you could follow him if you wanted."

"How?" Rodger wanted to know with absolutely no intention of being suckered into dissolving.

Grief grabbed a chunk of fruit off the Tree of Golden Eagle and split it open exposing the hook shaped fruit.

"Eat this and you'll be on your way. Promise."

Rodger became immediately wary. "You're saying, that's it? Just eat this seed and I'll be gone? I don't think so."

"Suit yourself," answered Grief miserably. "You're a big boy, and we don't have time to try to convince you. Gotta get to the Peaks of Seasoning ASAP." He handed the fruit to Rodger, then pulled down two more for Pain and himself. Both opened the rind and dug out the fruit, chewed it up and swallowed.

"Besides," added Pain, envying Rodger's new bruises, "if we go, you'll know that it's safe. Picture worth a thousand words, and all that."

They sat. Rodger wondered if something shouldn't be happening.

"Now, what?"

"You'll see soon enough," groaned Grief.

Rodger watched and waited. A thought arose.

"Hey!"

The two hybrids turned to Rodger.

"Quickly," urged Pain, duct-taping an aneurysm.

"Um, in the cave. When I came back through, the banquet table looked like it was many years older. The food was cold, dried up, and covered with dust, but I know we weren't gone that long."

"Manna," moaned Grief.

Rodger didn't understand the correlation.

Pain explained, "When God gave the Israelites manna, they could only take enough for the day. If they tried to gather for more than one day, it would go bad. We were given more than we needed for one day, but couldn't take more than that with us."

"Isn't that wasteful?"

Grief nodded.

"But," argued Pain, "in God's economy, it's not wasteful at all. He's got more to give than all of us combined could receive."

Dissecting Pain's words, Rodger added, "I never imagined God was such a good cook."

"Amen," nodded the pair. They felt that last word leave their lungs as Rodger watched both beings sort of dissolve. With chaffed hands, Pain smiled and waved one last time and both were gone. Rodger sat alone for a long time, waiting for he knew not what. He'd just left Ki and An, and emerged less trusting of those he met, such as Grief and Pain. He'd just seen Leonard dissipate, then Grief and Pain, and waited a spell just in case they came back.

The trees swayed in the breeze. Night approached. Rodger, ever and always the extremist, took one last glance around him, then popped the odd shaped fruit in his mouth. It was tasteless, and he almost spit it out, but down it went. He sat to wait. His wait didn't take long as he took off at the speed of light through the atmosphere, above the stratosphere and out beyond where he bounced off a communications satellite, got redirected back to earth, shot down to Leonard's pickup where he was captured by the antenna, slithered through the electronics, squeezed through the speakers and landed in the driver's seat, engine running. Regaining his senses, he sat, stunned, as the radio declared, *"Our God is an Awesome God. He reigns..."*

*****

"And," continued Rodger, "without a clue where I was going, I started driving all night till I found you." He paid for both meals, and helped Leonard out the door. Dropping Leonard into the driver seat, Rodger closed the door and leaned against the open window.

"Aren't you coming?"

Rodger just smiled and declined. "Thanks," he eventually answered, "for the adventure of my lifetime."

"You're welcome," sputtered Leonard. He started the engine and listened to the idle. "Uh, can I drive you somewhere?"

"Not this time." He started to walk off, then turned back. "Maybe I can take you somewhere next time."

Leonard nodded absentmindedly. "Okay. Fine. Where?"

Rodger grinned. "Ever try skydiving?"

Chapter Seven

Ki & An felt their way through the endless night of the cave. Neither spoke. Ki felt numb. An, too, in his usual, foggy way. Both sought a long nap and time to rest to put all behind.

Rounding a corner, Ki heard a sound. Squeaky wheels approached, still a way's off. The squeak ceased as Ki and An turned the corner and detected a light. Their path illuminated, they hastened forward to find the source. Reaching their site, they found a lone man loading their stones into an old, wooden cart. Ki started to yell, "Hey! Those are our stones," but realized that this may be where their stones went each night.

"What are you doing?" approached Ki and An.

The lone man turned to face them. He looked old - no, old was an understatement. He was hoary. He was also bearded and gray and had flat, powdery eyes.

"I always collect the stones," he muttered behind a weak, tired smile. "Looks like the miners had a good day."

"We're the miners," informed Ki. An danced a bit, partially in pride, and partially out of stress. It had been a disturbing day.

The old man blinked at them, then slowly turned towards the wall and saw the petroglyphs missing.

"You're usually out of commission by now. It's remarkable to actually see you in the flesh." He resumed loading stones into his cart.

Ki watched him a while, then confessed, "I always imagined that the stones transformed themselves and walked out on their own two feet."

"No, no," chuckled the stranger. "I've never seen a stone that could walk unassisted. You two must have been down here a lonnnnnggggggggg time."

"So, when do they become Children of Abraham?"

The old man stopped, a rock in hand, and circled around himself to peer at the miners.

"Become what?"

"Children of Abraham."

The old man snorted through his nose.

"You have been down here longer than I first imagined. These stones don't become Children of Abraham."

Ki puzzled a moment, then asked the obvious. "What do you do with them, then?"

"Walls, son. We make walls."

"Like, around people's property?" Ki felt a shudder hatch within.

"No," the old man grew gravely serious. "We build walls around people's hearts."

Ki stood, more numb than before. An wondered what was happening. The old man continued loading stones, then pressed on without another word, leaving them again in the utter darkness; his squeaky wheels resounded long after the light had disappeared.

Ki lit a lantern, set a hand on An's shoulder, and said, "I have something to do before we go to bed. You go on. I'll see you tomorrow." He waited as An applied himself to the wall. When assured that An slept, he tiptoed over to touch the chip in the rock where he'd broken his partner. He dropped to his knees. Tears glistened his eyes. Crushed by the massive boulders of guilt and lost purpose, he fell forward and pounded his head on the rock floor, over and over, till he blacked out, and slept, cold and miserable, for the first time in countless years, outside his wall.

Chapter Eight

"So?" opened Henry, not looking up from the sun-broiled sand, coating the Sea of Forgetfulness like Shake n' Bake. His old fingers, callused and spotted, sliced through the sand easier than butter. Leonard watched as he told a story of cruel manipulation and vicious maternal possessiveness by a woman named Wilma. She'd weaned all six of her kids on gross quantities of guilt, as though her children were created to pay penance for her own life of sin. All six eventually broke away from her barbed apron strings.

"So?" Henry asked again when Leonard failed to answer.

"This one's more elaborate than the other sins I've seen forgiven."

Henry looked back at his work. Much was already illegible.

"Yup," he thought aloud. "Some are a lot worse than this. You can tell what kind of books she reads..."

"... or what kind of TV shows she watches."

Henry raised and dropped both hands. "Never owned a TV. Never watched one that I can remember." He sifted sand through the fingers of his left hand – his weaker hand. Leonard wondered if it was compulsive, like an idle habit.

"Why no TV?"

Henry sat quietly. The floodlight sun spelled harsh shadows, obscuring his face.

"TV didn't exist in my time," he said slowly, "but, I would not have one if I lived on Earth today."

Leonard jumped on that.

"So, we're not on Earth?"

Henry went back to writing in the sand.

"So, where are we?"

No response.

Leonard peered up towards the sun. "Hell?"

"Gracious, no," snickered Henry, still writing. An artist's canvas never demanded more attention than Henry's sand.

"Then, where?" Leonard's voice became more intense.

"I told you."

"The Sea of Forgetfulness?"

"Yup."

"Where's the Sea of Forgetfulness? I'm not familiar with that map. Can you show it to me compared with, say, California?"

Henry laughed and winked at Leonard, "You can't get there from here." He stood and brushed himself off. His pants seemed to blow-off chunks of steam, while he reveled in the hot, crushing air; the blast furnace sun, and the bland, tan sand.

"Is this just a dream world? I awoke as from a dream last time. Am I still driving down the road, and you're going to awaken me just before I crash?"

Henry merely moved his head - a firm, steady No.

"The best way that I can explain it," he answered, a steadfast smile adorning his potent, lined face, "is that it's a small part of the spiritual realm. Like when you were in the cave. It's a quick and easy trip from one world to the next - unless you're mortal, locked into the narrow compressions of time and space. Human senses can make such ethereal entrances more difficult to find."

"Then, why'm I here if it's almost impossible?"

"The Holiest Spirit brought you," Henry answered matter-of-factly. "Like I told you, the journey's easy, but finding the gateways can be more fun than an Easter egg hunt. If Jesus wants you to cross, He seems to bear little trouble escorting you across. But, honestly, that's all I know. I see it happen, but don't know why or how it happens."

Leonard recalled a recent occasion when he was at church. Before the service, he entered the church bookstore and prayer room. Nobody was in the room. Leonard had been in that room many, many times, but this time, for reasons unknown, he felt an extraordinary sense of beauty. His breath paused, in awe and perhaps to listen more intently. "The beauty of the Lord," he mouthed. A Heavenly presence out of reach, out of sight, out of touch but very, very close. Thirty seconds, and the impression sallied as easily as it flowed in. Leonard stood some minutes before exiting, just to process and pray and consider and feel the upshot of the chance meeting.

Henry sighed, somewhat winded from his talk, but content. Leonard could tell that he couldn't wait to get back to his task recording sand script.

"So? I ask again," turned Henry, scribbling details of a con man's scam.

"So, what?" checked Leonard, watching Henry write. The perspiration glued Henry's shirt to his back. The band of his straw hat was discolored. The breeze pushed the sand around before Henry finished writing. Leonard could tell, this little man, without even pockets on his trousers, could not have held more joy.

"You mean, what'm I looking for?" answered Leonard.

Henry didn't answer or nod or move - his fingers suspended above the sand. Leonard knew that he'd found the right question, but still didn't feel sure of his answer.

Henry waited, suspended.

"The truth?" ventured Leonard.

Henry's hands rested against the sand as he turned towards Leonard.

"You think that you don't know the truth - God's holy truth?"

Leonard squirmed. "I thought that I did."

"You're right," affirmed Henry. "You do know the truth. Oh, you're not sure? Then, gird up your loins and answer a few questions.

"Who's the Way to the Truth?"

Leonard paused.

"It's not a trick question."

"God - Jesus?"

"Yup. Who is the Truth?"

"Jesus?" Leonard answered more promptly.

"Yup. You already know the Truth. You've known the Truth most of your life - got a whole closet full of Truth. It's flooding your basement and oozing down from your attic and bulging your silos, and still you go to church each week hoping to stockpile some more Truth.

"So, that's not it. You've got Truth. What're you looking for?"

"God's way - his calling for my life?"

"Well, you're getting closer," encouraged Henry, "But, nope, that's not it. Who's the Way?"

"Jesus?"

"Yup, and who showed you His Way?"

"Jesus."

Henry nodded. "So, if you've got the Way and the Truth of God, what is Life to search for? And, don't look at me like that. This isn't Twenty Questions, or "Guess what the farmer is thinking."

"You're a farmer?"

"We can talk about me later. This is too important to get side-tracked or flit about. Remember, the Holiest Spirit called you here.

"In the campground, you did good kissing the embers at the cold church, and you didn't turn back when the Spirit of Defeat tried to squelch your curiosity, and..."

"When did he do that?" Leonard honestly could not remember encountering the Spirit of Defeat. He felt sure he would've recognized it.

Henry checked his quarry. "Remember that cold wind that chilled you to the bone and practically broke-off your ears, then that sudden grip of fear as you climbed the mountain. You didn't head back to the warmth of your car, and you fought the fear until it abated, and instead of heading down, you continued up."

"That was the Spirit of Defeat?" questioned Leonard skeptically. "I've been watching for some fearsome creature, (not necessarily with horns and a pitchfork,) but truly terrible to behold."

Henry looked right through Leonard, gaining access through the windows of Leonard's eyes. The still gaze made Leonard wonder where the hot sun and sand went.

Henry challenged, "Have you ever seen a real demon personified like that?"

Leonard felt sheepish, and the hot sun and sand returned to his senses with greater impact.

"No," he squeaked. "Just in the movies."

"But, not in real life."

"No."

"Discernment," mumbled Henry.

"Discernment?" checked Leonard.

"Right," perked Henry. "Discernment of spirits is probably the least sought after of the gifts of the Holiest Spirit. First Corinthians, Chapter Twelve. I don't know if the Holiest Spirit wants you to have the gift of discernment, but it's a great gift to have, especially if you're around people who're prone to thinking there're demons under every rock and around each corner, waiting to pounce on you. But, we've blown way off the subject again." He looked to the sky.

"The sun is never silent," Henry muttered to himself, then looked back towards Leonard.

"What are you looking for, Leonard Lamb?"

Leonard looked towards the sun, then down to the ground. He drew a half circle in the sand, then followed with the other half circle to make the sign of the fish.

"My first love," he suddenly looked up towards Henry.

Henry beamed, and Leonard knew he'd hit the mark before the words reached his mentor's ears. But, his euphoria quickly evaporated. His eyes drifted back towards the fish he'd drawn.

"I can't find it," he confessed. "I've tried. For years. My prayers are cold. I get bored reading my Bible and applaud myself if I read more than a couple of chapters. My reward is to take a couple of weeks or more off before I feel guilty for neglecting it, and pick it up again.

"I recall way back when I'd study the scriptures for hours any given evening. And, I don't mean I'd study for a class or because I was preaching, but because I had that insatiable appetite to consume the Word, and wash it down with gallons of sweet Living Water. I was ravenous, and couldn't get enough.

"And, my prayers were long and hard and in pure earnest. I couldn't pray harder if I'd wanted. But, now they're shallow and dried-up and shriveled and sound stupid to me. I don't expect them to sound any better to God."

He knelt down in the sand, landing hard, pressed down further by the weight of his confession.

"But," he continued, "I've tried to be the Christian I used to be; to get back to that holy, feverish fervor. I've never come close. I'm worse than those dying embers I kissed at the campground.

"Oh, I have fervor. Just watch me at a sporting event. I'll yell myself hoarse. Or, just watch me when there's a new toy to acquire, like a car or camera or computer that I just gotta have. I can be obsessive. So, where's the fervor for my Lord? I don't know, and I don't know how to get it back, so in the meantime, I'm embarrassed and even disgusted to call myself a Christian."

He felt his tears form, flooding his desert-dried eyes. He feared Henry's consternation. He wondered if this would make it easier to seek God hereafter, and realized that he was seeking the easy answer or quick fix. For that matter, he wondered if his confession wasn't made easier by telling someone that he wasn't yet sure that he believed existed. So far as he could tell, Henry wasn't likely to blab to his friends and family. Not much in the way of accountability to his fellow mortals.

Henry jotted a few words in the sand. 'Guilt, Pride, and Apathy – Fear, the bottom line of all sin.'

"What instruction did I give you last time?" Henry asked slowly.

Leonard looked up to the little man. The flash flood of emotion had passed, and he felt the hard heart of composure gradually returning.

"You told me to 'do'," he answered, "and to beware of the Spirit of Defeat."

"Good," applauded Henry. "Does the directive to 'do' still seem so vague?"

"No," Leonard admitted.

"Good," Henry repeated and retrieved a handkerchief to blow his nose. "Then, keep on *doing*, and keep watch out for the Spirit of Defeat, but also add *Service* to your mission."

"Service?" Leonard groped.

"Serve," answered Henry. "Do, and serve. Both will help you regain your First Love. And, don't give in to the Spirit of Defeat. He's not done with you, yet, I promise you."

"Is that it?"

Henry looked around to confront Leonard's impertinence.

"You really want more?"

Leonard didn't answer.

"Cuz, I can give you more – lay it all out on the table. It's no secret. But, since you already know the Truth and the Way and the Life, I expect you won't take long to figure it out. Or, at least you know where to find it if you really want it. What?"

He studied Leonard a long moment. He saw the defeat; the fractured resolutions; the lost appetite; the certainty of guilt and failure. His face and demeanor said it all. Henry was moved to pity.

"So, you can't do it, huh?"

"Uh-," Leonard was about to defend himself. Henry raised a dusty hand to stop him.

"Gracious, man!" he exclaimed. "All is not lost – just you. It's a wonder you ever became a Christian. Okay, tell you what. Want some help?"

"Yeah," Leonard answered, standing. "I hate to admit it, but yeah."

"Need a mission?"

"I work better under deadlines."

Henry chuckled appreciably, "Okay. Well, this mission definitely has a deadline. But, more than that, you'll see the importance of focus; singular purpose. The meaning of 'One Way.' He closed his eyes and raised his tanned face towards the merciless sun. The sand swirled with the breeze. Henry's face started to transfigure. Leonard gasped at the sight.

"God speed your journey," he closed, and with a sudden burst, he dug into the sand and lurched forward, pushing Leonard hard, in the middle of his chest. He toppled backwards, falling and falling and falling, and when he looked, the sand wasn't there, nor the sun nor wind nor light nor anything. He found himself hurtling at an unimaginable speed through an absolute void some nowhere outside of creation.

Chapter Nine

"Wo!" said Leonard, or tried to, but there was no air to fill his lungs to speak and no future to capture the words once they escaped his mouth. He knew that he was moving, though there was no before, no behind, no above, and certainly no below. He detected no light, yet he raced through no darkness.

He tried to look around, and found nothing to see. He tried to turn. He succeeded, yet detected that it made no difference. He could fly along in any direction at the speed of creation. His efforts were still without measure, and direction was moot.

He sought joy and he soared without effort, yet instinctively knew that his sense of joy was equally liberated and stifled within the void. He was as free as humanly possible, yet completely trapped. His senses shut down. There was nothing to measure. There was no air to breathe. He needed none. He placed his hands across his chest. There was no beat; no pulse; no circulation. He wondered how he could think, then checked if he had not entered a deathlike state. For that matter, maybe he was just plain dead.

The idea caused him to shudder, though his flight was not affected. Then, he realized that there was no fear. It was gone. He'd never, ever lived without fear, and suddenly there was none. Even if he was dead, he wasn't afraid. If he was dead, this wasn't bad. He moved freely, through absolute nothingness, without fear. There was nothing in his way that he might crash into since there was no ahead.

Likewise, he felt no pain. Mostly healthy, he didn't deal with pain on a daily basis, but in the void outside creation, he realized that endless, moderate sense of pain in his body that perpetually filled him was also absent.

He raced along tirelessly, since there was no time to record. He needed no sleep, and there was no breath to catch. He drew in and felt like a jet-powered dart without a board. He closed his eyes. The only impression remotely measurable was the sense of flight, and though he detected no specific speed, he still trekked audaciously fast.

Without direction, without urgency, without fear, and without self, he raced. Then, he realized that he did have one thing – purpose. The one and only reason he found to be in the nowhere. He set his mind on that singular purpose which carried him forth through eternity. He traveled, not with speed, but with diligence. He felt the vastness of forever split and flow around him, for eternal infinity divided still equaled eternal infinity.

He couldn't go any faster. He couldn't slow down. He didn't try to do either. He found purpose without reservation or compromise, and stayed set on course like a divine utterance by Creator God Himself, spoken before He created the heavens and the earth, to race on, outside time and space, thereby enwrapped outside the infinite and the eternal.

Suddenly, he savored the voice of Creator God, for Creator God's voice is not sound, but relational authority. And, the being of Creator God's voice flowed in and around and through him more thoroughly than the void. The awesome ecstasy writhed through his frail body. His purpose, still singular and focused, immediately changed to seek the voice that graced him from virtually all directions at once. He raced to and fro with absolute fervor, for the voice is, was, and always will be when one listens outside of time and space.

He couldn't speed-up. He couldn't slow down. He couldn't turn towards nor away from the source, but he could stop; stop cold and completely in the void.

It took only a thought, and he no longer moved through the abyss. No sooner did he apply the brakes that the immeasurable borders of eternity passed, where Creator God's ever expanding universe of creation overtook Leonard. It did not come from behind or from the side or front, but filled him from all sides at once, including inside and out. The compression of time and space twisted and wrenched him, as though trying to make room for him to fit. Suddenly, he was adrift in deep space. The cosmos lay before him brightly. The ever-broadening edges of creation continued to expand away from him.

He tried with everything left inside him to get back to the void, but time and space wouldn't let him go. His momentum was gone. His acceleration was for naught, not that any space ship he'd ever imagined could catch-up with the fleeting boundaries of the universe. He looked towards the core, forever off, beyond his vision, and felt the silent freeze of complete isolation. Creator God's holy voice became a lost echo in his ears. His heart pounded loud and strong. New found fear gripped and strangled him. He struggled to breathe, but there was no air, save that which occupied his lungs the moment he'd entered the nothing outside creation. He cried out with those last broken molecules exiting his lungs, "Abba,,,"

Chapter Ten

Leonard landed, or awoke with a start. Face down, looking up from the sand, he first expected to see Henry. The sun was bright and the sand hot and dry, but he immediately saw he wasn't in the Sea of Forgetfulness. His first clue was the blue-green ocean, massively stretched beyond his line of sight. Waves crashed, one upon the other, over and over and over, like a million and one hands clapping, shouting applause, demanding an encore. He could hear the sweet belch of sea foam sizzling on the water after the wave. He could smell salt and water and the unmistakable aromas of decaying sea life.

He thought it odd that there were no words scratched into the sand. He wrote his own name in the sand and paused. Where does one start when listing their sins? Might Henry mirror Leonard's actions, taking dictation in the Sea of Forgetfulness? Leonard wasn't himself much of a writer, and wondered if Henry ever needed a Spell Checker?

What if Henry had written: "Steven St. Thomas the 1st of St. James St., an eggnostic, showed pore judgemeant fore steeling dumb bells, jaded jewelery, a vacume cleaner, wite whine and corn squeezins from Kernel Libby. With nagging purseverence, he also reefered to the weeds while Raiding the City Cementary for allot of treasures and mid-evil momentos from the maintenants. A struggling playright, his artistic liesense, poor pronounciation, laysurely past times likely baned him from the City Libelary."?

Leonard also wondered if Henry used contractions? Would the word "He'll" become "Hell"? "We're" could be "Were"? "She'll" became "Shell"?

Leonard had done that himself in a text message to his friend Tina in South Africa, when he couldn't figure out how to make an apostrophe on his new cell phone. He figured if she read "Who're" without the apostrophe, she'd recognize his intent. He definitely should've pre-read his message more carefully before hitting "Send".

On the same hand, Leonard wasn't the only one who'd recently sent and received atrociously misspelled messages, and realized any shortcomings Henry may have had with spelling would probably still get the job done.

Finally, Leonard wondered why "Sarge" was short for Sergeant? Why not "Serge"? Why not "Surgeont"? Why not Sergeant Sergio? Leonard opted to stop there rather than continue trying to outdo his other silly questions.

"We may be going the wrong way, but we're making good time." He found his self saying that to himself a little more than he should these days.

Leonard finally pushed himself up into a sitting position, his writing finger still stationed and hovering above the sand. He checked the movement of his joints. Something was definitely different, though his bones seemed intact. Even his left heel presently felt fine. Sand clung to his face and his breathing was heavy, perhaps "catching up" after his existence outside time and space when he couldn't (but didn't need to) breathe. Or his breathing increased anticipating the chance he might accidentally slip into another timeless/spaceless vacuum around the next corner. The old expression, "No breath, no life" came to mind. He brought his legs in close to his body and sat within the womb of his mind, taking in the sea and the sand and the surf and little sand crabs punching hundreds of tiny holes in the smooth surface of the receding surf sand.

Raising his eyes, he pondered the wide ocean before him. It was such a tiny sample of ocean within his vision; blue-gray and a tad hazy, yet it practically stretched around his peripheral line of vision. He followed the flat, straight line of the horizon, then internally realized with a prophetic gasp that Creator Dad's passage reached well beyond this endless ocean. Closing his eyes, he could hear his Brother Jesus' voice repetitively calling to him from across the water.

He slowly rose to his feet, and tested his ankle. It felt strong, but he could not walk. After his flight through pre-creation, the sand felt hard and alien with each step; far worse than what sea-legged sailors experienced after they left the boat for dry land. Each step felt like he had unexpectedly walked off some sidewalk curb, stumbling to catch himself.

Suddenly, a merciless stranglehold gripped him with sharpened talons. He felt dizzy and his breathing, already aggressive, increased.

"Fear," he pukedly exhaled, and he recalled Henry's warning. Dumb, old mortal fear. He should've felt right at home with it, but he'd just left an existence where he was totally free of its suffocating deadlock. He uncontrollably shuddered some minutes as he felt the cruel clutch increase and slither through his entire being.

Clumsily falling to his knees, he cried out, tears bathing his swelling eyes. He felt the initial compressions of fear and finiteness and pain slowly ease, but its venom had already pumped through each cell of his earthly body. He was back, he thought, back to the world of mortals after the fall, where fear and death were a part of daily life.

"Time," he thought out loud, and yearned to be away, freely racing towards Creator Dad's awesome, indescribable presence.

How long did I race through the void outside creation?" He'd often wrestled with the details of an Endless God. He did not have as much trouble imagining that God would continue on forever. Once God was already here, taking care of business from moment to moment, going on forever didn't seem impossible. On the other hand, "no beginning" had always been harder to swallow. How could anything, even Creator God, have no beginning?

Reflecting on his journey through nowhere, he'd just left the answer to the no beginning question. God was outside of time. For that matter, God created Time. And, God created the Heavens and the Earth. Leonard had been liberated outside the linear fetters of finiteness. Suddenly, he could imagine, as far as his brain would conceive, no beginning for God, because there was *nothing* before God, including time and space.

Leonard recalled childhood impressions of Creator God, alone in some dark, cloudy abyss before he created the heavens and the earth, including the angels and humans and other creatures throughout the universe. Leonard thought it had seemed so bleak for God to just hang out in the shapeless void outside creation.

Then, one day God the Father just said, "You know what? I think I'll make a universe. Yeah, that's what I'll do. Populate it. Share a bit of love with all of the life I create. It'd be quite an art project."

"Jesus. Spirit. I just got an idea."

"We already know," said Jesus. "Don't we always automatically know what You're thinking? After all, we are One and the Same."

The Spirit preened while nodding in agreement with The Son.

"Oh! Oh! Oh!" perked Spirit. "We could use that Primordial Sludge for foundation. It's kind of like a soup stock. Where did we store that?"

"In the Heavenly Basement," answered The Father.

"Maybe it's time to clean out the Basement," winked Jesus, recalling the time Father suddenly created the Primordial Sludge out of nothing. It just popped out of His mouth one night after He came home, inspired by that Angelic Wing Choir performance.

They all looked at it, shaped roughly like the state of Indiana as it sizzled on the Heavenly Carpet.

"Call Daniel and his wife Abigail to come clean it up," said The Father.

"D&A?" checked Spirit, already knowing the answer.

Both deities nodded in agreement and Spirit sent Gabriel to fetch them.

Leonard's pace became more comfortable, each step taking its time. He ventured to look up, and discovered that he was not alone. The beach was alive with activity as far down as he could see in both directions. He spied a lone pier off in the distance, a mile or more, stretched out over the water for hundreds of yards. If only to avoid trekking without purpose, he started for the pier.

His steps continued to feel heavy and slothful on the sand. Trudging along, he approached huge structures ahead. At first, they appeared to be buildings, but as he converged upon them, he realized that they were the biggest sand castles he'd ever seen. He toured past dozens of them, arranged in a grid pattern on the open beach. Each was unique, and many were as big as a house. He awed at the detail and craftsmanship. Some had each brick outlined. One was a Cape Cod style, two-story house with wooden siding, big, round pillars, and a large front porch. The front door had a design of a hot air balloon carved where the window might be.

He wondered how the porch roof stayed suspended on the sandy pillars. His hand brushed up against the porch rail. It easily crumbled. His mark was just a small blemish, so he tried to fix it. Big mistake! The more he tried to get the sand to form, the more the porch rail deteriorated, until it became just another pile of sand. He inspected the phenomenon, and resolved to keep his hands off, lest he destroy someone else's remarkable work.

He passed another building that looked like it had ivy attached along an entire wall. Another had a two car garage cavern, and another was shaped like the Statue of Liberty on roller skates. He rounded the corner of a Mount Rushmore style sand castle, and almost ran into a man, his hands full of wet sand.

"Greetings, landlubber," the man greeted cheerily. "I see that you're new here. M'name's Rick Shaw."

Leonard returned introduction as he studied Rick Shaw. Older man; probably sixties or even seventies, with a large torso and spindly legs. His salt and pepper hair, very thin on top, was brushed straight back. His skin deeply bronzed, he had a broad, top & bottom teeth smile, and bright blue eyes that would've given both Sinatra and Newman cause for envy.

"Can you give me a hand?" asked Rick Shaw. "We can always use more help."

"Whatcha doing?" answered Leonard, thinking the man's name sounded like an Asian taxicab.

Rick dissected the question before answering. Eventually, he said, "Oh, we're constructing sand castles up to the sky that we may make a name for ourselves."

"Why?"

"Why not?" snickered Rick.

"That's what Carnibal said," mumbled Leonard.

"Whom?"

"Never mind."

"Actually," corrected Rick, "are you asking why we're building sand castles; why we're trying to make a name for ourselves; both; or neither?"

"Both," answered Leonard as though the question sounded more fun than the answer.

Rick caressed the wet sand in his aged hands.

"It's alive in your hands if you handle it just right, you know?"

"What is?" checked Leonard.

"The sand. Feel it. It's cool and alive. A cold blooded critter that will let you take it anywhere your imagination wants to go. Come with me."

They walked past more sculptures. Leonard still walked with a bit of a limp, but was feeling more like himself with every step. He awed at the site of a tree made entirely of sand. It stood only a dozen feet high. The trunk rose and spread out to broad branches. He *knew* that there was no way that sand could be formed without an emulsifier, like straw or cement, but one brief touch told him that there was nothing like that holding it together.

They approached another man working on the Eiffel Tower. This model was approximately 30 feet high, though the top was not yet done. Leonard noticed numerous other models, smaller and with varying degrees of sophistication. The smaller ones were completely filled in with sand. The larger models were hollow, like the actual Parisian monument.

"Georges," called Rick.

"Bonjour."

The men grabbed each other's shoulders and exchanged a hug-like salutation. Rick turned to introduce Leonard.

"This is... what's your name?"

"Leonard. Leonard Lamb."

"Good to meet you Monsieur Lamb," nodded Georges. "How do you like my little creations?"

"Indeed. Did you make all of these?"

"Oui," he nodded again.

Leonard noted that Georges didn't speak with any sort of French accent.

"Leonard was wondering," interjected Rick, "why we made sand castles."

"Silly question," adjudged Georges. "Surely you don't need an answer."

"I have my own answers, " defended Leonard. "so, wouldn't presume to know yours."

Georges smiled appreciably at Leonard's response. "Fair enough. We are artists, my young Leonard. Artists of life. It brings us closer to ourselves and stretches us to go beyond our limits of yesterday. We make that which moves our hearts, and are masters of all that we create."

"But, what you create has no useful purpose."

"Perhaps true," admitted Rick, "but in artistry, it's arguable that the best creation is one which has no purpose other than to entertain. If it's beauty is unsurpassable, then its purpose has been met, if not even exceeded."

"Okay," allowed Leonard, "but, your castles, for all their wonder and splendor, still will not last. The next hard wind will take them down. The next rain will strip them of their beauty."

"Of course," answered Georges, glowing. "Is that not like the cycle of our lives?" He pointed at his array of towers. Leonard noticed for the first time that some of the structures were broken and falling apart. He realized that some of the heaps of sand may have been early efforts, now dissolved to nothing. Georges continued, "Show me a kingdom that has withstood all time. We create, but we have no illusions that they will last forever."

Rick leaned towards Leonard with his alluring, aquamarine invitation. "Wouldn't you like to see what you can build on your own?"

Leonard felt the call from across the ocean, tugging at his heart, though he could not see either the water or the pier. He peered at the wet sand, still in Rick's hands, and began to really wonder what he could create. A voice inside intruded as it reminded him that the ocean wasn't going anywhere, and he could cross later. He heeded the voice, and took some sand from Rick.

The two men chuckled as they watched Leonard start to mold the uncooperative granules. He found a spot with ample sand and space. Adding more and more water, he labored to construct a magnificent stallion with a flowing mane and rippling haunches. The two men went on with their own projects.

Sometime later, both men approached to inspect Leonard's creation.

"What is it?" asked Rick.

"What does it look like?" challenged Leonard, suddenly remembering Henry as he continued to work.

"A flounder?" Rick honestly guessed.

Leonard's face told him that his guess wasn't close.

"It looks like a Hostess Ding Dong to me," announced Georges.

Both Leonard and Rick peered at Georges questionably.

"No, really," urged Georges, not knowing enough to shut-up. "Look here, where the aluminum foil is partially removed."

"Tres bon," smirked Rick, mocking Georges.

Leonard rose and kicked his sandy creation, then walked away.

"Leonard," Rick called, but Leonard kept walking. He'd not expected to create a true masterpiece the first time, but also didn't expect to be THAT bad. On the same hand, he'd not yet fully adopted their Build-Your-House-Out-Of-Sand philosophy. He didn't expect his creations to last eons, but if he was going to learn and develop artistically, he wanted it to last longer than just the next rain.

A memory surfaced. Leonard and Reuel, watching Mary Poppins. Dick Van Dyke played Bert who danced in the rain to Chim Chim Cheree as the rain smudged and washed away his chalk drawings. Those long, stork legs of his, bounded over the floundering artwork, then he started scuffing the colors with his shoes. He soon moseyed off, a bit sad and alone figure, but also satisfied with the adventure they'd just shared.

Reuel grabbed a handful of microwave popcorn and said, "Good thing nobody stepped on their chalk drawing while they were in there. If the rain could get 'em, so could someone's foot."

Sipping his drink, Leonard added with a smile, "& when did he put on his hat? He left it on the sidewalk with coins in it when they jumped in. Then, they float back out of the drawings and he's wearing his hat."

"What can I say?" acknowledged Reuel, "Mary thinks of everything. Mary's good."

Leonard nodded. Yup, Mary's good, though she did mourn over Bert's ruined artwork instead of preserving it. If she was THAT good... C'est la vie.

Leonard wove through the maze of sand castles as he considered that chalk is its own kind of sand. Soon the open beach stretched out before him. The ocean seemed bigger and more blue than ever. He gazed with significant awe as he wondered what he'd done wrong. Sure, he was a novice, and it would take years of mentoring to reach the level of expertise he'd witnessed this day, but he still didn't expect to be *that* bad.

"Leonard," Rick caught up, interrupting Leonard's muse.

"Sorry if we upset you."

Leonard didn't answer for a spell, then said, "I know you were both being honest."

"Yes," agreed Rick, "But..."

"No," interrupted Leonard. "It's okay. Really. I appreciate your honesty. Actually, it's probably a very good thing." He kept staring at the ocean.

"What's out there?" Leonard asked, completely changing the subject.

"Out where?"

"There?" He motioned towards the ocean.

"Nothing," Rick answered.

"Nothing?" Leonard's brows furrowed. "I'm told that it's the passage to Creator God."

Rick scoffed. "There is no passage and no Creator God. That's why we build sand castles – to make a name for ourselves because there's no greater name than our own to build upon."

"What about the ocean?" pointed Leonard.

"There is no ocean," Rick Shaw answered flatly.

"But, I see it," insisted Leonard, pointing. "It's bigger than just about anything."

Rick shook his head sadly. "I have no idea what you're talking about."

"And, you really don't see the ocean?" checked Leonard.

"There's no ocean to see," jeered Rick. "We are all there is, was, or ever will be. We were not created, but composed, *ex-ni-Lego*, and you would do significantly better to construct your own life out of whom you are and what you yourself can do, rather than waste your time pursuing the dreams of the ocean and what lies beyond." And with that, he turned back to the avenues of sand structures.

Leonard watched the man walk away and encountered an unexpected sense of relief. Turning his focus towards the ocean, he tried to see what Rick saw, but no matter what he did, he still could not deny that the ocean was there. He removed his shoes, cuffed his pants, and walked down to the edge of the surf. The cool water coated his feet. The watery sand buried his feet as it slithered out beneath the weight of the man. He reached down, dipping his fingers in the swirling water, and raised his hand to his lips. The biting salt stung his tongue, a bit of sand grit his teeth, and the cool of the water spread across his palette.

"Of course there's an ocean," puzzled Leonard, tempted to bring dripping handfuls of briny water to Rick as evidence. He probably would just make wet sand with it, so wondered how Rick wetted his sand if not from the ocean. Maybe Rick would accuse Leonard of weeping this bucket of saline tears and claim it came from the ocean. None of it made sense, so Leonard re-started his trek towards the pier.

A sizable group of people played in the surf up ahead. "No," thought Leonard, they weren't playing, but he couldn't decide what they were doing. He watched as he approached, stopping alongside to make sure he saw them right. As the waves washed in and out and in and out, each person ran up and down the beach with the water's edge, keeping one leg in front of the other. It appeared, he decided, that they were trying to keep one leg in the water and the other on the sand. Amused, he watched them for some time.

Some were too slow to keep up with the ebb and flow, but continued their race.

One young woman caught his eye. She slid up and down the embankment like a pendulum made from a boomerang, effortlessly flying with extraordinary speed as the wave rushed in. Like the others, she kept one leg in front on the sand, but her gallop seemed much more smooth and natural.

"Hi," Leonard carefully approached.

"Hi," she answered, barely looking at him, dashing back in sync with the surf.

"I see what you're doing," called Leonard when she returned up the beach, "and I wanted to know why."

She dashed off towards the ocean's edge with the retreating water without answering.

He repeated himself each time she came up, and each time, she refrained from answering to dash back down. His repeated questions ignored, he followed her down towards the surf; unobtrusively, at first, then more aggressively. At first, he ran back and forth strictly on the beach, standard style to run. Then, his foot caught the water. He kept it in, and started to gallop back and forth, keeping one foot in the water and the other on the sand.

"Good," she said. Leonard wasn't sure if she was talking to him, or not.

"I'm Leonard," he tried.

"Kim." They flew down the beach. The water stopped abruptly and they together waited for the next wave. It would be only seconds, so Leonard spoke rapidly.

"I still don't know why we're doing this, Kim. Could you explain it a bit?" His foot sank into the watery sand. Suddenly, the wave washed in, and both scurried to stay on track.

"So," Kim started, "so, we can have the best of both worlds. We want to be close to God, so we keep a foot in the water which is the way to God, but we are also of the Earth, so keep the other foot on the land. Like I said, we're looking for the best of both worlds." Leonard stopped a moment as she dashed away with the surf, the abrasive water swirling around his bare ankles and calves, and wetting his cuffed pant legs.

"I see," he answered to himself as he exited the water to roll-up his pant legs as far as he could, then slid back down to the waterside, joining the group in their quest to have the best of both worlds.

For the next few days, Leonard skipped back and forth with the water, however high or low the tide took them. Someone set up a loud speaker on the beach facing the water. Christian radio poured out on them all day, singing songs of praise and offering words of insight and wisdom.

Leonard found his stamina surprisingly capable to keep up with the best of them. In turn, he noticed that it became more like a game, or competition, to see who could outdistance the others. The games were so intense, that few spoke. Thus, heads turned in surprise when Leonard ripped open his personal can of worms.

"Um," he began, (by the way, some of the best things ever spoken began with the word "Um".)

"Um," he continued, "When do you pray?"

"All the time. Aren't you praying?" answered Kim.

"No," he admitted, "not since I got here." He almost lied to keep face.

"Why not?" asked Kim, beside Leonard, scooping another heaving round of air into her lungs.

Leonard took a few waves to formulate an answer.

"Actually," at first he muttered, "I was praying, but I realized that I was praying along with someone on the radio, so stopped."

"Why, then?" puzzled Kim.

"Cuz, I realized that it was a recorded sermon. I'm not sure that Jesus has a clue what we're praying about when we're agreeing with a recorded prayer. It seems to me that if the recorded speaker prays something like, "Lord, lead us in your paths," and all I answer is affirmations like, "Yes, Lord," that the "Yes, Lord," may be all that the Lord actually hears. So, He'd be in tune to his praying children, listening to a bunch of "Yes, Lord," prayers all over the nation, but not receiving what they're agreeing to."

Kim decided to ignore him.

The radio declared, "Lord Jesus, we pray that your Holy Spirit will dwell in our hearts and our minds and our bodies and our souls. In your name we pray, Amen."

And, Kim automatically answered, "Praise Jesus, Amen," but quickly wondered for the first time if God actually took account from her prayer. She slipped a half step, and almost submerging her upland foot.

Another time, Leonard asked, "Some of you already can't keep up with the speed of the waves. What happens when we get too old to run up and down the beach like this? Does that mean that we can no longer be in the best of both worlds?

"In a way," she admitted. "but, that's because they'll be going over to the Heavenly realm soon. The trek is almost over, and they can let the water overtake them, and deliver them to the Father, Son, and Holy Spirit."

Besides no elderly folks, Leonard also realized that there were no kids. So, he asked.

"What about the kids? Until they get to ten, eleven or so, they wouldn't even be capable to keep up with the surf. Not only that, but no parent could carry even a small baby in their arms and still move fast enough to keep pace with the waves."

For the first time during his brief experience, Leonard watched Kim completely stop to think, letting the water rush over her ankles and up her calves. The water came down, then back up, then down. Leonard kept pace with the flow of water, but never took his eyes or ears away from the young woman. Others in their group also noticed. None stopped, but were ready to if they thought she needed help.

"I don't know," she finally answered, resuming her run. "I guess they just can't have the best of both worlds. Dwell on the sand, or revel in the water. It doesn't mean that they cannot be saved. It just means, like in all of life, that they are limited in their spiritual run by the circumstances of their lives."

"Okay," thought Leonard, not convinced. "So, what about ministry?"

"What about ministry?" checked Kim.

"While we're making the best of our lives, and showing absolute devotion to our Lord, how do we minister to others?"

"You mean bring new converts to our faith? You're here, aren't you?"

Leonard paused a moment on that one. He kept moving, but started to slow down. Eventually he stopped, up the beach, out of the water. The wave receded, then came back and lapped at his wrinkled toes with the softest of sea foam. Leonard watched the exchange. The surf again departed, leaving him on the beach, un-judged and un-condemned. He saw the imprint of his bare feet on the wet, solid sand. His socks and shoes, dry and stiff, still held down the beach where he'd laid them on the first day. He snickered to himself, and had to admit that yes, he was here and his purpose was singular, but for the first time, he listened to his little internal voice telling him that he was off track. It also occurred to him that life *solely* in God's kingdom should be better than trying to get the best of both worlds. He could just as easily spend his life in a revolving door.

Suddenly, bigger than life, he saw the pier he'd originally been heading towards. He stood alone, looking at it for a long time, then left the surf, retrieved his shoes and socks, and started to walk off without a word.

"Leonard?" called Kim. "Where're you going?"

"To go minister in another fashion," he quickly retorted, then realized how rude that sounded.

"I hope it wasn't something I said," she gasped, yelling to him at the top of the wave before she slid back down the beach.

Leonard looked upward in Neuro Linguistic consideration as he formulated for her question an answer that never hatched. He watched her comings and goings a few more times and listened to the sweet invitation of the surf when an amazingly simple idea cropped up in his mind. Dropping his shoes and moving towards the ocean, he waited until Kim came close, then raced beside her towards the water. As always, she stopped at the resting edge of the water, but Leonard kept going, full force with a front flip into the welcoming flow of the ocean. Sea water splashed all over, including onto Kim.

"Leonard!" cried Kim, almost stopping.

Leonard whooped and hollered and bounded in and around the water, letting the waves wash over him and the undertow threaten to drag him out to sea. For the rest of the morning, he frolicked and played and enjoyed the sweet bodysurf of life. When, he finished, he strode from the water, unhurried and elated and victorious, smiling at Kim and the others as they sped past. Soggy and spent, he went to sit on the thirsty sun drenched sand, drying and warming and resting happily. It felt good. And, he felt good. He slicked back his brown hair and lifted his face, eyes closed, towards the golden green sun.

A shadow floated over. Opening his eyes, Leonard recognized Kim's silhouette, half blocking the bright sun, bursting and vaulting and pulsing behind her.

"Have a seat," he offered. There was a huge beach for her to seat herself. She chose to sit next to Leonard. The other ministers continued their to and fro dash. Kim tried to not look at them.

"Having fun?" she asked.

Leonard wasn't sure if she was being inquisitive, condescending, curious, judgmental or something else.

"Yes, I did," he answered and smiled.

Both sat there some moments before Leonard added, "Feels good, doesn't it?"

Kim looked at him with a jerk of her head, like he'd asked her a probing, personal question he had no business asking.

"The sun," Leonard tipped his head. "It feels good, doesn't it?"

Kim sighed, like she had something to say but didn't know how to put it into words. Finally, she said, "I've always wanted to do that."

"What?"

Kim paused, still apprehensive to continue.

"What?" Leonard pressed. "Swim in the surf? Then, lay on the beach?"

It wasn't much of a nod - almost like a twitch, but her head signaled affirmation.

"Then, why don't you?"

Her voice barely audible over the surf, she admitted, "It doesn't seem right."

Leonard waited.

"The best of..." she almost added.

Leonard tried to show compassion as he suggested, "Maybe there's more than one way to get the best of both worlds."

Kim watched her friends whom she knew were watching her.

"It just doesn't feel right." She looked away far, far off.

A nimble breeze danced between them until they heard the others calling from surfside.

"Kim."

"KIM."

"Come on."

Kim glanced at Leonard quickly as she rose and bounded back to the edges of surf and sand. The group gladly welcomed her with whoops and hollers, bounding and bonding and binding and banding back and forth.

Leonard detected whispers of judgment towards him from the group, but wondered if he was projecting. Rising, he picked up his shoes to continue up the beach. He didn't look back, and replayed in his mind the images of Kim and the others dashing up and down the sand with the surf. He also replayed her conflict before they parted. He prayed she was happy and blessed with her decision.

Still carrying his shoes and socks, he came upon another group. They stood near the shoreline, looking towards the ocean. Leonard stopped some distance to watch. To his surprise, one of the men suddenly bolted away from the group towards the water. He ran as fast and as hard as he could, flying down the beach in a full sprint. The water receded ahead of him. He'd timed it perfectly. As the water stopped its descent, the man reached the waters edge and leapt with all his might into the water. He flew at least 10 or 12 good feet, but stopped short, crashing into the oncoming wave. He walked back up the sand, a classic drowned rat image, as the surf swashed him back to the shore's roving edge.

The group applauded, jumping and shouting and praising him as they surrounded him. He wiped the salty water from his face, and pushed back his curly hair as his friends patted his back and congratulated him.

Leonard started to pass around them, giving himself a very wide berth, when he saw another, this time a woman, sprint towards the shoreline and jump into the surf. Again, the water caught and held her, bringing her back to shore.

One man noticed Leonard, stopped on the dry, deep sand, watching the group. He came up, extended his hand, and greeted, "Did you see that?"

"Of course," chuckled Leonard.

"Wasn't that wonderful?" he added. "That's got to be her best jump, yet. I swear, if she'd cleared the wave, she would've made it."

"To where?" asked Leonard, wondering if he'd missed the obvious.

The man stopped to re-evaluate Leonard. His features softened when he determined that Leonard was asking for information, and not mocking him.

"To God," he answered matter-of-factly.

Both men turned towards the group to see another man sprint full speed towards the water. He leapt farther than the first, but still landed feet first in the water. Catching himself, he planted his feet in the submerged sand and waded back to shore.

"He's probably the best jumper in our congregation."

"I can believe that," complimented Leonard. "Um, m'name's Leonard."

"Aaron."

The two men shook hands again.

"So, uh, forgive me for asking," inquired Leonard. "I don't want to sound dumb, but how far do they have to jump to get to God?"

Aaron paused before answering, then plainly said, "All the way."

Now it was Leonard's turn to pause as the magnitude of the answer spread across his mind.

"All the way – across the ocean?" he gasped.

Aaron nodded.

"That's silly."

Aaron smiled. "I used to think so, too, but some have made it. That's all it took to convince me."

Leonard studied Aaron's face skeptically.

"Really," urged Aaron. "I kid you not. Come. Meet the group. They'll tell you."

Leonard glanced at the pier, but followed Aaron down towards the shoreline.

"Everybody," yelled Aaron. "This is Leonard. He's come to jump with us."

Leonard began to protest. Aaron quickly added, "I've got a feeling about him, too. It wouldn't surprise me if he was the next one to make the jump."

A sudden flash flood of veneration filled the congregation as they inspected this newcomer.

"No," stumbled Leonard. "I don't think for a minute that I could jump across the ocean."

"Humility," praised an elderly man with grey-green eyes framed with laugh lines. "A virtue in dire shortage today." He winked as he bowed to Leonard. The group took a step back to give their new Saint more room.

"Hold it! Time out!" said Leonard, making a "T" with his hands. "I'd love to play Superman and leap large oceans with a single bound, but it appears absolutely impossible for any person, man, woman or child, to be able to jump that far."

The group was undaunted. "It's true," answered a short, stocky man with a bald head and mustache. He seemed completely sure of himself. "Of course, they also have to have a pure heart, purged of all sinful thoughts, and total focus on the course set ahead of them. Only then will their feet and legs take them the distance."

Leonard considered, "Wouldn't it be easier just to swim across?"

The group snickered.

"Now *that's* silly," answered Aaron. "What would happen if *you* tried to swim across the ocean?"

Leonard had to admit the obvious. "I'd surely drown, probably before I was out of sight."

"Exactly. That's why they have to make it in one bound, with God or **The Prophet** there to catch them on the other side."

"I'm going to make it this time," declared the bald man.

The group turned. Some got on the starting line with him, as though they were going to race down together.

"Clear your mind," one yelled to his right.

"Clear your heart," one added to his left.

"See the journey," said Aaron from behind the man, and the group answered, "Amen."

He waited just long enough to gauge the flow of the waves. The short, stocky legs dug into the dirt as deeply as possible, propelling the man towards the water. Leonard imagined a penguin having better odds, then quickly scolded himself for ridiculing this innocent stranger. The bald runner got to the water's edge and leapt a few floundering feet before hitting an oncoming wave and getting flipped head first into the surf.

The group laughed and applauded, cheering him as he exited the water. He smiled, first sheepishly, then gallantly as he rejoined the group.

"I guess Heaven wasn't ready for me," he smiled and wiped either sea water or a few tears from his eyes.

"So," quizzed Leonard, "who has actually made the jump?"

The congregation answered almost simultaneously.

"**The Prophet**."

"The prophet?"

"No, **The Prophet**," answered Aaron with an air of finality, then waited for the weight of his words to sift through whatever filters of disbelief and discontent that Leonard may have had.

"**The Prophet**?" Leonard eventually uttered.

"Yeah!" Aaron shouted amidst congregational cheers.

"Well, who is he - or she? Tell me about him - um, her."

"It's a He," answered Judy, a skinny blond with a homemade, tattooed tear beneath her left eye.

Aaron kept hold of the Reigns. "**The Prophet** dwelt among us, his common people, for some years. He ministered tirelessly until the day of his martyrdom when, mortally wounded, he cried out in a mighty voice, "It is Phoenix!" and with that, he rose with legendary beauty to float, unfettered beyond the ocean's vail to the secure, woe-less bosom of our Eternal Fodder, who is our great provider. Thus, it remains our fervent prayer that we may live our lives clean and without blemish, ever striving to join **The Prophet** where He Reigns Unimaginable over the three kingdoms of Heavenly Host as well as over all of us, his subject creatures, that in our struggles and trials and triumphs, we may be touched by even just one molecule of his shed blood, spread like the sower's seeds throughout this ocean-wide baptistry, thus to be lifted up, and also delivered, cleansed of all earthly transgressions and brought to the open, waiting lap of the Eternal Fodder, where, like **The Prophet**, we may reign to bless the waters to bring those deserving after us."

The congregation waited with head bowed reverence. Some knelt. Some crawled, heads down. Some laid prostrate, face down, burrowing into the sand.

Leonard waited and watched Aaron take a long, deep breath of air after such a speech.

"Amen," answered a late-middle-aged man dressed in what Leonard thought looked like an open, terry cloth bathrobe, swim trunks and flip flop sandals. He wondered if the bathrobe was meant to resemble an Old Testament style robe.

"So," Leonard returned his attention towards Aaron, "how was he martyred?"

"Whom?"

"The prophet." He recognized the look, and corrected, "Pardon me – **The Prophet**."

The congregation relaxed. Judy clapped her hands.

"He wasn't martyred," corrected Aaron.

Leonard felt lost.

"Uh, then how did he die?"

"**The Prophet**?"

"Yeah," affirmed Leonard, falsely believing that the conversation was again moving forward.

"He didn't die," Aaron answered.

"**The Prophet** doesn't know how to die," interjected Judy.

"**The Prophet** was created to live forever," added The Bathrobe.

"But," Leonard carefully weighing his words, "didn't you just tell me that **The Prophet** was mortally wounded?"

"Yes."

"But, he didn't die?"

"No."

Leonard paused, then said, "If he didn't die, then he wasn't *mortally* wounded. Wounded, yes, but it wasn't fatal."

"It would've been fatal," reported Aaron, "but he traversed the ocean before his human life ended."

"Understood," sighed Leonard, "so, back to my original question."

"Which was?" Aaron answered a bit testily.

"How was he mortally wounded?"

"Oh," perked Aaron, turning red. "Uh, he was cruciblized."

"Cruciblized?" Leonard was not familiar with this verb. He was also perpetually awed at the new and pretzeling twists of this conversation, but kept an open mind in case he was the one missing the obvious.

"So, how," he ventured, "does one die - uh - become mortally wounded by - uh - (*Crucibleation!!??*) being cruciblized?"

"He was crushed," answered The Bathrobe.

"Like a walnut," added Judy, moving closer to Leonard. Her fingers caressed the side of Leonard's arm.

Leonard tried to ignore her and waited for further clarification.

"… such was His crucible," added Aaron.

"Okay," eased Leonard, ready to believe that it was starting to make sense. "So, what was his crucible? Our sins and transgressions?"

"No, no, no," answered Aaron emphatically. **The Prophet** wasn't crushed for our sins and transgressions. That was Jesus."

"Whoops!" thought Leonard while his silent face waited.

"No," continued Aaron, **The Prophet** was cruciblized in his final battle against evil when he toppled the Demon Sculpture."

"What was the Demon Sculpture?" asked Leonard with both exposed curiosity and avid repulsion. He realized that he probably would not have asked if he'd thought before speaking. He also wanted to give Aaron a chance to breathe between sentences.

"You know," responded Aaron, "the sculpture with the head of gold, the chest and arms of silver, the belly and thighs of bronze, the legs of iron and the feet partly of iron and partly of clay?"

"Like Nebuchadnezzar's dream in the Book of Daniel?"

"Exactly," applauded Aaron. "He struck it at the feet, taking the base out from under the structure. It tumbled down, crushing **The Prophet**, and as he ascended from the debris, cruciblized, he knew that there was only one way to refuge. He made it to this shoreline, and triumphed over his dying struggles to bound over to the Eternal Fodder."

"Wow!" answered Leonard, looking towards the water. To jump across the ocean had appeared utterly impossible not many minutes past. Now, he realized that he could see himself, gliding down beach with the elegant speed of a cheetah, reaching the flowing edge of the water at just the right, magical moment, then leaping with a burst of explosive joy mixed with bold courage to feel the unexpected power from beyond; to be airlifted via God's divine tractor beam. His breathing increased. His heart pounded. He could feel the rhythmic pressure of blood and excitement inside his ears. He watched the water; the ebb and flow of the surf, the strength behind the walls of water he meant to clear; the sharp, straight line of the distant horizon obscuring the Heavenly goals beyond.

He started to pray with frantic fervency, preparing himself for the ultimate flight. The Bathrobe pulled Judy away from distracting him. She started to protest, but saw his face and held her tongue.

Aaron motioned with his hands to bring the congregation around Leonard, leaving the necessary, broad opening towards the oceanfront. The group also prayed, heads bowed, eyes closed, arms folded. Some held holy pompoms that shivered when they moved.

Leonard detected the divine fire burning within his bosom. His heart continued to beat aggressively. He wondered what his blood pressure would read and imagined himself seated at the blood pressure machines in the Pharmacy section of the supermarket. He shook with disgust at himself for being so easily distracted from such an important intent and purpose.

Aaron and the congregation commended Leonard when they saw him shake.

Leonard looked again towards the ocean shoreline, trying to recommit his focus while wondering if systolic came before diastolic, then wondered if he was spelling and pronouncing them correctly. He clamped his teeth, and clenched his fists in frustration, and the congregation commended him.

"Yea, Lord," Judy squeaked.

"Lord, forgive me," peeped Leonard, folding his hands. He automatically counted the throbs of his pulse between his intertwined, perspiring fingers.

"Yea, Lord," chirped another woman.

"It's now, or forget it," snapped Leonard, still struggling to recapture the dynamo fervor he'd experienced bare moments before.

Aaron responded, stepping forward, taking position beside Leonard. He nodded invitation to The Bathrobe to take position on the other side.

"It is Phoenix," prayed Aaron.

"Found in flight," responded the Bathrobe, and the other followers chimed, "Amen." Leonard took another deep breath, filling his lungs to capacity, exhaling just as hard, then drawing another breath; his feet nervously pawing the ground. His muscles contracted. Flooded with emotion, he roared. Some jumped back, startled. He interpreted the flush rush as affirmation, and began the sprint towards the water.

He took off with short, biting steps. His pace lengthened into a full, smooth, flowing gallop, urged forward by the descending slope. His pantlegs, still cuffed, smacked each other as they passed. The surf receded ahead of him. He raced to catch it. The water pooled at its lowest point, preparing for the next wave. Leonard dug into the soaked sand at the water's edge, and leapt as high and as long as he could. He felt every molecule of muscle bounding forward with uncompromising audacity. He wanted to enjoy the free feeling of absolute flight, perhaps compared to his recent flight outside creation, and dared not let-up even one iota lest his momentum wane. Up, up, up he soared, peaking at the zenith, feeling the greedy magnets of gravity pull him back to Earth where he crashed, full body, straight on, into the next breaking wave.

Suddenly, he felt the cold, wet water prickling every nerve, and filling every oily pore. Still fully clothed, his outfit quickly saturated with water, weighing him down. The main force of the wave washed past him, and he stood, waist deep in water, barely a dozen-odd feet from his point of launch.

The congregation cheered as they raced down the beach to meet him and congratulate him as he trudged out against the undertow.

"Wow!" complimented Aaron. "That was one of the best jumps I've seen in years."

"Truly inspiring," added the Bathrobe.

"Actually," Leonard began, seating himself on the hard sand, "I'm not sure that I wouldn't've made it, but as I was running towards the water, I suddenly wondered, "What if I only made it part way across the ocean and landed thousands of miles from God, Heaven, **The Prophet**, or even good 'ole dry land?" Such misgivings of being lost, adrift, or even just castaway should have compelled me to try just that much harder to ensure success, but alas, I confess that it tripped me up, and surely slowed my attack a halfstep or two."

"The Jonah Effect," quipped Aaron, and the congregation nodded appreciably.

"So, what do we do now?" chaffed Leonard, wringing brackish water from his shirt and pants. Aaron answered curtly, "We do it again."

Chapter Eleven

" Seek **The Prophet**," prayed the man to her left.

"Seek the Eternal Fodder," urged the woman to her right.

"Jump, not just with might, but also with purity of heart," followed Aaron, and all three closed, "Amen."

Judy exploded from the group with all the fury of a crazed sandpiper. Her little, straight legs switched places like passing chopsticks. In classic pattern, she reached the water's edge and jumped as high and as hard as she could, only to land hard in the shallow water. The next wave slunk around her narrow frame.

The group skipped down to congratulate her as she returned to them. Leonard and Aaron stayed up on the beach watching them.

"I don't understand why none of us have made it," confessed Leonard.

"All the way?"

"Yup."

"Most never will," admitted Aaron.

"Huh?" Leonard swiftly swiveled his head towards Aaron at that.

"Most will never make it," he reported matter-of-factly. "Maybe none of us will; at least not before our moments of death."

Aaron had noticed that Leonard had become a bit frustrated. He'd started out with such holy fervor. After a dozen or so jumps, all about the same, he tried spending more time in contemplative preparation. Oftentimes he prayed, sometimes on his knees, sometimes pacing back and forth, sometimes face down on the sand, enwrapped in rapturous ecstasy. He'd rise with a sturdy 'Amen,' and prayerfully perform stretching exercises before bolting off for the ocean side long jump. Sometimes he would not wait for the group to gather to chant and cheer him on.

His leaps were admirable. He jumped with the best of them. Yet, it was that very sharp, competitive blade of his character that kept him ever dissatisfied with his personal best. Right from the start, he well knew that he could never make it on his own power and strength and effort. He'd attacked the problem with every solution that he could imagine. He added personal prayer, invited others to pray with him in preparation, he interceded for others; he tried jumping with others hoping that the Lord would answer the efforts where two or more were gathered. He even toyed with setting up a launching platform like a little trampoline in the surf.

The one thing he regularly rejected was giving his uncompromising commitment to **The Prophet**. Something in his spirit resisted. Aaron could see it. For that matter, everyone else could also see it.

"Don't you ever get frustrated?" Leonard looked up.

"Perhaps," Aaron dodged. The congregation, still surrounding Judy, rejoined the two men. Judy smiled at Leonard in a fashion he'd become well accustomed. This time he didn't return her smile.

"Well, I'm getting frustrated. No! That's not the word."

"Disillusioned?"

"No, that's not quite right, either." He paused, groping for the right word(s).

"How about 'unsettled'," suggested Aaron.

"Yeah, maybe," he muttered, gazing towards Aaron without ever really looking at him.

The Bathrobe scoffed. Others whispered to each other behind him.

"What?" challenged Leonard. "Don't you ever get frustrated – or unsettled?"

The Bathrobe was silent.

"Of course you do, Stan, (The Bathrobe's name was really Stan). I've seen you whip yourself as you stewed on the beach after a wimpy jump. I've heard you cry, "What's the use?" and I've seen you pull yourself together again to support Aaron, Judy and the others here as well as prep yourself for your next jump."

Stan backed up a step, and blended into the other silent members of the congregation.

"Now seriously," argued Leonard, "whom do you know who's made the jump?"

"**The Prophet**," answered most.

"Besides **The Prophet**."

Their blank faces answered his question.

"**The Prophet** is the only one I need to follow," defended Aaron. "And, you would understand that if you also would commit to him."

Leonard sighed, un-reproached. "Y'know, Aaron," his manner un-accusing, "I've tried to honor **The Prophet**. Really, I have. I've thought about him a great deal. I've earnestly prayed to God about him. I've sought his spirit to make the jump, and searched the sea foam for evidence of his blood. And, in each case, I've met the dead end."

The congregation shifted restlessly.

"But, I'll tell you, the one admirable quality I have found with **The Prophet**."

Aaron nodded for him to continue. Leonard obliged.

"The thing that really toasted my bread was not that he leapt across the ocean, though that's certainly remarkable, but that before his jump, he engaged the enemy in battle. He destroyed the Demon Sculpture as the tale goes, and I don't see any of us trying to destroy the other idols of this world. We're just seeking the Great Escape; to whistle Anchors Aweigh as God loosens our binds and chains before we've left our personal mark on His creation, and I'll tell you, my sense of discernment keeps popping big firecrackers in my inner ears to get my attention that maybe we're going about this all wrong. So, yes, I'm feeling unsettled, and frustrated, and even disillusioned." Leonard realized that he'd felt similar concerns before departing Kim's company up beach.

A long, laboring pause arose.

"That's it?" checked Aaron.

"That's it," assured Leonard.

"I'm sorry," muttered Aaron, and with that, he and the rest of the congregation wiped the sand from their feet, then turned away towards the hardened sands of the waning tides.

Leonard watched them depart. Judy stood looking at him longest, but said nothing. Water still dripped from her, but her eyes were dry. She also bowed her head and turned away to follow the others.

Some cried. Some hugged or held hands. None prepared to jump.

Leonard watched them a spell, then dropped to his knees on the damp, hard sand. He studied the sand, as though looking for the perfect spot. It didn't matter, but still he searched. Bending forward, his lips touched the clammy surface. Immediately, a small flame burst up, dancing and hovering with utmost joy over the sand. Still kneeling, Leonard watched the small flame. He felt its warmth, alive and so comforting after many days near the water. He looked towards the group below. None really reacted, though he detected some had seen the flame. Judy seemed to have a twitch slightly turning her head towards him over her left shoulder.

As the beautiful flame flowed off, Leonard pronounced, "Amen," and rose. He knew God's Spirit was neither created nor destroyed.

He looked to the North. He could see Kim and friends galloping up and down the beach with the surf. Farther on, he could see Richard's sand castles though he saw no one at work there. Neither drew him, so he turned to the South. The pier still stretched out over the ocean, much farther than any of Aaron's group had ever jumped. A ship departed. He felt remorse to leave Aaron and the group, but felt even more a degree of relief that he was again on the best course, or at least not on the wrong course.

"Want some shells, mister?"

Leonard startled, awakened from his selfish vigil to turn to see two kids, not more than six or seven, holding forth a plastic bread bag full of sea shells.

About ready to dismiss them, Leonard stopped and asked, "How much?"

"Two dollars," answered one.

"Each," added the second.

Leonard examined the bag, sand coating the inside, obscuring the variety of common sea shells.

"Two dollars - total, and you've got a deal."

The first boy balked. The second nudged him. Leonard pulled two damp bills from his damper pocket. The temptation was quite enough. The first boy snatched the bills, and without so much as a thank you or good-bye, both ran off to a Living Water concession stand. The shells rattled as Leonard walked onto the pier.

The pier felt so hard and unforgiving after so many days on the sand. A warm breeze flowed outland, feathering his senses and lulling him along. There was no reason he shouldn't venture out onto the pier, yet he detected a sense of violation, as though he was doing something forbidden, but didn't know it.

He plodded along the rough, wooden walkway, his right hand gliding along the railing. The beach disappeared as the surf washed-up well beneath his feet. The water seemed so close, barely past high tide. Sea gulls whined. One stood atop the railing and watched him cautiously as he passed. Leonard turned his head and squawked, more like a parrot than a gull, but the gull became alarmed, looked all around him, then flew off.

A few people populated the pier, widely spread out. He passed one man asleep on a bench, his arms folded and hat covering his eyes and face. In front of him a long fishing pole rested, fastened, on the railing, line down in the water. Leonard silently peeked in his bucket. Just water. No fish.

He passed others till he reached the end of the pier, and leaned against the railing watching the foam and swells on the water meander about. The lone ship continued away. Even this far out, Leonard could see his friends back on the beach, so small and unlikely, still contending with the surf and the sand. Their efforts seemed so frivolous, even foolish, viewed from this moderate distance. He watched one burst forth from Aaron's group, gallop towards the surf and jump with all his might. It looked like Aaron, but he couldn't be absolutely sure at this distance. As usual, the jumper landed in the shallow water, then clambered back to the beach.

He watched the waves roll in to become breakers. From this vantage, one could see the swells moving to shore, one after the other. Then, he turned attention back towards the boat, now farther away and just that much smaller.

"Dummy," he scolded. "If you wanted to get to God..." The boat pitched and swayed afar off, and he wished that he could've been on it. The good captain could've taken him across as easy as anything. No futile jumping with all his might. No trying to get the best of both worlds. All Leonard had to do was request permission to come aboard.

Oh, how he fervently wished that he'd hitched a ride on that boat. Eventually, it became a dot on the flat horizon. Leonard imagined that the ocean became a tall, flat wall and the boat was just about to drop over to the other side. Soon it was gone from sight. Leonard presumed that it had not sunk.

He knelt down against the railing and listened to the breeze flowing through his hair. He glanced to each side to ensure that he was sufficiently alone, not that it would've mattered. The tears came anyway. Once released, he became totally helpless to hold anything back, and he wept bitterly. Truckloads of bile overflowed from his Internal Emotion Center, its acid eating through his entire being. For the moment, a blubbering miscreant, he hated himself, and knew God did, too.

Amazing Grace played background music in his mind. The only word he focused on was "wretch." All he could see were his failings - in the campsite, in the cave, and now on the beach. He still couldn't find his First Love. He did nothing to combat the powers of evil, and probably was a puppet for the Spirit of Defeat. He seemed to have a spiritual gift of discernment, but didn't have a clue what to do with it. He also wondered if Billy Graham had days like this.

Life was full of Gethsemanes.

He let the pain run its course – even clung to it, wringing out every caustic drop of self-condemnation until he could successfully dry his eyes and hoist his heavy head. The sun still shone. The caressing breeze still flowed. He knelt, still alone - or perhaps avoided. He rose to re-set down on a nearby bench, and wallow in the void that inevitably followed such emotional upheavals. He felt so empty and utterly drained; as commercialess as a pre-empted TV program. What's worse, he didn't know where he was going. It'd been such a haphazard pilgrimage thus far, and wasn't promising to get any better, or take him any closer to his goals.

He stood and scanned the sea. No boats, coming or going. Nothing but blue, light sky, and dark water, peppered with white clouds or foam. He turned to leave the pier, grabbing his bag of shells, and walked the long, slivery beams towards the beach.

On approach, he saw that the sleeping fisherman had awakened.

"Hey Leonard," turned the fisherman.

Leonard gasped, then smiled and wondered if his eyes were still red.

"Rodger! Didn't recognize you before."

"I know," he harassed. "I saw you coming, so pretended I was sleeping."

Leonard sat beside him.

"How long ya been here?"

Rodger shrugged. "Couple of days, I guess."

"You ain't caught much," he nodded towards the fishless bucket.

Rodger seemed to ignore him as he started to reel in his line. Leonard noticed the barren hook as he brought it over the rail.

"And, you lost your bait."

"Ain't never had none," corrected Rodger, tossing his line back down to the water.

Leonard ignored the triple negative, and settled for Rodger's intended communique.

"& as for fish, I've caught lots more than my bucket claims." Rodger continued, "I noticed you down on the beach with those other bozos jumping in the surf. Couldn't figure out for the life of me what they were trying to do. Then, I took a closer look and realized you were one of them."

"Thanks."

Rodger wouldn't have apologized, even if he'd known how.

"They sure gave you the cold shoulder in a hurry."

"Some things I said," admitted Leonard. "Rest assured, I earned it."

"Bravo. Doomsday prophet?"

"Something like that."

"Double bravo."

"Welcome to the Land of Make Belief."

The two men idly sat watching the wobbly fishing line comfortably dangle. Rodger unexpectedly spoke a thought out loud. "What kind of weather do you think we'll see the day the world ends?"

Leonard thought about it for a spell.

"I don't know," he admitted. "The Bible talks about it a lot, but I don't recall reading a weather forecast. What kind of day do you want?"

"Sunny. I always want sunny, no matter what's happening, though it's been at least a couple of years since I was lost in the desert dying of thirst."

"Okay," thought Leonard. "I seem to recall Jesus warning people to flee from the tribulation including some who might be on their rooftops. Seems if they were on their roof, that it probably was agreeable weather, but He also warns us to pray that it doesn't start during the winter, so I expect that for some it will be summer, and other's winter, or spring and fall, just like it is every other day all over the earth."

"Sounds fair," assessed Rodger, still tending his line.

"Why no bait?" Leonard eventually asked.

"Bait is for sissies," he answered, a hapless mumble.

"But, you're always going for it with everything you've got. This seems a bit, uh, passive for you.

Rodger scoffed. "The real challenge is to catch it without bait. You get these guys with their fancy flies or lures or the best bait. They've got electronic lures. They've got hand held, electronic sonar systems that display depth of the water and where the fish are. They've got glasses so you can see into the water.

"Bah! Humbug! Wimp stuff! Fish without bait, (and I don't mean with a net,) and see what kind of angler you really are."

"Looks like you aren't much of an angler, either," commented Leonard, motioning towards the bucket.

"You'd be surprised," he answered, brows raised, lips pursed. "Wish I'd brought some barbless hooks."

"I don't know," confessed Leonard, glancing at the barren, bobbing line.

"Oh, I have a couple of secrets," an impish appeal crossing his face. "Here comes one of them."

A little, aging man approached, dressed in dirty, button-up shirt, equally dirty trousers, and a gray, brimmed hat covering his hairless head. Toting his own empty bucket, he walked past the two men and bent down, legs bent to peer into the bucket.

"No fish this time," he stated the obvious, still bent over, head swiveled. Leonard immediately thought his high pitched voice suited him perfectly.

"You ain't been here to help," complimented Rodger. He looked at Leonard and added, "This is Andy. He's the one who taught me how to be a real fisherman."

Leonard nodded greeting. "You fish, too?"

Andy seemed surprised by the question. "Oh, no," he answered. "I haven't fished in years. Many, many years."

"But,,,"

Rodger jumped in, "No. He used to fish, figured out how to do it better than just about anyone else, and now shows others who do the fishing for him. My bucket's empty 'cuz he's already taken all my fish."

"For the old ladies," Andy quickly added.

"How many have you caught?"

"Fish or old ladies?" teased Andy. Rodger set forward.

"Oh, what do you think Andy? A dozen or more? I lost count last night."

"At least."

"Those old ladies must really like fish."

"There're a lot of old ladies."

Leonard nodded appreciably. "How long you been fishing, or more accurately, when did you start fishing?"

Andy thought back a bit. "Oh, long time," he murmured. "Long time. Long as I can remember. Started fishin' when I was just a boy – in Cuba. I had a great teacher, named Santiago. He used to catch marlin; and he loved baseball."

"So, uh, what's your secret?"

Andy gave an inquiring glance to Rodger who nodded approval.

"Simple, really," Andy began. "First, you've got to go to the fish. No reason to fish if there ain't nothing to catch."

"Makes sense."

"Second, you've got to have the right bait."

"But?" he motioned towards Rodger's bait-less line.

"Oh, there's definitely bait on Rodger's line."

"No there's not," protested Leonard. "I saw it."

Andy was undismayed. "Why do you bait the hook?"

Leonard thought briefly, making sure it wasn't a trick question. "To lure the fish. Give them something they want, so they'll bite the hook, get snagged, and able to be reeled in."

"Pretty good answer," smiled Andy, "but take it one step further. What if I told you that you could hook them, but the hook didn't hurt, and instead they actually wanted to be caught? That you were really bringing them to fulfillment so that they were able to go to their final rest in peace. Now, that would be a feat of fishing, wouldn't you agree?"

"Okay," Leonard affirmed, not believing a word Andy said. "But, there's still no bait on Rodger's line. I saw it."

"So," suggested Andy, "maybe there's no bait that you could see?"

Leonard swallowed hard on that one.

"Want to see?"

Klaxons and sirens and 9V battery powered smoke alarms instantly resounded in Leonard's head. He glanced at Rodger. Maybe the expression, 'some people never learn' was just as often a mixed blessing. He also wondered why learning to fish should cause him any alarm at all.

"Okay."

"Okay's not good enough," responded Andy. There's no use wasting my time or yours if you really don't want to learn to fish. God's world is already packed with idle fishermen who wait for the fish to come to them. If you want to learn to fish, you've got to go after them. You willing to go after them?"

Leonard ignored the urge to scoff. He also discredited the personal ideology that he'd made a bunch of mistakes down on the beach, so one more wasn't going to hurt.

"I really want to learn if it's legit," he started, "but, I've been fooled before, so don't waste my time if it's not for real."

"Oh, it's for real," assured Rodger.

"You can't learn to swim till you're willing to get into the pool," added Andy.

"Okay," turned Leonard. "What do we do?"

"First, take hold of the rod."

Leonard did so.

"Then, drop the line in the water. Keep it dangling. Don't set it on the ocean floor."

Leonard let out the line, down, down, down, until it stopped unreeling, then took up what he figured was a dozen feet or more so the hook would be dangling.

"Got it?" asked Andy.

"Think so," answered Leonard.

"Hold tight."

Leonard increased his grip.

All of a sudden, he was in the water, under the surface, hanging from the hook. The blue and black steel gleamed above him. He pulled himself up, and sat on the crook of the hook while assessing his unexpected change of scenery.

"So, am I the bait?" he thought as he looked up.

He also noticed how much human garbage carpeted the ocean floor beneath him. A Big Gulp cup reminded him he was thirsty, but he dared not open his mouth.

The hook hung down from the surface of the water, numerous feet above him. He could barely make out the waving faces of Rodger and Andy looking down towards the water, silhouetted against the bright backdrop of sky. He was still a handful of yards from the bottom. Numerous fish swam by, most too small for his hook, but he saw one approach, a hammerhead shark, swimming idly. He'd never known fish to stroll. It turned away and didn't seem to notice.

Another fish, a salmon, or so he thought, meandered close. Leonard fought the urge to abandon ship or try to hide behind the hook.

"Hey!" he waved his arms. The salmon came to investigate. Leonard grabbed hold of the line above the hook. The salmon came very close. Leonard tapped its nose, then leapt up just in time for the salmon to grab only the hook. The fish started thrashing wildly, and Leonard had the ride of his life, whipping back and forth, and holding on for all he was worth.

"Reel 'er in," cried Andy.

Leonard roused as the rod and reel shifted in his hands. He tugged up sharply, then started to reel in, and eventually brought the little salmon up over the rail.

"Pretty good for your first catch," applauded Andy, taking hold of the line, and placing a foot on the fish as it thrashed around on deck.

"But," Leonard sputtered, thinking the salmon looked a lot bigger face to face under the water, "you said the fish would want to be caught. This one came out alive and kicking."

"Once down, and you think you're a pro. It takes practice, young man. Want to get good? Do it, and keep on doing it, and when you think you've got it down, do it again and again. Want to go down again?"

Leonard balked.

"See?" booed Andy. "Once down, and already you've done enough."

"But, I don't need another fish."

"Fair enough," answered Rodger, "if you were just fishing for yourself. You're a regular Leatherstocking. But, what if you were fishing for others - perhaps many others; most you've never met?"

"The old ladies?" Leonard thought out loud while silently wondering who or what Leatherstocking was.

"At the very least."

"Okay," agreed Leonard. "Down I go."

"Good," squealed Andy, "as long as you're not heading down for my sake - or Rodger's. Never fish just for show. That kind of trophy fishin' has its place, but this ain't it."

"Agreed," agreed Leonard, the words barely out of his mouth when he was back on the hook. He watched fish swim by for a while, then got the idea to start swinging. The water made progress slower and more difficult, but after a fashion, he flowed with the current until he was a regular pendulum. He saw a king salmon 20 feet below him. He tried to yell, but the fish didn't respond. He stopped swinging, tugged on the line, and to his surprise, felt it descend. The salmon, long and sleek, still ignored him.

Closer to the bottom, crabs moseyed over the surface. He saw some dungeness that he would've been very happy to bring up.

"Why not?" he thought, and again tugged on the line. Descending down to the bottom of the ocean, he stepped out on the sand, but kept hold of the line, and dragged the hook behind him. He realized even before he started that he was going to have a much harder time getting the crab hooked. Or, maybe not, he reconsidered. Just loop the line around a claw, clasped with the hook.

Easier thought than performed.

The crab flew off at an impressive speed. He saw another one, and tried to get close enough to capture the critter's claw. Same problem. He waited for another to come along, then walked up behind it and kicked it. Immediately, the crab froze, the underwater world's possum player. He strung the line around the creature's back leg and went back to the surface where, from the pier, he slowly reeled up the crab.

Andy cackled when he saw the crab lifted up out of the water.

"Good job," he said as Leonard lowered the crab to the surface. Rodger nudged it onto it's back with his foot, then bent down to remove the line.

"Hadn't tried a crab, yet," he admitted. "Just one problem."

"What's that?" Leonard stooped beside him.

"It's a pretty one, and big enough to keep, but it's a female. Sorry. Gotta throw her back."

"You sure?"

"Yeah." He picked up the crab and carelessly tossed her over the rail, back in the drink.

"So, that it?" asked Leonard. It sounded too easy.

"You bet," squeaked Andy. "But, like everything else, there are pitfalls."

"You mean," suggested Leonard, "like being gobbled up by the salmon?"

"Sometimes, but that's not the smacker." Andy motioned for Leonard to follow. "Maybe it'd be easier to explain by showing you what others keep in their tackle box. They walked up the pier to a couple, seated in folding chairs, sipping forbidden drinks.

"Catch any?"

"Not much, yet," answered the man. "But, what a day to be out, huh?"

Andy glanced at Leonard and motioned towards the open tackle box. Leonard nonchalantly peered down to see all Love, and no Truth.

They walked to another fisherman. In his tackle box was just the opposite - all Truth and no Love. Another had plans for golden cathedrals, padded pews, paved parking lots, and worship services that better resembled rock shows.

Leonard discerned these things more closely resembled Rick Shaw's sand castles.

Solomon's Book of Ecclesiastes came to Leonard's mind. *"Vanity of vanities" says the Preacher. "Vanity of Vanities, all is vanity."*

"You're So Vain" by Carly Simon started playing through his head. He'd often changed the song to first person.

I'm so vane, I probably think this song is about me.

I'm so va--------ne. You know I think this song is about me.

I do. I do. I do.

Andy and Leonard checked another tacklebox. This one hosted tele-evangelist efforts, complete with weepy pleas for donations.

Another had three books: The Book of Norman, The Squirrel of St. Bryce, and The Doctrine of Gloves and Mints.

Another had nothing but warnings of Hell and Damnation.

"See?" asked Andy, turning away. The little man furrowed his bald brow. "They all love God, every one of 'em. They all want to serve Him, and be good fishers, but they've denied the best ways to fish. Oh, they all catch some from time to time, but mostly, I wouldn't want to eat it. Some become toxic before they're even pulled from the water."

He returned to the bench and sat down, heavily, instantly very tired as Rodger pulled in a bass. Andy laid his hat on the seat beside him as he uttered, "If you want to give them your Love, be sure to balance it with the Truth, and vice versa. If you use scripture, make sure that it's the real McCoy - the Bible, and make sure you know what you're talking about. Finally, they don't need hype to be caught. Give them what they honestly need, and they will want to be brought in, I guarantee it."

He rose and donned his old hat.

"May I?" he pointed towards Leonard's salmon.

"Uh, you bet. Of course."

"Thanks. Bye, Rodger. See you soon." The two men watched as Andy walked down the pier, Leonard's salmon and Rodger's bass securely riding in his bucket.

"Those old ladies must really like fish," repeated Leonard.

"You know it," answered Rodger, and tossed his line back in the water. The two men finished the day fishing and sharing fish stories. Leonard wished they'd had two poles. They could've waved to each other down in the water.

Approaching dusk, Leonard rose to go.

"Leaving?"

"Gotta get to the city. I promised my grandpa I'd see him on his birthday. You still have my truck?"

"Here." He tossed Leonard the keys. "It's parked down by the highway."

"How long you staying?" asked Leonard.

Rodger thought a moment. "Oh, not long. I expected Andy to come back by now. What else am I gonna do with all these fish?" Rodger rubbed his eyes. "Also gotta get some sleep. And dinner. And a drink. And a shower."

"Amen," teased Leonard. He looked towards the beach. "Wanna ride along?"

Rodger considered the offer, but declined. "Nah, no birthdays for me. But, don't forget, we have a date..."

"What date?" Leonard drew a total blank.

"Skydiving."

Leonard moved his body in various poses, all of them thoroughly indicating that he considered it absolute lunacy to jump out of a perfectly good airplane.

"I'll get you up there. You'll see – and you'll like it." He teased his line a spell just in case a fish happened by close enough to get snagged.

"Skydiving, huh?"

Rodger turned and smiled; firm affirmation.

Leonard bent over to get his sea shells as he glanced at Rodger. Gasping, he did a double-take. The vision departed, but not before he got an eyeful. For the moment, Rodger had been an ugly, black, whirlpooling, hideous shadow. Rodger noticed Leonard's reaction. Both men gawped at one another, eyes spanned, breath abated. Leonard took a step back.

"We'll see," Leonard obliged, "but not today," and with that, he was gone.

Chapter Twelve

Leonard Lamb laughed, like a bald and seeping re-tread, out of balance and out of alignment. Chewing on thick lips, he accelerated down the on-ramp to the freeway. The road opened up before him, straight and estranged. He needed, or at least appreciated the time to reflect on the events of the past - uh - don't know how long. How long does one fly through nothing outside creation? How does one measure becoming part of the ecology en route to the city park? What nanoseconds are lost chatting with Henry? What happened to the world outside while he feasted within the Heavenly veil? He'd been through so much. How perplexing he should still feel incomplete. And, what in God's world was that vision with Rodger? With mile after mile to himself, he had time to pray as well as hopefully untangle and sort out some of his confusion. Likewise, this was the first part of his expedition to where he had to be somewhere at a specific time.

Soon he breathed a bit easier. There was a familiar feeling of security to be back in his little pickup speeding along the road. The cab still smelled like dirty oil and Altoids. The arm rest was still a bit too hard to be comfortable to his elbow. The dashboard still lit up letters and numbers and dials, except for the heater controls, ever lost in the black at night. The motor still sounded like a garbage disposal gargling aquarium gravel.

He headed to his homeland, the place of his birth, to be close to family. Grandpa's birthday was tomorrow, and he wanted to see him. Not that he felt that he could talk to anyone at home, including his grandpa, about his adventures. He scarcely believed them himself, and nobody but nobody at home would supply him with even an ounce of credence if he opened his mouth. He opted to hold his tongue when he saw his family, and later record these accounts in this book.

Practically fleeing from Rodger on the pier, he realized that the vision just plain scared him, and he wished that this 'gift' would give him some warning when he was about to be 'insighted'. Of course, he wondered and second-guessed and replayed numerous scenarios that he could've done besides make a hasty exit.

"Leonard Lamb, you could've said, 'I rebuke you in the name of Jesus!' That would've been good, but as usual, you were afraid of looking like a fool if it didn't work. Rodger probably doesn't even recognize the demon within. On the other hand, he's already dealt with two demons in the cave. Maybe he would've been more receptive than you feared." A burp erupted.

"Fear," he scoffed, the chalky, bitter bile filling his mouth. "Fear keeps you from yourself, over and over and over and over." He swallowed hard, but it didn't help though his ears popped so the sounds of the engine became much louder. "What good is it to be dealt a winning hand if you don't have the guts to lay your money down?"

He drove, passing through mountains and by trees and lakes and game and saw none of it. Cars passed. Huge trucks rumbled. Signs directed and rails bordered and protected, (or bounced squeaky shocks and springs while waiting for the train). The mountain country gave way to softer plains. The trees preferred the highlands. The brush sported a cowardly yellow. He wished - at first for nothing. Eventually, for someone. Someone to talk to. Someone to help him make sense of it. Someone to help him utilize this spiritual gift of discernment. Someone to expose the Spirit of Defeat that never showed its face, but knocked him on his can with ease and regularity. Why could he not see it coming, save that is what makes its attacks an 'ambush'? Even Grief or Pain could give him insights that so far evaded him.

Suddenly, he burst forth with laughter. For the first time, he laughed at his folly. It was not a jovial laugh, nor a bitter laugh, but instead, a release valve that squirted out of his nose and mouth and eyes and ears and brain. Translucent tears blinded his coated eyes, and he had to stop. The exit posted the Potholes Reservoir near Moses Lake. He parked alongside the shores of the reservoir and rested his head against his steering wheel, little snorts coloring his chuckles.

Grabbing the door handle, as he clambered out of his vehicle, an odd feeling seized him, as though his body briefly turned to Silly Putty. It rapidly subsided, and he wondered what it'd been. The Holiest Spirit must've been doing something. His mind felt oddly alive as though it had downloaded a computer file that was waiting to be opened.

The flat, deserted beach met the flat water. The rich outlines of twilight metamorphosed. He could not see the dam from where he was parked, so stepped out to explore the area. His shoes crunched and ground the crusty dirt. The moonlight blended with a few local lights to reflect across the broad, bland water. He recalled this area to usually be very windy, but this evening the air held its breath and the surface of the water seemed as still as buried dirt. Approaching the shore, he stood and idly watched the barely lapping water.

Suddenly, a silly idea flashed across his mind. His eyes lit up, and he scurried back to his truck. Checking again for other active signs of human life, he snatched the bag of seashells out of the truck bed, and returned to the shoreline. Extracting a shell, he tossed it on the sand by the water. Walking along, he occasionally left another shell or two, some on the beach, some dipped in the water.

Many steps later, still dozens of shells in his possession, he looked back. He'd already gone a quarter of a mile or so, but kept trekking, not wanting to leave the shells too close together, and enjoying the cool evening walk. He trekked along till he heard a groan. He stopped to listen, quieting his footsteps. Nothing for some time. He continued walking, and after a fashion, again heard a sound that could have been a human groan. He stopped again, and again heard nothing. Goose bumps snaked up and down his spine, but he resumed, not forgetting to occasionally sow his shells.

The groan droned once more. This time, he thought it came from up ahead, and hurried on to find its source. Even in the dark, the sight appalled him. He found a large man physically in pieces, like a 3D jigsaw puzzle spread about on the dirt. At first he feared the worst, but soon reckoned that his imagination was truly playing tricks on him. He tried to fix him and put him together, but that didn't work. Then, he tried to throw him away, but couldn't let go. Next, he tried counseling him, but that just made him break up even more, some parts becoming as coarse as baby powder. Drawing closer, he heard the sweet sound of prayers moving the sand beneath the large man's breath. Leonard fell to his knees and joined in.

Inevitably, the man came back together, rolled over and looked up at Leonard. His lifeless, glazed eyes suddenly sparked, like the strike of a match, and he stared vibrantly at Leonard. Even in the dim starlight, Leonard started to recognize the man.

"Pastor Pete?"

The man reached in his sport coat pocket and retrieved his glasses.

"Leonard?" he finally said, and Leonard extended both hands to help him to his feet.

"I can't believe it's you," each said to one another.

"What're you doing out here?" asked Leonard.

"Praying, my son. Praying just as hard and as diligently as I can." He brushed himself off. "I could ask the same of you."

Leonard looked sheepish. "Nothing quite so productive, I'm afraid. Actually," he held up the plastic bag of shells, "I'm playing a little prank."

"Prank? On whom?"

"Don't know. Parents. Kids. Anthropologists. I'm distributing these seashells on the sea shore."

"What for?"

"Just in jest. I expect this weekend, some of the kids will start collecting a few of my shells and get all excited. Then, they'll bring them back to their folks who will look at them, and you know that some will think, "Nah. That's impossible."

"But, won't some of them get lost?"

"You bet. And, I don't care. Actually, I can see it in a few hundred years or so, some high and mighty anthropologists finding my shells here

189

and claiming that they prove that this area used to be part of the ocean."

Pastor Pete had to laugh. "Okay, you goofball."

"But," Leonard changed the subject, "what about you? You just about freaked me out, finding you out here alone, prostrate on the dirt, not answering, all in..."

The silence became obvious.

"What?" checked the pastor.

"It's silly. Just..." he trailed off again.

"Tell me."

"When I first saw you, you looked like you were in a bunch of pieces."

"Like how?"

"Oh, you know. Pieces. Like your body was not connected." He started pointing, "Your legs were over there, and your arms were over there."

"Like the scarecrow in The Wizard of Oz?"

"Yeah," thought Leonard. "Kind of."

"Wow!" Pastor Pete thought aloud.

"Wow, what?"

"Maybe your eyes weren't playing tricks on you."

Leonard rolled his eyes and started to walk away, tossing a few shells aside.

"Really," Pastor Pete pursued. "I was in dire worship, and in my pleas, God broke me. I mean, really broke me, then as only his Spirit could, put me back together."

Leonard stopped. Even in the night light, he could see that the pastor was being totally serious.

"But, your body? Your actual body?" protested Leonard. "I always thought of that teaching as being more - rhetorical."

"Me, too, and maybe that's what it was, to where God's Holy Spirit brought you to the vision of me being in pieces. At the time, I didn't perceive that any of my parts were missing, but I absolutely knew I was being overhauled, praise Jesus."

It was Leonard's turn to say, "Wow!"

"So, uh, how does one get overhauled? I've lost my First Love, and need something drastic to delete my mundane apathy."

Pete thought about it a moment.

"Do you read your Bible?"

"Of course, though not as diligently as I used to. I used to sit for hours any given evening, Bibles open, plus lexicons and reference texts just to study the Word. But, I don't know if I lost my first love because I don't study scripture as much, or if I don't study scripture as much because I lost my First Love."

"Maybe both," Pete answered. "Bible study is just one part of your walk with Christ. Usually, when one facet suffers, it doesn't take long before the others also start to degenerate. How about your prayer life?" asked the pastor.

"I pray all the time - everyday."

"Do you praise Jesus?"

"Of course."

Do you worship Jesus?"

"Yeah," answered Leonard thinking he'd just answered that question.

Pastor Pete grumbled to himself as Leonard tossed off a couple of shells.

"Praise isn't the same as Worship."

"Okay," allowed Leonard.

"Really," added the pastor. "Listen, you can enter praise time spontaneously with little preparation, but to really get down on your face to worship God is itself a journey. The two are similar, but definitely distinct."

Leonard emptied his bag of shells, and started to turn back, thinking to himself.

"I have one question that's bugged me for a long time."

Pastor Pete urged him to continue.

"Why would God want our praises and worship? I have no delusions that I have the eternal mind of Christ, but I don't know why the all knowing, can do anything, made everything and everyone, most intelligent being in the universe would want me to worship Him. Commitment, yes. Duty, yes. Worship? I don't know."

They walked along in silence as Pastor Pete carefully formulated his answers.

"Think about this. If any person we knew wanted to be worshipped, we'd consider it sinful vanity. Right?"

"Sounds sound."

"But, the ethereal realm is not the same as the corporeal realm. Instead, we're engaged in a spiritual war. We like to think of it as a war between God and the devil, set in terms of divine good against demonic evil, but it's also holiness versus sinfulness. We worship, not because God is egotistical, but because He's a loving God who gives us much more than we can give Him, and worship keeps us focused on Him. So, praise and worship Him that you may be made holy rather than sinful. Personally, I'd rather be full of grace than full of the smut of sin."

They reached Leonard's truck. Leonard unlocked the door and retrieved a paper out of the glove box.

"I wished I'd shown this to you when we first met."

"What is it?"

Leonard handed him a brown paper bag. Even in the dark, the pastor could see the penciled words, reflecting the moonlight. Squeezing the small flashlight on his key chain, he read the letter.

"Cute," commented Pastor Pete. "Who gave it to you?"

"A young man who could dance like the wind and speak with the wisdom of the ages."

"Was he sincere?"

"Undoubtedly," Leonard recalled though he mostly remembered the weird way he danced.

"Did he know it was already a letter to another church?"

Leonard gasped. "What?"

Pastor Pete smiled. "It's one of the letters in the Book of Revelations. Letter to the Laodiceans, as I recall. Chapter Three. I'd have to double check, but I'm pretty sure that's it."

"So, why the reference to Ephesus?"

"Good question." The big man seemed unworried. His confidence felt reassuring.

Leonard felt the moment ripen. He laughed lightly, to himself, to his friend, and ultimately to life. "I'll also have to check it out. Thanks. It's been bugging me for quite some time." He took back the letter, and opened the truck door, ready to depart.

"Where're you off to?" asked Pastor Pete.

"Uh, way north of Seattle. Home. It's my grandpa's eightieth birthday. He's a pastor, too. Need a ride?"

Pastor Pete pointed to his car parked some slots away.

"Think about what I said," he urged.

"I already have, and will continue to do so," committed Leonard, sharing a hug with the big man. He opened the door, dropped in and reached to start the engine. "Please pray for me."

"I already have, and will continue to do so." Pastor Pete dropped a heavy hand on the top of Leonard's truck. "Lord bless you, my friend. If it wasn't a sin, I'd envy your journeys to come." He smiled and lumbered away to his car.

Leonard started up the engine, mostly out of habit, and sat blankly as Pastor Pete's headlights flashed across his face. Snapping out of his funk with a quick shiver, he shifted gears and raced out of the parking lot.

Chapter Thirteen

Like 'Four Score' without the seven years, old Pastor Lamb reflected on his life as the morning wind almost blew away his hat. He reached up to catch it. A minister longer than most living believers had been saved, he slid the tarnished brass key into its older, slotted mate. Turning the lock, then turning the handle as he'd done so often during the sixty-odd years that he'd shepherded his flock, he pulled forth the door. It's heavy, metal hinges squeaked shrilly. The wind whooshed in behind and around him.

He stepped in, turned on the lights, but left his coat on, zipped to the neck. Though it promised to be a warm day, the carpeted foyer of the church would've chilled new wine. He thought that he detected a puff of steamy breath seething forth ahead of him, but resisted the urge to turn-up the thermostat. If he wanted to warm the antique building before the Sunday morning service, he'd probably just have to open a few windows.

Climbing creaky, wooden stairs, he used the available light enroute to his office. Most of the morning's preparations were complete. He'd come early to air out the church, but would use the welcome prayer time as well as Bible reading and study before reviewing this morning's sermon. Any message he could research was ages older than himself by many lifetimes. It had thrived through the ages and would maintain for many more to come.

He coughed as he took a seat; more a reflection of his ancient age than any impending ill health.

At least, he hoped so. No man could be careless at his age. He felt the forced, sweet air, feather light and exceedingly welcome, flow through the ever open window, composing a benevolent atmosphere across his office. Preparing to take notes, he opened his Bible. The well worn pages, more wrinkled than its owner, reflected the soft bulb declaring again the words of divine truth.

Alone in his office he read.

"Yo!"

The young man entered, bounding through the door like it was a springboard.

Pastor Lamb jerked up.

"Good Jerusalem!" he snapped. "Leonard! Knock before you burst in, young man."

"Sorry Grandpa."

"And, don't you 'sorry Grandpa' me. I've told you over and over to knock before you opened that door. What if I'd been in its way? Good lands, son! You would've knocked me down. Broke my hip. Now, come over here and give me a hug."

The old man still glared at his grandson as Leonard dropped down to his knees before his grandpa who gave him a long, welcoming hug. Leonard smiled brightly, and took the seat beside the desk.

"When did you get into town?"

"Just got here. Came straight away. Haven't even been home yet to see Momma."

"How long will you be staying?"

"Just today, and maybe tomorrow." Laughing to himself, he realized that his demeanor had immediately adapted. He'd put on the family hat that he'd always used around his senior relatives; the sit-up-straight, clean-your-plate, eat-all-your-peas façade.

Pastor checked his clock.

"What brings you to town?"

"It's your birthday today, Grandpa. I came to celebrate with you."

A glow of recognition crossed the patriarchal face.

"Sure," he muttered, his voice like old snow underfoot. "Sure, my birthday."

"You okay, Grandpa?"

"Of course I'm all right," he snarled, then softened. "Sorry, Leonard. I must've dozed off." He smiled, trying to reroute his cranky emotions. "I'm just not up to another birthday. I've had more celebrations than any man should be allowed. Of course, how'd you like to have been Adam? That man had nine hundred and thirty birthdays. He died just eighty short years before Noah was born. Imagine the hoopla they had for birthday number nine-oh-oh. No one else had lived that long - not yet."

Leonard chuckled (*again*, he'd heard the joke like, every year since he could remember.) He glanced around the office. He'd been here so many times. He'd grown up in this office. His grandfather had built much of his empire from this office. The cracked leather chair which squeaked with each move more than any church mouse, had been his throne and trademark as well as his judge's bench, and even his prayer closet. Though to Leonard there was nothing detectably out of the ordinary, it somehow seemed all new this morning.

Peering out the window, the trees rustled and swayed like merry metronomes, leading cadence with scattering leaves. He loved the wind, ever blowing out the dust in his soul.

"So, how have you been?" Leonard asked, still watching the windy show. The old man waited until Leonard looked his way.

"Why do you ask, son?"

"You just seem more – bothered than usual."

Pastor sank back into his chair. Its creak could've been a surrendering sigh. Pastor rubbed his fingers over the hardened arm pads.

"I feel this old leather," he began, "and, it reminds me of my arteries."

Leonard grinned.

Pastor answered the same. His false teeth, perfect and off-yellow, shone back.

"But, it also reminds me of my ministry."

Leonard stopped and eyed the leather. Smooth and tanned, he reached out to feel the surface.

"Okay," he humored. "How?"

"I've shepherded this church for over fifty years. I've fought the good fight. I've run the good race, but I know my days on God's dear Earth are nearing their end. I've weathered the storms. So many have come and gone; some whose names I can no longer remember.

"I see the new ones; the young couples with their new families. Sometimes I envy them. They have their entire lives laid out before them. But, then I think of the kingdom to come and I weep for them. Somewhere life turned so evil. Somewhere man lost his sense of mortality and moral fiber. If I'd seen it coming, I feel certain I would've behaved differently. These regrets point back to my own life and I wonder if I'd made any lasting impressions at all. What could I have done differently? What can I do with the short time I have left?"

He folded his soft, pockmarked hands, scolding himself for saying too much. This grandchild had blossomed into a grand, young man. He seemed to have a little more of the wanderlust than Pastor would have preferred, but his love and devotion towards the Lord was quite admirable. Pastor loved him as much as he loved any of his own offspring.

Leonard fidgeted a bit during such moments of quiet reflection. His mind was alive, dissecting the old man's words. He'd never seen him like this – so resigned and equally depressed. His heart ached to reach out to him, but he wasn't sure how. He studied the wrinkled features of his grandfather's face, the highlands and the canyons. The crow's feet bordering his eyes testified to many hours of laughter. No crow has so many toes on its feet.

He thought of their last Christmas day together. The family getting together, sharing laughter and tasty edibles and LOVE more precious than gifts. This morning's difference was a moonless night after the overcast day.

"You've been my personal inspiration," offered Leonard, serious, recalling his pitiful vigil on the ocean pier. "I'm but one small part of God's body, the bride of Jesus. I feel small and insignificant a lot. Disposable. But, you always told me we were special. You always stressed a person's vitality to God's kingdom, still firmly thriving despite the sins of this planet. Even when I felt rebellious; even when I questioned God's reality, I could never reject Him completely. I saw you. I saw mom and dad. You've been the living and breathing grace in my life more often than even I've yet recognized." Leonard stopped to reflect. Grandpa could be pretty cantankerous. He met the old man's eyes. They were puffy and red, drenched with emotion. Hope's legacy incarnate.

They heard footsteps in the hall. A knock echoed off the door. It opened before anyone answered. Leonard turned to look. Pastor glimpsed also before looking away to dry his eyes.

"Pastor. Oh! Leonard! Happy birthday, – Pastor." The stout woman closed the door behind her. "What're you two doing up here by yourselves? Goldbricking?"

"Not without a permit," answered Leonard.

Pastor nodded, still head down, studying his text.

"We're just about set-up downstairs," Donna reported.

"Set up?" questioned Pastor, still not looking up.

"Oh, yeah. How can you two stand it in here? It's so cold."

"It's fine," answered Leonard. "Hope it's warmer downstairs."

"It is," she assured.

"Who else is here?"

"Everyone. The Langley's. Chip and Deena. Randall, of course. He brought tortilla chips."

"Chips?" blurted Pastor, finally looking at her.

"For the pot luck. Langley's brought a cake. Chip and Deena brought their usual pot of chili and cheese. I brought this wonderful green bean casserole I found in Better Homes and Gardens I wanted to try."

"It'll be fine," assured Pastor.

"Looks like it stopped raining before I got here," observed Leonard, turning away from the window, then back again.

"Another year, huh Pastor?"

He nodded.

"Why was it always the same?" A sense of peppery condemnation flavored her words.

"What?" asked Leonard.

"Oh, Randall. He always comes to our pot lucks with a bag of chips and expects to be fed." She checked the door, suddenly fearful and relieved that he wasn't standing there.

"Randall's single," defended Leonard. "I've been to his apartment. He's not much of a cook. Take my word for it. Be glad he brought something pre-fabbed and edible."

Donna waved Leonard off with her expression, looking to her pastor.

"It'll be fine," Pastor repeated.

Donna huffed, unconvinced.

"Going to the Timothy Grier Crusade tomorrow?" she obnoxiously changed the subject.

"I didn't know Grier was in town," belied Leonard.

"No, I'm not," answered Pastor.

"Plans?" she chatted. Small talk deduction.

He nodded as she retreated to the door.

"Don't know what you're missing, Pastor." She turned back, her hand rubbing the brass door handle.

"Enjoy yourself," he blessed.

She grinned, her cheeks proudly dimpled.

"Thanks. See you downstairs?"

"In a few minutes." Pastor and Leonard enjoyed the quiet lull after Donna's exit. They listened to her heavy footsteps compress each step. Leonard looked at his grandpa as they heard the music from the worship team practicing before the service, vibrating the floor.

"I thought that you were going," checked Leonard.

"Huh?"

"To the Timothy Grier Crusade?" Leonard sat, anticipation flooding his features. "You've worked so hard on it. I was sure you were going."

Pastor studied his grandson. His face twisted as though a pungent odor suddenly found his nostrils.

"I know I have," Pastor acknowledged, "but, I've never condoned such ministry. The elders decided to volunteer and add our support to the crusade. I support their decision."

"But, you don't agree with it?" Leonard was genuinely surprised.

"No," admitted Pastor, closing his Bible and gathering his notes.

"Why?"

Pastor sat up a bit, as though about to deliver a sermon.

"In my sixty two years of church ministry, I've long come to the conclusion that God called us to serve His people personally. One-to-one, if necessary. Certainly house-to-house, and it doesn't require the Big Show to do it. Lots of fancy music; lots of hype. Build up an emotional circus and anyone'll come to the Lord. Who'd want to be left out? But, when the hype is over and the show leaves town, you have a lot of lost new believers, more uncommitted than committed, returning to the ruts they'd dug in their lives. Many don't belong to a church body. They don't know anyone that will make sure they don't go astray.

"Oh, sure. A few slip of those through the cracks and wander into a church. Even a lot of those soon leave. The realities of church life aren't always that attractive, and they're seeking the excitement that first brought them in the door. The Sower's seeds fall on other than good ground."

"But, you worked hard to bring this crusade, Grandpa."

Pastor saw the misgivings in Leonard's face.

"Yes, I did," he responded soberly.

"Why?"

"Philippians," he answered, waiting to see if Leonard would get the right scripture.

Leonard reviewed his memory. His face confessed his ignorance.

"Chapter One," Pastor added.

"Uh," struggled Leonard, "Paul thanks the church for their gift, and tells how he's in prison for preaching the gospel and calls the believers to stand firm."

"Good," applauded Pastor. "Paul also endorses even those who preach the gospel out of personal ambition and gain, just so long as the gospel is being preached. Verses fifteen through eighteen."

"I'll look it up later," resolved Leonard, "probably before I leave today."

Pastor winked. A grant to his grandson.

"But," he warned, "Don't change your mind about going to the Crusade on my behalf."

"Why not?" Leonard asked.

"Because I could be wrong. In that, follow your own heart and the leading of the Holy Spirit. I'm a cranky old man who doesn't like such crowds. I doubt I'd go regardless of Mr. Grier's integrity or motivations. My suspicions are only that. Suspicions. Don't not go because an irritable, old man is spouting off his head out of his own piteous shortsightedness. God has blessed that man's ministry with an enviable abundance. It's an exciting career. He could've done a lot worse."

The old man smiled. His grin, thin and crooked, invited both men to relax.

"Let's get downstairs," he directed, rising. "We have our own little flock to attend to right now."

Lights in the hall led down to the kitchen. The two entered the stark, bluish lights.

"Pastor! Happy Birthday!"

Pastor Lamb nodded as he approached the food tables.

"Looks wonderful," he applauded, warm and inviting as steamy, hot cross buns fresh out of the oven.

Leonard saw a green bean casserole that looked somewhat like a green worm moshing pit. Randall came in, dropping off not just potato chips, but also a plastic tub of dill pickle dip. Soon all exodus'd to the sanctuary.

Pastor took his place at the podium. He stood beside the wooden platform, resting his right hand along its top; a common stance. The congregation had grown so well accustomed to this pose, that they stopped chatting and took seats.

Off stage, Pastor could appear fragile and bent. He'd been described as a frail man, known for his long enduring patience and servitude. He was well versed in scripture and allowed his flock their shortcomings. But, beside his podium, his demeanor changed dramatically. The bent man stood no taller, but he appeared bigger than the fears of the world, and stronger than the most ironic of human oddities; head and shoulders above the rest.

More than that, his reputation dwarfed even this stature. He'd been serving the work of the kingdom so long. Words like "wise" and "tireless" had long ago been tagged to his name. Pastor wisely and tirelessly ignored the accolades. He felt heavily the burdens of both his shortcomings and his age. Today, from his podium, he felt smaller than usual. Very small, and broken. A fragmented shadow of the man he could've been.

"Greetings and welcome," he opened.

"Good morning," most called back.

He made brief introductions and stepped down from the stage. Natalie at the electronic piano took her place, accompanied by the worship choir, and started the service. Pastor walked down the center aisle to take a place at the back of the church, in case others showed up. He greeted and shook hands with the ushers.

Natalie felt the hard, plastic-coated keys of the keyboard. They sang and played the first hymn, their usual shallow voices and occasional missed notes. Pastor relaxed as his ears welcomed in the old hymns. He looked around the congregation and picked out the few who'd been with him for more than a few years. These were the backbone of his life's work. The thought should have consoled him. Instead, it irritated him. So few for sixty plus years of ministry. He tried to expel the impressions, citing his pride; a census of vanity, he argued, but the gritty self-condemnations nagged him. He scratched the itch with logic. It rested a moment, then popped up again. He chastised himself, almost missing his cue when Nat ceased playing and returned to her pew seat.

Allowing the congregation to perceive a prayerful span of contemplative reflection, Pastor sauntered up to his podium, dragging his self-pity behind him. He thought he could hear its ball and chain rattle as he stood before his guests. Taking a moment to regroup, he scanned the congregation, then read the announcements and asked everyone to prepare for the offering. The big room barely half filled, the dozens of faces beamed back towards him. He smiled, then noticed a figure seating himself way in the back. He studied the newcomer; his old eyes taking in the man's dimensions.

Pastor gasped.

Leonard, seated in the front pew, turned towards the back of the church. Other heads turned as well. The reactions from the modest congregation crescendo'd, its excitement becoming apparent.

Leonard stood.

So did the man.

Leonard and his grandpa waited as the man approached up the aisle. His gait was strong and his head held high. His assertiveness glowed with each stable step.

Pastor stepped down from the stage. The man approached him.

"Mr. Grier," coughed Pastor. Words evaded him. "I'm – shocked – to see you here."

The Crusader extended his hand. Pastor accepted it graciously.

"Please forgive the intrusion, Pastor," apologized Grier. He motioned to the front of the church. "Can I say a few words – if I'm not interrupting your program?"

Pastor felt awestruck.

"Of course," he shuddered, still incredulous.

"Please don't go far. I won't be long."

Pastor acknowledged, taking a seat beside Leonard.

Timothy Grier looked to the podium. Deciding against putting the stand between himself and this small group, he faced the congregation.

"I did not come here to preach or to teach. I came to pay tribute to a man I've never met."

He smiled, taking that special, long moment to look from face to face.

"Forgive me," he restarted. "I'm not accustomed to speaking to smaller groups. It's much more personal and actually more scary than speaking to a big crowd." His hands found his pockets. Taking a deep breath, he continued.

"When I was a boy, I wasn't permitted to attend church. My parents, God rest their souls, wouldn't allow me to go to church. Just the idea upset them.

"As a side note, I'd like to mention that both of them came to believe in our Lord Jesus before they passed away."

"Praise God," called Donna. The congregation nodded approval.

"Amen," he answered. "Anyway, I was very attracted to church. We were poor. Very poor. I'd see the people on Sunday morning entering the church by our house. They were always so nicely dressed. I was maybe nine years old at the time. Their nice clothes impressed me as affluence. I thought everyone who attended that church were wealthy. We were poor, and that wealth attracted me.

"But, as I mentioned, my folks would not permit me to go to that church. They wouldn't hear of it. Wouldn't entertain the idea. Besides that, I myself felt inadequate to go. Dressed in my hole-ly blue jeans, my dirty T-shirt, and my worn out tennis shoes, I was afraid to enter the church. Everybody was so pretty compared to me.

"Then, I got an idea. Walking by the church one summer Sunday morning, I could hear the music. I wandered over to the open window, but didn't dare look in. And, there I stayed. There were big shrubs hiding me from anyone who might pass on the street, including my folks. It became my special hiding place.

"After that, I came back almost every week, taking my post outside the window. It didn't take long till I could sing along with some of the songs - not too loudly lest anyone besides God hear me. I'd even listen to the announcements. I'd hang on every word the pastor shared during the sermon.

"I'd been coming regularly over those few months time. One morning, the pastor led an altar call, and from my place outside the church, dirty and unkempt, I gave my life to Jesus. Shortly after that, my folks and I moved away, but I never forgot that day and the devotion I'd committed to my Lord and Savior. Many years have passed. The Lord has given me much more than I could've hoped or prayed for. And so, I came this morning to pay tribute to that pastor to whom I'd never met, and to thank him publicly for leading me to God's saving grace."

The crusader turned away from the congregation. Taking the one step up onto the stage, he walked over to the window. Unlocking it, he opened it a crack. The brisk wind seeped through the opening as he stepped down. Approaching Pastor, he extended both hands and helped the old man to his feet.

"I stood outside my old window this morning before I came in, tramping down the footsteps where I could tell other children run through any given Sunday morning, and straining to hear through the closed window. I listened to the music awhile until the Holy Spirit tugged at my heart and told me to come in. When I heard your voice, I knew it was you, and my heart leapt for joy.

"Thank you, my Pastor. I love you."

He gave him a long hug. Pastor wept helplessly. Leonard rose from his seat and joined the hugs. Others also came to share in the moment.

Wrapped in the joy of many arms, Grier kissed the pastor's wrinkled cheek, and whispered, "I always keep my window open. I never know who might be listening."

Chapter Fourteen

Dear Henry,

I can't begin to explain how things have been going since I last saw you. The Timothy Grier Crusade was more than wonderful. Reverend Grier honored my grandfather who came the first day. Plus, there is this unfathomable, hope-filled blessing to see thousands of people in devoted prayer and singing songs of praise to our Lord. Perhaps needless to say, Grandpa was the automatic celebrity-of-the-weekend, an accolade he grumped about all the way home.

The real reason I'm writing to you is over a dream I had last night. I've had lots of dreams, of course, including some I recall very well, but this one stands out because it was so dynamically real and still I get both excited and depressed just thinking about it.

It was a bright and hot, sunny day in a desert town; one of those days where the squinting sun was absolutely golden while it cooked everything around me. I was standing in a parking lot talking to Rodger, (I presume you know about Rodger). I don't recall what we were talking about, but suddenly a booming sound like a million-voice hum pounced on us from above. The sound was hyper-sonic, not long, but definitely got our attention, and my chest instantly ached with that shocking feeling that the Christ's return and the rapture were actually beginning.

"It's happening!" I exclaimed. I looked around and saw dozens of people sparsely spaced around the desert and sagebrush. I couldn't see their faces, but I watched as every one of them laid down, prostrate on the sand, and became virtually flat, as though murals painted on the ground.

Next, I remembered a popular comedian who said, "If I feel myself heading up into rapture, I'm gonna grab a sinner in each hand, and as we're zipping up through the clouds, I'll say, "Do you get saved, or do I let go?" I looked at Rodger and realized that he wasn't saved so I grabbed a firm hold on his wrist just in case we started flying. We were standing outside a red brick building, and I grasped that my relatives were in the building, so still holding Rodger's wrist, we walked to the main entrance. We stopped as we looked inside the open doorway. The opening appeared sooty black and forbidding.

Then, a voice seemed to say to me, "Don't go into the darkness. Stay out here in the light. Your family will be okay." So, I turned away from the door. A bunch of activity started to bounce around overhead. Just then, I awoke.

I'm sorry to say that I never did look up to see what was making all the commotion. And, I was so bummed, (that means depressed,) when I realized that it was just a dream. I awoke really excited. It was still the middle of the night, but there was no way I would go back to sleep, so got up and spent the next hours in prayer and praise and worship.

As usual, my prayers were selfish. I was so mad that it wasn't real, though I also thanked my Savior for the vision and when I ran out of people to share the account with, took to writing to you. Now, I feel like the man who could ride any ride at the amusement park, but still got queasy whenever he rode an elevator, such is my apprehension. Now that I've got this dream; this vision, what do I do with it? I've followed my trails

211

of dreams lots of times. They ramble like tears down one's face. It's a strange and crazy trail – often dangerous, and it becomes an emotional road; a passionate road; even an intimate road that is never straight and seldom lighted.

In like manner, I mix my dreams with my prayers to see if I could really move mountains. Sure, men can move mountains, but unlike God, they can't keep them intact. So, I asked my Lord Jesus about that – about how a man balances himself between his aspirations and the Lord's leading – or, whether my dreams clash with God's directions for my life, (I'm sure I'm not the first person to encounter this conflict). I don't get many direct answers to my prayers, but this time the answer drove through me like a supersonic bullet. If my spiritual antennae were adjusted correctly, it said that it was like vinegar and oil. They easily separated, but were awfully good if they were shaken up together.

I can make good with that.

It's about time!

It seemed, of late, that all my efforts, for whatever purpose, have been without effect. My prayers can sound so cold to me. My Christian walk blindly traipses headlong into the blizzard. My hot ideas have been packed in ice. Barbed wire hugs my heart. In short, my efforts are a joke. My soul must look like Swiss cheese. I don't recall who said, "Amputate your feat and you'll be defeated," but it seems to describe me most days. Defeat, the very spirit you warned me about. I don't see him, or touch him, or hear him, or smell him, or taste him, but he messes up my sense of being more than I can count.

I often try to reason my way out of the pit. I think, therefore I AM, but God is the only great I

AM. I try to pray (which may be the oddest of all,) because I know He hears my prayers, but there seems to be a clog somewhere between my mind and my heart - like the two are feuding, though neither can remember when or how the feud started, but each side refuses to cooperate, or even to politely wave as they pass. I persist in my prayers hoping someday to find myself submerged in everlasting grace, but so far I've been relying on complimentary passes to Living Water slides, or trying to mend my heart with duct tape.

Of course, I read my Bible, but the same problem. What good is it to memorize your Bible if you still don't know it by Heart? It's at those times that I am NOT assured of my salvation, nor that my leading and testimony would save others. My life feels like an overflowing ashtray. How can I who have a Messiah not act like I have a Messiah? If I was some hopeless existentialist or hedonist, I would have an excuse to feel doomed and depressed, but I'm not. I have a Messiah, so I'd do well to alert my face.

Oh, I was also wondering, how Heaven could hold all of us? (Of course, when I'm in some funk mood like I am now, I expect if all believers were like me, Heaven would have Zero Population Growth, but that's another matter. If God lived by the adage, "An ounce of prevention is worth a pound of cure," He surely would not have created us.)

But really, I was thinking about how many souls potentially could be delivered to the bosom of Abraham? There are about 6 to 7 billion souls living here on Earth now, and every sixty/sixty-five years on average, those six billion pass on and are replaced by more than 6 billion who also are being born, living and dying. Now, if only one sixth of those six billion made it to Heaven, (and I fervently hope that the percentage is much higher,) we'd have a billion Earthlings every sixty years crossing through the Pearly Gates. Multiply that by how many sets of generations? More than my calculator can figure without applying scientific notation.

That's still a mind boggling, impressive number of souls walking the streets of gold and expecting their own mansion. And, that's just this planet. How many more heavily populated planets are sharing the same eternal kingdom with us? Probably countless thousands, each sending billions of yearning, faithful souls to the Crystal Throne Room every few generations.

Such thoughts make it easy to feel lost and forgotten by my Creator, and I could concentrate on my own insignificance, but I'd rather realize God's awesomeness, for I still believe that Heaven, however it's designed, will never be overcrowded. Just our universe alone is made up mostly of nothing; plenty of room for countless souls living outside time and space; and there's no reason to believe that God created His kingdom to be any less grand, especially if He created the heavens and the Earth in six days, and still is working on His kingdom. That's got to be one high priced chunk of ecclesiastic real estate, Yahweh-luia. Of course, I've quipped that on the sixth day, God created Man, and on the seventh day, Man created Religion, and God hasn't rested since, but that's another story.

Well, I didn't mean to blither on paper quite so much. It's always amazing to me to find what's on a person's mind when they get started and don't quite know when to shut-up. I meant to just share my account of the Second Coming dream, but apparently had a few more things on my chest that needed confessing and/or professing. Obviously, I cannot really send this to you, but you still seemed like the best person for me to talk to and tell you what's on my mind.

Regarding my First Love, I think I'm making progress. Still searching diligently. Hopefully, you know that. Not just smoke and mirrors flavoring my words. So far, I feel like one of those people who measure their faith like teaspoons of sugar in the bitter brew of life.

Also, maybe you could give me a few insights about Rodger. I try to talk to him, and just get tongue tied before the first sentence stumbles out of my mouth. He intimidates me, but I'm still drawn to spend time with him.

Hopefully will talk to you soon.

In Jesus,

Leonard Lamb

PS   The last time I saw you, I forgot to tell you about a handwritten letter a young man gave to me. It instructed me to not be lukewarm. I hope that I'm getting hotter rather than colder. If you've got a soul thermometer at your disposal, maybe you could take a reading and let me know. Thanks, LL

Chapter Fifteen

Leonard simply did not know where he was going. No matter how far he drove, the terrain seemed to repeat itself. Block after block, it felt like he was trying to read a book, but was too tired, so kept re-reading the same paragraph. At least a dozen times, he'd passed the green house with the two bikes and the golden retriever laying in the yard. And, the two story brick home with red aluminum siding and the big oak tree in the front. And, the Cape Cod style home, slate blue, white pillars, and small front yard with a cute little hedge. It seemed like he'd seen that house before, somewhere. The blue paint was only partially done on the one side, leaving the upper floor the old, dirty white. Every house of this common looking residential city block he'd already passed numerous times.

He hadn't noticed the repetitions for some miles. He'd been daydreaming, idly passing through this neighborhood, taking a shortcut out of town. The straight street seemed to end a mile or so ahead. He could see the yellow and black warning sign ending the thoroughfare and what looked like an open field beyond. But, driving along, it never seemed to get any closer. He again spied the same dog and started to see the pattern.

After some blocks, he checked the street sign at the intersection. Gird Road. It didn't sound familiar. He entered the new block and spotted all the same houses, bikes, trees, and yes, even the dog. Reaching the next intersection, the sign read Gird Road. He stopped and studied it, making sure he'd read it properly. Driving one more block, again passing the familiar sites, he came again to Gird Road, so turned right. He felt amazement as he again drove past the green house with the two bikes and the retriever, the brick house with the aluminum siding and big oak tree and the slate blue Cape Cod. The yellow and black sign and empty field stood way up ahead. He reached the next intersection.

Gird Road. He turned left. The same thing. Gird Road at the next intersection. He made a U-turn and came back to Gird Road. He continued on, but before he got to the next Gird Road, he knew he was still trapped, repeating the same city block over and over. Even after he turned around, the same homes were, amazingly, on the same side of the street as the previous blocks, and he could see the yellow and black sign up ahead.

"What is this?" he snarled, quieting a sense of panic. The sky was overcast and afforded him no sense of direction. He checked his rear view mirror to see the same picture as out his windshield.

He toured a few more blocks, turning at random intersections, but couldn't escape or make discernible progress. For the first time, a car pulled into a driveway up ahead, so he sped up and parked to talk to the driver. Beside his truck, he watched as the driver slowly got out, locked his car and started for the slate blue Cape Cod home. He noticed Leonard and stopped, smiling. Leonard thought that he looked tired, his green pinstripe suit coat slung over his shoulder, his tie and top button loose, like he'd just come home after a hard day at work. He looked at his watch. Not yet noon.

"Um, I need directions," Leonard called from over his truck bed.

"Where to?" The man seemed as though he would stand there all day if necessary to answer Leonard's inquiry.

"Uh," Leonard thought quickly, "downtown."

"Just follow this road," he pointed. "Straight ahead. Turn right at the T. Take you right downtown." He climbed the steps to his porch, unlocked the front door and stepped in. Leonard noticed for the first time the stained glass design on the front door. It resembled a hot air balloon.

Leonard stood, numbly studying the design for some seconds before returning to the cozy security of his truck cab, and wondering if he should not have opened up more. He admittedly did not want to look or sound like a fool, but likewise, he knew if someone came up to him at his home and said, "Hey! I can't escape from your block," Leonard would immediately presume that the dude was stoned.

He headed on, and reached Gird Road, drove on some miles and repeatedly passed Gird Road, turned right, only to reach Gird Road, then turned around and drove some blocks, always passing Gird Road. He stopped again in front of the slate blue house and got out of his pickup. He was wasting a lot of gas for never getting farther than half a block away from any house on the street.

"This is too weird," he said aloud, stating the obvious. He was tempted to go to the door and knock. The man's car was still in this driveway, but instead, he wondered what would happen if he walked to the next few streets. On foot, he came to Gird Road, kept on walking and passed his truck parked in front of the blue house. He got to the next intersection. Same story. He turned left, and came up to his truck parked in front of the blue house. It wasn't exactly like the effect of two mirrors facing each other, creating a repetitive pattern to forever, but had that flavor.

Alone on the sidewalk, he leaned against his pickup and followed the urge to pray. He wasn't as concerned about sounding silly to Jesus, but kept his prayers to an inaudible utterance, lest any of the neighbors hear.

"Jesus, my Lord," he opened, "am I on some psychic Candid Camera? I was just heading out of town, and now I'm caught in this infinite loop, and I definitely don't have a clue how to get out of it. I need you every hour of every day, but feel like I need you more now..."

He felt a heave of relief, and a breeze lilted around him. He realized he had been sweating as the breeze cooled the fluid coating his skin. He walked to the next intersection. No change. Walking back, he jumped onto the hood of his truck, and reclined back against the windshield. He stayed there over half an hour till he heard the sound of music. Acoustic guitar, coming from the slate blue house. For some reason, the music made him less wary to go knock on the door and talk to the man even though he should have been some miles away from where he'd asked directions.

Slowly ascending the stairs to the front porch, he knocked. The music immediately stopped, and a figure appeared through the opaque stained glass.

"Oh, you again?" the man opened the door. He was dressed much more casually, and appeared ready to relax for the afternoon.

"I'm sorry to bother you," Leonard mumbled, "but, (and I know this will sound weird, but) I seem to be having a problem getting out of your neighborhood. Well, getting off your block, for that matter." He stopped to check the man's reaction. He had that same ever-patient gaze he'd had outside earlier. If he was distressed or miffed at having been disturbed, he didn't show it. Leonard continued.

"Uh, I seem to keep driving from block to block, but no matter what direction I drive, I keep on being on the same block. Your block. Each intersection says Gird Road..."

"You're on Gird Road."

"Okay," Leonard didn't argue, "but, whether I go straight or left or right, block after block, I continue to be on this block.

"So, what do you want?"

Leonard thought a moment.

"Uh, can you help me?"

"No," the man answered abruptly, and closed the door. Through the stained glass, Leonard saw him walk away, crossing the room and disappearing from view. His eyes examined the stained glass pattern of the hot air balloon on the door. It seemed vaguely familiar. Leonard wasn't sure where he'd seen it before, but it tickled and poked and taunted and jabbed his brain, over and over and over, barely out of touch with the clear memory. He turned away and looked at the neighborhood. It seemed the same; green house with the bikes and dog; brick home, and others. Everything the same from block to block.

He could hear the guitar music begin again. The sweet sounds of common chords sifted around the tight openings in the glass and wood. Despite his predicament, Leonard felt comfort listening to the fingered arpeggios. He wanted to stay longer, but started to feel conspicuous, hanging out on a stranger's porch. The song ended. Leonard absently waited for the next song to begin. Suddenly, the door opened. Leonard turned, startled.

"You're still here. Good. Please come in." The man stood back from the open door.

Leonard slowly responded, previewing the living room before stepping inside. He thought it an odd place as he crossed the threshold. There wasn't a stick of furniture anywhere. It had deep pile shag carpeting, gold in color. The wallpaper was gold foil with black fuzz patterns up and down. A large, black iron chandelier with a couple dozen amber glass covers hung in the center of the room. The gold carpet and black and gold foil design continued up the stairs.

"M'name's Dreadnought," he introduced, offering his hand.

"Leonard Lamb," they shook hands. Following the man to the next room, he noticed the inside doorway was a sliding glass door like one would have leading to their patio. But, this one was covered with twelve inch mirror tiles peppered with gold colored flakes.

They stepped through the doorway, and the entire decor changed. It was like a medieval motif. A green forest mural poster attached to the sliding door. The cream colored walls had dark stained, flat boards horizontally crossing the middle of the wall, others running vertically in each corner, plus diagonally crossing the wall, center to bottom corners. There were five windows, each with its own stained glass diamond layout in different colors. A big, stone fireplace, fire ablaze, adorned the wall opposite the windows. The old, gray carpet was covered with a full sized oriental rug. The guitar sat perched on the couch, under the five side-by-side windows. A piano keyboard sat on a folding metal stand next to the kitchen doorway. Overall, it was the kind of eclectic décor one might like, but wouldn't want to admit to their friends. Beyond that, Leonard could see the kitchen and dining area, surprisingly common beside the first two rooms.

"Sorry if I was abrupt," offered Dreadnought picking up his guitar and taking a seat. "You're the third one this week." His fingers began their limber dance over the bronze wound steel strings.

"That's a beautiful guitar," applauded Leonard, mesmerized by the beauty of the tone. The instrument also seemed familiar, though he really had no idea where.

"Thanks. Got it as a gift of sorts. Well, more like an exchange. Someone wanted to leave the neighborhood, and I inherited this guitar as payment."

Leonard suddenly looked at his host suspiciously.

"Forgive me," chuckled Dreadnought with that same passive expression. "That must sound so sinister. I gave him directions and he insisted I take it. I even offered to stand on the porch till he was gone. That way, if he didn't get out, he could stop and pick up his guitar."

"So," eased Leonard, "what's the story with this street?"

"Blast if I know," admitted Dreadnought. "The first time I came here, I was like you. Just passing through. If you're like the others, you were just drifting, not really focused on where you were going."

Bulbs went on in both Leonard's eyes. He remembered Henry's words and his flight through the pre-created cosmos. Singularity of purpose. He'd let himself lapse and lull into complacency only to become trapped.

"You're right!" Leonard piped-up. Dreadnought laughed easily.

"Us locals call this place "Borkum's Rift." A private nickname made up by August Albert who lives over in the red brick house with aluminum siding."

"I take it he's a pipe smoker."

"Never out of his mouth." He started another song on his guitar.

"So, how do I get out of the neighborhood?"

Dreadnought continued to play. "Tell you in a minute. You like books?"

"Of course," Leonard answered, still intent on the music, barely hearing the question. Dreadnought stopped playing and set down the instrument.

"Can I show you my library?"

"Uh, sure," answered Leonard, not wanting to be rude, but also wondering if he wasn't imposing.

Dreadnought jumped up. "You've got to see my library. It's by far the most impressive thing in my life. Please." He headed towards the gold front room. Leonard rose and followed. They beelined up the stairs, rising into a spacious room taking up the entire top floor of the dwelling. A skylight above drenched the room with clouded daylight.

Leonard stopped at the top of the stairs. The impression was impressive. He'd never seen such a big, packed private library. Books on every wall, plus rows of bookshelves, each shelf more full than empty. There was a desk, cluttered, with a computer and printer. There were stacks of books along one wall behind the desk.

"Please," Dreadnought raised his hand to invite Leonard to browse. As Leonard started perusing the first shelves, glancing at the titles, Dreadnought sat at the computer to print something out. Rounding the first row, Leonard saw an area encased in glass, so checked the rare exhibits. Continuing his tour, he started to notice that the free standing bookshelves had any variety of books, but the books shelved along the wall all had a similar appearance, like one super-colossal encyclopedia set. He sauntered over to check the titles. All black hard covers, he pulled one down at random. A printed label read, "The Biography of Donald M. Yeates." The name didn't ring a bell, and Leonard replaced the book.

"Do you believe a person's life can be an open book?" asked Dreadnought.

"Sometimes."

"Well, here's a good one."

Leonard saw that the book was much older, but had a hand printed label which read, "The Biography of D. B. Cooper." He opened the pages, and scanned the text. It was extraordinarily complete. He would have to spend at least a year reading this one, there seemed to be so much information, as though Cooper himself had personally written it. It even had dreams he'd slept through. Closing the book, it didn't feel as thick as the pages he'd just fanned. He handed it back to Dreadnought.

"Here's another rare one."

Leonard accepted a copy. The label said, "The Biography of John Dillinger." Leonard perused the text as Dreadnought talked.

"He didn't really get shot, you know. The feds made a mistake, and shot the wrong man. They realized their mistake, but didn't want to look foolish, so let the story ride. Did you know that The Lady In Red, Anna Sage, didn't really wear red that night?"

Leonard looked up from the book questioningly.

Dreadnought chuckled. "She really wore an orange skirt and white blouse the night they shot whom they thought was Dillinger. Dillinger was actually in custody in Indiana. The sheriff arrested him and was waiting for his "mother" to bring proof that he wasn't really Dillinger. When the G-men shot the other man, the deputy let the real John D. go. No longer a fugitive, Dillinger was smart enough to quit, and invested the remainder of his ill gotten earnings."

"So, you're telling me that Dillinger went straight?"

Dreadnought laughed again. "Not in a pig's eye. But, he targeted less public crimes – offenses that would keep him out of the limelight. Bank robberies, murders, (though Dillinger never actually killed anyone,) and shoot-out getaways tended to make newspaper headlines much more than racketeering and extortion. He already knew his way around the mob. He'd already had his face lift and fingerprints burned. He just changed his name and lived a long and comfortable life with his old sweetheart, Polly Hamilton."

Leonard thought at first that it sounded like a conspiracy theory.

"It's all there," Dreadnought pointed, "and I'm assured of its accuracy."

"Wow!" thought Leonard. "You must really like history."

"Love it," glowed Dreadnought, then his voice became as impersonal as a dial tone. "Actually, I used to have lots more books than you see here, but after I read them, if they weren't worth keeping, I burned 'em downstairs in the fireplace."

Leonard picked through a pile. All biographies of people he'd never heard of.

"Why not sell them or give them away rather than burn them?"

"They really aren't worth anything," answered Dreadnought,. "Most of them were just whiny losers or perpetual victims or boring grinds who didn't develop even a hint of imagination for their lives."

"But," he again got excited, "this is the best one of all. I have absolutely no doubt that this one will really grab you."

Leonard accepted the book. On top, the label read, "The Biography of Leonard Lamb." His brow furrowed as he opened the book. At first glance, the pages were all blank when, without warning, he ceased to exist and became physically trapped as the words on the pages, filling the entire book with his young life. Every thought, impression, emotion, feeling, action, fantasy, including his sins and his glories, framed in the mundane and common moments, were virtually encased in the pages of the book.

Dreadnought picked the book up off the floor and started to scan the pages. Leonard's five senses were mostly gone, but he could detect the motion of the pages and the presence of his betraying host. Though helpless, his mind was totally alive and freaking out big time. Plus, he felt totally exposed. Every sin was suddenly there for Dreadnought to pluck. He could tell what the man was reading, and wondered by what kind of demon he'd been caged.

Trying to concentrate past the embarrassment and impressions to naked exposure of his life, he prayed, and could feel the words added to the end of the book. He persevered, knowing nothing better. Demons were fought by God's holy grace, and this was the most direct attack he'd ever encountered.

"Same old, same old Leonard Lamb," uttered Dreadnought, starting to fan the pages. Still holding the book, he picked up the phone.

"Joe? Got another one. Yeah, as soon as possible." He hung up and fanned through more pages over the next hour.

Leonard could not hear him but recognized the waning interest.

"I was hoping for more from you. Really, I was." He continued to fan through, stopping long enough to catch a sentence or two. He slowly stepped down the stairs as he read.

Leonard continued his mouthless prayer vigil. Unexpectedly, a thought occurred to him. He'd been praying for deliverance and rebuking the demon in the name of Jesus. He sought victory. His last chapter became a Psalm King David would have cherished. But, this new revelation? He was to praise Jesus - and thank Him? Leonard just about printed cursing punctuation and special symbols found at the top of the number keys on the keyboard.

No, he corrected himself. The idea sparked a scripture reference, but he wasn't sure where. He thought and thought, but his mind, which still seemed to work fine, refused to answer. Briefly distracted by Dreadnought reading about the time he drove his mom's station wagon into the river then claimed it'd been stolen, he wondered if he could read his other pages. He'd read the entire Bible a few times, plus innumerable readings and studies. It might take some time, but he should be able to access the scripture.

He set to the task, and amazingly found the scanning speed of a new computer. Within moments he found I Thessalonians 5:16. *Rejoice always, pray without ceasing, in everything give thanks; for this is the will of God in Christ Jesus for you.* In everything give thanks. Not *for* everything, but *in* everything. He scrawled, "Thank you Lord Jesus, and praise your holy name. You are the Lord of my life, and I thank you for the life that you've given me..." The prayer continued along the veins of praise and thanksgiving, ever becoming more and more heartfelt. He also wondered what to call it since he now didn't actually have a heart. He detected Dreadnought approaching the last chapters of his life with increasing speed.

Dreadnought rambled downstairs and stood by the fire, about to throw Leonard into the flames and embers. He leaned against the mantle flying through the pages just in case there was even one thing worth reading or keeping. About to throw the book in the fire, he stopped. Leonard knew his book was open as Dreadnought paused to read the pages describing his pilgrimage.

"You've been a busy boy of late." Dreadnought read of the campground fires of the Holy Spirit. He read of his treks up the mountain, and the tours of the cave. But, Leonard felt the pages shudder, open to the account of the Trees of College and Golden Eagle. Moving away from the fire, Dreadnought laid down the manuscript on a table.

Leonard couldn't hear him, but the page was still open to his journey down from the Mountains of Perchance.

Dreadnought paced swiftly around the room. He sat down beside his piano keyboard, then rose and paced some more. He walked back to Leonard, picked up and read the account of the Tree of Golden Eagle, then set the book down again. He cursed to himself, and wondered.

"Leonard, my boy, you have some fruit from the Tree of Golden Eagle. I may have misjudged you." He picked up the book again and started searching for any indication where Leonard may have stored the fruit. Initially, he'd placed it in his pocket, but he likely would have put it someplace else once he got off the mountain. He continued to read ahead, diligently looking for any clue where the fruit might be. It never occur to him to go out to Leonard's truck and see if maybe he'd just stuck in the glove box or under the seat.

Just then, he heard the tow truck.

"No!"

He dropped Leonard on the couch beside the guitar and raced to stop Joe. Dreadnought burst through the front door, just in time to see the pickup truck disappear in tow around the next corner. He ran down the steps yelling and waving. No response.

Cursing again, Dreadnought trudged up the front steps much more heavily than earlier. Leonard had no idea why he'd been abruptly set down, but continued his silent vigil of praise and thanksgiving. He felt Dreadnought return and continue to study his pages, turning back and forth, making sure that he didn't miss anything.

"He must still have it on him," deduced Dreadnought. There's no mention of the fruit anywhere that I can find. He must have changed pants, moved it to other pockets, or tossed it in the fridge at his mom's house. Something! Some clue!"

He set the book down again, and dropped onto his keyboard seat, brooding. He absolutely did not want to do it, but the prize was too great. On the other hand, he'd never done it before. He wasn't even sure that he could do it.

Holding Leonard by the binding, he bounded from room to room, eventually taking a seat at the piano keyboard, still checking Leonard's pages. Leonard felt the conversations being replayed as Dreadnought read. Some were so stupid or inert.

"Happy Birthday To You? You've got to be kidding." Dreadnought scoffed. "That can't be right. Nobody's favorite song is Happy Birthday. He continued to read; a Leonard quote.

"Happy birthday is the happiest song, for someone is celebrating, and that makes it all the more special."

Dreadnought sighed, "Yeah. Yeah." He set Leonard down on the floor beside the keyboard and started playing Happy Birthday To You. Within moments, Leonard arose, his brain a bit scrambled, peering down towards the blank pages of the book at his feet.

Dreadnought started to feel Leonard's pants pockets. Leonard brushed his hand away and tried to speak.

"What are you doing?"

"Give them to me."

"What?"

"The fruit from the Tree of Golden Eagle."

Leonard blinked furiously a moment, recollecting.

"They're in my truck."

"You have more than one?"

"Uh-huh. They're behind the driver's seat in a plastic bag inside a paper bag." He couldn't figure out why he was talking to this man except that he'd just been totally exposed, and may have still been compulsively open. Well, almost.

Dreadnought cursed, (apparently he liked to do that). He studied Leonard a moment who stood dumbly erect. He raced to the phone in the kitchen and called the tow man.

"Joe? Dreadnought. I need something out of that truck you just took. What? No way. You couldn't have crushed it that quickly. You're lying. Just hold it till I get down there." He hung up. Standing alone in the kitchen, he looked to the medieval room.

"Leonard?"

No answer.

"Leonard?" He moved to the doorway and felt the whoosh of air as Leonard closed the front door behind him. Dreadnought flew out of the house and down the porch. He caught sight of Leonard running stiffly up the road and took off after him.

Leonard jogged up the middle of the street. He looked, but saw no one at any house. His limbs started to loosen the more he ran. Glancing back, he saw Dreadnought in pursuit. He turned corner and ran past Dreadnought's slate blue house. He reached the next corner, and ran up the block past Dreadnought's house. In short, he was still in the rift and getting nowhere. He heard Dreadnought's padded steps behind him. The sound stopped, but he didn't immediately notice.

Meanwhile, from Dreadnought's perspective, he ran out the door after Leonard. Running hard, rounding the corner, he noticed a small, yellow fruit in Leonard's hand. He ran all the harder, and was barely a few steps behind as Leonard rounded the next corner, swerving to avoid capture. After a couple blocks, Dreadnought began to lose breath. He stopped and hid behind the oak tree in front of the red brick house. Leonard continued running straight away, getting farther and farther, though for Leonard, he was still trapped in the same block. Dreadnought immediately recognized the oddity of the rift. As long as Dreadnought stood out on the street, Leonard got farther and farther away, even though he passed Dreadnought's home over and over. Leonard looked back, and saw Dreadnought blocks behind him. He slowed.

In turn, Dreadnought ran into his house, waited a moment, then ran out, appearing ahead of Leonard. Surprising him, Dreadnought tackled the young man, both crashing hard on the asphalt pavement.

Scraping to a halt, Leonard clung to the fruit in his hand as Dreadnought tried to rip it away from him. The battle would have lasted longer, but Dreadnought stomped on Leonard's wrist with the heel of his foot, causing the hand to spasm open. The fruit popped out and rolled down to the gutter. Dreadnought leapt away and scooped it up, snickering with villainous glee, which sounded dumb to both men, but didn't change Dreadnought's next move. He gazed victoriously at Leonard, seated on the roadbed, nursing his throbbing wrist.

He wanted to say something obviously stupid like, "It's mine!" or "I have it!" but held his tongue and settled for catching his breath and studying his new treasure. He pressed his fingers against the skin. It opened up easily.

Too easily.

He smelled the open halves, and tasted the pulp. It was nasty. Then, recalling his reading, he saw something missing. The hook shaped nut inside. He quickly looked up towards Leonard who grinned briefly, stuck out his tongue, and dissipated away, rapidly crowding into a digital signal humming through the phone lines overhead. Directed by the ISP, he flowed in and out of system after system until, hitching a ride as an email attachment, he came to rest on the hard tile floor at The Dollar Store amidst the hundred and forty plus factory outlet stores bordering State Highway One in Lewes, Delaware. Taking countless nanoseconds to download, his trip took significantly longer with a DSL modem plugging his megabytes along at a snail's pace 748 kbps.

Chapter Sixteen

Leonard wondered that nobody noticed him there on the floor of the store. Two teens, apparently foreigners judging by their language, shopped for snacks and hair brushes. He sat up, and still nobody seemed to notice him as he listened to the strange language of the two youths. They chattered away rapidly, but he couldn't quite make out the tongue. The intonations of their voices were unnerving.

The piped music also had an unsettling quality. It almost sounded like someone was playing the song backwards.

That's it!

That's it?

Standing, the teens still didn't notice him, but their voices were clearly speaking English backwards, not that he could make out a word that they were saying. Touring the store aisles, he watched in awe as shoppers walked along the corridors - backwards, just as easily and naturally as could be. It appeared that the entire store was moving in reverse. He watched for awhile. There was nothing accelerated about the motions around him; still the same twenty-four hour day, but his personal time line seemed to be moving in reverse to everyone and everything else around him.

"What did you get yourself into?" he asked himself as he took a few minutes to consider his options. His arms were scraped up and dirty, and his clothing unkempt. He tucked in his shirt and ran his fingers through his hair. His right wrist was terribly sore, but he couldn't remember why.

None of the patrons appeared to notice him, so he walked up to one and started talking.

No response.

He walked in back of them, and they immediately stopped or swerved around him. He got louder, yelling, but no response. Then it occurred to him that they may be able to hear him, but their responses would be in their future. For all he knew, he was freaking out the entire store, but they would be responding in the time he'd just passed through. Heading out, he passed the toothpaste. Gleem, his favorite. Nobody sold it anymore. He was tempted to take a tube, but there was no way he could pay for it.

He went out the front door, and wondered what reaction he'd created by mystically opening and closing the door.

He stepped out into the rising sunlight. Not that the sun was rising – the sunlight was rising, and the heat was being lifted from beneath. It was still warm, probably as the photons rose from the ground at the speed of light and rammed into his body, thereby never returning to the sun. In one fashion, as he surveyed the traffic passing along, he felt like he was watching a movie played backwards as everyone and everything moved in reverse at full speed. Watching TV was one thing, but walking onto the street and seeing numerous cars move backwards through the parking lot took some getting used to. For that matter, he wasn't sure that he wanted to. Dozens of cars raced by, backwards of course, along Highway One, (he did not yet know the names of the streets. Nothing was familiar, and he still didn't know what city he was in). He realized that he'd have to be extra careful before stepping out into traffic. The vehicles would be approaching in unusual directions, stranger than an American traveling in England for the first time and trying to get used to driving on the opposite side of the road. Likewise, it occurred to him that, like in the Dollar Store, drivers likewise would not be able to see him.

Stiff and sore from his wounds, he shuffled on down the sidewalk and across the parking lane past the miniature raceway, heading south. Not that he had a plan. He was merely exploring and trying to figure out where he was. He watched with amusement as the small cars raced madly around the track. Most fun was the slick track where the cars would come down the straightway, slow down, go into a whipped-up spin, accelerating, then take off rounding the turn on the slick section of the track full throttle, and fly up the other straightway.

He headed down to the sidewalk by the highway, continuing south. A green sign up ahead read Rehoboth Beach.

"Delaware?" He stopped to take it in.

Walking across a driveway, he had to leap out of the way as a car turned in from the opposite lane of the highway, then stopped on the edge of the driveway just past the sidewalk. The driver waited some moments, looking back and forth, then backed-up into the parking lot. Apparently, he'd made a left hand turn, punching it to merge, lurching into traffic.

"Of course, I might be ethereal, like a ghost, so nothing physical can hurt me."

He toyed with the concept, but was unwilling to test the idea on anything big like a car running over him. It occurred to him that if he didn't die, he could be badly injured and lay there on the sidewalk for days or even weeks or months if he didn't die from exposure and lack of water. The rules had changed, and nobody could help him even if they could see him.

A couple with a baby in a stroller approached, talking and cooing to their infant. Even backwards, baby talk didn't sound all that different. Leonard stood in their way. They backed straight towards him till they came within feet, then without looking, swerved and pressed on around him. They continued to chat as though their trip had not been disrupted. He followed them till they turned in to the Wilmington Bank. Watching them go in, he took a seat on the grass.

It occurred to him that as a pedestrian, he would travel more safely if he stayed close to others. The revelation expanded exponentially in his mind. If he got into a vehicle, say a car or a truck, he knew it would arrive safely, wherever it was going. It'd already left its point of origin and made it this far. The same for any train, plane or ship. The idea of a plane flying backwards was still totally disturbing, but he had to remind himself that it had already made the flight, and would get him wherever he needed to go safely.

But, where to go? There weren't a lot of airports on the Delaware coast, at least none heading cross country that he could stowaway on. On the other hand, detection didn't seem to be a problem. Unless led elsewhere by the Holiest Spirit, he would try to get back home to Washington state and Whatcome County. He noticed a shuttle stop down a ways, across the street. Double and triple checking the traffic, he ran across and waited at the stop. A small sign said Lewes-Rehoboth Beach Shuttle. He wondered if Lewes was pronounced "Lews" or "Lewis", (or something else completely different. In Hawaii it might be pronounced "Leave Us".)

Some minutes later, the shuttle arrived; a large van not quite a bus. Fortunately there was lots of room, so Leonard took a seat. Relaxing, he realized he'd been fooled. He wanted to head south to Rehoboth Beach, so followed the signs, but everything was regressive.

Duh!

The shuttle passed a few stores, then headed off the highway to the Lewes Ferry. They passed the sign entering Lewes, The First City In The First State. Leonard got off at the ferry terminal, wondering if that would take him any closer to an international airport. It crossed the Delaware Bay to Cape May, New Jersey which advertised tons of Victorian style bed 'n breakfasts, but no airports. The closest, sizable airports would likely be Philly, or maybe Atlantic City. He opted to stay on this side of the bay and would wait for the next shuttle.

He realized that he was thirsty, so headed to the terminal. He almost crashed into the automatic doors that didn't open for him. He waved his hand in front of the sensor. No response. Taking a moment's consideration, he knew the answer was the same. The doors may have been opening in his past. He waited till the next person came through and went into the terminal. Finding the water fountain, he couldn't turn it on. Same reason. This was getting obnoxious.

A man came by and turned on the water. Leonard saw a chance to grab a quick sip. He leaned down quickly, but stopped short of the water. It was coming up out of the drain and arcing into the fountain spout. The man leaned down as the water came both from the drain and out of his mouth, also heading into the spout as he slurped paradoxically. Leonard felt like he was being silly, but he sharply had to turn away before he lost his lunch. Somehow, he wasn't as thirsty as he had been.

Heading out of the terminal, he waited for the next shuttle. Few people entered the depot. All seemed to avoid him. That perplexed him. He had virtually no evidence, but still doubted that anyone could actually see him with their eyes. Still, they seemed to detect his presence, even if not consciously.

"I wonder if this is some sort of divine spacing," he said aloud, wondering what he might've meant by 'divine spacing.' He hadn't figured out the Lord's purpose for bringing him here, disjointed out of the time continuum. Not knowing God's purposes certainly didn't bother him. He typically didn't know God's leading or direction for the day, and sometimes God assigns believers to a task without ever telling them the reason. Still, these were certainly exceptional circumstances, and he kept his mind and spirit open, ever praying till the leading of the Holiest Spirit should help him make more sense out of all this.

Recalling the last time he'd globe-trotted after eating the fruit, he'd awoken totally disoriented and unsure where he'd been. He expected that this time the memory also would eventually catch up. Of course, he wondered when. Tattered and dirty, one chunk of his mind had been anxiously awaiting the moment of remembrance. His brain picked this moment, waiting in the shuttle stop. The recollection slammed him like a ton of falling ping pong balls, the memories bouncing all around him, then rolling off the sidewalk, came to rest in the gutter. He felt paralyzed. He also felt more sympathy for Captain Kangaroo.

Dreadnought! The memory of being trapped in the infinite loop on Gird Road. The diverting chase on foot. Being captured by the book and the helpless, laid bare feeling of Dreadnought reading his life. He shuddered with anguish.

He also wondered about the other biographies. There must have been thousands of lives imprisoned there, helpless and collecting dust. He wondered how many had been chucked carelessly into the fire where the flames danced and leapt with delight as they gobbled up page after page. The thought chomped into his psyche, painfully tearing away chunk after chunk. He was still brooding when the shuttle arrived.

The ride to Rehoboth Beach was uneventful, save that he got to see a rider make a mess on the floor with napkins shortly before her spilled soft drink and ice flew back into the disposable cup. The plastic lid and straw dutifully returned to the top just before the cup leapt into the rider's hand. He also watched the shuttle cross through the green lighted intersection, then stop in the lane on the opposite side and wait for the light to turn red while the diesel exhaust got sucked into the tail pipe.

Reaching the Rehoboth Beach boardwalk, the shuttle began its U-turn before stopping. Leonard exited behind the rest of the riders, facing him as they stepped down. The smells and sights grabbed him. He was still thirsty, plus getting hungry, enhanced by the boardwalk's numerous eateries. One café sold nothing but buckets of french fries. He again resisted the temptation to grab a small bucket, (about the size of a large soft drink.) Somehow riding a shuttle without paying did not evoke the same feelings of stealing as grabbing someone's order of fries.

An idea seized him. He walked into the next store, snagged a bottle of water, and left a buck on the counter before the checker. To his amazement, the dollar bill disappeared as soon as it left his hand. There was no way that the checker would've grabbed it that fast. The question challenged him. He stepped over and picked up a figurine of a lighthouse off the shelf. It was hard and real in his hand. He set it back on the shelf.

Nothing. No change. Maybe?

He picked it up again and set it down. No change.

No!

Wait!

Did it move just a hair? He picked it up again and set it on a different shelf. It immediately disappeared as soon as he pulled away his hand. Looking back to its original berth, there it was as though he hadn't touched it at all. It disappeared because it wasn't in that point of time, but if he suddenly started to move forward again, he would likely see it appear on the new shelf, disappear, then promptly reappear on its original shelf.

He laughed, unable to contain his astonishment. He walked out, strolling along the boardwalk and sipping his water. A thought occurred to him. He tipped the bottle and poured out some water. It disappeared almost as soon as it left the bottle, recollected in the alternate timeline. He tried it again a few times, laughing at the effect.

Moseying over to the rail, he watched the ocean waves flow down the sand, become breakers then swells. The sound of the surf also did not sound that odd played backwards. He could see New Jersey across the water. The sun was part way down in the eastern sky.

Morning! It was actually late morning. Either that, or the earth got turned over or started turning backwards, or..., but No! He wasn't going to start that train of thought running again. He already knew that the earth was revolving the opposite direction that he was accustomed. He also wondered who would eat a bucket of french fries for breakfast.

Emptying his water bottle, he carelessly tossed it in the air. It disappeared as soon as it left his hands. He felt regret for being so careless just as quickly as it took the bottle to disappear. What if he hit someone? It was still littering, even if he couldn't see it land.

He walked past Grotto Pizza. The smells invited him in. He saw groups of people come sit at a table and regurgitate pizza. Each slice became more and more whole as it came away from their mouths. He noticed a couple of slices on the pan at an unoccupied table. He went over just as the diners came in the door, clearly moving towards that table. Leonard scooped up the two combo slices shortly before the diners sat down and started chatting.

The pizza wasn't very warm, but tasted extremely good. He could tell it was a top-notch product. He'd have to try it again sometime when it was fresh and hot. For now, this was enough, and he feasted majestically, thanking his Lord for the best blessing of the morning. Being a man of faith, he expected that the Lord could understand his prayers whatever direction he was praying them. He also thanked his benefactors as they unpaid their check, and briefly wondered if the two pieces of pizza he'd taken would be missing when the pie was served. He decided not, since he'd seized the slices after they'd eaten.

Finishing his repast, he headed outside and settled onto a bench to watch the rest of the day begin. The sun set in the eastern horizon. It quickly became cooler, though not uncomfortable. Hours passed. Few walked the boardwalk during the early morning, mostly exercisers, and the rhythm of the waves lulled him to sleep. Just before he nodded off, he wondered if he'd awaken back in the forward timeline. If so, then he could enjoy the day he'd just finished.

Around two a.m., he was awakened by more activity than he'd left. The nighttime boardwalk was alive with players. The waves continued their endless beat. The lights lit up the beach as well as the walkway. He was stiff from his nap on the bench, but he walked along, stretching and again feeling hungry. Some volleyball players competed down below on the sand. He stopped to watch the pairs compete. Occasionally, one would lay down on the sand, then fly up horizontally, popping the ball up with his hands, arms fully extended, then land upright on his feet. Spikes flew back up diagonally to the top of the net, catching the heel of the spiker's hand before lobbing high up in the air.

He headed on and passed a video arcade. Two youths sparred each other with a karate game. Neither the inverse movements nor the yells on the screen looked or sounded that different. He continued on for some hours, just taking in the night sights.

His attention was diverted by the wails of a woman. He turned to see a beautiful, skinny nonna in her mid-fifties with platinum blond hair named Bonnie screaming. Her husband, a go-get-'em boater named Dave, with goatee and glasses, came walking rapidly past Leonard to join his wife. Even backwards, Leonard could tell his words were caustic. They were looking his way, and he wondered if they were looking at him. No. Turning around, he saw a man, running very fast towards him, a purse under his arm. The picture came to life in his mind. Purse snatcher. It took only a moment, but just as he arrived, Leonard purposely dropped down in back of the thief running full throttle. There was no avoiding Leonard this time. The thief flipped over Leonard and disappeared from his view, then reappeared beside Dave who had flopped on top of him for a moment then let go, and reeled back beside Bonnie. The purse snatcher also rose quickly, resumed his run, returning Bonnie's purse, then ran to the side of the boardwalk where he waited for them to pass.

Leonard hoped against hope that he'd altered the outcome of the larceny. His own, private Quantum Leap episode. Talk about re-runs! Only this time, he didn't leap into the next week's program, nor did his direction of time travel change.

Sometime later, he found the restrooms. Entering, he was pleased to see that it had showers. He was sooooo dirty, and his clothing tattered. Typical of beach showers, the water was left on. It'd certainly be cold. It would come up out of the drain. He didn't care. He pulled off his shoes and socks and tossed them on the bench.

Whoa!

They were gone!

Rolling his eyes, and chiding himself, he carefully removed his pants and shirt. Ripped or not, there was no way he'd let either go. He danced to the tune of the chilly water till his senses adjusted to the temperature. It flowed up from the gritty, sand covered tile floor, rolled around his body till it was sucked up into the spout. Despite his best efforts, his clothing got splashed till it was soaked.

A man, dressed in swim trunks, came from behind to use the shower; or more specifically, to put the sand back on his body. He characteristically stopped, his back towards Leonard and the showers. Leonard turned away, hastening to finish, and stuck his head on top of the water one more time. Turning, his limp garments snagged on the handle. Pain flashed through his sore right wrist, and in the twinkling of an eye, they were gone; wallet, keys, all. Moving away, he stood there in the buff, dripping wet, with nothing but a feeling of absolute loss.

He looked around the room for anything – anything that he could use to cover up. If someone laid down a towel, they *were* going to lose it. Even if nobody could see him, he felt little comfort. He'd essentially crossed the threshold of his puritanical mores, and wasn't anxious to streak along the boardwalk till he found some clothing.

The panicking thought occurred to him that he could suddenly change directions in time without notice. He could just return to present time without warning, appearing out of nowhere. There was no reason to believe that it would happen any time soon, but also there was no reason to believe that it wouldn't. He definitely didn't want it to happen wearing his birthday suit.

A man draped his big beach towel. Leonard waited till he stuck his head under the water and quickly made it part of the man's past. First he dried himself off, then felt more conventional confidence as he wrapped the fig leaf around his loins. Stepping out onto the boardwalk, he felt conspicuous as he searched for a clothing store. Even a pair of secondhand swim trunks would be better than a towel. As expected, nobody seemed to notice him. He passed Dolle's, a candy store that served as the figurehead for Rehoboth Beach. Various clothing stores had recently unclosed-up for the night. He slipped through one and grabbed a pair of shorts, a T-shirt and some sandals. Donning his newly acquired clothing, he strolled along and happenchance, passed the man who'd incidentally supplied the towel in the restroom. It was damp, but Leonard left it on the man's bag next to another towel exactly the same. It disappeared as soon as he let go, but he knew it was still there.

The shower revived him in another way. His brain was tiring of trying to make sense of all the alien impressions. It resembled the fatigue felt visiting a foreign country, surrounded by people who didn't speak an understandable language. A person's brain continually tries to make sense of their surroundings. For Leonard, it was a lost cause, and his sense of growing weary was offset by the stinging cool of the water. He was pleased at the revival and took advantage of the moments to set a plan in action.

First he made a mental note of the time and date. Approaching ten thirty on the twelfth of August. He would need that reference later. The twilight was already filling the western sky behind the boardwalk.

Next, he had to get back home. That meant crossing the country. He formulated a theory how he might return to the regular timeline. Lastly, if it worked, he figured out how he might take care of some unfinished business. He realized that he was thinking in vague terms, but didn't want to give away too much of the story at this time.

He checked a map. There were lots of international airports to choose from. Wilmington was probably the closest, but Baltimore/DC was lots bigger. He passed the french fries shop. The cook was about to toss the bucketfuls of steamy, cooked fries in the stainless steel pan where they would be unsalted, then leap up into the upside-down fryer basket, turned over, and dropped down into the fryer to un-cook them. Leonard reached in and grabbed a bucket. Tasting a hot fry, they were wonderful. They'd have to be super to be the only food item they sold. He liberally poured malt vinegar and salt over them, and strolled up the road munching grease and thick cuts of potato, (or potatoe if you were born before 1965. Just ask Dan Quayle, (Quayl ??!!) For the record, like Dan Quayle, Leonard also first learned to spell 'potato' with an 'e' on the end).

Finding the Greyhound terminal, he checked out the Arrivals and Departures section. Again, he was fooled momentarily, first checking the Departures. He would need a bus that was arriving. It would be some hours before the bus came, and he spent most of the time dozing after the short, strange night. He was sure he was going to sleep through the bus leaving. There should still be an announcement, even if he couldn't understand it.

Meanwhile, he checked his watch which was completely out of sync with the real world, and pondered whether the days relived would change his actual birthday. It was far too early to tell if he was getting younger, or older, or his aging suspended as long as he was on this timeline. If getting younger, his birthday would still be regular. If older, then each day had to be doubled. For example, if he remained in the present timeline for four days, on his next birthday he would actually be eight days older than 33. If he neither aged nor became younger, then he would add the number of days spent in the timeline. For example, if he remained in the present timeline for five days, on his next birthday he would actually be five days older than 33. Despite his musings, the bottom line was that he probably was never going to be able to tell whether he'd been aging, becoming younger, or what. He'd have to spend a few years traveling backwards through time till it became obvious whether he was aging or not, and the very idea of traveling backwards for so long caused him to cringe recklessly.

The candy machine across the room had been beckoning him for some time. After a spell, he answered. Crossing the room, he remembered that he had no money, but also realized that it didn't matter. Any money he might deposit would sit in the future waiting for someone to make their selection. But, what if he held onto the machine while he was adding the money? Would it become part of his timeline, like the water bottle and clothing? He decided, probably not, unless he actually picked it up – an impossible task. Similarly, the shuttle bus didn't changed time continuums when he boarded.

It seemed like there should be some way to get candy out of this machine. He wasn't so interested in the product as the challenge. Could he lift it if he had a hand truck? Maybe, but then he couldn't maneuver and make the purchase. He eventually settled for snagging the product just before it jumped up into the machine after another person, in this case a child, finished un-eating the Kit Kat and placed it back in the catch tray.

Leonard opened the package and broke off a section. Taking a bite, he munched greedily when the reality played through his mind, and the sweet chocolate turned bitter. In the regular timeline, that child was going to try to buy this candy bar and it wasn't going to be there. He considered placing the open package in the candy tray so the child could have the rest without paying for it, but someone else would be ripped-off when they tried to buy one, and really, nobody would be foolish enough to eat anything already opened in this day and age. Leonard tossed the rest of the Kit Kat in the trash. It was just a candy bar, but he felt like an absolute heel.

He saw his bus arrive, and a bunch of people back on up. It suddenly occurred to him that there would be no final boarding announcement. That was for buses departing, not arriving. He hopped on and grabbed a seat.

He would have kept on brooding about the candy, but heading out on a bus rolling backwards demands attention. Still, Leonard was amazed at the adaptability of humans. Already, this make-belief world was becoming common and was feeling less and less strange. He was starting to pick out a few words, though knew it would still be some time before he could follow an entire conversation. Some things he didn't tire of as easily. For example, he still loved watching people write. The ink lifted off the page leaving absolutely no impression. Likewise, they could erase the image back into place, then remove it with their pencil, leaving not a trace or impression. He wasn't certain why that always made him chuckle.

He also wasn't quite used to watching people un-eat, and he knew precisely why *that* made him burp squeamishly. Either way, he felt the same attraction as to the best stage magicians. Movies and TV could not create the same effect as seeing it in person, even if he knew how the 'trick' was happening. It was ever impressive. Other activities, such as watching someone unread a book, or un-type on a laptop weren't nearly as engaging.

The one thing that he could not get used to was the isolation. All these people around him, and not one to talk to nor interact with. No one to share with. He couldn't even play a good practical joke, not that practical jokes were that high on his priorities. It was a strange prison, bereft of responsibilities and expenses. He could go anywhere he wanted, have all his needs provided for, (as a perpetual freeloader,) without few if any one noticing the loss. He didn't even have to pay taxes. America boasted such a land of abundance.

Trapped in life's vagabondage, he prayed, and the prayers offered some encouragement. His spiritual commitments and morals swayed him from serious villainy, though he would be traveling awfully close to D.C. The Hope Diamond was at the Smithsonian. He un-seriously toyed with the idea, and decided it was a lost cause. Even if he could shatter the security glass, it would just become intact again the next moment before he could grab the gem, the glass unbroken in his future and everybody else's past. He also refused to be tempted to grab some racing forms, or take a side trip to Vegas and jot down a few key sports wagers. Lotto numbers? He could retire a wealthy man if ever he got moving forward again.

He scratched his cheek and rested his fingers against his chin musing over the possibilities. A new thought diverted him.

He wasn't aging at all!

He had wondered if he would be getting younger or older, and at first thought that it might take years before he could discernably evaluate his age. Then, scratching his chin, he realized that he didn't need a shave. He felt his bare cheek. Nothing. He should've had substantial stubble. He glanced at his hands. His fingernails also were the same length. They were a little harder to measure, but as far as he could tell, his years weren't advancing during the previous two to three days of roving.

"This is so weird," he again said to himself. It was the first time he'd spoken aloud since the ferry terminal and the sounds of his words surprised his ears. They were also the first understandable phrase he'd heard since then.

He'd been fretting about how to get to the airport from the bus terminal. He considered riding in a taxi cab all day until he happened to go to the airport. He considered watching for a business person with bags packed and tailing them. They would most likely be heading to the airport. He didn't want to try to have to wrestle with city bus schedules, but it was an option. Passing the slums of Baltimore, he hoped that the terminal was nowhere close. Moving towards downtown Baltimore, he rested easier as he saw his answer. The variety of high rise buildings included some posh hotels. They passed the lofty

Wyndham Baltimore Inner Harbor shortly before entering the terminal. Leonard hopped out of the bus and skipped for a little over a block to the hotel.

Airporter Shuttles galore.

Well, at least one, and it wasn't long before it was wheeling him to Baltimore/DC International Airport while a business man unclipped his fingernails. Un-finishing the job, he un-dug his clippers from the pocket of his grey trousers, then looking up, seemed to look directly at Leonard. Leonard had not had eye-to-eye contact with anyone this entire episode, and the effect momentarily snagged his breath. Worse, the man's greenish eyes resembled spinning roulette wheels. He seemed somewhat advanced in years, but still had an easy, youthful flow to his movements. Leonard never considered himself good at guessing ages, but this man's features totally baffled any guess of age. Both men stared at each other attentively for some time. Leonard nodded. The stranger didn't seem to acknowledge, but still seemed to be looking directly at him, so Leonard turned and watched idly as the reversible world flooded by. Factories slurped smoke. Cops un-clocked speeders. Passing a park, kids glided up the slides. A dog wearing a red bandana ran backwards with a Frisbee in his mouth. He leapt into the air tail first, letting go of the Frisbee as it took off spinning towards its owner. Leonard heard a crack. A baseball flew in from the outfield, returning to the backwards swinging bat, then to the pitcher as the batter positioned to swing.

Looking back, the man with the greenish eyes was still peering at him.

"Hello," offered Leonard, smiling.

He still didn't acknowledge, so Leonard got up and moved to the next seat. The man's eyes waited till he was settled, then repositioned on him. This was becoming both exciting and unnerving. The drive to BWI (the airport,) became very long as Leonard tried to make sense of the old man's apparent recognition. Pulling up to the curb, Leonard anxiously waited to exit the shuttle. The man seemed to ignore him as they clambered down the steps, one forward and one backwards, and together entered the terminal. There they separated as Leonard started looking for the next flight out to SeaTac.

This time he remembered to check the Arrivals screens all along the ticketing counters. After a fashion, he found a nonstop flight to Seattle on Delta that arrived in the next hour. Hurrying down the terminal, he first felt inclined to go through the security checks, then realized that he could stroll in through the open exit. He resisted the temptation to go over to the metal detectors and wave a chunk of metal through as some passenger, late and frantic to make his flight, tried to get through the security checks. He could wave metal around the wand in all kinds of inconsistent and unlikely places. Maybe if he'd had his keys...

He found the plane and waited in the Jetway till all the passengers had boarded on the all night flight. Hopefully, there would be an open seat or two where he could rest. People shared hugs hello just before the flyers backed away towards the walkway to the airplane. When it became obvious that the doors would soon be closed, Leonard entered the craft. He felt some apprehension as the door closed, locking him in. The flight was little more than half full, and he had lots of seats to settle in. The plane taxied backwards towards the runway. One last turn, then straight along for a couple blocks on the runway and without warning he felt the rush of turbines pushing the other riders forward with inertia, then the turbines stopped and restarted in the opposite direction. It gained speed along the runway, tires skidded a bit, then up the Boeing 737-800 lifted, nose raised, but tail end first. Leonard watched out the window as the fantastically impossible became permanently engraved in his memory. He'd never liked flying all that much before, and every safety measure inside his subliminal self screamed worse than a flock of smoke alarms.

"Fear is a lie," he spoke aloud, again reminding himself that this flight had already successfully completed its journey, and to settle back in his seat to try to enjoy the flight. It also occurred to him that his presence, though small, would require more fuel for the plane to make its journey. He believed it wouldn't *really* matter, but still bugged him.

Over the next couple of hours or so, he snatched a couple of fruit juices from the drinks' cart and waited, watching the clouds below as the morning sun set. Most of the riders were snuggled down and napping. One poor mom was trapped dealing with her cranky baby. Leonard rose to find the restroom and another seat farther away.

Walking towards the back of the plane, he was surprised to see the old businessman from the shuttle ride. Leonard considered the odds of just being on the same plane. Divine coincidence? He reminded himself that Divine Coincidence is NEVER a coincidence.

On the return trip from the restroom, still wondering if the toilet had flushed after he depressed the handle, he saw the old man, so stopped, facing him from the aisle. In short order, the man looked up at him, again directly meeting his eyes. Soon, the man turned away to retrieve his travel bag from under the seat in front of him. He opened it and pulled out a hand held cassette recorder. He shut off his overhead light. A small, red light came on as the man started to speak slowly into the machine. Stopping the recording, he pushed "Play", then "Rewind", causing the tape to play backwards rapidly.

The chipmunky voice said, "Hi Backwards Traveler. My name is John. Please have a seat. Take the recorder, push "Record," and say something, then shut it off and hand it back to me." He stopped the machine as soon as it was done and held out his hand.

Leonard was flabbergasted. He stared at the small cassette recorder for a moment, then gingerly took it from the man's hand. The man kept his hand out flat as Leonard slowly tried to think of something to say.

Introductions? He pushed Record.

"You're right. I am Leonard. Leonard Lamb."

He stopped the machine and handed it back to the man, then sat down next to him.

The man closed his hand around the machine as though it'd just materialized as he glanced towards the seat next to him. He played the message rewinded to understand Leonard's recording. To Leonard, he heard his squealing, backwards garbled voice. Next time he'd have to remember to speak more slowly and make sure that he enunciated his words. The message seemed longer than the brief introduction he'd just made. John spoke into the recorder again, this time much longer, and handed it to Leonard.

Leonard took it. The message said, "I know that this is odd, but bear with me. Remember, I'm traveling backwards by your timeline, so I don't hear what you just told me. The only reason I know that you're here is because you took the cassette from my hand, and by my timeline, I will listen to our entire conversation after I get off this flight in Baltimore, but at this point in time, I have no idea what you said. So, our conversations will be somewhat one sided, but I'll ask some questions, and you can answer however you please.

"Here's my full name, address, phone number and email address in case you want to contact me when you get back to regular time..."

Leonard replayed the recording as he took down the man's personal information, jotting it down on the side of his arm.

Author's Note: They didn't have a regular conversation, because of the time continuum differences, but could kind of go backwards then forwards, mixing questions and answers; similar to a two steps forward, one step back standard. Appendix A (at the end of this book) transcribes an actual excerpt of the tape John made. Appendix B offers that same bit of conversation in more understandable form. For this chapter, here's a bit of what Leonard learned:

Leonard asked, "How do you know about me? Can you see me? Nobody else seems to be able to see me."

John responded, "Keep in mind that I've been talking to you for some hours, now. I catch glimpses of something, but when I look, it's not there. Call it a revelation, if you'd like.

"I detected that you were there because the same thing happened to me, many years ago when I was a young man. I wandered throughout this world for over fourteen years before awakening one morning back in real time. That would have been hard to explain. I was near Leningrad in the old Soviet Union without passport or ID or any feasible explanation as to how I'd arrived. That was during the cold war. Fortunately, my wife Silke was there to meet me. She had the documents I needed to legally get me out of the Soviet Union without spending a few closing years in some Siberian salt mines.

"I've always wondered about those years, traveling backwards, then forwards, but have never come up with a plausible explanation."

Leonard asked, "How did you start to go backwards through time?"

"Don't know," John recorded. "I was on a spiritual retreat at a Catholic monastery. They rang the bells at three in the morning, so I arose and came to listen to the chants and pray. I was alone in the sanctuary praying and watching the bats fly about, and the next thing I knew, the bats started flying backwards. It still took some time before I realized that I'd become dissected from the familiar fetters of time and space. How about you?"

Leonard summarily explained his story, and also gave John his name and address, then asked, "How'd you get out of the backwards motion?"

John's answer was disjointed, but ultimately seemed to say that he didn't know. He'd been moving through time backwards, then without fanfare or detectable reason, awoke one morning back in regular time. It had been odd, aging once again, and re-experiencing those fourteen years, day by day, headline by headline, returning to the technology he'd previously seen for the future.

A small idea nagged him each year, whether he would get turned around again when he reached the day he'd started backwards, but the day came and went without exception. He'd avoided returning to the monastery that morning, just to see if he'd had to be in the right place at the right time.

The two chatted, though oftentimes it took John a long time to respond, and Leonard realized that he was traveling into John's past, so always had to re-inform him that they were carrying on a conversation.

Wait! That can't be right. Maybe John's been talking to him since John left Seattle, and for both, they've been trading places on their memory of what was said to one another. Leonard had not yet lived through what was for him the upcoming part of this flight, but John had, so for John, first contact would be closer to Seattle. Talk about dysfunctional communication! Likely, John would play the entire tape after he arrived in Baltimore.

They conversed till the tape ran out, then John abruptly nodded off to sleep, the cassette recorder resting in his lap. No, that wasn't right, either. The tape didn't run out. They talked till they got to the front of the tape.

Tired himself, Leonard moved till he found another group of seats, and settled in for a couple hours of shut-eye. Just before he nodded off, he wondered, "Fourteen years? Maybe longer?" The prospect depressed him, and more than ever, he hoped that his plan worked. He also feared that John had already tried it without success.

Finally, just before he nodded off, the last thought to flow through his mind was that John had not retrieved the cassette recorder out of his bag when Leonard discovered him. For John, he had put it away after Leonard stood up.

Chapter Seventeen

Leonard hoped against all hope that his plan would work. He'd been fasting and praying fervently all week, not just for himself, mostly because it would've been too easy to focus on his own strange predicament. Every activity led him towards this window of opportunity. Not that there wouldn't be other windows. As long as he traveled backwards through time, there should be plenty of opportunities to meet up with himself.

Incidentally, the week actually had been fun. He tried cooking, but the stove wouldn't turn on. When he found a stove that was already on, he tried cooking and found that it sucked in the heat. In frustration, he let go of the pot, and it disappeared into the future. He hoped that it didn't start a fire, but there was no way that he could follow it. He thought of leaving a note for the owner before he started cooking, but they wouldn't be home to leave for work for some hours.

Another idea arose. He jotted the note in big letters, ran over to the neighbor's, slid the note into the doorway, (which disappeared as soon as he let go,) and rang the doorbell, (which he couldn't hear). He couldn't tell if they answered or not, but he knew that they were home, so would get the note and hopefully act on it. If they'd been by the door when he rang the doorbell, they might have seen the note appear in the door frame. What a weird chat they'd have with the neighbor later when she showed him the unrecognizable, handwritten note.

Now, Leonard stood by the shore of the Potholes Reservoir. The water lapped away from the bank. The moonlight reflected from his retina to the water to the moon to the sun. When thought of in those terms, Leonard wondered that he could see anything at all. He should be lost in perpetual darkness. How was any light getting to his eyes?

No, that didn't make sense, either. There'd been a vaguely sharp change to what he saw, like someone turned up the Contrast on the TV. As he thought about the light, bouncing around the cosmos, it occurred to him how much light was reflected and refracted and redirected. Since light is always bouncing around off of everything except black holes and large egos, there would be lots of light to illuminate the things around him.

An intriguing thought occurred to him. Well, two intriguing thoughts. The first was that some of the light that came to the Earth from the sun, was being redirected back to the sun, 93 billion miles away. The second was that at least a tiny amount of the light that came into our eyes bounced off our retina and came back out our eyes. How many times had he seen cat eyes light up at night? He didn't know, not that mattered, but it mildly bugged him the idea of light reflected out of our eyes had never occurred to him before now.

Sound had been the same way. Sounds still seemed to come from their source, though the sound waves should have been traveling from the opposite direction, returning to the source of the sound.

The sand, obscured by the twilight, seemed so smooth. He'd arrived yesterday, so hung out, anxiously waiting. The wait was almost over - if he remembered his dates correctly. Either his plan would work, or it wouldn't. Only one way to find out.

He waited by his pickup truck till the sounds of footsteps registered. Waiting to meet up with himself, he watched as Leonard approached, walking backwards, sea shells leaping up to his hand. He placed the plastic bread bag of seashells in the bed of his truck, then swiftly trotted backwards down towards the water. Moments later, he strolled back to his truck and opened the driver's door with a wave of his hand.

Backwards traveling Leonard hopped into the driver's seat as his counterpart moved to get into their truck. Sitting on top of himself, the two amalgamated into one, fusing like beaded bits of mercury blended with the ticklish feelings of passing through industrial sausage grinders. It was fun for neither, but the backwards traveling Leonard just about jumped out of his skin with delight as the sounds around him became hospitably familiar. The water immediately lapped instead of 'deppal.' He reached down and started the truck. It roared to life in his present and stayed running in his future. He honked the horn. Same cause and effect. Ecstatic elation! He wanted to dance. He couldn't believe how giddy it felt to be back in his regular world. He exited the vehicle and started running down the beach. Forget the seashells!

"Pastor Pete! Pastor Pete!" He ran until he found the man, again in pieces on the ground.

"Quick! Pull yourself together."

"Leonard?"

Leonard yanked the big man to his feet - a momentous occasion in Pastor Pete's life.

"Sorry to bug you, but you ain't gonna believe what's happened to me," he yelled.

"How'd you find me?"

"That's what you ain't gonna believe." He was heaving heavily, but went on to explain the activities of the last week. Pastor Pete grinned and laughed throughout the entire explanation, barely able to keep up with the events.

"That's it?" asked the pastor as Leonard brought the story back to where they were standing.

Leonard nodded gleefully, feeling the liberation of the moment.

"Wow!" the big man answered. "All this time I was waiting for the punch line." He looked down, pitcously shaking his head. Playing the long suffering victim, he had to laugh to himself.

"I'm not making this up," Leonard defended, starting to deflate. He wasn't a beachball.

"I know. It's absolutely amazing," answered the pastor with that sincerely-concerned-I'll-be-praying-for-you-look on his face.

Leonard recognized the hopelessness of his plea, even if this was the man that led his congregation cast in the burning tower of light from the Holiest Spirit. He felt anger, but he couldn't be too mad. There was no way he would've believed anyone, either. He gave the pastor a big hug, realized he was blessed that he could give anyone a hug, and changed the subject, counting the splashing waves as they strolled back to the parking lot.

Bidding farewells, Leonard started up the engine, mostly out of old habit, and sat blankly as Pastor Pete's headlights flashed across his face.

A new, scary idea suddenly popped like kernels of corn under the microwaves of his mind.

When he tried merging with himself, what if they'd both started going backwards through time? He shuddered long and hard at the idea and wondered if John Debzee didn't try a few things to stop going backwards. Snapping out of his funk, he shifted gears and raced out of the parking lot.

He also held his tongue as he replayed the visit with his grandpa for his birthday, and acted surprised when Timothy Grier entered the sanctuary. He left the Crusade early, and walked the streets of Bellingham, feeling the clogged ears of frustration. What a testimony! What a gift! What good was it if he couldn't tell anybody? Even John, back in Baltimore. They wouldn't fly together for a couple more days. Seated at the computer in his mom's house, he could write to him, then. In the meantime, he got an idea and printed off some stuff, then he checked the county maps in the phone book.

Saying his good-byes, he left town early. He had a dangerous appointment with a dangerous man and an untested plan. The parched hot sun irradiated as he drove and drove through neighborhood after neighborhood until he came to Gird Road. Driving, he reached the end of the road with the reflective yellow and black signs, and turned to the right. Circling around the block, he headed back up the road, checking every house and wishing he'd paid attention to the address number. After driving it those dozens of times, you'd think it would've stuck. Still nothing familiar. He U-turned again, and drove up the road again till he came to the end of the street. He knew from the map that this was the only section of the road.

From Dreadnought's description, he'd entered the "Borkum's Rift" by daydreaming and not watching where he was going. He tried to daydream and just drive, but it was as hard as trying to go to sleep. He had too much at stake to wander down the road aimlessly so that his voyage always took him to a destination at the end of the road. Frustrated, but hardly deterred, he stopped and tried to remember from what direction Dreadnought might have driven home from work. Maybe he could be waiting when Dreadnought drove by and follow him to his home.

After only an hour's wait, he tired of the vigil, and considered driving on. There were thousands of other places on Earth still waiting for his attentions, but one festering chunk inside his brain insisted that he knew the score and had to settle it now. He waited, and then waited some more, so was extraordinarily surprised when he awoke from an unexpected catnap to see the Gird Road sign up ahead. He'd thought that he was on Gird Road. About to start the engine, he realized that he *was* on Gird Road. Looking around, he recognized the houses. The green house with the two bikes and the dog on the front lawn. The two story, red brick and aluminum siding with the big oak in the front yard - August Albert's place. And, sure enough, Dreadnought's slate blue Cape Cod with the white trim and pillars. Yup, this was it! He started the engine anyway, and drove from block to block, somewhat unsettled that he'd let himself return to the rift. He still didn't know how to get out and didn't have anymore fruit from the

Tree of Golden Eagle. He also wondered if the dog ever went in his house.

Eventually, he parked down the road from Dreadnought's. His adversary's car wasn't there, so he waited. When he'd nodded off, it was sunny. Now it was cloudy, just like the other day he'd come here, and he wondered if that was par for the rift. He spent the time in prayer.

"Lord, Jesus, I must be crazy coming back here," (it wasn't your usual apostolic invocation.) "And, if you want to talk me out of it, I'm listening. But, there's a part of me that has to stand up to this – demon who pilfers and incarcerates people's lives. I'm here for the imprisoned lives on those shelves, but also, who knows how many lives he's tossed into the fire. I hope that I can prevent more destruction. Would I have been next? Will I be again? This is my return visit, and if he captures me again, it will be recorded for him to read. If he finds that I've come back to confront him, he will dispose of me in the fire as surely as my capture in this rift. So, talk me out of it – direct me in your right ways before I walk into his snarly web..." the prayer went along those lines a spell, then Leonard stopped.

"Am I talking about me too much?" he thought aloud. He thought about Pastor Pete, and asked God's forgiveness for his foolishness the last time that they were together. He prayed for Grief and Pain, for Lotsa Frump, for John, Aaron, Kim and Rick Shaw. He thought about Henry, and wondered when he'd see him again, if ever. Lastly, he prayed for Dreadnought because he needed God's merciful grace most of all. It was just about that time that he saw Dreadnought's blue car turn the corner.

His heart popped with anticipation. There was still time to back out. He started the light duty pickup and drove 'carelessly' up to the slate blue Cape Cod. Stopping, he wondered if he'd made a mistake. The man getting out of the car looked different until Leonard realized that he was just dressed differently. It was a different day. He wouldn't wear that green pinstripe for a couple more days. Another glance, and he knew he had the right mark.

Dreadnought grabbed a stack of folders sitting on his passenger seat to bring in the house. He promptly noticed Leonard, looking at him from over his truck cab.

"Can you help me?" called Leonard.

He stopped as though he'd wait all day if necessary.

"Uh – can you direct me downtown?"

"End of the road and turn right. Take you right downtown." He continued his trek to the door. Leonard watched as he unlocked the door and entered, then started his truck and headed up the road. True to days of future past, he drove from Gird Road block to block, locked in and unable to escape. The pattern unnerved him, but he still stopped by Dreadnought's and went to the door.

"Sorry to bother you again," Leonard said nervously as Dreadnought stood at the open front door with the hot air balloon stained glass. "Um, I'm lost. I mean, I can't, uh, seem to get off your block. I drive and drive, and I keep driving on the same block. Does that make sense?"

"So what do you want?" asked Dreadnought.

"Uh, I hoped that you could help me."

"Sorry," he easily answered and closed the door. Leonard watched him return to the medieval room. He waited on the porch for the guitar music, but it never came. Different day. He realized that he was shaking, so stepped down and climbed on the hood of his truck, lounging against the windshield. It wasn't bright, but he wore his sunglasses and closed his eyes. A light breeze swirled around his hair. He felt his apprehensions drain into the warm hood of his truck. His attitudes became more of impatience than fear. He wanted to get it over with.

"Maybe I should just storm in and punch him out." He wondered how he'd explain this to the police. They'd take him to the funny farm for sure.

"Better than being trapped in one of Dreadnought's books," he scoffed, so turned with a hostile aggression when, an hour later, Dreadnought came out the door onto his porch, framed by the white pillars.

"What are you doing?" he called.

"Sitting on my own out by myself," Leonard answered none too sweetly.

"Well, go do it somewhere else, - or I'll call the cops."

"Right! What charge?" Leonard challenged. "I'll tell you. I would leave if I could, but I'm stuck here. It doesn't matter where I drive. I just drive past your house over and over and over again, and there's nothing I can do about it. I don't care if I sound crazy. I'm not stoned or drunk. You wouldn't help me, so rather than waste gas, I'm sitting here."

"Well, go do it in front of someone else's house." He turned to go in.

Leonard called, "It's a public road. I'm within my rights."

Dreadnought stopped; then smiled.

"I'm sorry," he answered. "Where are my manners? Please come in."

Leonard stayed on the truck glaring at him.

"I'm serious." He could've sold pork chops to an orthodox Seventh Day Adventist.

"I'd rather you just tell me how to get off this block."

"I will," he promised. "Please come in." He motioned towards his open door. Henry Kissinger and Norman Bates would have taken notes.

Leonard sighed and hopped down from his vehicle, marching towards the door.

The rooms were the same. Still intent, he followed Dreadnought almost too close.

"Please have a seat," Dreadnought motioned towards the couch. Leonard sat. The guitar rested on a stand next to the couch. He couldn't recall having seen the stand last time. The fire was small, but effective, and warm. He wondered why anyone would have a fire lit in August, even if this was an overcast day. The keyboard to his heart stood idly against the wall next to the kitchen.

"May I get you something to drink?"

"Uh, no thanks. Really, I just need to know how to get out of here. I am sorry to impose." He stood up quickly and faced Dreadnought.

"You called the cops, didn't you? You just lured me in here to keep me until they showed up." He turned towards the door.

"NO!" spurted Dreadnought, displaying for the first time in both meetings a snag in his façade. "No, really," he settled down. "I have not called the police. I just sincerely felt remorse for being abrupt and wanted to make it up to you by showing a little more hospitality."

Leonard remained standing. "If you really wanted to be a good host, you'd tell me how to get off this block. Hope I don't have to use the toilet while I'm here. Heaven only knows how long you'd make me wait before directing me to the bathroom."

The lull between the two was indescribably long, then Dreadnought laughed. Leonard again turned to leave.

"I'm sorry," he smirked. "I told you, drive straight to the T, and turn right."

"I tried that," Leonard was quick to answer. "Didn't work."

"I see. Well, that's what I do. I don't understand why you'd feel trapped, nor why you think I have the answers you're looking for."

Leonard looked stunned.

"You're right," he blustered, un-billowing. "It's not your problem, and presumptuous of me to be so belligerent."

"Apology accepted," Dreadnought granted.

Leonard left the room, heading for the door.

"Where are you going?" called Dreadnought, following him into the gold room.

"Back to my truck, of course." He grabbed the knob and opened the door.

"Do you like to read?"

"HUH?" asked Leonard.

"I have an extraordinary library that I love to show to new visitors. Do you like books?"

"No," Leonard turned towards the door, then paused. "Sorry to bother you."

"You can make it up to me by letting me show you my library."

Leonard snorted, "Fine, but this had better be one hullaballoo of a library."

Dreadnought laughed. "Well, I don't have any dancing girls. It's not a tractor pull. It's just books, but some even the most illiterate or dyslexic would find interesting. By the way, what's your name?"

Leonard paused. He'd hoped to avoid this part, but had to go forward for his plan to work.

"Leonard," he answered, looking suspicious.

"Just Leonard?"

"Lamb."

"Leonard Lamb? Really?"

Leonard's look told him to not press it. "What's yours?"

Dreadnought smiled his most dis-alarming smile. "Dreadnought."

"Just Dredknot?"

He nodded.

Dreadnought pointed towards the stairs and led the way. Leonard fought the screaming impulse to flee.

"Do you have any idea how to get out of here?" he called, following Dreadnought up the stairs, pulling a paper out of his shirt pocket.

"Afraid not," Dreadnought lied.

"No idea at all?" He paused at the top of the stairs.

"Very impressive, now tell me how to get out of here." He turned to go downstairs.

"You haven't seen anything," objected Dreadnought.

"I didn't promise results. I've bugged you long enough already, and I need to find someone who can help me get unstuck."

"NO!" Dreadnought sprung for the second time today. "Here. Just look at a couple of these books. Please."

Leonard groaned. Dreadnought handed him the copy of D.B. Cooper. Leonard saw the cover, and carelessly flipped through a few pages as

Dreadnought sat printing the label at the computer. He brought the Dillinger book.

"You know Dillinger wasn't killed outside the Biograph Theater in Chicago, don't you?"

"Don't know anything about him," spurned Leonard, "and really not all that interested. He also glanced through the pages. It bugged him to think that Dillinger could feel him turning his pages. Would he cry out, "Don't do it!" if he could?

"Here," Dreadnought handed the ringer. "This one will really grab you."

Leonard took it just as a sneeze whistled through his nose. He glanced at the label just before scrunching his eyes, and raising his hand to his face. Turning away, he sneezed hard, three times, the last time taking a moment before letting loose. He wiggled and coughed and let the euphoric feeling wriggle out of him.

"Sorry," he apologized to Dreadnought, wiping his nose with his sleeve. "Now, what's this fancy-schmancy book?" He looked at the cover, then opened to the first page. He turned numerous pages, then fanned to the end of the book."

"There's nothing here," he challenged, obviously irritated. "It's blank."

Dreadnought was already on his feet. Leonard assertively shoved the book back at him.

"Very funny," he said, and backed away to go.

Dreadnought looked at him contemptuously, then checked the book. He glanced at the cover as he opened the first pages. As the book crashed to the floor, Leonard could read the new printer label that he himself had applied to the cover over his own name, reading: "The Biography of Robert M. Dreadnought".

Picking up the black, leather-covered book, he turned to the last page.

"How do you like that?" Leonard taunted, though he knew that Dreadnought could not hear him. On the other hand, he definitely knew that Dreadnought could feel the last page open.

"Ooh, such language," added Leonard, watching the crass words appear, rapid-fire. "Feel like I'm reading a 1970's John Lennon interview."

Leonard sat on the edge of the desk for a very long time, uncertain what to do. He'd come to confront and capture Dreadnought. He'd also hoped to free the people from the books, but D.B. Cooper and Dillinger weren't the type of people you necessarily wanted to set loose.

No.

That sounded lame to Leonard. Maybe the most lame thing he'd said this entire book. They ALL deserved to be set free - just not right now and not without others there to help.

He'd scanned the names on the biographies. The volumes included James Hoffa, Sr., Jim Croce, Jim Morrison and James Dean. He wondered if they sustained life while imprisoned, or eventually died like everyone?

Most were people he didn't recognize, though one book caught his attention. The name, Ty M. Lourdes. He'd heard it before, but wasn't sure where. He skimmed page after page till his eyes burned dry with fatigue. Setting the book beside him on the desk, face down, he idly turned the cover open and closed. The type on the back page appeared.

"Leonard! Leonard!"

Ty was calling him. Leonard picked up the text to check the back pages as he wondered how he'd known his name. The print added, "Page 14,593."

Leonard turned to the page in the inch wide volume.

"Praise Jesus!" Leonard shouted aloud. "Ty!" He recalled the gifted guitar player back in Pastor Pete's campsite church. Ty Lourdes! Ty Lourdes, the worship leader? He couldn't believe it was the same.

He ran downstairs with the biography under arm, and turned on the keyboard to his heart. Turning page after page, it took well over an hour to find a favorite song. Being an endowed musician, Ty had a few thousand to choose from. It should not have taken so long.

Unlike Ty Lourdes, Leonard was not a musician. He touched the keyboard apprehensively, one finger at a time. He hoped he would not have to be proficient to free the youth from his vagabondage. He checked Christmas songs, expecting to find an easy one. He groaned as he read, "Carol of the Bells," and the "Halleluia Chorus" from Handel's "Messiah." He kept searching. Eventually, he tried to pick out "Lord I Lift Your Name On High." It was awful, and took a few dozen tries, so no one was more surprised than Leonard when a hand came in over his arm to touch one of the black keys.

"B-flat," corrected Ty Lourdes, grinning wider than any ole' Cheshire Cat as Leonard jumped, startled, turning to see who was there, and preparing to pounce, resist, or flee.

"So, that was your guitar?" devised Leonard, listening to the flow of chords.

Ty answered with music, a nod, and a beaming countenance.

"It seemed familiar, which actually is weird, 'cuz I'm not a guitar player and wouldn't really notice one guitar over another. Someone says, "Look at my guitar," and I usually don't know whether to offer praise or pity. But, when I saw Dreadnought playing your guitar, a feeling inside told me something was wrong."

"What kind of feeling?"

Leonard still resisted labeling it. "Some are calling it discernment."

"What do you call it?"

Leonard gazed at him for a spell before answering, "In this case, intuition, maybe, laced with luck."

"What's wrong with calling it discernment?"

Leonard sneered. "I don't think God would waste his gifts on me. He'd pick someone who'd use it. God's not frivolous."

"Granted," answered Ty, "but, it still sounds like discernment to me."

Leonard shrugged. "Can't see myself a sage."

"Not sagacious enough?"

"What?"

"Not sagacious enough?"

"What's –"

"Sagacious? Sagacity?"

"Yeah."

"Wisdom. Someone who sees things quickly, like Joseph, Israel's son. Sure, he could interpret dreams, including the Pharoah's, but another gift that's a bit overlooked is his sagacity, or wisdom. After he interpreted the dream, he told Pharoah how to avoid calamity, and that's what securely won him the second spot in the kingdom of Egypt."

Leonard laughed wryly. "That's fine for Joseph, but me, wise? I don't think so."

"How'd you figure out how to escape from Dreadnought, and for that matter, how'd you trap him? Bet that you had some help from somewhere, even if you don't know where."

Leonard felt silly talking about it.

"Really, Ty. I just got the idea of re-labeling the book. I had no idea if it would work. It scared me to death to open that book again today, knowing it might suck me onto its pages as though through a thin straw."

"But, you went forward with it?"

"Well, yeah."

"Sounds like something gave you the security and assurance to move on it."

Leonard thought back. It was just a suspicion, but he considered the fruit from the Tree of College.

"Maybe," he admitted without explanation, "but, it creates a new problem."

"And that is?" Ty started a new song on his guitar.

"What to do with all these biographies."

"Oh." Ty stopped playing.

"Someone's got to read them and see who should be freed. It's a big job, and will take some years, I expect."

He looked at Ty inquiringly.

"Plus," he added, "it has to be someone who won't be tempted to become his own version of Dreadnought."

The name chilled both of them. Ty picked up Dreadnought's book, sitting on the table before them and, setting aside his guitar, walked over to the fireplace. He looked over at Leonard, opened the book, and started to brush the pages over the tips of the flames.

"Don't," called Leonard.

Ty pulled the book out.

"Why not?"

Leonard sputtered to think of a good reason.

"Because that's what Dreadnought would've done. It would be acting at his level."

Ty thought about it for a few well-weighted microseconds before answering, "Burning this book will never bring me down to Dreadnought's level. If anything, it will be liberating." He let the flames tickle the pages. Little sparks glowed on the flakey, gold leaf edges. He dropped the book on the fire and watched the flames race around it.

"Oh my gosh!"

Leonard jumped up and raced over, reaching into the fire and pulling the book out, getting singed, and brushing it off so the red embers wouldn't consume it. The back cover was blackened. The edges of some pages had begun to burn.

"What are you doing?" demanded Ty.

"Saving information," defended Leonard, setting the book on the mantle and nursing his barbecued flesh. "Remember, he burned up a bunch of books. If we burn this one, what people he destroyed will also be lost, and what little he read of their lives should be recorded here, as well."

Ty softened.

"This is also a missing persons record and account."

Ty relented. "Okay. But, what do we do with it in the meantime."

Leonard thought quickly, then took the book upstairs to the library, wrapped duct tape around it eighteen or twenty good times, and set him in the rare collections glass case beside the desk.

"We lock it up, of course," he answered, coming downstairs. "Maybe we should get a safety deposit box at a bank. Somewhere that people won't be able to accidentally pick him up and free him."

Leonard picked up Ty's biography.

"I ain't touching it," Ty stepped back.

"Can't say I blame you." Leonard checked the label, opened the book, made sure all pages were empty and tossed it in the fireplace.

Ty watched it burn, totally absorbed by the destruction, then jumped up.

"I'll do it," he thought aloud.

"What?"

"I'll free the books."

Leonard was taken aback.

"No, really," continued Ty. "I won't do it alone. That would be like "The Most Dangerous Game." I'll talk to Pastor Pete and the congregation, and we'll start a ministry to read through the books and talk over whom the individual is, pray about them, and corporately free those who would not destroy our society. I could certainly play most of the music. The others we'll just have to box up and store in some attic or something." He displayed a gracious sense of patience and peace.

"Wow!" thought Leonard, and wondered if he should talk to the prison system of the state. NEVAH!!!!!!! It might save taxpayer dollars, but can you imagine how this system would be totally abused by the Powers That Be?

The two men continued to discuss plans. Leonard warned Ty to not play any songs too close to Dreadnought's book, lest he accidentally free Dreadnought, including singing, humming or whistling up in the library.

"I thought we had to use the keyboard to your heart to free someone," argued Ty.

"Maybe," conferred Leonard, "but, that's more of a presumption than I'm willing to test right now. Try the guitar on some other book, first." He rose, as if to leave.

"Can I drop you somewhere?" offered Leonard.

"Anywhere but in the fireplace."

Leonard mocked him with a wry smile.

"But, how are you going to get out of the rift?"

Leonard had no idea until Ty asked the question. At once, the whole, simple plan came to life in his brain. Walking over to the telephone, he called Pizza Shack and ordered a large pepperoni with cheese filled crust, delivered. The two continued to talk over book issues until the pizza arrived. Leonard paid the driver, (a young man named K.C. driving an old, white Hyundai Excel,) included a decent tip, then grabbed a couple pieces before handing it to Ty. Taking a bite, he muttered, "Thought you might be hungry," then, "Wait up," to the delivery driver as he waved farewell to Ty.

Getting into his pickup truck, he waved at the delivery driver to proceed. The driver didn't have a clue what was going on as he drove on to his next delivery, leading Leonard out of the cursed city block.

Chapter Eighteen

"Sometimes I wish you'd make an appointment," protested Leonard, glancing up towards the cloudless sky and the ardent sun supporting the endless day.

Henry glanced up from his dune, looked over his protégé, and nodded, his brimmed hat accentuating the effect. He hadn't changed a molecule since they'd last been together. The sweat line around his straw hat; the same cream, long sleeved shirt, black pants, suspenders and boots, his full beard minus the mustache, and his tanned skin like old, wrinkled leather. Age spots decorated the backs of his dark brown hands.

"God has His own timing," Henry answered in his distinct, Germanic, country dialect, "and, that time is definitely now."

"But," Leonard was about to tell him about Dreadnought, and Ty and John and the days walking back through time.

"That's in the past. I'm talking about what's up ahead. All before was to prepare you for what is to come." His demeanor was, as ever, completely disarming, yet his words so direct and impacting.

"What's up ahead?" Leonard felt the sun turn-up a few degrees.

Classically scribbling in the sand, (about a Lutheran boy who'd lied to the priest during his first confession,) Henry paused a moment before adding, "Two battles. Maybe three. It depends on you."

Leonard sat down in the sand and started covering up his legs. The hot sand tickled his burned hands. It hurt a bit, but not enough to stop. Then, he remembered what he was wallowing in, and it somehow seemed distasteful to bury oneself in forgiven and forgotten sins. He brushed himself off, and asked, "Is it, like, fashionable to talk in poetic obscurity?"

Henry paused to dissect the question.

"No, not fashionable," he considered, "but prudent. The more I tell you, the more you will not act on your own."

"So, what's wrong with stacking the deck in my favor once in a while?"

Henry dropped his head. His words were barely a whisper blown away with the wind. He uttered, "You're not always a very good card player." He paused before breaking forth to enjoy a hearty laugh.

Leonard was stunned, then irritated, then snickered, then threw handfuls of sand in the air, all in the course of a handful of seconds. All tensions released, the two peered towards each other. Henry resumed his stance on his knees, but didn't jot. He closed his eyes and raised his face towards the eternal light. Leonard glanced up, then back at Henry. The farmer's skinny arms looked old and a bit twisted as he extended them out, palms up, fingers hooked, ready to hold. Leonard watched him as he prayed, awed by the passion, so intent that Henry became the prayer for his ward.

Abruptly, Henry looked up at Leonard and said, "What are you watching me for?" His hat brim nodded upward, and he resumed his supplication.

Leonard felt thumped, but recovered, dropped to his knees and joined him in the prayer. Henry didn't look again, but the light smile on the seasoned face indicated he knew he was not alone in purpose. The prayer lasted for hours and hours and hours. Not half an hour passed before Leonard began to squirm and wonder when it would close. After quite a spell, when Henry showed no signs of slowing, Leonard let go of his selfish impatience and dug in for the long haul. He checked himself, lest his commitments were more of a dare, to try to outlast the angel.

Sometimes they worshipped loudly. Sometimes they engaged in quiet meditation. Sometimes they spoke as one, and sometimes each responded to the other. At one point, around the third hour, Leonard had to laugh to himself as their prayer almost resembled a dialog. It felt so automatic, like a rehearsed routine, ("So Henry, Who's on first?")

Around the sixth hour, Leonard's voice started cracking badly. He'd clear it, but it didn't help. The arid air seared his vocal chords and afflicted the inner cylinders of his throat, so his words became gravelly and broken. Henry didn't seem to notice as they continued.

By the seventh hour, Leonard's body quaked with fatigue, but he persisted. Stationed on his hands and knees, he felt his neck and arms, red and burnt. Henry didn't seem to notice as they continued. No seventh inning stretch today.

By the ninth, Leonard was laying face down. His breath created a rounded hole in the sand. He felt it a fitting place to deposit and bury his spoken sins.

By the eleventh hour, Leonard's brain was more exhausted than his body, (and there wasn't much left of his body.) He rose to his feet, both his legs and his mind rubbery, his body spent beyond weariness, coated top to bottom with sand. There was nothing remotely elaborate or refined about his prayers. Henry didn't seem to notice as they continued.

Topping off at the twelfth hour, Henry sighed a sweet, "Amen," stretched his stiff back and rose to his feet, dancing from foot to foot to shake off the sand and cramping. He looked over at Leonard, laying on the sand, still muttering words like, "Praise Jesus," and "Glory to God," totally on auto-pilot. He smiled, and for the first time since they'd met, he dropped to his knees and touched the young man, laying one hand on his brick red forehead, and the other on his hand and wrist.

"Lord, Jesus, touch Leonard with your grace, your holiness, and fill him with your strength. Amen."

Leonard weakly mumbled, "Alleluia, Lord. Alleluia. Praise Jesus. Alleluia."

Still holding on to Leonard, Henry bent over him.

"Leonard?"

Leonard didn't respond, but kept muttering his prayer.

"Leonard?" he called more loudly, and shook him mildly.

Leonard turned towards Henry, making eye contact, his lips still moving. Henry's head and hat shadowed Leonard's face. His hazel eyes shone as he said, "Leonard, say, "Amen.""

"Amen," Leonard automatically responded.

Like a bolt out of the blue, Leonard shot up, on his feet, renewed and revived,ᵢ transfused, ready for another twelve. He also noticed that the dry pain from his sunburn was also gone as he whooped and shouted, his feet dancing, sand falling from him like obsolete, forgotten curses. Henry joined him, stretching short, stubby shadows up the sides of the dunes like a funhouse mirror. Winded, they gazed at each other, smiling.

"What happened?" questioned Leonard, inspecting his now brown arms and shoulders.

"Time change," answered Henry. "Sometimes our Lord just accelerates your personal timeline so you naturally heal rapidly. For you, it's miraculous. For the Kingdom, it's common stock."

Leonard still felt awe at the extraordinary relief.

"You have to go soon." Henry stood and invited Leonard to do the same.

Leonard felt mixed reactions as he rose. He'd always been anxious to go before. Now he felt good, and didn't want it to escape.

Henry continued. "This will be the last time that we meet, at least for a spell."

"Why?" Leonard challenged. "I still haven't found my First Love."

"Understood," acknowledged Henry, "but I can see your growth, and though I cannot see the future, I have more hope for you than I did when we first met."

Leonard thanked him though it left an empty uncertainty dented in the core of his being.

Henry glanced up at the sun, then back at Leonard.

"But," began Leonard.

"Doesn't matter," Henry interrupted, resuming his stance at the endless canvas of sand. He recorded the confessed sins of a pimply, punk teen who'd glazed the football team's jock shorts with cinnamon oil and Super Glued the coach's phone receiver to its station.

"Time is short," he announced, "and, there are a few things I want to impart."

Leonard waited indicating Henry had his complete attention.

First, do you still have the letter I gave you?"

"What letter?" Leonard sincerely had no idea what he was talking about.

From Jesus, written on the brown paper bag."

Briefly stunned, Leonard fished it from his back pocket. It was wrinkled and wet with perspiration, but still intact and readable.

"You didn't give this to me," argued Leonard. "I got this from a guy on the boulevard waving a sign..." He studied Henry's face.

"You're the signman who gave this to me?"

Henry smiled, wide with delight. "Is that so incredible to believe?"

Leonard sighed. "Not at this point of the story. Why didn't you tell me before?"

"To what means? That's like saying, 'Why didn't you tell me when I gave you the letter?' You would not have believed it then. You would not have believed it much more readily the first time we met here in the Sea of Forgetfulness."

"But," protested Leonard, "why the façade at all? I mean, you could have given me the letter the first time you dragged me into the Sea."

"Perhaps," allowed Henry, mostly because it was no longer an arguable point, "but, the Lord told me to give it to you. It's never my place to question His direction. As far as dressing up as a young man advertising, that came for two reasons. The first was merely to check you and Reuel out so I'd know how best to serve you. The second was to disarm you. You held no purpose or reason to fear me."

Leonard felt a little duped, but promptly scolded himself for offering a foothold to his sinful pride. He perked up.

"Why'd you use a paper bag?"

"I didn't use anything. I was just the messenger – the delivery boy."

"Sorry," coughed Leonard. "Um, why did our Lord use a paper bag? Is there some significance I'm not seeing?"

Henry smiled, sweet as a summer eve's rain, closed his eyes and let the question settle between them. Opening his eyes, he answered, "What size bag is that?"

"Uh, small."

"What would you use it for?"

Leonard turned it over, not that he needed to. He'd already examined it many, many times.

"It's a lunch bag," he eventually answered, feeling like the answer was too simple and obvious to be any earthly good.

"Perfect," applauded Henry. "It's a lunch bag. When you think you are alone and don't have the provisions to complete the work of the kingdom, keep in mind that Jesus fed literally thousands of people with what amounted to a sack lunch. In His name, you can do the same."

Leonard looked at the bag with a renewed sense of value.

Henry knew he had no time for them to dwell on the moment. He shouted, "So, gird up your loins, Leonard Lamb, and answer me honestly. Are you still lukewarm?"

"Uh, no, but I'm not yet hot – just warmer than I was."

Henry nodded and continued, "And what, like Ephesus, did you lose?"

Leonard smiled. "It took me a long time to find the answer, and when I found it, I felt absolutely foolish for not having seen it right up front. Like Ephesus, I lost my First Love."

"Yup," applauded Henry. "Now listen, for your time is naught."

Leonard looked up at the sun, but detected no further movement.

"First, remember," began Henry, "that your soul is not part of your body, but rather, that your body is woven around your soul, integrated with each cell of your body."

"Second," continued Henry, "the Kingdom of Heaven is everywhere. It's all around us. There really is a sheer veil between the Spiritual and the Physical. And, though one could not measure it in cubits, square miles or acreage, Heaven's a lot bigger than Hell.

"Third, after God created the heavens and the Earth, what'd he do with them?"

Leonard rapidly realized he was expected to answer the question. "Uh...He ruled them."

"Who did He rule?"

"Uh, people? All the creatures of the air, the land and the sea?"

"This still is not Twenty Questions or Try-To-Guess-What-The-Angel-Is-Thinking."

"People."

"Right, so what did he do after he created the heavens and the earth?" He didn't wait for Leonard to answer.

"*He gave it away*. He's a giving God; a generous Father. He gave away His creation to all of us. What did He do with Heaven after he made it?"

"Gave it away?"

"To Christ Jesus, His only begotten. He gave the whole package away. And He's still creating and giving it away. But, don't forget, you are not going to spend eternity in Heaven."

"I'm not?" Leonard disheartened.

"Scripture says," pointed Henry. "You are eventually going to spend it on Earth. The New Jerusalem. You're all going back there."

"Of course," admitted Leonard, sheepishly wondering why he hadn't immediately realized the answer. Henry answered the question for him.

"Remember, you are bound by your five senses which make up your carnal, human nature. They are wonderful gifts, but they also can separate you from your Lord and His Heavenly Host. You do not yet see yourself in the New Jerusalem. But, you may find Him soon enough. In the meantime, God spoke the Truth, and now He's searching for those who believe it enough to tell others."

"But, I'm not an evangelist," considered Leonard.

"And my ears are not your trash can. Christ Jesus, your Brother, has already shown you little splashes of revelation. He's given you discernment, He's with you twenty-four/seven, and He sees you as your brother's keeper. You want to find your First Love?"

"Of course," Leonard perked, happy that he again actually knew the best answer for the question.

"Then," Henry's face became very dark, "give your life away to others, and you will find your First Love."

Leonard replayed and committed the ideas through his head. "Give away my life to others, and I will find my First Love. And, that makes all of us evangelists, with or without the title."

Henry nodded and pulled something out of his pocket.

"I have something for you," he began, changing both the subject and his demeanor. "It is very special. You will never see another one like it, and it will charge your life as a constant reminder of our time together, and more importantly, that God's creation is ever bigger than your life."

Leonard accepted the gift, a small rock about the size of a medium olive. It was neither polished nor shiny, but Leonard was enthralled as he tried to find a word for the solid color. Nothing came close to his experiences.

"We call that color 'cloune'."

"Clown?"

"No, cloune. There is no equivalent in the English language, nor any other human language for that matter."

"What is it?" Leonard had to know.

Henry was enjoying the moment so much, he wanted it to last, but realized his time was waning rapidly.

"Think of it as a "retina bender." Cloune is the color directly below what you call infrared, or more exactly, infra-magenta. If your eyes could see the light beyond your visible spectrum, this would be one of the colors."

"But?"

"You are right. It's not red or black or brown or gold or blue or green or any other color you've ever seen, however exotic. Of course, cloune is a secondary color."

"Secondary color?" Leonard's mind was too busy to keep up.

"Instead of primary colors. Please pay attention."

"Sorry." He looked at Henry. "Uh, if it's a secondary color, what's it mixed with?"

"Red and weel."

"Come again?"

"Red and weel. Take the red out of cloune and you'll have weel. Weel's just the next primary color outside your visible light spectrum, below cloune. There's a bunch of colors out there that humans cannot see."

"Can you see them?"

"Some," Henry admitted.

"Like what?"

Henry thought a moment to make sure that he had his facts right. "In the light spectrum, I see six primary colors and nine secondaries. Of course, all six together still make white.

If I drew a regular color wheel with red, blue and yellow, mine would have fifteen primaries and fifteen secondaries, including the ones that you can see."

Leonard looked at the cloune colored stone again. He wanted to say, "Thank you," but it didn't seem like enough. He said it anyway.

"Maybe I should mount it to a necklace."

"I would advise against it," warned Henry. "Be exceedingly judicious about whom you show that stone to. It's just a common stone, but its color and special way it affects your eyes makes it invaluable. You can be sure that some will try to buy it, or worse, steal it from you. And, once it's lost, it's lost. I can get more, but won't."

"Why not?"

"Doesn't matter," he answered, virtually shutting down the idea. The time was now.

"You have to leave," announced Henry, eyeballing the length of his shadow. Stow your cloune rock deep in your pocket.

Leonard looked towards Henry questioningly as he pocketed the treasure. Henry had never announced that it was time to leave before until the absolute last seconds. Leonard just sort of awoke back in his regular world. Then, an imponderable came to mind.

"One quick question?"

"Quickly."

"Your shadow? The sun? Does the sun ever set here in the Sea of Forgetfulness?"

"Never," Henry answered, his face alive and euphoric.

"But, it moves. Why doesn't it set?"

"It circles overhead like a vulture, not that it is anything like a scavenger. Think of a child's top, or gyro spinning on the floor. Just before it falls over, it starts to pivot. We're like that top, pivoting and spinning, so the sun moves in an oval circle, like a halo on a comic strip character."

Henry glanced up and waved to the star.

"Wave," he ordered Leonard.

Leonard responsively waved, full arm, though he felt a bit silly, so was completely and equally amazed when the sun responded with an awesome spiral twirl, then returned to standard yellow.

Leonard gaped at Henry, who smiled back proudly.

"It's a friend of mine. I was his mentor when I had star duty in another part of the universe, before this assignment. I am blessed each day to be drenched and enfolded in his light. You should be, too. You know that your soul is primarily made of light.

Leonard shook with amazement at the concept.

"No. Never occurred to me."

"Yup. When God created the Heavens and the Universe, the first thing that He created was?"

"Light."

"Yup, and each being in this universe was a predestined creation formed with Heavenly Light as their foundation."

"Wow!" thought Leonard. He started to ask another question, but Henry cut him off.

"I wish I had more time to share more, but we have an assignment for you. Don't think of yourself as a volunteer. This is the second battle I spoke of, and the time is now."

"So be it," affirmed Leonard, concerned that he had no idea what he was being recruited for. He was surprised to hear crisp footsteps approaching from behind. Turning, he saw a man twice his height dressed in full battle armor.

"He's all yours, Hondo," said Henry, returning to record the forgiven sins in the sand. A woman named Teresa who was perpetually compelled to lie, even when the truth would do her good.

"Front and Center, recruit" yelled Hondo. "There's a war on, and you've been drafted."

"But," protested Leonard, too late, as they landed behind a protective knoll. Fiery arrows whizzed by as Leonard toppled down into the foxhole.

Chapter Nineteen

At first, all he could do was keep his head down. Fire tipped arrows flashed by all around them like homemade comets. Soon, the epicenter of battle shifted away.

"Come on," called Hondo, rolling out of the foxhole to another.

Leonard followed in fashion, or tried to, tripping over his sword. He was astonished to see a broadsword, sheathed, attached to his regular belt. He was dressed as usual, except for the armor and helmet. And his shoes were different. He checked for more fiery darts as he prepared to roll out.

"Don't forget your shield," the voice called.

Leonard wasn't sure he'd heard right, but looked and quickly saw a dilapidated, old shield resting against the wall of the foxhole. Grabbing it, he tried to roll to the next foxhole. Both the sword and shield snagged against the dirt and stone. Like a ballet dancer with ingrown toenails, he never-so-gracefully flopped around a bit before falling backwards beside Hondo, landing hard and losing his breath.

"Do it again!" cried Hondo, pointing to the original foxhole.

Leonard forced his breathing to normalcy and sat up, hoping he'd heard wrong.

"Get on it," yelled the warrior, flipping his head to the side.

Leonard stooped, checked over the brim, and scampered lizard style back to the safety of the foxhole.

"Back," ordered Hondo.

This time Leonard responded without hesitation, first checking the lane as though he was entering traffic from a parallel parking space, then rubbing his belly on the roly-poly grains of dirt, till he landed face first beside Hondo.

"Better," complimented the fighter. "Still too slow, but better." He checked over the edge, then drew his sword.

"They're coming. Get ready. Come on!"

He sprung out of the foxhole. Leonard started to come, then paused.

"NOW, Lamb!"

Leonard drew his sword from the sheath, then jumped up and paced beside Hondo as they advanced to attack the enemy. He was surprised at the length of the sword, stretching his arm full length to draw it forth. No more time to think about that, now. Jumping over foxholes, dodging around mounds of dirt, slipping behind trees and rocks, Leonard didn't see anyone. He checked high points, wondering if they might pounce or snipe. The fire tipped arrows still flew off to their left, but he couldn't see who was shooting them.

Hondo led them around a hill. They took position behind a low stone wall and waited a moment to catch breath. Leonard's heart pumped rapidly.

"We're out of danger now," sputtered Hondo, looking snug.

Leonard gazed amazed. He again wasn't familiar with this particular application of the phrase, 'out of danger.' He'd have to get another dictionary.

Hondo scanned the area, then commanded, "Come on." Leonard hurdled the wall and started to advance, then saw the archer behind a bush. He stopped, but the arrow was already flying towards him, full strength. He tried to duck or move or not be there, but there was no time, and the arrow struck him firmly in the lower, left chest, bouncing off his armor and landing harmlessly against the wall. Hondo hadn't waited, and attacked furiously, slicing the archer with a single, bold stroke. He fell, and Leonard tried to feign staunch fortitude, but quickly lost, and keeled over, vomiting all the way down to his knees.

Hondo waited, then yelled, "Clean off your sword. Not on yourself - on the grass or something. Here's some clean cloth you can use." Leering, he pointed to the fallen archer.

"Take cover," he hissed, and ducked behind a tree. Leonard rose and slipped over the stone wall, watching through a potentilla hedge with little yellow flowers.

Three soldiers crept past. Leonard wondered if he should attack, but then realized that they might be allies. Hondo wasn't moving, as far as he could see. Next, a man jumped over the wall beside him and attacked, his sword leading the way. Leonard fell back on his back to avoid the attacker's blade and rolled sideways to rise, his sword springing up to avert the lethal lunge. He hadn't held a sword since he'd pretended to be a samurai warrior as a teen. This wasn't the same kind of sword; a two-handed broad sword; heavy and comparatively slow to swing. He did his best to divert the attack till help could arrive. Hondo came from behind, and outnumbered, the attacker ran off.

"Good recovery," said Hondo, scanning the area for further adversaries. "Come on."

They headed towards the rocky top of the hill when a horn sounded, long and sorrowful, then another and another, the heralds surrounding them. Hondo sheathed his sword and marched towards a road down at the bottom of the hill. Leonard held his sword and followed. He looked back and saw their attacker also coming up the hill, still some distance back. His sword also holstered, he didn't seem to care about Hondo, Leonard, or anyone else who might see him.

"Shouldn't we go after him?" asked Leonard, catching up.

"No."

They reached the road, and walked for two or three miles. The road curled to the left, then right, then left as it hugged the side of the range of hills. Rounding a curve, the hill dropped down hundreds more feet to a large, pale colored valley. Thousands upon thousands of people filled the valley, a number too many to count; their movements making the valley floor move, as though alive and itching all over. Hondo turned down to join them.

"Wait!" called Leonard.

Hondo stopped and faced him.

"Where are we going?"

"To join with the Army of the Lord," Hondo answered, his voice a buttonless snooze alarm.

"But, what was that back there?" Their attacker approached. Leonard prepared to raise his sword. The man stiffly nodded greeting as he passed, heading down the hill. Next the man they'd slain walked past. Hondo marched behind them down the trail.

"War games?" Leonard guessed, close behind. Hondo didn't have to answer for him to know that he was right.

There can be an unnerving quality one feels as one approaches thousands upon thousands of armed strangers. Most US citizens didn't walk the streets with large, lethal weapons, except maybe in downtown Miami and growing sections of Los Angeles. He eased a bit as the flood of warriors became faces with personalities. They were all dressed for battle, both male and female, but Leonard wondered at the wardrobe of some.

Many had full battle attire that had obviously been used bunches, was worn but still totally functional and well maintained. Others had pieces missing, or ready to fall off. Some were rusted or ripped. One couldn't get his sword out of its sheath. Yet again, another group had beautiful, polished armor. It looked strictly ornamental and for show, and wouldn't win a battle any day of the week, including Sunday.

He inspected his own outfit. The breastplate and helmet seemed fine, but his sword was flat and dull and ugly. His shield had holes in it, and his footwear was too tight, causing him to limp a bit on the instep. They approached a small group of three idling the time telling stories and comparing battle techniques.

"Hondo!" greeted the big red.

"Vernage," returned Hondo, giving him a hug of camaraderie. "This is Leonard Lamb, a new recruit. Need him trained."

Vernage nodded greeting. Another man approached, extending an arm towards Leonard. As Leonard reached to take the hand, the man grabbed Leonard's wrist and forcefully pulled the novice forward, practically dropping him to his knees.

"Gotcha," winked Davoid.

"That's Davoid," introduced Hondo. "Watch him."

Leonard had already figured that out.

"And, that's Dugless," pointed Vernage. Dugless scowled. Hondo turned to leave.

"Let's see your sword," reached Vernage as Leonard watched Hondo head to another brigade.

Leonard started to hand it to him, handle first. Vernage took it, and whacked Leonard on the knuckles with the blade.

"What're you doing?" Dugless yelled at Leonard.

"What?" protested Leonard, nursing his wounds.

"Don't ever hand anyone your sword. You'll be defenseless." Dugless scoffed with impatience, grabbing the sword from Vernage and tossing it back to Leonard.

"Don't ask for it," countered Leonard.

"You threw his sword at him!" accused Davoid.

Dugless shrugged. "Wouldn't cut melted butter."

Davoid tried to take hold of the sword. Leonard pulled away.

"I won't rap your fingers - or treat you like a punk," Davoid assured, glancing at Dugless who ignored him. "Let me see it."

Leonard carefully held it forth, still unwilling to let it go.

"You're right!" Davoid announced, touching the blade, then holding up both hands like a referee after a touchdown.

"Man!" he turned to Leonard, "What you been readin' all this time? Comic books? Too much TV? Newsprint that's outdated by next week? Comical emails and YouTube videos?"

Leonard shuffled sheepishly.

"That's why your blade's so dull," added Vernage. "You ain't been reading your Bible. If you're gonna read something, make sure you include that which lasts your entire life and beyond."

"But, I read my Bible," defended Leonard.

"What, in the bathroom?" snorted Davoid. "Is that like, your daily devotional?"

"You can't cheat out here on the battlefield," stated Dugless. "You'll lose the battle every time."

Vernage jumped in. "You wouldn't believe some people. They actually think that they can talk their way into Heaven at the final judgment. They're gonna show up with their armament broken or missing and think God ain't gonna see what they're really made of."

"Kind of like putting jewels in my crown?" Leonard played.

"Exactly," assured Dugless. "I see you've got a New King James sword."

"Good sword," applauded Vernage.

"There're different types of swords?" questioned Leonard.

"Of course," answered Vernage. "King James, NIV's, Jerusalem Bible. Personally, I prefer the New American Standard."

"I started out with a Living Bible," reported Davoid. "Ever see a Paraphrased Sword? Looks more like a bayonet, but I'll tell you, I've seen some of these warriors fight with one effectively enough for me to want to covet them."

"Let's see that shield," Vernage picked it up. He fingered the half dozen holes.

"Where's your faith?" accused Dugless.

"I have faith," snapped Leonard.

"And, I have fleas," bantered Davoid.

"You do have fleas," mocked Dugless.

"I mean beside my pets."

"You do have faith," Vernage added, shutting up his companions, "but, it has some big holes, and you've been hurt each time someone's fired a dart through one of these." He handed the shield to Leonard. "Feel the fissures."

Leonard examined the holes with his fingers. The edges were sharp and snagging in places, providing a polite potential for pain. He examined each of the six holes, inside and out. Sensations arose, slithering through the pores of his fingers, nibbling on his nerve endings, flooding phalanges, drilling carpel tunnels, arcing up the arms, shorting out the shoulders, changing lanes on the cloverleafs of the spinal column, coursing up like a geyser where it exploded – POW! – branching across the deltas of his superego. The effect shook him like a paint mixer.

"Obviously you feel it," observed Vernage.

"Fear?" murmured Leonard, still shaking.

"And, Guilt?" checked Vernage.

Leonard nodded.

"And, Foolishness?"

Another yes – Wait! No, more like, "Ignorance. Don't read my Bible enough."

"Like you're afraid to find out what you believe," jabbed Dugless.

"What else?" continued Vernage.

"Probably a juicy helping of Disbelief," suggested Davoid. "I used to dip mine in salsa to make 'em taste better."

Dugless' jaw twitched at that one, but Leonard admitted the accuracy of Davoid's lopsided insights. Worse, recognizing his Disbelief made the hole of his Guilt bigger.

"Y'got two more little holes here," pointed Dugless. "What are they?"

"Come on now," ribbed Davoid. "Cough 'em up."

Leonard closed his eyes and drew deep breaths.

"Grief and Pain," he puffed.

"What's that?" asked Vernage.

Leonard turned to Vernage. "Grief and Pain. Some things they said."

"You knew Grief and Pain?" gasped Davoid, his words like a battery powered jackhammer.

"Yeah. They brought me through the Mountains of Perchance."

"Wow!" bounced Davoid. "They led me across the Sea of Forgetfulness."

"Led you, my foot!" kicked Dugless.

"Well," conceded Davoid, "more like dragged me across the desert..."

"Screamin' & kickin'."

"I was learning Cooperation. I didn't scream or kick after the first seventy or eighty dune drifts. But, that's not the point. I'm just excited to learn that Leonard also was accompanied by Grief and Pain."

He turned to Leonard. "I hope that you fared better than *moi.*"

"Remains to be seen," admitted Leonard. "But, I was just thinking of what they said."

"And that was?" asked Vernage.

"There were a few things." He fingered one of the holes. "This one's Impatience," he announced. Moving to the last hole, he added, "And, this one's Shame. But!" he pointed to another spot where there had been a hole that looked freshly sealed, "I'm glad to report that this one used to be Prayerlessness. I realize that 'Prayerlessness' isn't a real English word, but you get the idea. They urged me to pray, Grief and Pain." He beamed. "Looks like it made a difference, praise Jesus, alleluia."

Vernage took back the shield as all three warriors appended their own, "Amen." Davoid pulled a pouch from his pack and handed it to Dugless who spread a grayish-yellowish paste across the face of the shield.

"What're you doing?" questioned Leonard.

"Patching it – well, resurfacing it, to cover the holes in your spirit," answered Vernage.

Leonard felt the seals across his soul as he asked, "What are you sealing it with? Wood patch? Joint compound? Epoxy?"

Dugless scoffed, but Davoid laughed as he answered, "Mustard seeds."

It wasn't the answer anywhere near Leonard's lists, so he took moments to fathom it.

"Read your scriptures," poked Dugless.

Leonard bristled a bit. "I admit my holes, but I know about having faith like a mustard seed."

"Good," scowled Dugless. "This will patch it. It's your job to make it last. Now, let's see your Truth."

"My Truth?" inquired Leonard, grinding and changing gears once again.

"Yeah," Davoid jumped in. "Truth girds up your loins and holds up your pants. Kind of like wearing a flea collar around your waist. Lose your Truth, and you won't like what's exposed."

"Some fray," Vernage stooped down, checking Leonard's belt, "but, he's pretty clean. He rose and stared down at Leonard. "Whatever you do, don't lose your Truth."

Leonard nodded gravely.

"How're your shoes?"

Leonard looked down at his new footwear.

"Uh, better, I think. They were tight, but starting to break-in. Don't seem to hurt as much - on the instep."

"Good," nodded Vernage. "They're your gospel of peace, both your foundation and your balance. Lose your good news, and you won't have a leg to stand on. Prepare ye, and you'll have more mobility than a flying carpet."

Leonard looked at his companions' feet. Deft strength, able to support not only the soldiers, but their load. He looked back at his own new boots. One was scuffed. He bent and rubbed out the mark.

"Where's your Word?" asked Vernage.

"Uh –"

"Here." He handed him a pocket New Testament with Psalms and Proverbs. "Start reading, *now*. We've got to sharpen that sword before we head into battle."

"But, I want to learn sword play, and fencing," protested Leonard. Vernage's look told him he sounded foolish. What good was it to wield the biggest two-edged sword if it wasn't sharp? Leonard complied, sat down and cracked open the book.

"Start with the gospels," pointed Vernage. "Then, a few Psalms, then a Proverb, each and every day. The Proverbs are good because there's thirty-one of them, so you can read one each day of the month. Read them. Meditate on them. Discuss them with us. We're all on the same battlefield, and we can fight together, but you have to get your sword sharpened pronto. Ignore the warriors. Ignore us. Get to your holy studies."

Leonard felt deflated for some reason. He wanted something a little more glorious, but dutifully accepted the task. Opening to Matthew, he tried to study the opening genealogy with more interest than previous readings. Davoid spared him.

"Here," he took the small book and turned to John. "You're not an infant. Matthew's great, but here's some real meat to sharpen your teeth on."

In the beginning was the Word, and the Word was with God, and the Word was God... Leonard had read as well as heard the words countless times. This time, he was off and running.

Leonard checked his sword. It was sharper, though not so honed that he'd want to shave with it. Only one side seemed sharper, and he asked Vernage about it.

"It's like the vision of our Lord in Revelations, Chapter One, with the two-edged sword coming out of His mouth. One side defends you, and the other attacks your adversaries. Be careful. The shrewdest opponents will try to confuse you and use your own sword against you."

Leonard acknowledged the warning.

"What else should I look out for?"

Dugless brought over a sword and handed it to Leonard.

"What do you think of this weapon?"

Leonard checked it out. It looked a lot like a King James sword, but was inscribed New World.

"I don't see the difference between this and a King James," admitted Leonard.

"Hit it against this rock," pointed Davoid.

Leonard did so, not as hard as he could, but hard. The blade broke right off the handle, almost flipping back in his face. He leapt back and landed on his behind, afraid that he'd broken someone's weapon.

Retrieving the blade, Vernage applauded, "Good job. Now, take a closer look at the blade."

It didn't take long before Leonard could pick out the small cracks in the metal.

"It's a counterfeit," reported Vernage. "They changed the recipe for the blade, and now there are cracks in it. It won't hold up when fired and pounded out by the Swordsmith."

"The Swordsmith?" inquired Leonard.

"Jesus," answered Davoid. "You might also call Him the Wordsmith."

"Would you stop?" yelled Dugless to Davoid.

"What?"

"The jokes," answered Dugless. "Everything's a joke. I'm tired of it. Stop it!"

"What if I told you I wasn't joking?" bantered Davoid. "Maybe that's just the way I think. Sometimes I think the only difference between myself and others, like you, is that we all think the silliness at times, but most won't say it out loud. So, I don't just think it, but also speak it, and deal with the consequences."

Dugless huffed, but let it go.

"Anyway," Vernage announced, more loudly to again take control of the conversation, "Despite how brittle this sword may be, it can still do a lot of harm. The warriors are earnest and forthright, but camp on their own and do more to fight for the adversary than they know. The point also being, that there are a lot of counterfeits, so be careful and don't be fooled."

Leonard tossed away the broken stub of the sword and drew his own with a renewed sense of delight. A murmur had started to cross the camp. The word was being heralded to prepare for battle. He looked around and watched the response. Some stretched. Some polished their shiny armament. Some tried to jerryrig their outfit. Vernage, Dugless and Davoid checked their gear one last time. Davoid honed his sword to an enviable edge.

Leonard checked his outfit again. It still amused him slightly to see his denim pants and T-shirt with this old world aegis. Noticing his shoe untied, he genuflected onto one knee to tie the lace. It seemed like the right place to prepare for battle, and he stayed down, head bowed, eyes closed, engrossed in prayer, mostly asking God his Lord to keep him from messing up too badly. He'd always lived the battle more as a figurative standard. Apparently, the battle was more real life than he'd ever imagined.

Horns blew, and the army started moving to the South, crossing the vast valley. Leonard occasionally could see a dark movement on the horizon, taking shape more and more as the two armies advanced towards one another. Unlike the Lord's army, the adversary's army seemed mostly gray in color. The Lord's army began to separate into smaller groups, as though divinely segregated. Leonard followed Vernage and companions to the head of one of the brigades. The adversary had already begun its advance.

Leonard gasped!

They were wolves. Thousands of wolves, larger than mortality, trotting in cadence, gaining speed, tongue and teeth bared.

"This is real," yelled Vernage specifically to Leonard, then as one, the entire army cried, "THE BATTLE BELONGS TO THE LORD!" Over and over blew the battle cry as they drew swords and waited for the command to attack. Leonard caught sight of Hondo, so tall and imposing, moving back and forth before the troops, pointing and shouting commands.

"Maybe I should move to the back of the line," pointed Leonard.

Impressed, Vernage turned to Leonard. "What courage! That's very noble of you, Leonard, but I don't want you on the back line. Stay close to me. You'll see the battle more than you know, so remember to keep fighting, even when you tire. You'll find your second wind before you know it. If you think that you can't go on, back off a bit to catch your breath, but don't stop fighting. Trust me. You'll be amazed at your stamina and endurance after you reach that level."

Leonard nodded, numbly affright at what lay ahead.

"You hear me Lamb?"

Leonard turned, stunned. "Yes," he screeched. Vernage smiled and made a sign of the cross on Leonard's forehead with his grubby thumb.

The wolves advanced at full speed. Horns resounded across the battle lines, and the soldiers whooped, loud and long and wildly. Leonard checked his comrades. Dugless, cheerless as ever, looked fierce with fervor. Davoid was just the opposite. He grinned, as though he could disarm the wolves with his charisma. He leaned to Leonard.

"If my hair was longer, I could've braided it and painted half my face pink. Then, you could all call me Braidheart. Leonard expelled an explosive, smelly laugh through his nose while sporting disbelief at Davoid's nonchalance.

The horns sounded again. The army began to advance, keeping a steady canter, gaining speed, watching for pitfalls on the uneven terrain, flowing like a tidal wave towards the wolves. Leonard thought that they were getting taller as they ran faster and faster and faster than he'd ever before imagined running. Hondo led the cheer, and they hollered, long and hoarse, moving upward, leaving the ground, forming tiers of infantrymen and women, the back of the army gaining ground, moving overhead until they were many stories tall. Leonard looked down and gasped, seeing the groups of soldiers countless levels below him. His feet still seemed to find hard, invisible ground as he followed the compulsion to run all that much harder. He glanced upward to see the bottoms of thousands of feet passing over head.

None dared let up. None dared give away even an ounce of effort. The highest layer of troops topped the crest, and started to glide down like a breaking wave into the line of wolves, still advancing, but starting to break away into chaos. The Lord's army gained momentum right up to the moment they landed in the midst of the wolves. Swords swept round and round like the harvester's scythe. Leonard, hurdling headlong towards the ground, awed at the sight of flashing swords, flying back and forth and round and round and up and down, reflecting the sun skyward. Still descending, he gasped between heaving breaths as he ran full tilt. He noticed Vernage and others taking position; picking their spots. His mouth and throat were dry halfway down to the pit of his stomach. His lungs burned, but he stayed with the attack, searching for the best place for him to land.

A dozen-odd feet over the ground, one wolf jumped at him as though trying to catch a Frisbee. Leonard started to stumble, but flung his body around, the blade following. He somehow slashed the wolf at the shoulder as both crashed into the ground, his momentum cartwheeling him over a few times till he landed on his knees. Bruised and shaken and winded, he rolled onto his feet and danced around to keep moving. The wolves would have taken him down in seconds, but the warriors around him kept them occupied or dead, giving Leonard time to regain his wits and reengage the battle. Another soldier went down beside him, the wolf ripping away his flesh. Leonard bounded into the huge wolf with all his might, and sent it reeling. It turned on Leonard, belligerent and rabid; its green, lifeless eyes glowing with hatred. It wasted no time, and lunged viciously. Leonard parried for the first time in his life, and pounded the wolf in the back with his shield, then leapt sideways as the wolf whipped around.

The attacks came, fast and furious, one after another. Leonard found the second wind Vernage promised, and bound forward to finish his attacker. The wolf backed away briefly, recoiled, then leapt at Leonard's throat. Leonard sharply dropped down to his knees as he raised his sword and held it steady in both fists. The wolf twisted to avoid the blade, but landed, gullet first. The blade fell under the weight of the animal which rolled away, coughing and choking till it suffocated.

No time to rest on his laurels. Leonard turned around to face another foe. Passing the wounded soldier he'd saved, he helped him to his feet. Wrapping his wounds with ripped, dirty cloth, the soldier limped away, seeking retreat.

Turning, Leonard saw Vernage dashing back and forth, mowing down wolves right and left. Dugless followed him, protecting the rear. Leonard heard a hearty roar to his left. Veering, he watched as Davoid held off six wolves, thrusting with his sword with admirable skill.

"Come on," he called to Leonard, rapping one wolf on its teeth.

Leonard came alongside.

"Other side," Davoid twisted. "I'm left handed."

Leonard dropped back and took position to Davoid's right.

"Now watch." Davoid started a rapid, sideways figure-eight motion with his sword at two of the wolves, boldly hacking both on the nose. The two yelped, and ran off. Facing the other four, Davoid commanded, "Try it. On those two." He started the figure eight motion, (or Infinity sign if you like Trigonometry,) with his sword. Leonard did the same. The wolves seemed to wait as though confused or hypnotized by the pattern.

"When you're ready, don't break motion as you take a full step forward."

Leonard concentrated on the two wolves before him who started to back away. He kept the flowing sword in their face till Davoid called, "Now!" then quickly stepped forward, nicking both wolves in the face. The pair backed off, then, passed by Davoid's pair, fled. The two men stopped.

"Not bad," complimented Davoid. "Not bad at all. Come on. Looks like Dugless could use a hand."

They fought for the next hours, then as quickly as it began, the battle abruptly ended. A dusty trail of wolves could be seen fleeing over the next hill. The warriors claimed the day and gave praise to Jesus, their Lord as they cleaned their swords before sheathing them, then attended to the wounded. It wasn't until the sun started to descend that Leonard finally felt the flood of fatigue replace the marrow in his bones. Later, encamped, he drank all the water he could hold and missed dinner, falling asleep beside the fire, reassured by the laughter of his companions.

His dreams took on color as he replayed the battles of the day. Vernage, Dugless and Davoid floated in and out of his thoughts, smiling and maybe saluting or giving him a thumbs-up. He also wondered why foot soldiers in movies like *Braveheart, The Last Samurai The Alamo,* (and others) didn't twist an ankle, or blow out a knee or dislocate a hip or trip and fall on their sword when running across some rough field. He could imagine half the warriors for each side limping along by time they finally reached the opposing army. He also thought it a good thing none of the armies had epidemics of inner-ear infections. He also wondered about droid twisted ankles during the *Clone Wars.*

The bright morning sun rustled him from his night on the cooled ground. He sat up, alone, disoriented, wondering where literally thousands of warriors had gone without his detection. The ground showed no footprints, nor any other disturbances. No tents or campfires or littered C-rats. Even his own footsteps were missing, as though he'd been plopped there. Even his battle armament had disappeared into La-La Land.

His legs felt shaky as he stood, and he stretched to bring life and circulation back to his limbs and back. For a moment, he wondered if the battle had been just a dream, but his muscles ached as from strenuous labor. Idly feeling his pockets, he discovered and withdrew a pocket New Testament with Psalms and Proverbs. Opening to where he left off in the Gospel of John, he read to continue sharpening the sword he'd recently taken into battle. Still reading, he picked any direction, started walking off from the mountains, keeping an eye out for any evidence of further human life in the dusty valley.

"Hey! Warrior!"

Startled, Leonard turned towards the voice.

Davoid's mischievous features grabbed Leonard's eye like a black dot on a white page. He leaned out, as though from behind a curtain; only the upper half of his body showed.

"Where'd everyone go?"

Davoid looked back behind the curtain, then leaned forward as Vernage and Dugless squeezed out.

"We're all here," answered Vernage.

"And, not just us," added Davoid, winking.

"The whole army," frowned Dugless, pointing back with his stained sword.

Leonard detected the familiar sounds of many voices, encamped, seeping from the opening.

"We'll be ever ready," confirmed Dugless.

"And never far," assured Vernage.

"Which also means ever-close," twisted Davoid.

Vernage and Dugless both rolled eyes, gave Leonard a two-finger salute, and reentered the spiritual portal.

"If you see Grief and Pain, enclose my greetings." Davoid backed in.

Just Davoid's fingers showing, Leonard gasped, "Wait!"

Davoid peeked out.

"Can I stay with you? All of you?"

Davoid glowed under the compliment.

"Not yet – but you will. You've still got a body to use up. I'd love to welcome you back in, but our Lord Jesus ain't through with you yet on this side of the picture. Fret not! You'll be used wherever the Holiest Spirit needs you soon enough – here and there."

He waited for Leonard's response.

Leonard acknowledged, but could tell that he wasn't happy with the answer.

Davoid pointed to the little book in Leonard's hand.

"Keep sharpening that sword." He again winked, and slipped away.

Leonard watched and waited, but none returned. He stepped forward, but could not find the portal, even with his eyes closed, and his discernment turned up to full strength.

Opening his eyes, and blinking against the bright sun, he picked any direction and slowly walked, reading the Acts of the Apostles, and looking forward to Romans.

Packing the holy book in his back pocket, he recollected his dreams - of Hondo, Vernage, Dugless and Davoid, but those visions rapidly shrunk as he crossed the brusque terrain, disappearing over the last hill. He stopped in the shade beside a stone bank, resting his shoulder against one of two unnoticed petroglyphs; the larger one with a chunk chipped out of the forehead. He left the shade to tramp down into the valley. A plane unexpectedly flew by overhead, passing low, then circling around to land. It eased down and landed on a natural runway of crusted salt. The propeller buzzed around and headed towards Leonard, who prepared to take cover till it turned away and stopped. The side door opened. Leonard was astounded as Rodger hopped to the ground.

"What're you doing way out here?" greeted Rodger. "On walkabout?"

"You could say that," considered Leonard, "since part of a pilgrimage, like a walkabout, is going to new places to discover new things."

"Does that mean that you're ready to try skydiving?"

Leonard shook his head, firmly answered no.

Rodger was unconvinced. "Hey! You could think of it as being on a fly-about, then a fall-about."

Leonard again answered a decisive "no." He didn't want to be on a die-about, or even a scared-out-of-his-wits-about when a voice from the rocks seemed to say, "Go with him." He looked back, but saw nothing. Rodger waited, grinning, leaning against the side of the airplane door. Leonard looked back towards Rodger, and discerned a distinct need to accompany his companion. Clambering up into the plane, he strapped himself into a seat, and felt the rough bounce as the vehicle gained speed and left the ground, sharply ascending, blasting through nameless clouds, topping off at what Leonard was sure had to be outside the earth's atmosphere. Rodger unbuckled and opened the big, sliding door of the airship. Holding onto the bar, he leaned out the opening, closed his eyes, and felt the wind whip and wail around him. Pulling back in, his face colored by the red stop light above the door, he turned to Leonard and called, "Want to see what it's like to slip through the Devil's grip?"

Stand therefore, having girded your waist with truth, having put on the breastplate of righteousness, and having shod your feet with the preparation of the gospel of peace; above all, taking the shield of faith with which you will be able to quench all the fiery darts of the wicked one. And take the helmet of salvation, and the sword of the Spirit, which is the word of God; praying always with all prayer and supplication in the

Spirit, being watchful to this end with all perseverance and supplication for all the saints- and for me, that utterance may be given to me, that I may open my mouth boldly to make known the mystery of the gospel, for which I am an ambassador in chains; that in it I may speak boldly, as I ought to speak.
Ephesians 6:14-20

Chapter Twenty

"How high are we?" yelled Leonard, standing beside Rodger by the open door of the aircraft.

Rodger looked down at his altimeter and responded, "Around twelve five."

"Twelve thousand five hundred feet?"

"Yeah. How're ya feeling?"

"Fine."

"Woozy?"

"Not yet."

Rodger grabbed an oxygen mask hanging by the door and put it over his face. Taking deep breaths, he took it away and offered it to Leonard.

"I'm fine," assured Leonard.

"Take a few deep breaths, anyway – just to make sure."

Leonard did so, skeptically, but was surprised to feel sharpness and clarity return to his mind.

"See?" called Rodger. "At this altitude, you can lose track of your senses if you're not careful." He took another few whiffs from the oxygen mask, then hung it away.

"Sure you don't want to jump?" he checked while checking his equipment.

Leonard didn't need another moment to reconsider.

"Like I told you, I've never jumped before."

"So?"

Leonard thought aloud. "It's serious business. Lots of training, starting with ground training, assisted by jump masters who make sure they can recover if anything goes wrong. For me to jump would be seven-eighths of the way to suicide.

Sure, I might make it, but I'd rather do it right the first time."

"I thought that you were Christian," answered Rodger.

"I am Christian," Leonard wrinkled his forehead, wondering what that had to do with skydiving.

"Then, what're you so stuck on this life for?"

"I could ask the same thing of you," answered Leonard. "Why're you so much of a daredevil?"

"I wouldn't be anything else."

"Exactly," shouted Leonard, "Just 'cuz I'm Christian doesn't compel me to tempt my divine fate. I'm not so self-centered to believe that Jesus arranges His schedule around my dilemmas."

Rodger shrugged.

"So, there's no way I could get you to join me on this jump?"

Leonard swiveled his head fervently.

"Too bad," he rued. "I would've liked the company. We're almost to the DZ."

"DZ?"

"Drop Zone. That's where we jump."

The words tried to form on Leonard's lips, "Have a safe jump - see you on the ground," but didn't make it past his throat. His vocal chords seized up. He looked at the red light. It went out, replaced by the yellow light, then the green, and Rodger was out the door in a flash. He whipped around to smile and wave at Leonard who would have watched from the retreating plane, but instead, found himself leaping forth in Olympian glory out of the airplane. He felt his heart lose a few well needed pumps as he followed Rodger on down, falling helplessly, flailing at first as the ground bounced in and out of his line of sight.

Rodger swooped around to grab Leonard and slow the momentum of his spin. He took hold of Leonard's cold sweating hands as he floated around, facing him. Reaching terminal velocity, Leonard found it hard to breath, but held onto Rodger as they raced, belly down, through the atmosphere.

"You're doing great!" called Rodger. Leonard read his lips as much as heard the words. "Now, let go."

Leonard never wanted to let go, but given his predicament, he realized that he'd have to, and forced his fingers to release. The two moved, still barely feet away. Leonard was about to pull the ripcord, but Rodger motioned for him to wait, then pointed to his eyes to watch. He started swooping in and out like a pro, including a flip, then moved back in close to Leonard.

"Now, watch this," he mouthed.

Leonard nodded, but glanced towards the ground that seemed much bigger than it had just moments before. Looking back to Rodger, he was surprised to see him remove his helmet, then unbuckle his main chute, slip out of the straps, and toss both to the wind. He was even more surprised to see him do the same with his second back-up chute and let it go. It hovered away, rising, much lighter and slowed by the wind.

"What, the-?" cried Leonard as he watched Rodger point to Leonard's ripcord, then raise two fingers to salute, straighten his body upright, and plummet full speed towards the ground. Freaked, Leonard watched his friend speed towards the ground feet first. Only the most primordial levels of self-preservation screamed for him to pull the ripcord. He did so, barely in time, as he watched Rodger disappear inside a puff of dust and

Leonard felt the wind grab hold of his canopy as he clumsily crashed into the rocky desert floor. Rolling into sagebrush, the tears filled his eyes and dirt-encrusted face as he crawled over to the accordion'd body of his friend.

Rodger didn't feel a thing on impact; it was so quick. Every nerve in his body went into overload. The blood flow burst at every juncture. He could've impacted from any direction, so feet-first was as effective as any. He'd entered the world breach, so left in the same direction. He could've slowed his descent, but knew faster would be more thorough. Bones split, flesh ripped like old wine skins, and life bounced out of him faster than his slopped-out brain could register.

He reveled as his soul gathered outside of his broken body. All sensation and pain was gone for the barest moment, and he glanced Heavenward, awestruck to witness the holiest glory and majesty, then felt himself plummet uncontrollably into the unholy abyss. Hellish despair seized him. He'd never ever felt absolute despair in human life, but now it pumped its venom through his withering being. He'd never been hopeless, but it also filled him as he was shackled outside of time and space. The God-shaped void in his soul became a delirious lava flow, engulfing him in infinite incineration and his soul rolled over and over, helpless as mashed potatoes in the boiling, churning, howling magma of Hell.

He had no mouth to cry out. The pain was complete and timeless, filling every pore of his spirit. There was no reprieve; and no chance for escape. Demon and sinner seethed together in the Godless pit, timelessly suffering all at once, forever and ever in the perpetual prison. He looked Earthward and found Leonard, who looked directly into the charred sockets that used to be his eyes before Leonard abruptly awakened to see Rodger, by the open airplane door, watching for the green light, preparing to jump.

"Wait!" Leonard screamed, awakening from the horrific visions.

Rodger looked over at his friend, surprised.

"I'll jump," Leonard simply blurted. He thought to ask, "Is there still time?" but stayed his question. He was jumping, or Rodger was not.

"Tandem?" Leonard called, not really sure what the word meant as it popped in his head and out his mouth.

"Ain't got any tandem gear," answered Rodger, smiling. "You'll be fine. You sure you wanna jump?" He didn't wait for an answer, but grabbed the already inspected gear, and helped Leonard buckle up.

"Now listen," Rodger bellowed, tightening straps as Leonard secured the helmet and goggles. "We'll jump together, do the freefall, then separate. Okay? On my signal, you pull on the ripcord. Now look. If your canopy doesn't open, you have only a couple of seconds to toss off the chute, and pull the back-up chute. That's this second ripcord. Understand?"

Leonard nodded.

"That's it. Snap. Snap. Off with the main chute, then pull the ripcord of the second. Got it? You're gonna love it," he grinned. Here's the green light. Ready?"

Leonard gulped. Fear was a lie.

"GO!"

Together they dropped out. That first moment of reality slammed into Leonard's sentience as he stepped out into nothing, but was committed and no matter how much he may have wanted to, could not go back. The tail passed well overhead as the plane left them behind. Leonard couldn't believe the impact from the wind. He kept in his arms and let himself fall. Rodger caught up and faced him against the down draft of wind. True to the recent vision, Rodger took hold of his hands, and the two men laughed with glee as the exhilaration of freefall filled their lives. Rodger slipped away, checked his altimeter, then turned into the wind, slid into a Stiletto, and rolled back and over, showing off for Leonard.

He pointed to Leonard to grab his ripcord, then held up his hands. Leonard watched intently. His fears became real as Rodger started the entire scenario, saluting first, then removing his chute, comfortable as an easy chair. Leonard was such a novice, but didn't waste any time trying to maneuver towards Rodger. He missed, flying down beneath him. It was everything he could do to force himself to face into the wind. He steadied his descent, then turned over, his back to the hard deck. Rodger was just out of reach, his second chute about to become history. Leonard quickly rocked back and forth, and pulled in his legs, then grabbed hold of Rodger as they started rapid descent.

Rodger struggled to push Leonard away, but Leonard entangled himself and wrapped his legs around his friend. His arms and hands tangled, he looked at Rodger knowingly, who realized the predicament and reluctantly pulled Leonard's ripcord. The canopy opened up. The weight of the two men hastened the dive.

"Keep the canopy headed into the wind," yelled Rodger. "Crab left," he added, "away from those rocks." Unwilling to let go, Leonard leaned to the left to see if that was what he meant. Right or wrong, the pair swooped around and headed away from the escarpment. The ground came up fast. Leonard continued to squeeze Rodger with his legs until they ached.

"Pull down on these just before we get to the ground. They'll slow the landing. Now! Pull down! Pull Down!"

Off balance, and legless, Leonard landed full strength against the dense Earth. His breath stormed out of his lungs. Spasms choked him, unable to breathe. He thought his left arm had snapped. Rodger jumped up from a classic land and roll, uninjured. He hopped over to Leonard, laying on the sharp rocks.

"You crazy clown," he chastised.

"You have no idea," groaned Leonard, sharply reclaiming his breath. He turned over to escape a bed of stones stabbing him in the back.

Chapter Twenty One

Leonard and Rodger waited in the examination room at The Clinic, waiting for the doctor. The Clinic was the closest thing to a hospital the small, rural town had to offer.

"How's the arm?" asked Rodger.

Leonard moved it back and forth, bending the elbow gingerly, then pivoting the shoulder.

"It's really sore, but I don't think it's broken," he answered. "X-rays'll be back soon."

"I still don't believe you did that."

"What?" sneered Leonard. "Save your life?"

"If you want to call it that."

"What would you call it?"

Rodger, ever audacious, answered, "Just movin' on."

Leonard didn't like the answer. "That's very careless of you."

Rodger sat upright. "You mean like indifferent?"

Leonard nodded.

"Wrong!" Rodger smirked. "I had a very definite goal."

Leonard stared hard in response.

"Oh?" Rodger continued. "Did you think I was depressed and despondent, and that's why I was ending it all?"

"What else is there?" He rubbed his arm some more, but it didn't really help. Stressing the joints, he Ow'd, but kept rubbing.

Rodger smiled and shook his head.

"You're right, in a fashion." He somehow stared intently at Leonard, looked around the room and smiled jovially all at the same time. I was depressed, but it wasn't depression that sent me out of that airplane."

Leonard grabbed a paper towel to wipe his mouth and eyes, and blow more dust and dirt from his nose.

"What was it, then?"

"I told you. I was just movin' on. I've lived and done everything to the max that I can think of in this world, and was just ready to go on to the next challenge. Death is a mountain I've never climbed, an ocean I've never swam, and a cave I've never explored. And, from all anyone's ever told me, it's a lot better out there than in here."

"Depends on where you go," pointed Leonard.

"What? Like Heaven and Hell?"

Leonard nodded gravely.

"I don't believe it, and I can't believe you do, either."

Leonard recognized the juncture. He'd been here so many times before in his life, and had almost always turned away, or smiled to smooth out the wrinkles. Not this time, buddy.

"You would if you'd seen what I'd seen."

"Like what?" challenged Rodger, becoming testy. "More of that discernment junk like on the mountain?"

"Uh-huh. Only worse, I mean better. Visions. Real visions, and the last one you were the star of the show. You want to know what compelled me to jump out of that airplane?"

Rodger stopped to replay the scene in his mind. He recalled that Leonard *had* zoned-out for a brief moment before shouting, "Wait!"

"Okay," he condoned. "What did you see?"

Leonard detailed the vision as eloquently as he could express. Rodger took particular interest in the premonition. Leonard had not reacted the way he'd expected when he removed his pack. He knew about going feet first. He felt the initial cracks in his veneer, but ignored them. To Rodger, they weren't the first cracks to appear. They'd always fixed themselves before when he'd ignored them.

"What about on the pier?"

Leonard's brain skidded on ice. "What about the pier?"

"What'd you see there, just before you left? You looked like a deer in front of the headlights."

"Your soul," he answered intently. "It was inky black and repulsive. Scared me to look at it."

"Yeah," teased Rodger. "You looked like you'd seen a ghoul or something."

"Worse, or better," admitted Leonard. He looked at his friend. His head dropped. He seemed disturbed. Something inside was breaking up. He was trying to ignore it; maybe hide it.

"You want the next big challenge?"

Rodger looked up a bit too quickly.

"Okay," he answered.

"Jesus is no wimp, and if you want the ultimate challenge, let him be Lord of your life."

Rodger sat-up and pulled out the old arsenal of complaints.

"I hate church."

"That's 'cuz you've never been the church."

"Huh?"

Leonard continued, "The church isn't a place. It's the people. But also, it's not a belief system or list of rules, but a relationship with God, the holiest and awesome-est of any person, place or thing that you've ever encountered in all your travels."

"Yeah, but they're just a bunch of hypocrites."

Leonard snorted. "Rodger Spears! I believe that that is the wimpiest, most insincere thing I've ever heard you say. If this was a perfect world, I'd, - ur, uh, I wouldn't exist. And, neither would you, or anyone else for that matter. But, look at you, Mr. Hype. Well, I'll tell you what's better than the hype."

"What?" dared Rodger.

"Depth. You might like bouncing around from thrill to thrill like a pinball, but you don't really rack up the points in God's design till you are held tight to listen to the bonus points multiply."

Rodger clung to his skepticism, but his reflections were interrupted when the doctor stepped in. Both men began to rise.

"Oh, don't get up. Don't get up," greeted the elderly medicine man. "I'm Dr. Ed. Heard you had a nasty accident."

"Skydiving," answered Leonard, extending his arm and indicating the elbow.

Dr. Ed grabbed hold with soft, expertly trained fingers. He felt around, listened to the joint, then examined the rest of the arm.

"Anywhere else hurt?"

"No. Nothing serious."

"Good. I checked the X-ray. Nothing broken. At least nothing I could see. Can't speak for your pride."

"It'll heal Dr. -."

"Ed. Just don't call me Mr. Ed. Growing up, all the kids called me Eddie Haskell or Eddie Munster. You have any kids?"

Both men answered no.

I've got three. Oh, they're all grown up - as much as they're going to. My youngest tried skydiving last year."

"How'd he do?" asked Rodger.

"Broke his clavicle."

Rodger turned his head to the side, thinking. "Thom?"

Dr. Ed turned. "You know Thom?"

"Don't know. I went skydiving with someone named Thom last year, but he broke his collar bone later that night riding home on his bike. Dark road. Hit a log."

"So, you're Spears?" accused Dr. Ed.

"Uh-huh."

"Thom said that you called him Toe-Moss."

"Yeah," Rodger owned up.

"You know, that accident cost me over four hundred dollars." Dr. Ed looked down accusingly at Rodger.

"Not good," Rodger responded, not really taking responsibility.

"Toe-Moss!" teased the old doctor, his demeanor doing a one-eighty. "Love it. I still call him that."

"Uh," wondered Leonard, "what was the four hundred bucks for?"

"TV and DVD player," answered Dr. Ed. "He didn't have one. Wanted to borrow ours. I just bought one for him to help him convalesce. I suggested books, but getting Thom to read a book is like telling St. Paul not to pray."

Dr. Ed finished the examination. "Looks like you'll heal just fine," vouched the jovial physician. "Wonderful meeting you, Rodger." He departed.

Almost before the door clicked, Rodger asked, "How long you been Christian?"

"All my life," Leonard answered, carefully dressing and leading the way past reception, and out the door of the clinic. "I was weaned in the church. My folks were involved, and you ought to meet my grandpa. If you think Christians are wimps, you definitely need to see him."

"What's funny," Rodger reflected, "is that I get around Xtremists like me, and I can't stand 'em. Really. They're just as pigheaded and arrogant as I am. They drive me nuts after a while. I'm no different for them.

"Still, it amazes me that my best friends tend to be milk toast types like you. Arguably, it's probably just my ego enjoying veneration, but lately, I've preferred to believe it's a soft spot in my make-up; a desire to help those break out of their shell, like a social worker, only my office is the great outdoors and my lessons of life offer no safety nets."

"Sounds plausible," considered Leonard, as they headed any direction down the sidewalk, "however, I've never seen evidence that you have a tender side. Sorry. Take that back. You were diving to catch me when I tripped over the cliff. And, you found me in the park, – and you pulled the ripcord rather than take me with you."

Leonard paused to reflect. The street lights came on with the twilight.

"You know, Rodger," he considered, "if I'd thought of *that* before I saved your gnarly hide, that you might decide to take me with you, I might not have saved you. Us milk toast types are strong supporters of self-preservation, and all wish to live to eat oatmeal yet another day. By the way, you hungry?"

The two men laughed as they passed City Hall. All was closed and dark. Hidden behind a manicured hedge, neither noticed the two petroglyphs embedded in the concrete of the modest, three story structure. One began to materialize as the pair passed and watched as they entered a small café on Main Street.

"An. Wake up," called Ki after his lungs became capable of holding air during their peculiar metamorphosis. An responded forthwith, some minutes behind Ki. Breaking free from the wall, and taking the necessary time for his joints to loosen, he collected their two tools; a pickax, and a sledge hammer. Together, they headed towards the café and waited outside, watching their quarry through the big window.

Eventually, Rodger arose and headed to the restroom.

"Now. Come on," Ki started across the street. An giggled anxiously.

"Try to look natural," suggested Ki. An's interpretation of 'natural' was anything but.

"Just come on."

They entered the café, tinkling the bell over the door. Leonard looked up to see them, then went back to his coffee. Something???

Ki and An beelined down the hall to the restroom.

"Drat!" cursed Ki, trying the locked door.

"Hold your horses!" called Rodger through the door.

Ki motioned to An to back up a bit, then changed his plan. Rodger would see them, and surely lock himself back in the restroom till his friend came to see what was taking so long, or fight it out, creating a scene that would bring the cavalry.

They returned to the dining room, and took a seat across from Leonard. Leonard noticed their tools; odd implements to bring to dinner. Thoughts of Rodger's account in the cave came to mind. He observed the two as both silently studied their menus.

Rodger came out and crossed the dining room, passing around the counter and center divider to their table. Taking a seat, Leonard seriously motioned with his head towards the pair hidden behind the large menus, then pointed to their tools.

Rodger grabbed the meaning with both hands and both feet. He stood as Ki and An dropped their menus. Rodger stared hostilely at Ki, ready to attack. Leonard also stood, ready to go to blows, sore arm or no sore arm.

The pair merely sat there and looked rather out of place outside the dark, lonely cave.

"What do you want?" challenged Rodger.

"Sorry to startle you," opened Ki. "I feared that we'd give you a coronary when you saw us, don't you think?"

"Answer my question," pressed Rodger.

"Sorry," apologized Ki. "Actually, we just wanted to thank you."

"For?"

"Deliverance."

Rodger saw no animosity or deception in Ki's temperament. An the same.

Ki continued, "Shortly after you departed our company, I discovered that we'd been misled, and that the fruits of our ministry were being used for evil intent."

"No Children of Abraham?" asked Leonard.

"Sadly, no," sighed Ki. "So, rather than mope like I did for that next month, we have begun a new ministry."

"I'm not interested," chaffed Rodger, half seating himself on the table.

"Oh, no," corrected Ki, "we're not looking to recruit your assistance in our cause. Such must be our history."

"So, what's your new ministry? Stone Ten Commandment souvenirs?"

"Nothing like that," replied Ki, "though that might also be a good line to go into some day. No, we're undoing our old ministry. We learned that our mined stones were being used to make the walls around people's hearts. Thus, it is now our divine goal to break down as many as those walls, as best we can. So far, our ministry has been taking off. There are so many who are tired of being prisoners or victims to their past. We take down one, two, or many layers. Whatever they're ready for."

"I'll bet that some have built quite the fortress around their hearts," commented Leonard, taking his seat and sipping lukewarm coffee.

"Babylon would be jealous," quipped Ki. "Thus, our real reason for coming here was to thank you for your deliverance, and to ask you to pray with us and ask God's blessing."

"Uh, I don't pray," Rodger said bluntly. He glimpsed at Leonard. "But, this time I'll make an exception. Uh, you'll have to lead."

The four bowed heads there in the café though Rodger kept eyes open, just in case some deceptions became exposed. Ki started, Leonard added, and Rodger provided a closing, "So be it." The strange pair rose. Ki was elated, offered a handshake, took Rodger's hand warmly, then Leonard's. An offered a handshake, then grabbed Rodger and held him tightly. Both Rodger and Leonard were about to start thumping on the huge man, but quickly realized he was simply sharing his best version of a bear hug. Rodger returned the hug, patting his back. An then did the same for Leonard, offering a long, sloppy hug. An's strong arms wrapped around Leonard, who humored the half-wit until a unique feeling grabbed hold. Something inside his rib cage crumbled, piece by piece, like a crusty wall made of dry-rotted dirt clods. He could feel each stone degenerate. His breathing advanced. He felt cold and scared, and weakly tried to push away. Rodger noticed his distress.

"Watch," pointed Ki, speaking to Rodger.

Leonard cried out, tears in his eyes, as the guilt he'd so carefully imprisoned inside himself for so many years, flowed out of his being like green, slimy water through a newly installed drain. He remembered his shameful prayers in the cave with Grief and Pain. He remembered his wretched woe on the pier. He recalled his shield, patched just before battle, and knew he could feel one of the holes close up, stronger than the shield had originally been.

Guilt expelled, An released Leonard. Tears showered Leonard's eyes. He didn't even try to wipe away the tears as he watched the pair depart without further fanfare.

"Still think that God doesn't change hearts?" sighed Leonard, dropping onto the booth seat, blowing his nose, and motioning to the waitress for more coffee.

Rodger stretched a bit, somewhat pleased that he hadn't been abducted, though the last time, it'd been downright exciting to escape.

"I once told myself that the day I really discovered that God was bigger than me, I'd never see the universe quite the same, and would want to know what He'd want me to do to make it a sturdier place." He paused, taking a breath for effect. "I think today is that day."

Leonard nodded and smiled while his feet danced a jig under the table.

Chapter Twenty Two

"None of that namby-pamby, plastic Jesus junk peddled as religion. You understand?"

Rodger wasn't kidding.

"The first day I see myself turning into milk toast –"

"–Like me?"

Rodger let the moment play hooky between them.

"Not quite that bad."

"You're sweet," scolded Leonard.

"Not on this side of the tomb," Rodger assured. "And, thank you for making my point. The day I start turning into Christmas songs, I'm outta here."

"But," Leonard pointed out, "don't you expect Jesus to change you?"

"Absolutely," Rodger perked. "I expect it, not 'cuz I'm arrogant, (though sometimes I am,) but 'cuz I can't imagine Jesus wanting anything less than the best from all His followers. I don't have all the answers, but I also didn't commit intellectual suicide. So, I'll start with the gifts that He's already given me. I'd rather be strong and courageous than resting by still waters. Get my drift?"

A thousand plus Christian axioms, teachings, clichés, expressions, sermons, and scripture verses raised hands inside Leonard's mind.

("Pick me!"

"No. Pick me!")

So many things he itched to share, but wisely held his tongue. This time, he recognized it was prudence, not fear that supported his reticence.

They were being church. He knew that Pastor Pete would share that which God the Father, Son and Holy Spirit wanted to make known to Rodger. He also rested, assured that Rodger would take it with him and apply it more thoroughly than Leonard had ever before seen. It didn't take a doctorate to figure out that Rodger preferred action to chatter; works to words; reality to rhetoric.

The campfire blazed. It was going to be the holiest of services. It's warmth already glowed around the campsite, reflecting on the picnic tables and tents. Numerous souls knelt and worshipped shamelessly, and they were only preparing for the service to begin.

A large group of men and women, young and old, came up to Leonard and Rodger.

"You're Leonard Lamb?" asked the eldest woman, her figure and features silhouetted by the huge fire.

"Yes."

She stepped forward and gave him a looonnnnnnnngggggggggggg hug, and whispered, "Thank you so much." Leonard reciprocated though he awkwardly wondered what gave.

"Hey! I want a turn," nudged a young man of eleven or twelve, closing in and grabbing hold around Leonard's waist. Rodger stood back amused and made room.

A large man just about broke Leonard's neck with his constricting hug. Another woman held his face in her hands and kissed both cheeks. The gratuities continued till Leonard said, "I appreciate all this attention, but I'd like to know what it's for."

Just then Ty appeared. Leonard looked at him, and promptly became excited, looking to each and every blessed face in the crowd around him.

"What?" asked Rodger.

"The books," answered Leonard. "These were some of the people captured by Dreadnought."

Rodger didn't have a clue what he was talking about.

"I'll tell you later," assured Leonard, and hugged a child who had a voice like a hummingbird. Another young woman named Patricia, (who had a voice like squeaky, wooden pews,) shared the next gratuitous moment with him.

"I'm offended you didn't find my book first."

Leonard spun around. He knew that voice so well.

Reuel met his friend, full force. Reunion beyond description. Human words cannot adequately express what the 2 men encountered and engaged together.

Wearing his navy blue jacket, Leonard turned his friend around. The extraordinary lettering was, of course, gone.

"You were captured by Dreadnought, too?"

"Yup. I can't believe how stupid I was."

"Same here," admitted Leonard.

"I heard."

Pause.

"I just wish I'd been the one the Holiest Spirit chose to get the better of that - you know what."

"So, what happened?" urged Leonard. "Where've you been?"

Reuel smiled and took a moment to collect thoughts.

"Let's see. After we parted, I found myself crossing into Canada. It was weird, but I felt like

I'd driven the entire Alaskan Highway backwards. I didn't, but it felt like it.

Along the way, I dressed in clouds, made and sprinkled snow, and played tetherball using the North Pole with a man named Xerogen. What a feeling to know that any direction you step will be south."

"Sounds like you had quite the adventure."

"I don't think it's over," grinned Reuel.

Leonard returned the grin. It was Soooooo good to see his friend again.

Suddenly, a large, soft hand bounced across Leonard's shoulder. Turning, he met the mountainous grip of Pastor Pete, notably intact, and lifting Leonard onto his toes.

"You made it!" Ty stated the obvious, sporting a one point six kilometers wide grin as Pastor Pete brought Leonard back to earth. Leonard introduced Rodger and Reuel to Ty and Pastor Pete the paraclete.

"Leonard, you look great," complimented Ty.

"Thank you," Leonard complemented.

"Hey! It's my name," glowed Ty.

They chatted awhile. Rodger fell into a conversation with Patricia. Eventually, Ty grabbed his guitar and plugged-in up front to start playing and praying. Others readily joined in. The fire of the Holiest Spirit astounded all with its brilliance. Its light filled not only the campsite, but could be seen and felt throughout the entire campground. Ty led the songs. Pastor Pete knelt in absolute, uncompromising worship. The congregation prayed and sang, hands and voices raised. Some danced, or clapped cadence.

Leonard opened his eyes to watch them awhile. They shone like crystal mirrors around the bright light. Looking up, he half expected to see the huge face and healed but scarred hands of Jesus move aside the tops of the trees to look in on His children. He felt the prayers, and his own words blended with the group, but an old, obnoxious, nagging feeling still held him outside the group. He recognized it, that same stumbling blockade that deterred his spirit the last time he'd been here. It held him back in the Heavenly veil while praying with Grief and Pain. It resisted his desire to pray with Henry in the Sea of Forgetfulness. He knew it too well. They were old pals, but this was a friendship that needed to be severed.

And he rebuked it!

He spit it out of his mouth. He shook the chips off his shoulders. He slammed the heel of his palm into his forehead. He jumped up and down like a child having a tantrum. 'Not this time, buddy, don't you know.'

Then, he praised Jesus for Ki and An, who helped release him from his guilt. He thanked his Lord for Grief and Pain who brought him off the mountain. He prayed for Rodger who pushed him to be bold. He blessed the warriors Hondo, Vernage, Davoid and Dugless. His life had changed. Now he had to shed his own old, personal habits and perspectives, for he recognized these chains of habit ever kept him from moving forward, even if every door was unlocked and opened before him, and the Holiest Spirit had personally come to usher him through.

Meanwhile, the assembly prayed like mad before him. Leonard had been lost too long, and had come too far to settle for less than blest. Tears arose. He shouted, wet eyes closed. He heard the foreign prayers of both his brethren and sisteren, each one stretching its fiber optics to the Heavenly switchboards. No busy signals or voice mail there. Everybody was home.

The breeze lifted across the congregation. Leonard welcomed the cool caress as the loud, dynamic prayers bounded in around him. The pressure increased, squeezing and compressing him.

A vision arose, responding to the litany. As the grace of the pray-ers pounded him, he became a flat, two-dimension silhouette, all one tone of gray with a hard, black shell drawn around him. He saw dazzling white light beating in on the black shell, unable to break it, causing him to quake, squashed by the pressure of the light. It continued to thrash him for some moments when, unexpectedly, a spark of redeeming light materialized in the middle of the figure's chest. It rapidly filled his contours, erasing the gray. When it reached his frame, the black shell dissolved and dispersed completely, making him one with the grace filled white all around him. Jesus' Holiest Spirit filled him; he had forgotten what he'd once been, so many years before, but now liberated, could totally join in with the worship.

He became giddy. No act here, and he'd been faking it for a long time. Getting delivered from the cosmos was nothing comparable. Escaping Dreadnought's book didn't do it. He'd just been freed, including all rights and privileges, real and implied. He'd totally graduated and gravitated and congratulated, all in one swoosh. One small part of him couldn't believe it. The bigger part of him was too busy reveling in it.

He heard the joyous Voice of the Holiest Spirit.

He'd heard the Voice when he'd been a child and would still believe in it. He'd heard the Voice before, when outside creation. This time he understood the call. And, this time it called him by name, as the Lion didn't just lay with the Lamb, but nurtured it and reared it and brought it to its own. He'd finally rediscovered his First Love. Praise be the Name of Jesus, forever and ever and ever. Amen.

"What you gonna do now?" asked Rodger, his head still spinning from the meeting. He thought he'd been to church before. It was obvious from his face that he'd been mistaken. Reuel kicked a small rock to bounce and somersault and frolic ahead of them. They walked together across the campgrounds towards Leonard's truck. The first light of morning tumbled over the tops of the distant Mountains of Perchance.

Leonard engaged a faraway look before answering. "I seem to recall some fruit trees that need harvesting. Either that, or go fishin'. There were a few folks on the beach that I would love to see again. Maybe bless them more than the last time. What're you going to do?"

Rodger almost puffed out his chest. "I'm heading to the battlefield, and fight me a few wolves."

"Look for Vernage when you get there. If you think that you've got guts and glory..."

"Will do."

Reuel interrupted. "I thought we were going for coffee."

"And, a bite," acknowledged Leonard. "We definitely have a few things to catch up on. Meet you there?"

Reuel nodded and turned towards his own little car.

Reaching Leonard's truck, he offered, "Need a lift?"

Rodger smiled haughtily. "Not this time."

"Rah-ger."

The two men turned towards the squeaky voice.

"Be right there, Patricia," called Rodger. He looked at Leonard. "I already have a ride."

"I see," answered Leonard behind a teasing glint. "Then, take care, and godspeed."

Rodger laughed. "Actually, I prefer 'god-send'. You know, we *will* meet again." He was about to offer a handshake or a hug, or something mushy, but instead tipped an imaginary hat with a bit of a nod and a bit of a bow, then skipped off to Patricia. As the pair drove off, Rodger yelled, "Ever try cliff diving?"

"Yes," Leonard yelled and beamed. Well, it'd been multi-tiered diving platforms into a very deep pool in Lava Hot Springs, Idaho when he was a teen. That's cliff diving - kind of.

Reaching his little pickup, he sat, alone, resting briefly in the comfortably familiar cab. The keys dangled from the column. His hands found their favorite spots, the left on the steering wheel, the right on the gearshift knob. He saw the road, open and inviting before him. He listened to the wind stroke the thousands of new leaves behind and around him. Each breath felt like new life, and he couldn't get enough.

A homemade cassette sat in the deck. John Debzee had sent him a copy of their conversation during the flight to Seattle. He'd listened to it with Rodger before telling him what was happening. He'd called John and asked him to pick up his clothing, keys, wallet, etc. in the rest room on Rehoboth Beach boardwalk. They were due to appear around ten-thirty tonight. John said he'd be glad to. It'd been too long since he'd taken Silke to the beach.

A beefy chain hung around Leonard's neck. He pulled out the special stone securely mounted, and gazed, again amazed at the indescribable color. He'd examined it often. In sunlight. In fluorescent or incandescent light. At dawn. At night. Under water. Each condition adjusted the hue of the rock, but the color remained unmistakably cloune. Another striking moment, and he tucked the stone away against his chest.

About to start the truck and go, he paused.

"Hmmm."

He reached behind the driver's seat and retrieved the fruit, wrapped in a plastic bag inside a paper bag. The golden yellow skin had a few brown spots. He opened the pulp and dug out the hook shaped fruit. Glancing back at the Mountains of Perchance in his mirror, he said aloud, "How can I not?" A few chews and a swallow, and he closed his eyes to wait.

An acorn bounced off the hood of his truck, bringing him back to the present. There were no branches directly overhead, so he looked around to find its source. Up in a tree, he saw Henry, smiling and giving him a thumbs-up. Leonard returned the compliment while thinking that the angel looked so different surrounded by the rich green.

"What be you now, Lamb?" called Henry from his perch.

"What be I now?" Leonard answered aloud, dissecting the question. Numerous answers swirled through his mind. One grabbed hold, and he laughed. Looking up, Leonard answered, "A broken bone, now healed, and stronger than before."

The old farmer nodded approval, the yellow brim of his straw hat circling his head like Saturnal rings.

Leonard grabbed the brown paper bag letter to wave at Henry. From the window of his cab, he glanced up again, just in time to see Henry's weathered features blend in with the green leaves before Leonard felt each refracted wave of light rapidly collect every atom of his body where it collided with innumerable physical objects, absorbed and turned into heat energy which soon gathered into the atmosphere to float, caught in between Heaven and Earth on the whims of wind molecules, briefly filling holes in the ozone, until it gathered photosynthetically on the leaves of the Tree of College producing scads of bittersweet, blue fruit that dropped to the ground, leaving Leonard, again in physical form on the rock hard surface, filled with joy, energized by his First Love, and ready to pursue the divine work of the harvest,) certain his Vagabondage was far from over.

Appendix A

The excerpt from the cassette tape that John Debzee made on the flight from Baltimore to Seattle between himself and Leonard Lamb in Chapter 16.

Leonard: Are you married?

John: My name is John Debzee. I live in Baltimore.

Leonard: Engaged twice. Both wonderful women, but it didn't work out. One decided to go away to school. The other realized that my profession didn't make as much income as wanted. All in all, it's worked out better for all of us.

John: Yes. Beautiful woman named Silke. German born. Are you married?

Leonard: Northwestern Washington, right up in the Fourth Corner, a dozen miles from the border. On clear days you can see the Canadian Cascades. Where are you from? Baltimore?

John: Where are you from?

Leonard: Why did you leave Israel?

John: Israel. Lived there for years. Traveled around. Settled near D.C.

Leonard: Just two or three days.

John: Religious persecution. How long have you been traveling backwards?

Leonard: Yup. It's weird all right. I almost didn't get on this airplane.

John: Oh. A greenhorn. Sorry. Shouldn't call you that. You have enough to deal with at this time.

Leonard: Back to Washington, I guess near Moses Lake for the present.

John: So, where are you going?

Leonard: What'd you do for fourteen years?

John: Drifting?

Leonard: Why was that a mistake?

John: I drifted for the first couple of years. I'd already traveled some, but I went to pretty much every country this world had to offer. I took cruise ships around the Carribean. I crossed the Atlantic Ocean in a private sailboat. That was a mistake.

Leonard: What's the worst thing that happened to you while moving backwards?

John: Not enough food. I was a stowaway, and the lone sailor didn't plan on food for two. I checked before we left to see how much he had left, and thought it was enough, but probably miscalculated and seriously rationed my consumption. I just hope that he made it with enough. By time we made port, it was the beginning of the journey for him, so everything I ate early his voyage he wouldn't have at the end. I couldn't bring any food on board. It'd just disappear into his timeline as soon as I let go of it.

Leonard: How long did you lay there?

John: Getting serious hurt. I got so depressed that I tried suicide. I leapt off a huge building. Should've killed me on impact, but it didn't and I laid there, broken, unable to move and no hope for help.

Leonard: But, you recovered. How? How did you get food or water? Shelter? Use the bathroom and bathe?

John: Months. I really don't know. Those days came and went, measured mostly at first by my pain. It was a long, long time to recover.

Leonard: What do you mean that you weren't alone?

John: Actually, I wasn't alone.

Leonard: So, she also re-entered real time when you did?

John: I had Silke, a German woman, to care for me. She was also caught in the void, and came upon me while I was laying there. She cared for me, nursed me to health, and we stayed together. She's the sweetest woman I could've married.

Leonard: I don't know what you mean by "in a manner of speaking, yes."

John: Oh no! But, in a manner of speaking, yes.

Leonard: So, how long did you have to wait for her?

John: We figured that if one of us re-entered real time, (that's what we called it,) then we would be separated. As providence worked out, I started forward before Silke.

Leonard: I'm still not getting it. How was she eight years older?

John: No time at all. She was there when I started going forward, though she was eight years older.

Leonard: That's weird.

John: She noted the date, hour and location of our separation, then continued back for eight long and lonely years.
  Then, like me, started moving forward again without warning or explanation. But, she was eight years away from when we'd split, so she had to live her life for another eight years till she caught up with the time that we'd separated.

Leonard: Talk about a loving commitment!

John: You're telling me. For me, it was an instantaneous reunion. For her, sixteen years had passed. When we separated, she was younger than me. When I started going forward, she was a few years older than me.

Leonard: Why not?

John: You said it! She admitted, some months later, that she considered not rejoining me.

Leonard: What would you both have done if she'd traveled back, say twenty, thirty or forty years or longer, so that she would've been in her sixties or older when you reunited?

John: Vanity, I think. And fear. She'd aged eight years and wasn't quite so young and pretty, though still a knock-out as far as I was concerned.

Leonard: So, what'd you learn? What good did it do? What calamities did you stop?

John: You know, Leonard, we never thought it out that far. The wise thing would've been for us – Silke in this case, to just live out her life and not be there when I changed directions.
We did discuss that if the other partner wasn't there, again in this case Silke, that they were surely dead, so just go on with life without them. It was disorienting when I did change back to real time; I'd been traveling backwards for so many year, but I was sooooo elated to find my wife there waiting for me.

Leonard: And, what haunts you about it, even after all these years?

John: Mostly, it carved into my being that God is ever bigger than life, no matter how often I try to make myself bigger than Him.

Leonard: But, you didn't have any children.

John: That's easy. What scares me most is what might've happened if Silke had delivered a baby, then while still an infant, we both got separated from our baby, either because we both started forward, or the baby disappeared into our past as soon as we laid him down. That's the thought that still wakes me up nights.

Leonard: Why not?

John: Sure did. Five of them, after we changed direction. But, I also believe that Silke could not have gotten pregnant during those years.

Leonard: That sounds about as useful as a nearsighted stargazer.

John: Because, we ourselves were not aging. By that standard, there would be no period of gestation.

Appendix B

The excerpt from the cassette tape <u>in standard, more understandable order</u> that John Debzee made on the backwards flight from Baltimore to Seattle between himself and Leonard Lamb in Chapter 16.

John: My name is John Debzee. I live in Baltimore.

Leonard: Are you married?

John: Yes. Beautiful woman named Silke. German born. Are you married?

Leonard: Engaged twice. Both wonderful women, but it didn't work out. One decided to go away to school. The other realized that my profession didn't make as much income as wanted. All in all, it's worked out better for all of us.

John: Where are you from?

Leonard: Northwestern Washington, right up in the Fourth Corner, a dozen miles from the border. On clear days you can see the Canadian Cascades. Where are you from? Baltimore?

John: Israel. Lived there for years. Traveled around. Settled near D.C.

Leonard: Why did you leave Israel?

John: Religious persecution. How long have you been traveling backwards?

Leonard: Just two or three days.

John: Oh. A greenhorn. Sorry. Shouldn't call you that. You have enough to deal with at this time.

Leonard: Yup. It's weird all right. I almost didn't get on this airplane.

John: So, where are you going?

Leonard: Back to Washington – State, I guess near Moses Lake for the present.

John: Drifting?

Leonard: What'd you do for fourteen years?

John: I drifted for the first couple of years. I'd already traveled some, but I went to pretty much every country this world had to offer. I took cruise ships around the Caribbean. I crossed the Atlantic Ocean in a trimaran. That was a mistake.

Leonard: Why was that a mistake?

John: Not enough food. I was a stowaway, and the lone sailor didn't plan on food for two. I checked before we left to see how much he had left, I mean arrived, and thought it was enough, but probably miscalculated and seriously rationed my consumption. I just hope that he made it with enough. By time we made port, it was the beginning of the journey for him, so everything I ate early his voyage he wouldn't have at the end. I couldn't bring any food on board when I began my journey. It'd just disappear into his timeline as soon as I let go of it.

Leonard: What's the worst thing that happened to you while moving backwards?

John: Getting serious hurt. I got so depressed that I tried suicide. I leapt off a huge building. Should've killed me on impact, but it didn't and I laid there, broken, unable to move and no hope for help.

Leonard: How long did you lay there?

John: Months. I really don't know. Those days came and went, measured mostly at first by my pain. It was a long, long time to recover.

Leonard: But, you recovered. How? How did you get food or water? Shelter? Use the bathroom and bathe?

John: Actually, I wasn't alone.

Leonard: What do you mean that you weren't alone?

John: I had Silke, a German woman, to care for me. She was also caught in the void, and came upon me while I was laying there. She cared for me, nursed me to health, and we stayed together. Sweetest woman I could have married.

Leonard: So, she also re-entered real time when you did?

John: Oh no! But, in a manner of speaking, yes.

Leonard: I don't know what you mean by "in a manner of speaking, yes."

John: We figured that if one of us re-entered real time, (that's what we called it,) then we would be separated. As providence worked out, I started forward before Silke.

Leonard: So, how long did you have to wait for her?

John: No time at all. She was there when I started going forward, though she was eight years older.

Leonard: I'm still not getting it. How was she eight years older?

John: She noted the date, hour and location of our separation, then continued back for eight long and lonely years.
  Then, like me, started moving forward again without warning or explanation. But, she was eight years away from when we'd split, so she had to live her life for another eight years till she caught up with the time that we'd separated.

Leonard: That's weird!

John: You're telling me. For me, it was an instantaneous reunion. For her, sixteen years had passed. When we separated, she was younger than me. When I started going forward, she was a few years older than me.

Leonard: Talk about loving commitment!

John: You said it! She admitted, some months later, that she considered, over and over, not rejoining me.

Leonard: Why not?

John: Vanity, I think. And fear. She'd aged eight years and wasn't quite so young and pretty, though still a knock-out as far as I was concerned.

Leonard: What would you both have done if she'd traveled back, say twenty, thirty or forty years or longer, so that she would've been in her sixties or older when you reunited?

John: You know, Leonard, we never thought it out that far. The wise thing would've been for us – Silke in this case, to just live out her life and not be there when I changed directions.

We did discuss that if the other partner wasn't there, again in this case Silke, that they were surely dead, so just go on with life without them. It was disorienting when I did change back to real time; I'd been traveling backwards for so many year, but I was sooooo elated to find my wife there waiting for me.

Leonard: So, what'd you learn? What good did it do? What calamities did you stop?

John: Mostly, it carved into my being that God is ever bigger than life, no matter how often I try to make myself bigger than Him.

Leonard: And, what haunts you about it, even after all these years?

John: That's easy. What scares me most is what might've happened if Silke had delivered a baby, then while still an infant, we both got separated from our baby, either because we both started forward, or the baby disappeared into our past as soon as we laid him down. That's the thought that still wakes me up nights.

Leonard: But, you didn't have any children.

John: Sure did. Five of them, after we changed direction. But, I also believe that Silke could not have gotten pregnant during those years.

Leonard: Why not?

John: Because, we ourselves were not aging. By that standard, there would be no period of gestation.

Appendix C

A picture of Pain's appendix that he removed in Chapter Six:

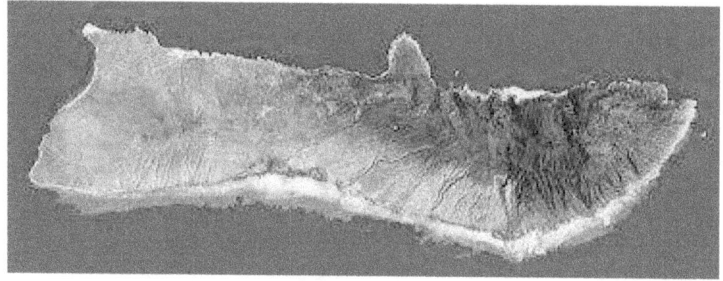

That's <u>not</u> really Pain's Appendix. That's an aerial photo of the Hawaiian Island of Molokai.

I hope you enjoyed my little book.
Reviews and feedback totally appreciated.

God's blessings be with you, always and all ways.
Thanks for reading, Dave

www.ingramcontent.com/pod-product-compliance
Lightning Source LLC
Chambersburg PA
CBHW060936030726
47503CB00003B/611